Praise for Claire G. Coleman's debut novel

Terra Nullius

WINNER, black&write! Indigenous Writing Fellowship
WINNER, Norma K Hemming Award
WINNER, Tin Duck Award
SHORTLISTED, Stella Prize
SHORTLISTED, ABIA Matt Richell Award for New Writers
SHORTLISTED, Aurealis Award Best Science Fiction Novel
SHORTLISTED, Reading Women Award
LONGLISTED, Indie Book Award Debut Fiction
LONGLISTED, Dublin International Literary Award
HIGHLY COMMENDED, Victorian Premier's Literary Awards
RUNNER-UP, MUD Literary Prize
SHORTLISTED, Neukom Institute Literary Arts Award

'Artfully combining elements of literary, historical and
speculative fiction, this allegorical novel is surprising
and unforgettable'

Publishers Weekly

'The truth that lies at the heart of this novel is impossible
to ignore'

Books+Publishing

'A delightfully duplicitous noodle-bender that flips the script on
the Indigenous Australian survival narrative'

Kirkus Reviews

THE
OLD LIE

ALSO BY CLAIRE G. COLEMAN

Terra Nullius

THE OLD LIE

CLAIRE G. COLEMAN

hachette
AUSTRALIA

Published in Australia and New Zealand in 2019
by Hachette Australia
(an imprint of Hachette Australia Pty Limited)
Level 17, 207 Kent Street, Sydney NSW 2000
www.hachette.com.au

10 9 8 7 6 5 4 3 2

Copyright © Claire G. Coleman 2019

 A catalogue record for this book is available from the National Library of Australia

ISBN: 978 0 7336 4084 1 (paperback)

Cover design by Grace West
Author photo courtesy Jen Dainer, Industrial Arc
Typeset in 12/17.1 pt Bembo Std by Bookhouse, Sydney

Printed and bound in Great Britain by Clays Ltd, Elcograf S.p.A.

 The paper this book is printed on is certified against the Forest Stewardship Council® Standards. McPherson's Printing Group holds FSC® chain of custody certification SA-COC-005379. FSC® promotes environmentally responsible, socially beneficial and economically viable management of the world's forests.

For my grandfather and the other Black Diggers,
who went to war for a country that did not see them as people

For Kate, you deserved better

For Lily, Always

The old Lie: *Dulce et decorum est*
Pro patria mori.

- WILFRED OWEN, *DULCE ET DECORUM EST*

My subject is war, and the pity of war.
The poetry is in the pity.

- WILFRED OWEN

CHAPTER 0

THE CITY OF Melbourne was sweltering under a damp, oppressive forty-six degrees centigrade, the sweat-enveloped citizens cocooned in air-conditioned rooms, escaping to others when the air-con in their offices failed. The streets were mostly empty of pedestrians; even the homeless were indoors, hiding in the shopping centres which were showing unexpected mercy and letting them stay. Drivers stared out at a white-hot world from their climate-controlled cars.

The 'whoomph' could be heard in every corner of the city – in the forest of grey stone they called the central business district it blew out windows letting in the heat, and popped eardrums, protecting those victims from the sound of screaming, even their own. The flash had been bright enough to turn night into day though few noticed in the heat and light of the daytime city, wrapped as it was in the throes of global warming. Then, for those who could still hear, came the sound of sirens, echoing through the man-made canyons, approaching from everywhere and converging on the west end.

Those in surrounding buildings evacuated into the heat – receiving as they did a view of the Department of Births, Deaths and Marriages afire, the flames shooting up as high as the surrounding skyscrapers, the vortex the heat created throwing burning paper and sparks into the sky, there to settle on the city, on the people. People scattered to the nearest climate-controlled safety as firefighters came from all around the city and pumped water on the fire but the flames would not die.

Passers-by, people watching the inferno from their windows, spoke of how lucky it was that nobody worked there any more, well, almost nobody, only a couple of guards and an archivist or two, protecting the paper from mould and insects; there was paper in that building from all the state's bureaucracies, backups stored in case digital copies were lost. Despite advances in technology, data rot had been discovered to be inevitable, a paper backup was a vital precaution.

Four days later, when the fire had burned itself out, the pavement was buckled around the building, the road melted by the heat, the façade of the building, already ancient for that young city, was crumbling and threatening to fall. Debris, turned into shrapnel by what had been more of an explosion, a string of explosions, than a fire, had embedded itself in the surrounding buildings, not one of which still had windows. Investigators entered the mess, but there was not much left to investigate, not much that was not burned to ash or cinders, broken or fallen. The building, full of records that nobody needed, was gutted and nearly completely destroyed.

After weeks of the wounded city holding its collective breath for news of what had happened, an arson specialist devised a theory; it was mad, ludicrous, too crazy to believe, but it was the best available. All the investigators, the journalists, the citizens latched onto it as a lifeline – better to announce a half-crazed, half-baked, ludicrously implausible theory than say they knew nothing. The attack, they knew it must have been an attack, was as spectacular as it was old-school, as brilliant as it was mind-bogglingly meticulous.

People could not even imagine the sort of mind that could think of it.

It must have taken years, some said a decade or more, to set up and execute. Every day, day after day, one of the archivists or one of the guards, more than one person, surely it must have been more than one. Page by page, sheet by sheet, book by book, the paper in the building had been turned into nitrocellulose, flashpaper. One of the guards, or the archivists, whose carbonised bones had probably turned to ash then to vapour in the heat of the explosion, had spent countless days turning the entire contents of the building into a bomb.

Fear then a desperate, dangerous paranoia swept the city. How was this possible? Who could have done this? Why would anyone do this? People spied on people, reported their friends for suspicious behaviour. The surprising, impossible nature of the attack turned everything into a reporting matter, anything could be another attack. Trust melted and dissolved in the heat.

People passed the ruin, the ring of fire, the surrounding buildings that were still not safe to enter – maybe never would be. People asked 'What is next, what is next, who did it, what is next?'

Nobody could answer.

CHAPTER 1

Bent double, like old beggars under sacks,
Knock-kneed, coughing like hags, we cursed through sludge,
Till on the haunting flares we turned our backs
And towards our distant rest began to trudge.
Men marched asleep. Many had lost their boots
But limped on, blood-shod. All went lame; all blind;
Drunk with fatigue; deaf even to the hoots
Of tired, outstripped Five-nines that dropped behind.

– WILFRED OWEN, *DULCE ET DECORUM EST*

THE SKY WAS dull, dark, granite-grey overhead, the kind of grey that sucks all joy from a face as it steals the very breath from terrified lungs. It had stayed that way for days, maybe even weeks, for so long the beginning of the gloom was immemorial. At least the hammering of the rain, its rippling spatter so like the marching of tiny boots, had finally stopped, though there was nothing to say it would not return. Sticky mud lined the bottoms of the mud-coloured puddles and the sides and bottoms of Corporal Daniels' boots, was splattered up the corporal's legs. The sludge, once grey-brown, had grown over the last days steadily redder until the mud, even the water, was tinged a dull maroon.

Corpses floated, drifted, forming log-jams of bodies, leaking themselves bloodless, bone white, staining the once fertile plains with their life, their loss. There were so many corpses, so many, too many, how could so many die? How could there even be that many people in the world to kill?

Corporal Shane Daniels was lost, the grey uniformity of the sky and dirt, the rain, the muck, had rendered the flat, bomb-wracked plain featureless. What trees, what buildings there must have been were long since gone, all there was to navigate by was foxholes, trenches and bomb-craters, all now full of corpses, rainwater and diluted soupy viscera.

Sticks, timber, broken, leafless limbs poked up out of the mud — some buried enough to be invisible in the slush, sharp enough to penetrate the rubber sole of a boot; some embedded well enough to trip the unwary. Some were almost certainly trees, dead and half-destroyed, almost completely buried, where they had grown for years, for decades. Nothing living was visible.

Tangled barbed wire was a constant obstacle, tangling, tearing, hidden, trampled into the soupy mud, it stopped walkers dead, it cut through the sides of boots, it chewed away at feet. The holes in boots let the filthy mud and water in — there to rot the skin.

Momentum stolen by the heavy, coated footwear, by despair and the bone-cold damp, Daniels collapsed, knees down, then face-down. Only instinct, head turned sideways, preventing death by drowning in the bloody puddle.

Pure luck, there was nothing dangerous in the depression but the mud and water itself.

It was peaceful there, it felt safe, lying in the mud, nothing to smell but the scent of dirt, miraculously clean mud – wet soil from which one day, after the war had ended, life might spring. Seeds were in that mud, there would always be seeds – no matter how much death the war rained down upon it. Shane would not be there when life returned but could smell it, feel it in that eternal soil. The smell spoke of potential still there; it would be heartening, in a heart still capable of hope.

'Daniels,' the familiar voice, parade-ground loud, tore through the restless silence between the relentless screams and whomps of shells, between explosions, between the wails of cannon fire, the wails of the wounded, the soft touch of sound from falling globs of mud and viscera. 'If you are not dead yet, don't just lie there like you have nothing to do, get moving, we are leaving.'

Shane rose to the voice like an automaton, complete lack of impetus converted temporarily into utter lack of will. Standing there, swaying slightly from the after-effect of the burst of energy it had taken to stand. Shane stared at the shouter, the sergeant, with an expression both sheepish and impertinent.

There were other survivors milling around, just as muddy, as bloody and bent with despair as Daniels, so covered in muck they were barely human-shaped. If not for the slight swaying of the human-height mounds, the swaying of people who were only standing at all by pure will, they would not be readily recognisable as people. They could have just been columns of mud, holding shape by some miracle, or mud-coated tree stumps, cut off at about human height and left to die. No uniforms, no insignia, were visible under the thick coating of muck, it was only their universal air of defeat, of dejection, that identified them as being on the same side. The other side were entrenched, secure, warm if not actually dry, hiding in wood-lined crevices in the mud. Surely they were happier and better fed.

'Retreat finally, Sarge?' There was hope in Corporal Daniels' voice, flavoured by relief and the fear that the relief was unfounded.

'They just called it in, thank fuck,' Sarge replied, 'we are finally getting off the front line, heading for a hot meal and a warm bed. Hopefully someone else's warm bed.' Only Shane seemed too tired to laugh at that one, the giggle moved in a wave through the crowd before it stumbled and stopped. 'I won't even ask what the fuck happened to your gun, Daniels.' It was only then that Shane realised there was indeed no rifle at hand. Shit.

'Almost time for a beer,' squawked a voice from the back of the milling, undisciplined mob, 'for beer, for beers.'

The talker was known for his whining, you could tell he was a whiner from the tone in his voice. Everyone called him 'Shut-up'. Shane barely managed the energy for a brief smile, knowing what was coming.

'You still owe me a beer from last time, Shut-up,' came a cry from the left. Laughter again bubbled and washed through the mob.

'I think I owe everybody beer from last time,' said Shut-up with a strained whiny laugh.

Corporal Daniels wondered how everybody else had enough energy to laugh, it wasn't even funny.

Corporal Daniels was trudging, in the rear, boots heavier with every laboured step, herding the stragglers, keeping them in line, despite standing itself having, long since, become a chore. The mud at the back of the migrating mob must be even worse than it would be up front because every soldier who went before had churned the puddles into soup; left sticky, ankle-breaking foot holes in the few patches where the mud was thick enough to hold a shape; left holes in the thick sticky bottoms of puddles to get a boot stuck in; tripped and left what they tripped over exposed, a bony arm, a limb of a tree, more dangerous as each seeking, tripping foot lifted it higher. Someone had found a spare rifle, or could no longer carry theirs. Shane held onto this one, kept it ready, tried to keep a watch for the enemy, but was too tired.

The rain had returned, the incessant hammering rain that some would say was trying to drive them all mad, sapping the energy they needed to understand: the falling water was impersonal, of course it was, though the rain on their heads, on their helmets, felt spiteful.

Someone fell in the line with a splatter, when the mud settled they were face-down in it. Someone tried to help them stand, yet they could not, the faller was too weak, their joints flopped like cloth. Daniels gave the order, someone unrolled a stretcher, the unconscious man was rolled like a bundle of linen onto it.

They marched on, slowing to the pace of the slowest, four terminally tired troops lugging the dead weight of a poor half-dead bastard, even worse off than them, on a stretcher. Daniels ordered the troops to rotate the stretcher-bearers out, give those wretched souls a needed rest. There were heartfelt, tired and mumbled moans, shouts of complaint but the change went smoothly. Briefly they marched a little faster and Sarge, always cranky, had less to whine about.

Sarge noticed those in the back were lagging, dragging in the mud, and ordered a rotation, the troops at the back to the front, troops from the front, relatively clean, to the back; everyone but Daniels. Corporals were meant to be harder than the privates and were constantly forced to prove it. The other corporals were dead, or hiding from those expectations among lesser soldiers.

To an observer the column might have appeared to be the walking dead, rough-made statues, golems of myth, creatures of mud, not men; they looked barely formed, as if a creator had breathed life into a child's mud pie. Blood stained the mud they wore, blood dripped and trailed behind them from myriad small wounds. Death stalked in their footprints.

Rolling the collapsed man off the stretcher, nobody had noticed he had died, they rolled on another who had simply fallen over onto his face; no warning, no clue why he fell. There was nothing they could do for the dead man, the mud claimed him, embraced him. His flesh would become part of the mud, his bones would abide there forever, he might have friends, family, there in that mud, so many had died, he would join them.

Corporal Daniels wanted to take him home. His dog-tags would have to be enough, at least his family would know he was dead, not missing. The death report, the paperwork, was already being composed in Daniels' overwhelmed, tired head. It was technically a sergeant's job if the lieutenant was missing, but shit rolls downhill.

Daniels took out a photo, wet and mouldering, the last evidence of a life before the war, of a family, of something to live for; something to fight for, maybe to die for. Maybe it was a mistake to let thoughts go that way, towards family, towards home. The photo was disintegrating, age, time and mud were the enemy; the smiling faces from a better time were fading, only memory could fill in the features of the people worth dying for. Shane stared at it in hope of memorising what was left before it disappeared completely and forever.

One day, at the end of the war, the embrace pictured would be repeated. It must be, for what else was worth fighting for, what other reason would there be for the ultimate sin: leaving them.

Their numbers had swelled during the long march. Men without their comrades, men who had lost their units, men without orders, without officers, without even sergeants, accreted to them like the sticky brown muck. The rain ceased, suddenly, miraculously, their hearts lifted until the mud dried to the texture of dog-shit with the smell of an abattoir.

Corporal Daniels could no longer see any familiar faces in the crowd when they stopped to eat whatever scraps or reserved treats they could find from their packs. Except Sarge, he was everywhere Shane turned, learning all the mob's names, finding out where they all came from, not just which unit they were lost from, but where they called home.

Home, best not to think about Home. It was so far away, maybe never to be seen again. They were dying to defend a distant home they might never return to; family they might never see again. Maybe it was worth it, knowing they had kept home safe. Knowing they had kept loved ones safe too. Maybe. At that moment though, the cost felt too great.

Shane Daniels walked in a daze thinking of beloved books, of remembered stories, of poems about Home. The only stories memorable were about blood, blood and rain and death, pointless death, gory death, cold-soaked-freezing slow death. All the poems were compressed tears.

All around was the scrawled signature of a massacre, a rain of fire had descended through the coming storm, catching so many unprepared as they advanced, or as they retreated. People still lay where they had been blown to bloody bits or cut down by shrapnel as they ran.

There were bodies already half buried by mud and dirt where explosions had upturned the land they stood upon. No doubt some had drowned in the mud, nobody had been there, standing, able, to help them to their feet, to roll them from the sludge, dig them out. Somewhere nearby there would be soldiers buried alive by the mud that had flown in the fury of the assault. The tortured earth left no evidence, kept no memorial, of these burials.

They found a pair of uniformed legs, shins and feet sticking out of the mud like sticks, miraculously undamaged. Not knowing if there was someone alive down there, not willing to give up on them, the exhausted soldiers dug their comrade out. Dead, his face contorted, his mouth open to scream, filled with the mud that had drowned him.

The hammering of artillery fire, the wailing of shells returned with the rain and did not cease. Attacks came without warning, with no regularity, all they could do was react and fatigue had slowed their reactions. There was nothing that Daniels and Sarge could have done to keep their people alive that day, there was too much death, too much fire – those who had survived that far could do nothing more to load the dice.

People lived or did not.

From the ruined camps and trenches, from the scatterings of corpses, Daniels could see the survivors had simply been luckier than most others. Whole squads lay dead and bloodied where they had been hit.

As they retreated.

Having no idea what else to do, Daniels and Sarge collected the scattered remnants, the lost and bewildered, the walking wounded. There were no orders to do so, there seemed to be nobody left alive to give orders.

A man walked blind, his eyes destroyed, nothing there but bloody holes. Someone covered his sockets with a rag, not because they thought it would do him any good but because they could not bear to look at his ruin.

A soldier stared at the stumps of his legs, no sign of pain on that lost, confused face. Another man carried him as best as he could.

Someone lay, no sign of a face, the only sign of life a bubbling and fizzing, bubbles in the blood coating a side of meat. Another soldier stood, mindless, eyes clouded, unreacting, the back of his skull sheared open as if he had been hit with a giant's axe.

An officer lay in the ground, his face the only part of him visible in the field of mud, the only clue to his existence. Two men dug him out barehanded, the cleaner one gaining mud-smears up to his elbows; the other was so dirty he would not have noticed.

The officer seemed unharmed yet his eyes were blank, no reactions to stimuli at all. Insensible, half mad, incapable of giving orders, his rank insignia all but invisible under bloodstains and crusted mud, he was nothing but another burden. A soldier the same height gave him a shoulder to lean on, they led him blindly forward.

All around there was nothing visible but devastation. The shelling, the bombing, had reached their rear, had hit the command post where officers went to be safe while their troops died. Tents, mess-tents, motor pool, all were in shambles. The bodies were uncountable in the camp as they had been in the field but here the density of death left Daniels breathless. The men tripped on the dead, they picked their way between limbs, between faces of their friends and comrades. Viscera-stained tent canvas, scattered among the bodies, was all that remained of the medical post.

Some bodies were contorted yet had no visible wounds, faces twisted in pain, mouths stained, brushed with bloody foam.

'Gas,' one man hissed and all desperately fingered their gas masks, some men found their masks were missing, their faces assumed rictuses of terror.

'Everybody look sharp,' Sarge hollered, 'check your masks, if your mask is faulty or if you have somehow lost your mask, and just this once I will not bust your arse over it, find someone who was too slow to put theirs on and take it. They don't need it as much as you.' He stalked around the chaos, searching for who knew what, maybe for a conscious, coherent officer. They could sure use one, or maybe not, they had done all right without one so far.

'Move,' Sarge roared at a terrified soldier, 'get yourself a mask, I don't care whose, they are all the same, get cracking.' He turned on the spot, glared into every pair of eyes looking his way, so all could absorb how angry he was. 'All of you move!' he screamed.

'You and you and you,' Corporal Daniels did not bother to try and read the muddy name tags on the three nearest soldiers who were apparently still capable of standing. They were all from other units, tag-alongs, comrades for the moment rather than dear friends. 'Keep sharp, fan out, guard the perimeter, we can't have the enemy catching us here unprepared.'

Sarge must have heard, he looked over and nodded to Daniels faintly.

Sarge was so loud the enemy must have heard him. 'I need a working party, we need to find whatever we can that is of use: ammo, rations.' He laughed pre-emptively, 'A tank, artillery, we need to search for survivors. Corporal Daniels has the perimeter guard sorted already, if there are any other corporals out there ask yourselves why you didn't think of it then organise the work parties. If there's a sergeant out there hiding among the troops, gods help you if the rain cleans the mud off your stripes. Get moving people, food, supplies, guns, ammo, a first aid kit, if you can't guess what we need you clearly shouldn't be here.'

'None of us should be here, Sarge,' said a moaning voice.

'Shut up, Shut-up,' someone said. Laughter moved in a wave through the group.

Soon, they marched on although many of them wished they were dead. Perhaps in an hour or so some would have that wish granted. It was no longer a retreat, it felt like a death-march.

'This is the place,' barked Sarge, not even needing to shout for the rear to hear it, moments before Shane would have collapsed. He had stopped the troops at a nondescript patch of mud in a vast, uniform field of mud – it was impossible even to guess how he had identified, or chosen, that particular place.

Corporal Daniels followed the stragglers as they staggered in, making sure none of them completely ceased moving or wandered off in a daze, caught up, shrugged and sent out perimeter guards again. They were faster to react this time, they had recovered somewhat from the disastrous battle, they were taking orders like good soldiers. Maybe they were simply too scared or too tired to rebel or whine.

Even the inveterate whiners had ceased to make noise at every order.

The troops fanned out into the mud, they stood waiting. Nobody but Sarge seemed to have any idea what they were waiting for.

A wailing noise chased a shell overhead, it hit the ground nearby, fireballed, splattering them all with steaming water and dangerously hot mud. The troops scattered in a chaotic cacophony, desperate for whatever poor cover they could find. Sarge had already disappeared – you don't live long enough to make sergeant if you are not faster to react, more paranoid, than everyone else.

The wail of shells came and, again, the air filled with the boom of ordnance, with flying mud, with fire, with whirring steel, with screams as soldiers were hit by shrapnel, with mud hot enough to burn the skin through clothes, to soak through and keep scalding until, after an eternity, it cooled.

Drizzling rain grew into a relentless hammering storm yet brought no cool relief to the scorched soldiers. More boiling mud from the thumping of shells, still falling, was mixed in the rain, fell trailing steam. Daniels could see almost nothing through the mist, through rain so thick it was like standing in the bottom of a lake. More shells, then more fell.

Corporal Daniels screamed through a smoke-hoarse throat over the violence, hoping someone would hear the orders despite knowing nobody could. There was another scream, louder than even imaginable, a terrible wail, a tall building afire, the crack of thunder, a hurricane, it was all these things but somehow louder; louder even than the wail of shells. Daniels saw others look up and did the same.

A column of fire was descending from the clouds.

Silence, there was just too much sound, it overwhelmed Shane's ears until hearing shut down.

The mud sizzled, hissed then boiled, filling the air with steam and the smell of scorched earth, with the screams of the soldiers standing too close to the inferno. Daniels dashed from the heat, hoping everyone else had too, certain some would not be fast enough, yet there was no time to do anything about it. The roaring stopped, Corporal Daniels stopped running and turned tentatively, ready to restart running at a breath.

In the middle of a circle of cracked ceramic, burned mud and stinking, smoking, still afire corpses – there would be words with the pilot about that – sitting jauntily on its struts was a scorched, battered lander. Its cooling engines clicked and clattered as the loading ramp lowered with a roar and hiss of pneumatics. Shells were still flying, one, a lucky shot, landed on the ship with a splashing explosion. Parts Daniels hoped were not critical to their flight careened noisily into the burning crimson sky.

Sarge was somehow already at the loading ramp. A magic trick Daniels would love to learn one day.

'We are leaving, get the fuck up this fucking ramp now!' His voice was somehow audible through the ear-shattering roar of another shell hitting the ship. 'This bastard pilot was happy to cook some of us landing so I am sure he would be bastard enough to leave some of us behind if we are not quick enough. Everybody move!'

In the silent chaos of running soldiers, Daniels fought towards the quivering ramp, scrambled towards the hatch, helped someone stand, dragged them through. Fighters flashed overhead, there was a rattle as they strafed the transport, screams as men were hit, as more men died. There was a shudder, Daniels was thrown to the floor of the transport as it lifted off, the ramp was still down, wind blasted in, a soldier fell out without even having time to scream.

A hand helped Daniels stand, it was Sarge and his smile was feral. They fought their way in through the standing and fallen troops in the entrance tunnel to safety just before the ramp started lifting. Others were slower, they tumbled and fell off the rising and tilting ramp, landing in a bloody, moaning mass of scattered limbs just inside the hatch, a moment before it closed with a whoosh. At least they had fallen inside, not out.

'Daniels,' Sarge snarled, 'let's go have a little talk with our friendly pilot.'

'Don't shoot anyone,' Daniels said with a faint tinge of hysterical laughter, 'they don't like it when grunts shoot the bus drivers. Pilots are officers, or so I have been told.'

CHAPTER 2

CORPORAL SHANE DANIELS had no strength left with which to mourn, as another shovel of sand and rubble rattled down over another piece of meat that had been a friend. It had not been a good idea to make friends among the infantry. Death had no respect for friendships. There were no words adequate to talk about the hell in which a soldier's heart walked, nothing to say by the graveside that did not catch in a throat, no tears left to water the thirsty sand. Every soldier wished there was a way to take that friend, that body, with them back to Earth, but they were not leaving, they were under orders to stay here, right here, and hold the city.

That was a soldier's hell: to miss dear, dead friends while glad to be alive. Guilt, despair, self-hate, desperation.

Maybe one day, after the war, somebody would return here and exhume all the bodies, but maybe they would not, maybe this friend would lie in this alien land forever, their soul walking this place looking for a home they could never reach, for loved ones to whom they were lost forever. So far from Country, trapped on a planet light years from Earth. Shane could not even imagine being that lost.

It was a strange, unfathomable city; the buildings, the layout of the streets, a confusing labyrinth to the human mind. Nothing was recognisable as a dwelling or a shop, nothing like a house, with a bathroom, beds, kitchens. It would have been as confusing as hell even before bombing had turned it into little more than piles of smouldering rubble and pieces of dangerously torn, twisted metal.

What colour there might have been had been erased by the war, the rubble was almost uniformly charcoal grey, coated thick with choking grey dust. It was everywhere; the troops coughed it out of their lungs every morning, they could taste it in their food. Shane did not want to think what might be in that grey filth.

They had not been there when the city was bombed. There was no clue which side had dropped the first ordnance that had torn the buildings and everything in them to pieces.

Their camp was in one of the more stable buildings. Despite the hammering of the guns, the plasma fire, the bombs that both sides were using even though far more destructive weapons existed, even though they might hit their own troops, the building still had three and a half walls and approximately half a roof.

They had arrived weeks ago, in the dead of local night, and were given no orders but to take, then hold, the city – the ruin that had been a city – regardless of consequences. There would be no chance of evacuation, no reinforcements were coming, until the attacks stopped. They could all end it there, add their weight to the grey dust. Too many had died already: snipers, shelling, bombing, mysterious deaths that might have been disease, others that looked like suicide.

People had fallen into open shafts, been crushed under falling walls, been scratched by rubble – the scratches infected, turning gangrenous.

Nobody had bothered to tell them where they were, they didn't even know what planet it was, in what sector of space, or even which species in the Federation called this place home.

Shane had never wanted to go home, to Earth, to family, to life and the kids left behind, so desperately.

They had found bodies and scattered parts of bodies, rotted, reduced to skeletons, draped in rags of flesh, rotting and still stinking or mummified in the dry oppressive heat. The flesh that had fallen off the bones was dust, mixed with all the other dust they lived in. Shane did not want to think how much of the dust was powdered corpse. The dead were civilians, they must have been, none of them wore anything that even resembled a uniform – the rags of clothes were more individual than the corpses they draped.

Nobody had yet found an intact body yet Shane felt certain of never having seen a member of this species before. The troops, those interested in xenology or those who were bored, studied the ruins of faces, examined the skulls trying to imagine flesh on those bones. Shane hoped this planet was home to a Federation-member species humans had not yet met, a people who had never been to human space, whose part of space humans had never before visited. If not, it must be a Conglomeration planet and Shane was part of an invasion force, destroying someone's home planet.

Shane was horrified at the thought that the humans might be the invaders; killing the civilians of this planet to take it.

The third option was even more difficult to accept; the path that led to that thought led also towards madness.

Maybe this planet was neutral. Maybe it was independent or a member of one of the neutral trade-collectives that refused to join a side – preferring to trade with both. Maybe this planet had not even made contact with either side of the war. Maybe they had no space flight technology and their first contact with other species had been when the troops of one side landed, followed swiftly by the troops of the other side who refused to let them take the planet without a fight.

It truly did not matter, in that case, which side had landed first. Shane could imagine the horror that would have struck the populace.

Because the same thing had happened to Earth.

Shane had been thirty-two when a thousand spaceships appeared abruptly in the sky above Earth. Nobody knew whether to cheer with excitement or piss their pants with terror. Parties erupted spontaneously on the streets in some places while other people hid in bunkers or armed themselves with whatever weapons they could fill their shaking hands with. The levitating ships ignored all communications, any overtures of peace and friendship, ignored all human attempts at contact completely. By the time the denizens of Earth suspected what was hovering above the planet it was almost too late. The invaders completed their reconnaissance flights, landed troops and attempted to wrest control.

It was soon understood that the enemy who had landed on Earth had no intention to share the planet with humanity.

Humanity faced extinction.

It was only the violent tendencies and irascibility of humanity that had saved the planet and prevented summary extinction of the species. Humans had fought each other, had squabbled over resources and ideologies, for thousands of years. When the ships full of alien troops landed, humanity did not go quietly. All the energy people had previously spent fighting each other was turned on the new common enemy, these Conglomeration forces, far more alien than another human could ever be.

The countries of the world that had peaceful relations with each other immediately handed control of their respective countries' military might to the United Nations, which scrambled to build the resources and structures for prolonged war. The others, which were fighting violent, very personal wars all over the world, soon, reluctantly, followed.

They knew no one nation could fight this enemy alone.

Even the full might of every army on Earth was not enough, the end of humanity was inevitable. Yet every human who was able to fight did. How could they stop fighting when their own survival, that of their loved ones, of the species was at stake?

Every human with a gun fought back, every human with an axe, a knife, a sharp stick and the physical fitness to fight fought back. Armies united and, where armies were unavailable, militias formed. Where there were not enough people to form a militia people fought alone, standing ground, solo and in couples, side by side with neighbours and strangers, before the doors of their houses, of their improvised bunkers as their children huddled, armed with what they could, inside. Armed families held houses, strangers banded together with whatever they could find to fight with, for whatever they could find to fight for. Still, wave upon wave of ships arrived and no human force could hold them back, humanity could not defeat them. In droves the people of Earth were dying.

In desperation the UN sent out a message in every frequency they could, even using a device from a downed Conglomeration ship they had not yet begun to understand. The Federation answered. The night sky was filled with fireworks for a year as the Federation attempted to blockade the solar system and the Conglomeration tried to take the planet. People died, ships fell from the sky, destroying homes and whole towns, missiles that missed their mark entered the nearest gravity well, that of Earth, killing thousands.

Maybe more died from the Federation's defence of Earth than had from the initial attack. There was no way to count.

The ships of the Conglomeration stopped landing, they were too busy fighting in space. Using the thousands of weapons looted from Conglomeration corpses, the combined UN forces turned the tide. They, with the aid of the militias, the independents, the violent, destroyed all the invaders left on the planet.

When the Federation, who had miraculously saved the world, invited Earth to join them, the UN jumped at the chance. There were few voices who objected.

CHAPTER 3

JIMMY HELD TIGHT to obsessive, forced silence like it was his last precious possession as he puked his last meal, the first solid meal to pass his lips in days, into the already unbearably filthy toilet. No groans, no exclamations, escaped from his mouth, only the splatter of his, mostly liquid, stomach contents hitting the bowl and the hacking sounds that he could not quite suppress.

He winced at every involuntary noise, terrified at the thought of who might be listening. He wanted to scream in fear and frustration, he wanted to punch the walls, tear the door from its hinges but he did nothing.

They might not have tracked him to this place, might have just been there by random chance; they might be everywhere but not aware of where he was, or who he was. There might not be anyone looking for him at all. Nevertheless, he could not risk it.

He would have been ashamed by his inability to control his body if there had been anyone in the toilet block to hear or see him. The part of him still rational, he hoped that part was right, knew that the entire ablutions block was empty, nobody had been there when he walked in and he had not heard the door to the outside open.

He feared, however, that someone was listening, somebody was waiting for him. It was his fear that had chased him there, into that cubicle, that had thrown him to his bruised knees, that had emptied his stomach contents noisily into the bowl.

Fear could make him careless, fear could lead him to error, could get him captured or killed. Yet, he could not completely banish it.

Closing the seat carefully, silently, afraid at that moment to even flush, despite the stench that permeated the air, he sat on the cold, scratched plastic. He did not know how long he would have to wait. They could be still out there, they might have never been out there, it was only a fleeting glance he got, a face that looked familiar, what could have been a police uniform. He had reacted with the reflexes that had kept him alive so long.

The unique scent of stomach contents and bile, strange how the smell of vomit bred more of itself, had been added to the already potent miasma in the toilet cubicle. The plastic seat was hard, the walls so dirty that to lean against them was unthinkable. The urine-yellow, pus-green light made him feel sicker, he closed his eyes to cut it out.

He could not imagine anywhere more uncomfortable to sit, waiting out the hours until he felt safe. Nevertheless he woke with a start, his face pressed, to near the point of bruising, against the hard, filth-encrusted, piss-coated wall of the cubicle.

He swallowed back the metallic taste that warned him more puke was on its way, disgusted at himself for sleeping in this piss-coloured hell-hole. There was one consolation: he felt rested, like he had slept for hours. They must have stopped looking for him by now, if they had been out there at all. His fatigue might have made him overreact, might have amplified his fear. Now that he was a little rested, it seemed likely that there had never been anyone out there to run from.

Flushing his puke down the s-bend he shouldered his bag. With laborious care, he opened the scratched and stained cubicle door. There was nobody in the restroom. He stepped over to a cracked sink and splashed water, barely cooler than his skin, on his face. He let the water run first in the hope it would be cleaner than the tap it was coming from or the sink it was flowing into.

There was a face in the mirror, surely it could not be his. Previously familiar features had disappeared into dark blush-coloured blotches and sunken, black-ringed eyes.

There might be people outside, it would not be clever to open the door in a way that might make them suspicious. How, other than opening the door, would he know if it was safe? Indecision was crippling, that was dangerous too, someone might walk in and find him loitering if he didn't move. Hoping his fear would not show, praying he was not too obviously scared, sick and tired looking, he opened the door and stepped out.

He needed a ride more than he needed to hide.

Another day, another station, this one was stripped right back to the bare necessities, nothing there but a fuel stop, which was no use to Jimmy, and a filthy diner even he was not quite desperate enough to eat in. The entire station looked prefabricated, built in a factory and towed into place. There were a few essential items for sale, covered in dust. He imagined even the desperate had long avoided shopping there. People in the diner looked horrified at what they were trying to eat.

Jimmy had made it to the concourse without even seeing the police. There he had loitered without being obvious until he could hitch a lift. He had not stayed long at the station where that freighter ended its run, he had almost immediately looked for and found another ride, keeping a fast courier company. Hitching two rides in quick succession was by no means an easy task with the Federation as paranoid as it was.

The Conglomeration were on the move, the Federation was no longer in complete control. Fear was everywhere, permeating the institutions of the Federation, visible in the searches, the extra law officers, the military on the move; it had overthrown the system. It was not a safe time to be on the run.

It was worth the risk though – any risk was worth it to get another step, another hyperspace jump, closer to Earth. He hoped to stay one step ahead of the authorities intent on catching him. He was fairly sure they had not tracked him to his last destination, so they could not have tracked him here, but on such a small station it would be too easy to stumble upon unwanted attention. That was why people like him, desperate, homeless, fugitives, lived so dangerously close to the edge.

Somewhere officers of the law sought him, stretching the tentacles of the system out towards him; to catch him, to take him back. Everywhere he looked he thought he could see police uniforms, but when he looked closer they disappeared. They would try and take him back there; he would die first.

Things were looking up, though; he was wearing neat, freshly laundered clothes; they even smelled nice. He had a backpack, stolen of course, and some food in his bag. A shop at his last temporary home had dumped some out-of-date, barely human-digestible cans. They were a reassuring weight on his back. He filled a water bottle in a bathroom basin, now he had water too. Taking a sip of water, he winced, it was foul, some of the worst station water he had tasted, but drinkable.

The next step, if he was to do something smart, would be to try to get another ride, a little closer to home, closer to his long-lost family. He knew he had a family, he could almost remember them. He wanted them back, prayed they missed him. He could not believe they had abandoned him; he could remember being taken from them, he knew they would have come after him if they could.

He had to get back; he had to get back. All his energy was concentrated on that one thing. He hugged his bag. He had to get back.

He wanted to celebrate making it a bit further.

Sitting in the darkest, dirtiest corner of the diner, careful nobody could see what he was eating, he took out a disposable plastic fork and one of his cans of beans. There was an abandoned half-cup of brown liquid he hoped was cola on the table. He carefully wiped the edge of the cup. Beans and cola, yes it was cola, the most exciting meal he had eaten in many, many days. For just a moment, he basked in the embrace of a meal, of cold beans and warm soft-drink.

Jimmy liked beans, tinned beans, they were not the most exciting food he had ever eaten but he must have eaten them as a child, back home. When he ate them he could feel his distant memories edging fractionally closer. There was a suffusion of happiness, a distinct feeling of being cuddled, when he ate beans. He only had two cans, they weren't expensive but you needed a card, a bank account to buy them, the grocers did not take cash. He had beans from the bin.

CHAPTER 4

WALKER SAT, CROSS-LEGGED, on his dusty, prickle-impregnated blanket, picking absent-mindedly at the wounds in his left arm, removing the crusty, filthy scabs. There was as much sand in those old wounds as there was congealed blood, the scabs were hard, sandpapery. Blood trickled unregarded down his arm and dropped off his elbow onto his swag.

His hunger was not helping, he had nothing, no kangaroo, no flour, no tin-a-meat. If he did not find something soon he would have no strength left to move on.

It was cold in his makeshift camp, the humpy of tattered canvas and sheet-metal had no insulation, the windbreak around his humpy could not keep off the cold night-time winds and the smoky fire outside the door could not quite contrive to push enough heat through the tiny opening to banish the chill. He crawled out into the chill desert night hoping he would be warmer closer to the fire. A full moon fought with the red firelight; the combination almost blinding after the darkness under cover.

Lacking the strength to stand, lacking even the strength to crawl any further, he collapsed onto the dirt. A puff of dust, red and black, swirled into the air. He rolled to his back staring at the moon-faded stars; the sky bright, almost too bright. Tears trickled over his temples carving runnels in the dust on his skin, disappearing into his hair, warming his face until they too cooled in the frigid desert air. The thirsty dust stole his tears, leaving his face as parched as his mouth had felt in the dry heat of day. He coughed, hoped there was no blood.

Rolling back to his knees, finding some small strength, he crawled away from his camp. It was agony, his hands hurt, his knees hurt when they took his weight on the ground. Why did it have to hurt so much just to crawl? Reaching what he hoped was out of smelling distance from the place he called home, he puked, certain from the taste that there was blood in the vomit. It felt like his entire stomach, not just its contents, was evacuating past his teeth.

The screaming of his nerves soon became so constant, so overwhelming he could no longer tell which parts pained him and which did not. It drove his mind from his skull, drove the sight from his eyes. He did not know where his mind wandered during that time of pain but he did know for certain he was no longer in the desert, no longer in his body. When sight returned, he could remember nothing of what he had seen or felt in that other, nebulous, place. All he could remember was that it had felt a lot like what he imagined dying must feel like.

'My god it hurts, oh fuck, it hurts, fuck, fuck, oh fuck,' he whimpered to the emptiness around him. He was utterly alone; all the others were missing and he didn't know where they had gone. He could not even remember where or even when he had lost contact with them.

Maybe it would be best not to remember.

What he remembered was too horrible. People had died – what a small word – on this unplanned exodus – this desperate run from an invisible poison, faltered, stumbled and then fell as they walked. Their weeping, fetid sores draining them dry of strength, of hope, of blood, then finally of life. People fell on their faces and their families could not make them walk, could not even stand them up, would not leave them behind. They sat with their fallen, sat there when the rest of the refugees staggered away. Nobody looked back, for all Walker knew those left behind sat there until they were too sick to carry on themselves, maybe they died there too. He could not remember any of them catching up.

Someone's leg had gone gangrenous and stinky even as they walked, someone could have lopped it off, if they had the tools, given them a chance of living but how would they have moved on – how could they have travelled afoot with only one leg? Nobody had the strength to carry them, they were left lying in the red sand screaming in pain, screaming for help, screaming to not be left there to die alone. They had no family to stay with them. Those who were still alert enough to know what was going on had tear-streaks in the dust and blood on their hollowed cheeks.

The black smoke had not abated for days, the stillness of a land holding its breath kept it in place. They walked in it, brushed the charcoal-grey dust it became off their skin, brushed away their skin with the dust. Smeared the dust into the blood that coated them. There was no water to wash off the death they were coated with, not even enough water to drink. Finally, when they, miraculously, found some water, it too was coated with black dust. Some of them drank it. They died.

Then thirst had become a new danger to contend with, all the waterholes they found were poison. A man, tall and wrapped in muscle, covered, like them all, with scabs and the black, weeping sores, dug a hole in a dry riverbed with his bare hands. Water trickled into the hole, life-giving water, it might even be clean so deep underground they thought.

Before the man could drink from it, the exertion overcame him and he collapsed. He would have fallen in the hole he had dug if someone had not grabbed him, held him until others could help. They dragged his corpse away from the water, lay it in the sand, in a place where there was less black dust, perhaps the dying tree had protected the riverbed there.

Everybody drank their fill but had no way to carry water with them. Some of them drank more than their sick stomachs could take. Their vomit added to the smell, made them weaker.

As the ragtag survivors staggered away, that strong man's family were not with them. The family he had died to save could not go on; his wife, his two little girls, sat by his corpse and wailed. Nobody wanted to listen, the wailing crawled into their ears.

Walker could not remember when he had lost the rest of them. He lay where he was, next to his fire, unable to stand; repairing this half-fallen humpy had sapped the last of his strength. Maybe tomorrow he would stand up, maybe tomorrow the people he had lost would find him. Maybe tomorrow.

CHAPTER 5

I know that I shall meet my fate
Somewhere among the clouds above;
Those that I fight I do not hate
Those that I guard I do not love;

– WILLIAM BUTLER YEATS, AN IRISH AIRMAN FORESEES HIS DEATH

'LIEUTENANT ROMANY ZETZ, call sign "Romeo" reporting for duty, sir.'

Romeo stood to attention before the captain's desk, having not the slightest clue which part of space they were in. There had been too many shuttle flights, from station to station to station, to get to this ship. She had seen the ship on her way in, a classic battle carrier, kilometres long, bristling with weapons, the black mouths of landing bays and hangars at the front and back. Approaching closer she was not sure what she thought of the words 'FSS *Yulara*' on the side; was it an omen or an insult?

'Ah, Romeo,' the captain spoke without even looking up at her. That was okay, she didn't want to look at him either. 'Your reputation preceded you faster than your files. Not surprising really, files move by hyperspace, rumours by some energy we unfortunately have not managed to harness.' He laughed at his own joke.

Romeo was uncertain whether a response was needed so said 'sir' in an emotionless tone. That usually sufficed. He was still pointedly staring at the screen inlaid in his desk, but that was no reason to let expression show on her face. She was careful, kept staring blankly at the captain's forehead. He might have cameras; if it was her office, her ship, she would.

The office was classic captain's office style: walls a boring, soft dove grey, lighter than the greys used in the rest of the ship; a wooden desk that looked real but probably wasn't. Wood was heavy and expensive. Art hung on the walls, Indigenous Australian art, desert art, overwhelmingly culturally dense and stunningly beautiful; a map of somebody's home, a portrait of their ancestors. Romany hated seeing it there, especially if it was an original; she always hated seeing her people's art in military offices where she knew it was nothing more than a status symbol or decoration.

It was not like the captain understood what he had.

She stared at it, lost herself in it, could feel, smell, almost touch Country. For a brief moment, for the length of a breath, she was Home. She hadn't realised until she saw it how much she'd needed to.

'Be aware,' the captain continued, sounding bored, 'that we do not like your type here, and if there was any way to not have you here I would ensure it.'

'My type, sir?' The confusion in her voice was genuine, there were so many things in her files he could object to that she had no idea which he had a problem with.

'I understand that you have been promoted to Squadron Leader on six occasions and busted exactly that many; that you would have possibly been demoted lower if it was possible to demote an active pilot below Flight Lieutenant.'

It was not a question so Romany didn't answer. Besides, his information must be out of date, it was seven times. She was not going to be the one to tell him that.

'You are lucky we are so desperate for skilled pilots,' he mused, almost to himself. 'I will not tolerate insubordination on my ship,' he continued, 'no fighting, no gambling, no trouble or I will see you court-martialled, I don't care how short on good pilots we are.'

I am the best pilot you are ever going to meet, Romany thought, and I am not under your orders, Captain, I am under the orders of the squadron leader, who is under the orders of the wing commander. You just fly the bus. Though she was not stupid enough to say that; maybe he really could get her court-martialled. Interesting that he failed to mention the real reason she kept getting busted back to flight lieutenant. He must be a prude, that was something to be wary of. Prudes were almost extinct, which was good because she rarely got on with them.

'Go get settled in,' he continued, 'and stay out of trouble.'

I don't look for trouble, she wanted to say, I just keep finding it lying around.

Dismissed, she went to find the fighter pilot barracks, winding down dull grey, plastic-walled corridors, ignoring the enlisted sailors who stopped what they were doing and saluted as she passed. Her soft-soled ship-side dress shoes made no noise on the hard floors. The pilot billets would not be hard to find, all the bloody ships were the same, no matter how different they looked from the outside, how big they were or how small, the inside always followed the same plan as much as possible. Fighter pilots slept right next door to the ready-room, which was right next door to the launch bay.

Convenient. Unless some bastard managed to blow a hole in the launch bay. Or a fighter and its ordnance exploded. Or some idiot crashed a bit hard. Or, best not to think about it actually.

She found her call sign on a hatch; logistics and their label-maker had beaten her there. The corridor was lined with hatches in columns of three, ladders up the wall between them. The hatch leading to her capsule was the middle one. She hated the middle, but she hated the bottom capsule even more.

The handle had already been coded to her handprint, to her DNA, or something, and opened easily. Pilots were theoretically officers, which meant they ranked a private room; not a bunk in a rack of them, in a stinking barracks. If you could stretch your imagination far enough to call a capsule a room.

Slightly longer than a single bed, the capsule was not a breath wider and the bed took up most of the space. There were hatches for storage down both sides, and half a metre of 'floor' space between the door and the bed. The floor space was mostly useless, the best Romeo could hope for was sitting or kneeling, if she was happy kneeling on institutional carpet like sandpaper with her neck bent, which she wasn't. If she sat up in the bed there was only ten centimetres between the top of her buzzcut head and the ceiling, and she was the absolute maximum 160cm height for a pilot.

She suppressed laughter unbecoming in an officer when she remembered the first time she was busted back to lieutenant. The executive officer had caught her in someone else's capsule, with them still in it. Up to that point she had wondered whether you could comfortably fit two people in a capsule. You can't, not comfortably, but it was fun discovering ways to fit. Apparently you were supposed to wait until shore leave before fraternising with the other pilots. You live and learn. It was then she earned her call sign, a stupid nickname that stuck. Or maybe it was the second time she got busted for the same thing.

Or the third. Some people would think she was a slow learner. She preferred to think of herself as beyond such petty concepts as 'the rules'.

At least pilots had their own mess and common room, maybe to stop them infecting the ship's crew with insubordination and bad habits. That was her next stop, if there was any trouble to get into she would find it there. What other people called trouble she called fun.

@

The fighter fit Romeo like a glove, she had always felt more comfortable in a ship – not much bigger than her – in vacuum than in somewhere safe with atmosphere. Out there, where the cold emptiness of space was just outside her window, she felt she could breathe. She really didn't want to talk to a psychiatrist about that.

The space between the stars was lit with fireworks, with flash and moving colour. There was little flame when a missile exploded in vacuum, but when it holed a ship the escaping oxygen would create a flash of coloured fire. The light-weapons were invisible until they hit something and flared brighter than the stars. Plasma cannon fire flashed across the sky like contained suns, like jarred lightning.

Ships were lit, the small lights bright in the darkness of space.

Far from Romeo's fighter, only visible because it was huge, *Yulara* just hung there in open space, adding ordnance to the already overcrowded sky. Romeo could not see the planet, although she knew from what humans insisted on calling radar that it was out there, behind and above, although 'above' lacked meaning in open space.

The planet had fallen to the Conglomeration and there had been no time to get all the local civilians safely off-planet. Freighters and ferries, doubtlessly full of refugees, were boosting off-planet in every direction. The ground-pounders, Federation infantry, would not be left on planet to die. Every pilot was ready to spend their life to save as many as possible.

It had become almost competitive: how many infantry lives could a pilot buy with their own?

The space between stars was filled with death, just waiting for someone to stumble into it.

Romeo flew with the skill and instinct she had become famous for. She had no choice but to fly inhumanly well, for so many were dying and she refused to be one of them. Before her flash-burned eyes another fighter exploded and she went completely blind for a few desperate seconds. She wrenched on the controls and lurched out of the way even before her vision cleared. She hoped she would not hit something else, had not dodged one danger for another. There was more than one rapidly expanding debris field to avoid. Every exploded fighter, theirs and the enemy's, had become a fresh source of further danger. Both sides were spending more time dodging than fighting.

'Romeo, you still breathing?' The crackle and hiss of her squadron leader's voice in her headset almost distracted her as she dodged a tumbling dislodged missile, somehow it had not exploded when it fell out of someone's missile rack.

'Ah, you know me, still here long after the party should have finished, drinking the last of the beer, I wish. I would fucking love a beer. Yet as long as they keep playing my song I will keep—' she paused to dodge half an enemy fighter that spiralled past spewing small pieces of itself '—dancing.'

'They've finished loading the last of the transports, the ground-pounders are almost all safe, we can go home soon.'

'Those of us still flying can go home, which is not that many. I hope, uh, they don't want us to engage,' Romeo was near breathless with the g-force of the turn, 'right now it's, uh, taking all I, ugh, have to keep from crashing into something.'

'One more transport,' the squadron leader said, 'the bogeys are hammering them, command have asked us to intervene. Can I have this dance?'

Romeo dodged a missile that had apparently missed someone else and was just going its merry way. How it had not yet hit some random debris was a mystery, why it had not locked onto the nearest random target was a bigger question. There was no guessing when it would find something to hit.

She saw the transport lumbering its way out of the planet's gravity well and turned towards it; the enemy fighters were indeed circling the transport, already firing. 'Shit, that's a bit hot for just two of us, Dodger, please tell me someone else has signed your dance card.'

'Well, I don't actually think there is anyone else left to join us, unless it's on their side and that's going to be a hindrance not a help. You'd better be as good as you've always said you are, Romeo.'

'Oh, what the hell – yeehaw!' Romeo was surprised by precisely how sarcastic she sounded. She did not want to die, but the soldiers in those transports did not deserve to die helpless, their ride home destroyed around them before they even knew about it. Romeo would not, while she was breathing, let that happen.

The problem was staying breathing.

The enemy fighters, four of them, roughly spherical, shiny like Christmas baubles, disengaged from the transport to defend against the coming fighters, that was a plus for the transport and a minus for the suddenly outnumbered Federation fighters. As good as she was, Romeo did not like the odds. Rather than defending the transport she found herself dodging missiles and plasma fire, light cannons and projectiles.

Both sides used the smallest people they could as fighter pilots. The maximum height for a human fighter pilot was about five foot three. Lighter pilot, lighter cockpit, lighter life-support, more guns on the ship.

In her eight years in space Romeo had only met two male fighter pilots and one of them had been female, according to his military records, when they first met. It was kinda cool to suddenly have a male friend who was not a total jerk.

Every kilo of reduced pilot weight was a kilo of extra ammo or fuel. Every pilot Romeo knew starved themselves as much as they could and still fly. Romeo didn't even eat for hours before a scheduled flight. There were rumours that both sides were working on ships piloted by disembodied, surgically extracted brains. She could not imagine anyone volunteering for that duty. Romeo had also heard some boffin had created a machine brain as good as a living pilot but the computer brain was heavier than a pilot and the machinery needed to keep them alive in space combined. Not to mention far more expensive.

Lives are cheap.

Romeo flew through another, fresh, debris cloud – she must have hit an enemy fighter with something, she had been throwing everything she could find at them. She would have thrown her helmet at them too if it was not a vacuum out there. She had run out of harsh language hours ago. Actually she never ran out of harsh language, she made sure she had enough for everybody.

There was no time for cheering, for talking, for fear, it took all her energy and concentration just to survive. From the glances she took at her squadron leader, Dodger, she was not doing any better. Dodger disabled an enemy engine with a lucky shot; another disengaged, maybe out of ammo, it had sure fired plenty. Inspired, or just lucky, Romeo scared the last one into dodging the wrong way, the fighter entered an area thick with the remains of ships and their pilots and failed to exit.

'Good flying Romeo, let's—' Dodger's voice disappeared into static as her fighter erupted into another cloud of fragmented death.

'Oh, for fuck's sake,' Romeo hissed before switching her comms on to the main channel. 'Command, the transports are safe, the flight commander has bought it.'

There was a crackling, scared voice at the other end. 'Bring the fighters in, Romeo, you are in command.'

'No offence, sir,' Romeo replied over the comms, 'but I am pretty sure there is nobody out here for me to command.'

CHAPTER 6

WILLIAM WISHED HE knew how long he had been in that cell; he wished he knew how much longer he could keep his mind from breaking free from its cracking home and escaping into the wilderness. He wished he could sleep.

He wished he knew how much longer he would have to stay there.

He blinked involuntarily; the overhead light was harsh, too bright, an eye-burning blue-white, the colour of fluorescent tubes, amplified to agonise; the colour of a migraine, of nauseating fear. He could not keep his eyes closed forever but to hold them open hurt; the light was bright enough to hurt even through closed eyelids. How long had he been in that room? How long had he been in solitary? He knew he had been in prison for years. How many years? He had forgotten.

He had never seen darkness in that cell, that bright white hell, only the eternal, unrelenting, agonising, hateful light. Someone had discovered that constant uniform illumination, so bright it was as bright as day through closed eyelids – it hurt, it never let the victim sleep, never allowed a moment of peace – was far more terrifying, more emotionally debilitating, than constant darkness. At least in total darkness sleep and dreams can come. How he missed uninterrupted dreams. In dream, for a time, is freedom.

He did not deserve to be in that cell, he had not even really injured the other man. It was self-defence, that bastard was always looking for a fight and had forced him to defend himself. The guards just didn't like his face, didn't like his race, didn't like him. If there was a fight it was always his fault; if there was a theft he was always blamed; a riot, his fault; too much quiet, so much it seemed someone must be up to something, his fault.

Later; William paced slowly around the gravel exercise yard under the hammering of driving rain. Rain ran in runnels off his flesh, he felt like he was being stripped clean, cleansed of the prison and all it stood for. The rain turned the dusty exercise yard into mud, mud that splattered his wet prison coveralls turning them brown up to his knees. Yet he was happy to be wet and cold.

It had come from somewhere else, this rain, this force of nature, from the clear open sky, from the land outside the walls. The sun, glowing somewhere far from his sight, had lifted the water from the ocean, from the lakes, from the river, from the breath of the forest. The breeze, somewhere outside, had carried the rain over the prison walls.

The rain was alive.

The rain would never know it would bring no life here, landing on concrete, on a place swept dead. It would disappear into drains when it wanted to become a river, would flow away when it desired to feed life.

Standing under that rain, while it hammered down on his skull, William could breathe.

He paced, feeling the cold water, the slippery dust–turned–mud, with his bare feet, revelling in the damp between his toes; a feeling he did not even know he missed. He hoped the growing numbness in his feet from the cold would slow, allow him to hold on to the feel of the cold water for as long as possible.

He did not resist when the guards took him inside, when they suggested he have a hot shower to warm up, when they whisked his wet jumpsuit away. They must have feared being caught leaving him outside in the rain – he nearly lost control and laughed at the thought as the warm water washed the cold away, washed the outside, that he had missed so much, down the drain. A guard handed him a clean jumpsuit as he stepped out of the warmth of the shower, a guard took him back to his cell, a guard locked the door.

Lucky for him there was surveillance on the guards, guards watching guards watching guards. They could not leave him cold or wet, could not return him to solitary without a shower, without dry clothes. The perfectly hot shower, the clean dry clothes were almost as comforting as the rain outside.

His eight-foot cubic cell was unchanged, still lit like day, still silent, still windowless.

The white walls were again covered with art, with views of the world outside, with photos of his children, of his wife, his mother. Among them, because it was family too, was his home, the forest of tall trees where he had walked his childhood away, the coast, the dunes, the white sand. He knew the guards could not see what he saw. It was hard to not be concerned he might be going mad, but he didn't really give a shit.

Solitary was interminable, eternal. He could not be sure how many days he had been there. Sometimes exercise time was during daytime, other times night, under too-bright artificial lights. That was when he was allowed exercise at all. The lengths of time between visits to the yard were irregular, if this had not been a plan to unhinge his mind it was working regardless.

They seemed to prefer letting him rot.

William was smiling as he drifted peacefully off to sleep. There were no dramas in his dreams, nothing more eventful than a birthday, no conflict greater than a struggle around the dinner table over the last lamb chop. It was little things his dreams, his memories showed him, hugs in the morning, smiles on faces, family meals.

He woke and held onto those dreams, to lose them would be to lose what was left of himself.

CHAPTER 7

SERGEANT SHANE DANIELS was curled up in a ball, would have been praying if there was anything out there to pray to; would have been screaming if there was enough air to spare for such luxuries. Sparks and fire rained down from the mesh ceiling above, spraying from the damaged wires, from the split pipes, from, well it didn't really matter where it came from, it was not going to stop. Shane uncurled because there was no other choice, felt sparks burn through the lightweight off-duty uniform, felt them burn into flesh.

This was not how Shane had intended to spend some well-earned R and R on this station.

The smell of singeing hair, of burning cloth was overwhelming. The growing pain was a clue this fire, and the smell, was personal. Crawling towards the nearest hatch hurt. The comms crackled 'Sarge' in a voice Shane did not recognise through the deafening crackle of static and fire, 'where are you,' crackle, hiss, 'Sarge, where are you?' The voice kept on, every repetition sounding more panicked.

'I'm crawling out of a fucking fire, and for what it's worth it fucking hurts,' Sergeant Daniels snapped through the headset mic, glad to have followed protocol and kept a folding headset in a pocket even when off duty.

'Where are you? Where is the lieutenant?'

A piece of ceiling was chased to the ground by burnt wires, sparks and the smell of ozone. It landed in clatter, loud enough to scare all thought from Shane's head. 'Shit,' Shane said through the mic, 'the roof in this room is collapsing.'

Then the decompression alarm went off.

There was a hissing scream and hidden jets sprayed thick banana-yellow foam into the room. Fires guttered out, crackling and breathing as they died, the foam set solid where it hit. Once the room filled with foam there would be nowhere to move, nothing to breathe, and the doors would lock to make sure no idiot tried to enter. The answer to the question 'What do I do if the decompression foam sprayers go off when I am in the room?' was always 'Don't be there'.

With a surge of panicked energy, Shane scrabbled on hands and knees to the door, used the doorframe as an aid to stand, and hammered on the 'open' plate.

Nothing happened.

Another harder slam on the plate; nothing happened. Above the plate was the emergency release lever, grip and pull. The entire plastic panel ripped off with a crunch and a groan.

'Shit.'

Ignoring the flames, the smell of burning hair, the flying sparks, the smoke, the foam that was coating everything and slowly taking away the air, Shane stood to stare calmly at the void where the panel used to be.

The mechanism was a tangled, smoking mess but it looked like there was a way to hack it. Reaching in left-handed, Shane grabbed a cable deep in the mangle, breathed slowly and calmly pulled with all the strength that could be mustered. There was a click and a clunk, a scream as a piece of torn metal penetrated Shane's hand.

Nothing happened. The door did not slide open but – it might have unlocked.

Grunting with the pain, Shane extracted the injured hand forcibly from the torn, mangled machinery, leaving behind skin.

Grabbing the closed door with the undamaged right hand, bracing, Shane leaned against the weight of the door and it began to slide just enough to slip through sideways. Sergeant Daniels fell through and landed on the floor with a thud. Two privates stood staring, mouths agape. 'Close that fucking door,' Shane screeched, 'that room is sealing up with foam and we don't want it boiling through.'

They jumped to action, dove to the door and pulled it closed as Shane stood with a grunt. The door locks clicked when the emergency lock button was punched; at least that worked. Something was burning, it smelled like a uniform. Shane beat out a small area of clothing fire. Standing, left hand dripping blood, still smoking, perhaps still smouldering, the sergeant stared at the privates, who looked like their bowels were loosening.

'Report.'

'We got cut off, we don't know where anyone is, the radios aren't working right,' one of them said in a rush.

'Pull your shit together,' Sergeant Daniels growled, 'and let's go find everyone.'

There was no way back to where Shane had come from, the room behind would be filled with rapidly solidifying foam. It would kill the fire and keep the hull integrity, seal any atmosphere leaks. The system was foolproof and uncaring, it would do its job no matter who or what was in there. By the time someone fixed the ship and dissolved that foam anyone trapped in there would be long dead.

The station was being bombarded, that was obvious from the damage it was taking; it had been holed, probably more than once, and was bleeding oxygen into space. They were also, obviously, near the outer hull, which was not at all the best place to be. Shane knew they needed to get to the core, as far from the outside of the station as possible.

Another shudder through the floor confirmed how heavy the bombardment was. It might be a precursor to a boarding, or the Conglomeration might just be trying to destroy the station. If the former, Shane and the two privates were needed at the core to help repel boarders; if the latter, the core of the station was further from the bombs, might lead to longer life, and was almost certainly closer to rescue.

'We have to get to the core.'

The privates nodded but just stood there.

'Get your arses moving.'

CHAPTER 8

ROMEO INSPECTED HER fighter with paranoid, almost obsessive care, for pilots who did not inspect their own planes, who trusted too deeply in the abilities of the ground crew, tended to have even shorter lives than the average for a fighter pilot. Above her call sign, in the boring block lettering the forces seemed to like so much, were new words, so new she was surprised when she ran her hand over them that they were not tacky. 'Squadron leader.'

The captain of the ship had called her to his office, stood her in front of his wooden desk on his plush carpet. He had made it perfectly clear he had no choice, there was nobody else available, not even a transfer from another battle carrier. He promoted her under direct orders from the admiralty.

He must have hated that.

She was delighted to have her old rank back but under no illusions that she would manage to keep it for long. It didn't matter how hard she tried to keep out of trouble, it seemed to land in her lap, on her head, on her lips. It was her mouth that had got her in trouble, in more than one way, on more than one occasion.

Finished with the inspection of her ride, she took her time strolling to the pilot's ready-room. It was inevitable some of her new pilots would be late to duty and she did not want to catch them out and have to reprimand them on her first day in command. It was their first day under her command too.

The other fighters were being inspected by ground crew. None of them saluted her, which was a good thing, tools get dropped and mistakes get made when techs stop working to salute. The previous squadron leader had made it clear that no pilot was to be saluted when crew were working. Romeo had made it perfectly clear the tradition was to continue, if the pilots had a problem with that they would have to talk to her about it.

Not that she had seen any of her pilots in the launch bay. It was possible that not one of them had bothered to visit. That would never do.

A few fighters were still wrapped in clear plastic, glistening and new, they looked almost like cling-wrapped food at the supermarket. They had been picked up when the battle carrier had returned to a spaceport for repairs and to replenish its supply of pilots. She needed to trust the crew were being careful making the scheduled modifications to make the fighters suitable for human pilots – she could not check everything, she had to trust somebody.

That last escort mission had been a triumph, rescuing the entire complement of infantry, armour and marines from the planet, yet it had been a disaster for the Starforce, they had lost every fighter, almost every pilot. The other surviving pilots, other than her, would never fly again: one destroyed physically, the other had been evacuated home, her mind completely gone. Romeo was lucky to be alive, her ship was still in repairs, she had requisitioned a new one.

When she eventually strolled in, the ready-room was pretty much full, every armchair had a pilot at relative attention, the big screens that made the place look so much like a cinema were showing nothing but the squadron's logo. The smell of coffee was ubiquitous, flowing from a cup in pretty much every hand. She had a full squadron, yet they were all as green as cabbages, a bunch of babies. She could see in all their faces that combination of terror and excitement all newbies wear on their first assignment straight out of pilot school. Shit.

'Ladies and enbies,' she said, the five foot three height require-ment for pilots continued to mean that nearly all the human fighter pilots she had ever met were women or enbies. She could see no evidence before her that anything had changed. 'You might have heard of me, my call sign is Romeo,' she paused while the pilots giggled and sniggered. 'I can tell from your giggles some of you have heard the rumours of how I got that call sign. Let it be a lesson on how long it takes for rumours to die off.'

They all stopped laughing, some of them were glancing at each other in near panic. She barely managed not to laugh.

'So,' she mused aloud, 'I won't bother asking if any of you have fought out here before, I can already see you have not.' There were no exclamations of disagreement, so she was right. 'We have just picked up a big bunch of brand-new fighters, we even have spares, and more fuel and ammo than we could reasonably need. Therefore,' she paused, 'manoeuvres.'

There was a chorus of heartfelt moans from the pilots. 'First things first, if you did not learn in training to check your own plane before every flight, it is time you learn.' She raised her hand to stop more moaning. 'I am sure you are all settled in your bunks, I am sure you have all met each other, played cards, gotten up to things that I don't want to know about.

'Move your arses, go find a member of ground crew, anyone who does not look busy and is not carrying anything heavy, and get them to show you to your plane because we could be in battle tomorrow.' Gasps of horror. 'The captain knows you are all cabbages and will be avoiding trouble until we get some manoeuvres done but this is a war, we could bang into a brawl without any notice. Get to work, dismissed.'

The pilots tumbled to their feet, hastening to their planes, desperate to impress. Someone swore when she bumped into somebody else and spilled her coffee on herself. Romeo smiled, took that as an omen, poured herself a coffee. Taking her time savouring her caffeinated beverage, she walked the short distance back to the hangar.

It was bedlam. Pilots searched desperately for their planes, for a tech to help them check their planes over. Then the scramble alarm sounded, harsh over all that other noise. For just a moment everybody in the hangar froze. Romeo felt the headset in her pocket vibrate and put it on. 'Squadron Leader Romeo, prepare to mobilise, we have been called to an emergency. We will exit hyperspace in twenty-two minutes. The situation is expected to be hostile.'

@

Romeo, first out of the launch tubes, could do nothing to stop the rain of death that was hammering into the stricken station and the troop transport attached to it. The ship and station, the Conglomeration fighters swarming around them, were above her, or that was how it looked at that moment, though there was not really any above or below in space, which was the hardest thing for some fighter pilots to learn. More than a few pilots were grounded forever the first time they tried to fly in open space with no up and down and nearly nothing nearby to use as a reference.

The ship she was flying was one the human pilots called a 'delta', an elongated pyramid with bristling weapon-mounts on the four corners and the pilot's seat right at the tip. It was terrifying for those who were new to them because space was right at the pilot's feet, nothing between them and the void but transparent stuff that looked like plastic.

Romeo loved flying in deltas, they were the most manoeuvrable ship she had access to in vacuum and zero-g, which was where she preferred to do her fighting. Let others fly the atmosphere fighters that looked like fighter planes from the old wars on Earth, or the heavies, flying tanks with armour plating and a tonnage of weapons and ordnance. Boring, slow, ugly. Her squadron, summoned there almost before they had unpacked their bags, had found itself in a hell of a fight. They were so clearly outnumbered that the radar and computers had ceased even attempting to analyse the battle. The enemy had brought a dedicated carrier as well as a battleship. There was not the slightest hope in hell of taking out the cloud of fighters that swarmed around the station.

Larger ships slid from the carrier's hangar, larger even than the bombers and heavy gunships that were already pounding the station – cutters, transports. Shit. 'We have what looks like a boarding party, that is something the station and that ship do not need right now' she spat through the radio, 'that is also something we can help with.'

There was a chorus of 'Yes, ma'am' and 'Affirmative', and even a yelled 'Geronimo!' as the fighters turned as a group and headed through the cloud of enemy fighters towards the transports.

Flicking a switch she changed channels. 'It looks like a boarding party, we are preparing to engage, attempting to contact the station,' she said to their mothership before switching again.

'Federation space station, and Federation ship,' she said, 'this is the fighter squadron leader from the Federation battleship attempting to save your arses, my call sign is "Romeo", acknowledge if you can hear me.'

'Romeo?' Did I hear that right?' Romeo thought she heard a suppressed snigger but it might have just been signal distortion.

'Yes, you did hear that right, do you have marines on board?'

'Negative,' the voice from the troop ship sounded worried, 'we were transporting a platoon of infantry to this station for medical and R and R when we were attacked. We were not meant to be endangered, isn't this well within our lines?' For a moment there was silence on the radio but for what sounded like panicked breathing. Romeo wanted to tell them to suck it up. 'We've lost contact with the infantry, they were all on the station.'

'I hope they have trained in station and on-ship combat,' Romeo hissed, dodging a missile, 'you have a boarding company incoming. I will try to contact your infantry.'

Romeo switched over to the fighter channel and spoke with false confidence, 'They don't have marines, people, only some ground-pounders on R and R, we need to take out that boarding party.'

A fighter exploded close in, one of her own, she dodged the expanding debris cloud. 'And bloody be careful, kids.'

Switching the channel again she put on her best officer's voice, 'Attention, this is the fighter squadron leader from the battleship *Yulara*, call sign Romeo, is there anyone from the infantry platoon stranded on that station listening?'

There was nothing but crackle and hiss.

'This is fighter Squadron Leader Romeo, any infantry down there in that station alive, over.'

'This is Squadron Leader Romeo . . .' crackle.

'Holy shit, Romeo?'

'Who am I talking to, over.'

'This is Sergeant Shane Daniels, when did they give you another squadron, tidda? Last I heard they had just busted you again.'

'What the fuck? What are you doing on that station? When the hell did they make you a sergeant?'

'When the Sarge didn't walk away from a firefight on my last mission, don't tell me you are out there getting shot at by the same total bastards that are hammering this station?'

''Fraid so, and I have even better news, despite the best efforts of my squadron that station is about to be boarded. Stand by to repel boarders, Sergeant.'

But the comms were already dead, blocked by the Conglomeration, she had no idea how much of that Shane had heard.

She fought the urge to scream into the comms. Outnumbered, outgunned and now her best friend out there at risk. If she was ever as good as people thought she was, as she always said she was, it was time to prove it.

Romeo dodged, wove and fired her energy weapon, for she was long past empty of missiles and bombs. Soon she would be out of fuel, all that jinking and dodging and using energy weapons would burn it away, she would have to return to the hangar soon. She was pushing the ship to fumes; she did not want to leave her fighters out there without her but if she judged it wrong her ship would be dead in space. Then she would be dead.

A warning flashed on one of her screens. If she kept manoeuvring she would lack the fuel to even make it back. She had to trust the ship, it would be better at the calculation than she was.

'Back as soon as I finish refuelling, kids,' she said with false calm as she turned her ship.

Almost back at the *Yulara*, she felt the cabin go hot, felt the delta kick against her back then start to shudder. Lights flashed on then off across her console. She knew that pattern of tell-tales: a main engine had been hit. Oh well, she still had one. The small explosion, and the venting of fuel, had blown her fighter off course, away from the hangar door.

Almost on instinct she hit the attitude jets, burned away more fuel she could not spare. The ship started spinning but at least it was following the right vector, towards the fighter bay. An enemy fighter, green, crystalline, shaped so like a flying saucer she suppressed a giggle, was flying towards her. It drifted, like a film-prop on wires, believing her crippled waiting for a clearer shot. She lost sight of it again as she spun slowly, held her breath.

When she turned back towards it she pulled the trigger on her barely charged energy cannon, watched the battery power depleting, the single engine she had working was unable to put enough power into it. The beam poured the last of her batteries into the enemy fighter, straight across the pilot's viewport, hopefully cutting the bitch's head off, if the bitch had a head.

Her energy weapon died as the enemy fighter lost control and started drifting in a straight line. Her console flickered off from lack of power.

Apparently the bitch had a head or something like it.

Her last working engine died. Dangerously slowly, having no way to change her speed or trajectory, she spiralled towards the open hangar, praying she was as good as she always said she was. In vacuum there was nothing to kill momentum, no friction, she spun through the open hangar door on her remaining inertia. Not quite: a corner of her delta hit the entrance, spinning her the other way, her head jerked to the side, she thought it was going to tear off – her helmet made a surprising 'spang' noise against the cockpit window.

The inertial dampeners in the hangar roof and on the deck fired something that looked a bit too much like fire extinguisher foam and her spinning ship splatted to a stop and slowly drifted in the foam to the floor of the hangar. Pumps and sprayers surged into life, spraying the foam off her ship, collecting it for recycling. She wanted to scream, imagined this was what a car crashing into the ocean would look like from the inside.

Romeo bounced out of the cabin as soon as the atmosphere detector on the outside of her ship pinged. She stumbled, nearly fell, was delighted she managed to stay on her feet. She jogged to meet the ground crew emerging to deal with her wreck. 'I need a ship, now.'

'Sorry, ma'am,' someone said, 'we need to deal with this mess you made.'

'I need a ship,' Romeo growled, 'now.'

The chief non-commissioned officer of the ground crew walked around her busted ship. 'Ma'am,' he said in the tone of voice usually used by someone trying to calm a madman, 'we have a crashed ship on deck we have to deal with, let's not even mention who crashed it, we have to secure it, we have to clean debris and inertial dampener foam off the deck, then we can consider wheeling out another plane for you to crash.'

Romeo had not even realised her hand was on her sidearm until she heard the gasps of the nearest techs. She stared the petty officer direct in the eyes, wondering who was going to flinch first.

'Ma'am,' the petty officer said, 'unlike the people around us I know you are just resting your hand on your pistol butt. I also know you need a new ship and we will clear this deck faster if you leave us to it.'

'I,' she said with false calm, 'am the squadron leader. My squadron is out there right now trying to stop a hostile boarding of one of our stations, where a ship is docked. They are so outnumbered there is no way to even tell you how outnumbered they are. Not only do I have to get back into the fight, but I need to command my squadron from somewhere.'

'I know, ma'am.'

'What you might not know is that my dearest friend, closer to me than family,' she hoped she didn't sound as anxious as she felt, 'is on that station.'

'Ma'am,' the petty officer said in a deliberately calm voice, 'there is a comms console in the flight control station, just over there.' He pointed as if she didn't know where flight control was. 'You can command your squadron from there, you can also see us through that window. When we clear this deck and get you a plane you will be the first to know.'

Grumbling, Romeo stomped away.

The floor shuddered under her boots, the lights flickered, as a Conglomeration missile blew more pieces off the ship.

CHAPTER 9

JIMMY DASHED THROUGH the maintenance tunnels at as much of a run as he could manage while remaining completely silent despite the hard walls that bounced the sound, despite the hard ceremetal floor under his boots. He could not afford to be seen in there without a pass.

Yet it was worth the risk if he could make it. Past the maintenance tunnels there would be openings into the conduit tunnels, the actual veins and nervous system of the station. Security were even more likely to object to his presence in the conduit. On the other hand, he was far less likely to be caught there.

People only entered the conduit if there was the type of breakdown that would cost lives.

He found a loose panel, the screws missing, and lifted it carefully; hands shoved inside plastic produce bags, improvised mittens, making certain he left no trace, no DNA, no fingerprints. His backpack went first, shoved through the hole that seemed suddenly too small to crawl through. Too late to change his mind though, he could hear slow, arrogant footsteps echoing down the tunnel.

Sliding head-first through the hole, he snagged the dangling hood of his hoodie on the access panel. Panic swept over him as he lay half in, half out of the tiny hole, its edge digging into the skin of his stomach in a way he knew must soon draw blood, leaving DNA traces.

The approaching footfalls were getting louder; the owner of those feet must be almost upon him. He wriggled and writhed but could not slide through. Contorting himself until it hurt, he managed to get an arm back through the hole, un-snagging his clothes. He slithered the rest of the way through the hole and prayed the panel had slammed shut behind his boots.

Lying in silence he waited until he felt the feet must have passed, then waited again, just as long, just in case, then a bit longer. Jimmy pulled out the tiny light he had stashed in his pocket and clicked it on. By the weak light it looked like the panel had miraculously closed flush, there was no leakage of light from the corridor outside.

He studied his surroundings by the pallid torchlight. He was in a long metal tube, square in cross-section, wires and pipes ran along the ceiling. There was enough room to crawl, though not enough to sit up. He had no idea where the conduit led but it had to go somewhere. He started crawling into the narrow choking darkness.

His light was back in his pocket as he felt his way slowly along the tube. He did not know if there were vents and holes to the outside where people would see his light, he did not know how long his light would last, how much was left in the battery. How could he, he had only stolen it that morning. He was lucky he'd found it, hanging on someone's keys; he had stolen the entire key-ring and dumped the keys on a table in the concourse.

Jimmy crawled through tubes that narrowed until he could barely fit his shoulders through then widened until he could not touch both sides at once, again and again, for what felt like miles, for what could have been miles; he didn't know the station was that big. The conduit ceiling lowered in places until he was sliding on his belly then, suddenly, new conduits appeared dumping plastic hoses and wires into his tunnel from above in tangles he struggled to negotiate.

He crawled on through darkness, punctuated by the sparse use of his light. Through conduits of mesh and plate steel, plastic and diamond-plate, hard and sharp on his knees and hands, through tangles of tubes and wires, over mesh-covered, heart-stopping drops, too deep, too dark to see the bottom of. Around bends so tight he despaired of negotiating them. In darkness, he crawled on.

After a while he worried there would be no end to the tube he inhabited.

I could die in here, he thought, I could die and maybe never be found – not even when the rot-smell from my carcase permeates the environmental system so the entire station can smell me.

Like a rat stuck in the walls of a house he would die when he could finally go no further; when the time it would take him to escape was longer than the reserves of water in his body would let him live. He would die screaming with his last breath yet nobody would hear him.

The conduit suddenly ceased, the wires and pipes bending up and away. He reached out into the darkness with terrified fingers but there was nothing ahead but an unfathomable, unidentifiable empty space, the square opening of the tube leading to nothing. He reached out again carefully, examined the invisible edges. The conduit had led to a junction box, or something of that kind, or maybe it had ended at a void – if he crawled out in that case he would fall to his death. No use lying there, no use thinking, he would have to trigger his precious light.

The pale blue light in his hand revealed a junction box. Conduits, carrying bundles of wires and tubes, came from all directions, he counted twelve, including ones above and below. He felt sorry for any maintenance guys who had to get in there and fix anything in that festooned mess of wires and connections. Sighing, he slid head-first from his conduit into the junction box, but he lost control and landed hard.

Pipes criss-crossed the low roof of the chamber; in the sterile environment of the station, even in the filtered air, they were dusty. Some pipes must hold water, he could sure do with some to fill his depleting bottle, but it was not worth the risk. He had no idea which pipe to cut and no way to reconnect it to stop it flooding the junction, setting off the moisture alarms, bringing maintenance crew running.

Sitting cross-legged, even the junction box was too low to stand up in, he examined the mass before him. The wires were all colour coded – stripes, dots, an eye-bleeding rainbow of colour – and completely beyond his understanding.

It took some fiddling, some feeling about, some risk, he cut his knuckles, nearly got his hand caught in a tangle of wires, but he found a coupling where a low-voltage power supply connected to another. The adaptor was in his backpack, he had stolen it with the tablet. Pulling the plug was a risk, somewhere, someone, some device, maybe an entire room, would lose power, though that was unlikely with a low-voltage connection, it was more likely to be a small device somewhere, like a security camera. Eventually it would be noticed, they would start looking for the fault.

He hoped whatever it was he disconnected didn't have a failure alarm.

His stolen tablet booted with almost forgotten music, he could not remember the last time he had heard music other than the abstract alienating sound piped into station concourses. The flickering light filled the room. Thank fuck, it worked. The screen was the wrong colour, far outside of the human spectrum. He moved his fingers on the screen in a pattern all humans practise and memorise from childhood and it flickered through colour changes at nauseating speed then settled down to the standard human colours.

Whoever had owned the tablet before, technically still owned it, had not been concerned about security because the device did not have a password, fingerprint reader or face scanner. Flicking the screen with his thumb, he tried to access the galactic map, the tablet flickered then went dead, casting the junction box back into disorienting darkness. Not enough power yet.

Weariness overcoming wariness, he tumbled into sleep waiting for the tablet to recharge. He woke in a panic when the cooling fans in the conduit stumbled on, with no memory of where he was. The darkness was broken only by a blinking blue light, it looked like an LED on a tablet.

In a rush, memory returned. He disconnected his adaptor, his tablet, and reconnected the coupling he had been forced to disconnect. Hopefully it would look like a temporary failure in the system correcting itself.

Hopefully the tablet would hold power long enough to do what he needed to do.

This time the machine worked, flashing on, lighting the junction, almost blinding after his time in the darkness. Wiping the sleep and fear-sweat from his eyes he loaded the galactic map, the tablet automatically orienting itself to where it was in Federation space. There was the station, he zoomed out, then zoomed out again and watered his eyes searching for Earth. There it was. Oh shit, he was so far from home, all the way to the wrong side of the Federation core, almost into Conglomeration space. It was going to be a long trip back to Earth.

He didn't know where he had started from but he must have been going the wrong way. He might die of old age before he got home.

The time display on the tablet seemed to mock him: midnight local time. It was never a good idea to walk around a station at midnight.

On a non-human station he had no way of predicting their sleeping habits. On a human station those averse to sleeping would be deeply involved in the antisocial behaviours that the Federation has been so bad at stamping out.

Best, therefore, to stay right where he was. He was relatively safe, unless someone came to investigate the power fault he had created. He had returned everything to how it was when he had arrived there.

Rummaging in his backpack, he pulled out a crumpled lump in a scrap of plastic. Careful unwrapping revealed a half-eaten, slightly squished, still hopefully edible sandwich. He had found the sandwich already half consumed on a table in the food court but that had been a couple of days ago, it was looking pretty gross. Other species had learned to like sandwiches too, some to the point Jimmy found it weird. Somewhere, no doubt, was a technician trying to invent a sandwich with infinite shelf life for vending machines, another human invention to colonise the stars.

How did the Federation survive before humans, before sand-wiches and vending machines, before beer and fish and chips?

Sipping frugally from his water bottle he lay back carefully against a thick bundle of wires, not too uncomfortable, not particularly comfortable either.

Memories flickered across his vision in the darkness, all of them too fleeting to even make sense of. He grabbed at them over and over and missed. What he did remember, mostly, was the colour; the colour of Earth, of his home there, unlike anywhere else he had ever been.

He was no longer even trying to understand what he saw when he slipped into a restful, fearless sleep.

CHAPTER 10

WILLIAM LAY ON his aching back on his brick-hard bed listening to someone in the next cell dying. He could easily guess what was happening, for he had been there, he had survived but only barely. He did not hold out much hope for that stranger. For whatever reason the guards, or the police, or both, had beaten the man to the very edge of death before throwing him in the cell.

The anonymous man was choking on his vomit, or his own blood, or teeth, or perhaps all three. The bubbling, gurgling noise was nauseating. Will felt, with his tongue, the gap where the two teeth he had swallowed had been. He could not remember how long ago, it could have been a decade for all he knew.

He had defended himself when the police laid hands on him but before they could cuff him. There had not been much hope of escape, there were five of them, all armed, versus him, he had not expected a fight, was no brawler. They had not used their guns, they must have thought it more fun to kick his arse, break him, bruise his face, kick in his teeth, put in the boot again and again.

Despite his spirited defence of his liberty, they had taken him to the lockup, the watch house, taken him in bleeding, with cracked ribs and loose teeth, with blood in his throat and a fuzzy punch-drunk head. They had thrown him in a cell while blood frothed in his lungs and bubbled out his mouth. He had vomited up blood and teeth and had nearly choked on them. He had screamed in pain, in the certainty he was dying, they picked him up, dropped him a few times on the way to a paddy-wagon.

The hospital had dismissed his concerns, had said he was drunk, when he had not touched a drop − the doctor had said he was okay, that he should stop his infernal whining. They did not check his head, full of fog and confusion, were not concerned he might have been dying. They dropped him a few more times on the way back to the wagon, then a few more, completely by accident they would say, on the way back to his cell.

He knew better than to make a noise after that. He lay in his cell in the watch house half hoping for death to end the pain, half praying for the miracle he knew he would need to survive.

Survive he did, somehow. Survive was all he could do after that, he survived the watch house, he survived his trial, if it could be called that. He was silent when they added assaulting a police officer to his list of crimes, when the only police he had hit was in self-defence when they were kicking his teeth in, the only injuries he could imagine the police sustaining were bruised knuckles where they had punched his bone rather than his flesh. He was silent when they sentenced him, when they threw him in jail for years.

He stayed silent now, listening to the gargle and hiss of the man beside him dying. He knew he could not help, knew they would do nothing to save that man no matter how much of a fuss he made, knew he himself would suffer for the effort. That stranger in the next cell was too far gone to appreciate someone else risking their lives to call the guards, that was what William told himself. If he shouted out, if they came, they would not help that man, that stranger, instead they would take William to solitary; no doubt they would claim he was fighting them, that he did not go quietly. They would hurt him on the way, he might die too.

Lying on his wafer-thin mattress he prayed the man in the cell next to him was already unconscious. He did not wish that man any pain. He did not wish for that man to lie there wondering why nobody was calling for help. That might be worse than dying.

CHAPTER 11

SERGEANT DANIELS CHECKED one more time that the door was secured – the two privates were standing outside the door, hopefully keeping watch – then limped across the tiny communications room and dropped down into a chair at the comms desk. 'Private Harper, please tell me you have managed to get communications open to the fleet above us.'

'I hope so, Sarge,' Harper said, her voice too small, too young for a soldier. She looked to be no more than fifteen, although she was probably more like twenty-one. She was so white her skin was translucent, the pink of her flesh burning through. The mousey-brown hair on her head was cut in a page-boy cut; a little too long for serving military. Her head would have fit neatly under Shane's chin.

'I have, um, routed extra power from the lights in the rooms connecting to the hatch the Conglomeration troops are attempting to enter through, used it to boost the power available to comms. I hope that's okay.'

Daniels' laugh splattered out. 'That's better than okay, kid, are you sure you work for us?'

'Excuse me, sergeant?'

'That was a bit more creative than I have learned to expect from our people, well done.' Daniels leaned forward, 'Are we ready, Harper?'

'Yes, sergeant.'

Sergeant Daniels picked up the communication handset; on this station, with at least some humanoid staff, there was a handset in the shape of an old-fashioned phone. Other species could request another handset, or tentacle-set, or if nothing for them was available, would have to use the equivalent to speaker-phone, or keyboard or whatever they needed. There was a sound coming from the ear-piece, like listening to a shell, or the hiss of static a great distance down a tube.

'Federation battleship *Yulara*, this is Infantry Sergeant Shane Daniels, we are besieged, the Conglomeration are attempting to gain access to this station. I have no contact with officers from my chain of command and I am by no means certain we have the resources to repel the invaders even if I can find an officer. Please advise.'

'Daniels, putting you through to the bridge, please hold.' The voice at the other end was crackly but at least she could hear it. The line went silent and she waited as patiently as she could manage. Going straight through to the bridge was never a good sign.

'Daniels, this is Captain Carpenter from the Federation battleship *Yulara*, you are the first person from that ship to communicate with us.'

'You can thank the signals private I found for that, sir.' Daniels hoped like hell that surprise wouldn't carry well through the weak connection. Private Harper looked about ready to cry, how cute.

'What is your situation, Daniels?'

'Sir, we have not managed to make contact with any of our officers. I have collected all the infantry I can find and I am looking for others. So far I have not managed to find any higher-ranked NCOs, any officers at all or even most of the soldiers trapped on station.'

'Daniels, we have a problem, the Conglomeration have us outnumbered here. We are in no position to execute a rescue nor are we leaving you there to die or be captured, not while we can still fight. Do you have a plan, Daniels?'

'Yes, sir, but it is not really up to me,' Daniels tried to speak with as neutral a tone as possible. 'I contacted your ship for orders. I was hoping your ship would patch me through to an infantry officer. I did not expect to be put through to the captain.'

'As I said. We have a problem, Daniels.'

'Sir?'

'If you can get to us from the station any officers would have been able to reach us already. That means that, in all likelihood, any officers on the ship or station are dead or incapacitated.'

'Yes, sir.' Shane, like all NCOs, knew that all officers have communicators implanted into the bone of their left wrists that will patch automatically through all Federation networks. It was possible that there was an officer out there without their left arm but Shane decided it would be a really bad time to point that out.

'You are also likely to be the most senior NCO still capable of commanding the infantry, and ship security, on that station.'

'Yes, sir.' Sergeant Daniels was beginning to see where things were going and hoped the worry was not audible. Harper choked and spluttered when Daniels covered the mouthpiece of the phone and mouthed 'oh shit' theatrically.

'We lack the manpower to defend or retake that station,' said the captain, 'we only have enough marines on board to repel boarders if we are attacked.'

'Yes, sir.'

'Do you have a plan, Daniels?'

'If I was in charge I would find all the infantry I could and repel boarders, then I would ensure we have control of the station's defences and attempt to utilise them in holding off the enemy battleship. Knowing you are out there I would also attempt to clear a path for you to land a crew to staff the station guns.'

'What is your ID number, Daniels?'

'Sir?'

'Your number, Daniels.' The captain's voice cut off abruptly leaving no sound but the crackle of the signal and the occasional splash of distortion when plasma fire interfered.

'Sir, 36733264587, sir,' Sergeant Daniels spurted out in a rush.

'Daniels,' the captain said in a tone that was firm but not harsh, 'we are cut off. The ship that took you to that station, the station you are standing in and my ship are the only Federation assets in operation within this system or immediately available. We need to defend that station until we can regain access to the transport and activate the station defences, or until more of our ships arrive. I could land a crew on the station but you are in the process of being boarded and it's a bit too hot for a flight crew.'

'Yes, sir.'

'I need you to repel boarders, we cannot offer you any assistance other than fighters to try and keep the transports from landing,' there was a crackle on the other end, 'more transports that is, there are already two. Most likely a specialist marine boarding team.' Through the crackle Sergeant Daniels could hear the captain breathing, slow but he sounded tense.

'Let the record show that effective immediately Shane Daniels, Federation Forces ID number 36733264587, has received a temporary commission to lieutenant until such time as a commissioned infantry officer becomes available.' The captain paused, the sound of tapping on a keyboard clearly audible through the signal. The pauses went on a bit too long. 'Lieutenant Daniels,' he said finally.

'Yes, sir.'

'Kindly go out there and kick the Conglomeration out of your airlock.'

'Yes, sir.'

'And if you find any officer equipment, such as a communicator or a tablet — not an implant, it won't work — log in with your ID and it should work for you now. Promotions start propagating through the computers almost instantly at this sort of range.'

'Thank you, sir.'

Harper was wide-eyed, looking even younger than she obviously was. 'Well, Harper,' Shane smirked, 'you heard the man, let's go kick some arseholes out of the airlock. But first we need to find the rest of our people. Move out.'

@

Lieutenant Shane Daniels skulked up a corridor. Ahead was the station food hall, someone must have been there when the shit hit the fan, soldiers were always looking for food, or booze, or both, or other things she didn't want to think about. Alarms would have gone off station-wide the moment Conglomeration ships were detected in the system. Shane had been too far from anywhere to have been useful.

The other sergeants from the other platoons on station must have been killed early in the bombardment or they would have managed to make contact with the ships already. None of them could be as freshly promoted as Shane, they would have known what to do; none of them must be alive.

Hopefully someone had fortified the concourse; it would not do her any good to have an accident with friendly fire. It would not do the friendly who fired at her any good either. Again, Shane tried the comms. 'This is Lieutenant Shane Daniels, is there anybody out there receiving?' Nothing came back but crackle and hiss.

The food hall was the closest fortifiable position to the only place the Conglomeration troops would be able to hack in. There had better be troops there or there would be words.

Taking point were the two privates that had been standing confused outside the burning room. They seemed more alert and less afraid. At the back was Harper, as a signals tech and a hacker she was too inexperienced at taking fire and was too valuable in this mission to be risked. Not that the back was safe, it was merely safer, they still didn't know if the station had been boarded.

As they passed a hatch one of the privates stopped. 'Lieutenant, this hatch must lead into a kitchen,' he said.

'How the hell do you know that?' asked Daniels in a tone somewhere between irritated and excited.

'That writing,' he said, pointing at what looked like scratches in the metal, 'it's the name of an Xuthu takeaway, they must have an outlet in the food hall.' He shrugged. 'I like Xuthu food.'

Daniels could see that Harper and the other private were staring at the speaker, Harper looked nauseated. Shane hoped to look not quite so bewildered.

'I know, I know,' the private continued, 'some of you think Xuthu food tastes like garbage mixed with compost and rotting onions, but I like durian and you probably think that tastes like compost mixed with onions too.'

'More importantly,' Shane said, interrupting, 'is the hatch locked?'

It wasn't and they stalked through into a kitchen littered with scattered pans and spilled food. 'You say we can eat Xuthu food?' Daniels asked.

'I do,' laughed the private, 'but I actually like the taste.' Shane stared at him, head tipped to the side, eyebrow raised. He looked scared for a moment. 'Yes, sir,' he said, 'medical have tested it, there is one spice that is poisonous to us but many Xuthu find it distasteful so it is only a table condiment – don't eat that.'

'Okay, people,' Shane said, 'help yourselves to anything that looks edible but be quiet about it and try not to vomit. I did last time I tried Xuthu food.'

Shane was hungry and tired but wary, yet not yet hungry enough to eat Xuthu food, absent-mindedly stuffing a can of something and a packet of something else in voluminous uniform pockets, while trying to watch the door they came in through and the swing door to the front of the shop at the same time. If the enemy came through the swing door their best chance would be that the Conglomeration soldiers would be a little more surprised than them.

'If you have all eaten,' Shane said, 'it is time to move on. Hopefully we have some friends in the food hall, or in the concourse. Let's hope if we do they ID us before they shoot at us. For their sakes too because I am in a hell of a mood.'

The private who liked Xuthu food went through the swing door first, disappearing from view. Then his hand waved through the just-open door, telling them to follow. The other private went through next, looking slightly green, then Lieutenant Daniels, motioning for Harper to stay back.

They were behind a counter, surrounded by the smell of rot, onions and off meat, though Shane found it impossible to determine if the food was rotten or smelled like that when fresh. The service area was covered with spatters of food from broken storage equipment that looked half-industrial, a little medical. The privates were crouched behind the counter, in a slippery mess of spilled food. Daniels skidded over and joined them. They were really going to stink.

Peering over the probably-steel bench in the low light, Shane stared where the entrance to the concourse should be. The blast doors between the concourse and the commerce zone were shut, that was good. There was carbonation around the door controls, someone was desperate to keep the door locked and had blown it. Maybe because there had been nobody around to hack the lock. There was a chance it was enough, though it might be best to weld the door shut just in case.

If they could find welding gear and preferably a sapper.

In front of the blast doors, barely visible in the half-light, was a barricade of tables, other furniture and smashed objects. People huddled in the half-light of the unlit food hall, lanterns and torches from infantry packs, salvaged from who-knew-where, providing the only light. All was grey like a pencil sketch, scribbled and smudged all over until only the shapes were visible. A barricade protected the huddlers from the airlock side, with a decent no-man's land to defend if the airlocks were breached. Which meant someone was aware they were being boarded or they just realised that if anyone tried to board the station it would be through there. Not too stupid then.

Not smart enough though – the enemy could have made it to an access tunnel from the concourse, could be behind them already. Shane hoped not. Most stations were secured against ship-lock failure or an exploding ship because the blast doors were the only access to the station from the concourse. Shane stood, handgun, the only weapon available, holstered – nobody had expected the station to be attacked.

Hand-signing the better-armed privates to stay where they were and provide cover, Shane vaulted over the counter. Calmly, like someone who owned the place, the lieutenant strolled towards the impromptu camp.

Nobody responded, no challenges, maybe nobody was alert enough to notice someone coming from behind. Shane stopped only five metres before the nearest knot of people, they were dressed in civilian street clothes and looked like they were sleeping. They had better be civilians or off watch or they were going to have their arses kicked.

Ruminating on what to say, what tone to take, Shane settled on informal, edging on sardonic, 'Good evening everybody,' at a volume loud enough to be heard over the murmur of voices but not loud enough to cause anyone to shoot. 'Could I speak to the NCOs please?'

Silence spread slowly through the group until finally a couple of startled voices spoke out. 'Who's that?'

'Lieutenant Shane Daniels, formerly sergeant, temporarily commanding whatever sorry-arse excuse for a defence I can pull together out of you mob.'

'By whose authority?' the same voice asked. Shane was impressed, had not expected someone to be alert enough to ask the right questions.

In a tangle of limbs, grey and twisted in the half-light, in the dead, flat glow of LEDs, they huddled. Sleeping, heads taking whatever cushioning they could, bags, bundles and rolls of clothes, each other, there were too few blankets, every blanket was being shared, two, three, four to a cover barely big enough for one. It was cold, the station must have taken enough damage for climate control to become unstable.

Shane hoped the cold would not get worse, with vacuum outside the station it was possible.

Close up the figures became clearer. A soldier lay with a rifle beside him, another had her head on his hip, he didn't seem to notice, she was unarmed but for a bar of steel, shiny, held across her chest. A bunch of civilians lay in a rough pile, so entwined it was nigh impossible to tell one from the other.

Among that tangle of limbs and sleeping heads, there were too few soldiers in uniform. No cordon of alert men, no guns at the ready, no order to the camp. Nobody acting like they were in charge.

A few troops, a couple of station security, a lot of civilians – who would mostly just get in the way – and a freshly field-commissioned officer. Not enough to repel an attack.

The floor shook, sent Shane's knees wobbling, something had hit the station.

Somebody invisible huffed up, somebody else screamed at the boot that half-crushed their hand.

'Whose authority,' the approaching voice huffed.

'We are being boarded,' Shane interjected.

'I know that, I can hear them,' the voice replied sharply, must be a corporal at least.

Shane tried to stare down the invisible eyes. 'One of our battle carriers is out there, attempting to keep the boarders off us, and failing.'

There was a grunt of disgust.

'My lieutenant didn't even make it here,' Shane said, 'what happened to yours?'

The corporal had a look on his face like he had trodden on something. 'She was green, straight out of the academy, when the attack came she ran to the escape pods and when the Conglomeration bombed the pods she was sucked out into space.'

Shane's urge to say 'dumb arse lieutenants' was almost uncontrollable. 'The battle carrier out there needs us to repel boarders so they not be required to retake this station and our transport while fighting the station defences, such as they are. Repelling boarders will help us live a little longer too,' Shane said. 'We need to hold the Conglomeration off long enough for reinforcements. Unless you have an officer here with full capacity, which I doubt from the mess you have made of your defences, I am in charge here.'

There was another grunt of disgust, quickly cut off and followed without pause by a 'Yes, sir.'

'So now we have that out of the way, rank and name.'

'Corporal Geth, sir, I am not the ranking NCO, but I am on this watch.'

'Okay, Geth, let's get our shit in a pile. Start by waking the senior NCO. If they were not a sergeant they are now and sergeants don't get to sleep.'

CHAPTER 12

JIMMY SLIPPED SILENTLY out of the hatch of the luxury yacht and surveyed the station concourse. It had been a boring few days but at least he had made it a little closer towards home. He had liked the ridiculously wealthy retired couple who had offered him a ride; how could he not. Then, after a day of hearing the same stories about their grandchildren, and great-grandchildren, incessantly he had wanted off their ship so badly he had been tempted to throw himself out of the airlock into vacuum. There had been nowhere to go until they reached a station so he had to zone out and pretend he was still listening.

He had wondered how much time he could reasonably spend pretending to sleep. How well did they know humans?

They were now turning the wrong direction, heading towards some holiday world he didn't even want to know existed. They had told him again and again about that too, some place he would never be able to afford to visit. Away from them he realised they had not been so bad after all.

He was still too far from Earth, from the single system, one habitable planet, one being terraformed and a few stations, that constituted human space. There were no humans visible from where he stood even though humans had the right to travel and work across the entirety of the Federation. He strolled towards the commerce zone, which on a way-station this small was bound to be not far from the docking concourse, examining the kaleidoscope of shapes and colours exhibited by the travellers arriving and departing from ships.

The commerce zone was close, the doors of the shops opened directly from the concourse. There were no blast doors, no decompression shields, no protection from vacuum if a connected ship exploded. He strolled to the food hall, looking for something, anything, to eat, anything he could buy with cash. Beside alien stalls with signs in alien languages selling products he did not know whether or not he could digest, there was only one thing he recognised.

Some human foods, mostly fast food, were appreciated by non-humans and tended to pop up in stations. Burgers, sandwiches, fish and chips, Vietnamese pho and especially sushi could be found all over Federation space, at least one of them at each station. He would have expected sushi here, he saw it at more stations than anything else, but here the random human food was burgers, a branch of the Hungry Human.

Hungry Human never took cash.

People of dozens of species filtered past his perch on a backless bench, few of them even glanced his way, people were seldom very friendly on remote way-stations. There must have been humans there before, otherwise they would have been staring at him regardless of their attitude towards strangers.

It seemed crowded for such a small station, maybe shifting traffic patterns had landed the station on a major route, perhaps the war was sweeping people this way, it didn't really affect him either way. At least nobody was wearing badges that identified them as Federation Law Enforcement. For now he had nothing to run from, instead he pretended to doze while contemplating what to do.

He surged to his feet as what looked like a giant spider, furred like a tarantula, with twelve legs, skittered past, politely dodging through the crowd. 'Excuse me, sir,' he said in his best Federal, hoping the spider understood it, 'please can you help me?'

'Young human,' the spider-like citizen skittered, the Federal words barely comprehensible coming from those pseudo-insectoid mouth parts, 'what seems to be the problem?'

That's Ziggys for you, Jimmy thought, always over-polite, over-friendly, they could be helpful if you managed them right. They seemed aware that many species found them distasteful and, already a polite race, they had overcompensated by dialling up the politeness to a level that bordered on weird.

Jimmy quite liked Ziggys.

'I have lost my party, my family and most of my luggage,' Jimmy said in feigned panic, 'I have been waiting here for hours and I cannot buy food without a credit chip.'

'Oh dear,' twittered the Ziggy, 'that must be terrible.' There was nothing readable in that fuzzy spidery face.

'I have money, cash,' Jimmy said in a rush, 'could you buy me a burger at Hungry Human with your chip? I can pay you cash for it.'

'Happy to help,' skittered the Ziggy before disappearing into the crowd.

Jimmy woke to a sound like bones rattling, it took him a long time to work out it was the Ziggy talking. 'Sorry, sir, I fell asleep,' he said. 'Please, sir, can I ask you to repeat what you were saying?'

'I have purchased you a meal pack, burger, a horrible human drink and those things humans call chips that are pretty dreadful,' the Ziggy said.

'Yes, kind sir, chips are pretty dreadful,' Jimmy agreed, 'but they do help fill a hungry belly.' Jimmy didn't want a meal deal, he couldn't really afford it, he reached into his pocket and pulled out his cash. 'Here, sir, how much do I owe you?'

The Ziggy was still and silent, Jimmy never did understand their subtle body language. 'Was that a human idiom,' the Ziggy said with curiosity in his voice, 'because I did not understand it.'

'Please, sir, I would like to pay for my meal,' Jimmy explained. 'How much was it?'

'Oh no, young human, you don't need to give me money, I am happy to help a fellow citizen of the Federation. Also,' the Ziggy made a sound that could have been a laugh, 'I cannot carry cash anyway; I have nothing in which to carry it.'

Jimmy did not dare ask where, if he had no pockets, the Ziggy kept his credit chip. He did not really want to know and it was likely an impolite question. When the friendly alien skittered away, Jimmy sat back and ate his meal, the bench was comfy enough and he felt no desire to move. Soon he would have to find somewhere on station to sleep but for now he would be okay.

After that, he would have to find transportation heading closer to Earth. There was a freighter leaving, he might be able to smuggle himself aboard. There were freighters whose pilots or captains might believe a sob story, smaller ships whose solitary pilots might be bored and enjoy his company. He would need to mope around the concourse to find the right ship.

@

The next station, and everyone on it, must have been as poor as the dirt on their boots even before the refugees descended upon them. Displaced people filled the hotels, overflowed the shabby emergency camp in the food hall, scattered through the filthy commerce area and into the concourse, creating more camps and shanty towns wherever they stopped.

No money left to pay their bills, they squatted; no money left to buy their meals, they stole, or begged. The station was close to the battle front, yet far from the usual trade routes, so there was nothing there to steal, not even the space itself was worth taking, that was why it was poor, and why the refugees were there. The station lacked the resources to send them elsewhere.

Jimmy was close enough to the chaos of the camps that the station police probably assumed he was a refugee too. They left him, huddled, alone, in his corner – he was far enough away that the refugees assumed he was not one of them and didn't talk to him. Or they did not want to talk to him because he was human.

On his first ever encounter on a station he had discovered that humans have a reputation for violence across Federation space. He had needed somewhere to rest and had sat in a place claimed by a local vagabond. They were prepared to fight Jimmy for space until their acquaintance had dragged them away, the words that came from their mouths were unintelligible except for one: 'human'.

The one whose turf Jimmy had usurped kept looking at him, the expression on their face might have been terror.

Here and there in the concourse were other lost wanderers, he could identify them by their air of dejection and the wiry, stubborn strength that would not let them surrender, would not release them to a simple, quiet death. Some were probably on the run like him, criminals or escaped servants, thieves. Still others had most likely been forced into homelessness and had decided that if they were not going to have a home they may as well not have a planet.

He had never seen so many wanderers and tramps in one place. The approach of the war, the movement of so many refugees, had swept them together. He could only assume that, like him, the other wanderers recognised they were safer alone, separate. A group of his type would stand out way too much.

The refugees had the same aura of dejection as the wanderers, yet did not have the quartz hardness, the strength, that would have kept them alive for years in the stainless-steel and plastic corridors that Jimmy lived in. Their belongings were too messy, they carried too much bumf, not enough of the stuff that would keep them alive. They had run with what they could carry with scant regard for what they should carry.

They made family camps on the plastic floor and surrounded them with towels and blankets, hid their treasures and babies in the middle, slept around them. Jimmy had watched them stagger from their ships, overloaded hulks, bulk carriers, hollow trucks. The refugees were sentient, whining cargo rather than passengers – dirty, lost and hungry, crying and helpless.

The station's guards had shot the pest-ridden pets until they ran out of bullets, bludgeoned the rest until there were no more. They had splattered the walls with the blood of a man trying to protect his beloved child's beloved animal, threatened the wailing children who tried to protect their pets.

Some of the refugees were robbed almost immediately, the poverty-stricken locals quick to take any opportunity, too desperate themselves to ignore easy thefts that had landed right in front of them. The refugees were not their species anyway, they mugged, pick-pocketed, profiteered, any small chance to turn the flood of invaders into any minute advantage, a way out of poverty, a meal.

The guards had tried to load the refugees back onto their ships, but even robbed, deprived of their animals, having nowhere to sleep, they refused to move. It had been too hard a trip, too recent in their memories, the ships too rough, even the authorities had to agree with that, they could not force people onto those ships, it would be murder.

Jimmy almost wept for the plight of the refugees, surprising himself. If he had been as fresh from safety as them he would have been as scared, as tired, as hungry and desperate as them. Yet no matter how he sympathised he had no desire to help them, he was close enough to the edge to feel for them which was too close to risk himself to help. Instead he buried himself deeper in his blanket to disguise his shape, his human face. He was not enough like them to disappear completely among them.

Then he saw it, or her, dirty, scraggly, starved almost to bone, dressed in rags, a human child, a little girl. She looked between six years old and a severely malnourished ten, wandering among the refugees like any child who had lost their family. Not crying, she looked, even from a distance, like she was all cried out. She was alone, shunned by the refugees, not taken into any of their family circles, none would even talk to her. Her face was partially obscured by a shock of red-black hair, it looked like it had spontaneously formed dreadlocks. It was her hair that made her appear human for he could not see her face. No species but humans grew hair like hers.

Hair like his.

She must not wander like that, someone might attack her, he thought, might rob her, if she had something worth stealing. They might hurt her in the attempt even if she had nothing worth taking. She might be raped, kidnapped, taken by the slavers that, despite Federation law, always seemed to haunt slummy stations. If station security saw her they would be forced to do something, to be seen doing something. There were many things they might do, none of them good.

A group of security changed direction, heading towards the girl, they must have seen her, or had been watching her. They would take her into custody, keep her there, place her with a family where she would be abused, he knew this in his bones. He would never trust station security.

He wrapped his blanket around his neck and over his head like a hood, he hoped he simply looked cold, hoped he did not look like he had something to hide. What he had to hide was his face, he did not want to look too human. There were many cold beings on the concourse, wrapped in blankets, he became one of them, invisible or at least unnoticeable. Many of the refugees were hooded, he had noticed, it must be part of the traditional costume wherever they had come from.

Weaving through the sleeping, the half dead, the terrified, trying hard not to attract attention by stepping on someone, he moved towards the lost girl. She seemed oblivious to his approach, to the approach of the station security, all he knew was he had to reach her first, she was human. She was human. She was the first human he had seen in a long time.

He reached her mere moments before security did, swept her into his arms like lost family, hoping she would be too bewildered, too shocked to cry out. She was as light as a bird in his arms, hard yet floppy like a bead necklace under her layers of clothes. Turning his back on security, hiding his face as he had seen the refugees do, covering her mouth and hoping security would not notice, he wove back through the crowd, into the food hall.

He grabbed an abandoned half-burger one-handed as he passed the tables. It was a risk, a bit obvious, but he had to get something. Days ago a homeless man – Jimmy never did know where he was from, or even his species – had, in desperation, sat down to someone else's abandoned meal. He had almost finished, almost eaten his fill, when station security descended.

Jimmy saw them take him, but did not see them bring him back. Hopefully he was getting a good feed in the station lockup, maybe he was dead, maybe he had been wanted somewhere for something, his identifying features – most species have something like humans have fingerprints – might have pinged a computer somewhere. That was what Jimmy really feared, a stomach-churning, mind-fogging fear, if security ran his DNA, his fingerprints, his face through the Federation ID system he would be taken somewhere he did not want to be.

There were many starving refugees in that concourse, soon many of them would be raiding any dropped food. Hopefully the risk of doing so would not be too great. Even the bins, generally a reliable source of food, would empty if the refugees got desperate enough.

Nobody followed Jimmy and the bundle in his arms to the darkest, most isolated corner of the food hall. In the crush of bodies in that overcrowded station maybe security were too busy; petty thefts, stupid brawls were like a plague with all those citizens out there in the concourse. They would have no time to spare for harassing a homeless human. Finally sitting, he lowered the little girl to the next seat along. She hunched in on herself, face almost on the table, knees pulled up to her chest, hugged by skinny arms.

Jimmy reached over gingerly, brushed the matted hair from the side of her face. She did not react, maybe was beyond responding, stuck in some internal hell. Her face was filthy, ground in muck and dust, the greasy film that accumulates on poorly maintained ships, a coating that had worked its way into her pores. Even through all that she was still recognisably human. Her eyes were closed, squeezed shut so as to not see, to not be seen, her eyelids crinkled with the force of her conviction to keep them closed.

'Hey, kid, you okay?' Jimmy asked finally.

The girl said nothing, only a hardening of her expression demonstrated she had heard anything at all.

'You okay, kid?' he asked again.

Gently as he could, Jimmy grabbed her under the chin, forced her head up slowly. Her eyes flashed open, burning with anger. She opened her mouth as if to scream and Jimmy covered it with his hand.

'Please, kid, if you scream security will come, we don't want security to come, that would not be good. Please. I will run away if you bring security here, you don't want me to run away and leave you alone, do you?'

There was not a sign in the girl's eyes that she understood a word.

Holding the girl's filthy, knotted hair back from her face, he let go of her chin and grabbed the scavenged burger. Even as stale and cold as the burger was her nose wrinkled at the smell – she was clearly at least half-starved, here was something she understood. She reached for it, Jimmy released the burger to her desperate grab.

He had to stop her, snatch the food back, before she shoved the whole half-burger in her mouth; if she was that hungry she would have to eat slowly. Tearing a smaller chunk of food with his hands he handed it to her, she shoved it in her mouth and started to chew, a small animal moan coming from her throat. Jimmy sympathised, he had been that hungry more than once.

He fed her the rest of the food chunk by chunk, noting her hunger did not seem to be abating. When there was no more a snarl escaped her lips when she noticed. 'Sorry, kid,' Jimmy said in as calming a tone as he could manage, 'no more.'

Again the expression on her face was bewildered, she stared at him with a disturbing intensity.

'Hi,' Jimmy said nervously, 'I didn't get around to introducing myself, my name is Jimmy.'

Her expression of confusion merely grew deeper, Jimmy found it deeply distressing.

'Jimmy,' he said pointing at the middle of his face. It was an almost universal gesture, most species did something like it, or had learned it from humans. She still stared at him in complete bewilderment. 'Jimmy,' he said again, surprising himself with his patience.

He pointed to her and raised his eyebrows.

A noise came from her mouth. It sounded like 'Itta', he hoped that was her name.

'Well, hello Itta,' Jimmy said, 'where have you come from, are you travelling all alone?'

Again she looked at him blankly. It seemed that despite her human appearance she did not speak English. That was not impossible: although English was the most common language spoken by the humans of the Federation, it was not the only language. He stared more at her face, she was olive-skinned, like he was; most modern humans were, there was no obvious reason why she would not know English but no reason why she should.

There was a sound, a terrible wailing, from the speakers, filling the food hall. It must have hit the concourse even louder. There was a cacophony of noise, a frenzy of panicked movement. Jimmy craned his ears, concentrated on the words, alerted by the panic in Itta's face. 'Approaching', he understood, then some words he did not know. 'Conglomeration', then more he did not know, 'prepare to evacuate.'

'Prepare to evacuate, prepare—'

The battle lines had moved.

They were coming.

The refugees were wailing, shoving, grabbing their belongings, getting ready to run. Itta grabbed onto Jimmy in panic, he didn't even know if she had understood the announcement, she might have grabbed onto anyone in her fear but it filled him with unaccustomed emotion, protectiveness. They had to get off the station.

Grabbing his backpack, his blanket, his only belongings, he grabbed Itta by the hand, she seemed to own nothing but herself and the clothes on her back. There were too many scared people in the concourse, the screams of the crushed echoed into the food hall. The crush of the fearful was a wall, an impassable forest of limbs. He saw someone fall, trampled almost instantly by people squeezing into the space created by their sudden tumble. He could feel Itta shaking, she was scared, even more than he was.

Behind them the locals were surging from corridors, from hatches, holding whatever they could grab, carrying children. Their yells reinforced the wails from the concourse, they surged towards the already overcrowded space.

He held Itta's hand firmly when she tried to run and waited until the crush subsided. Cordons of ship security stood at attention before the open doors to the ship access tunnels, protecting the ships from the crowds. There was a shout and then a grunt as a terrified, desperate refugee slugged a guard in the face, followed by the buzz of stun guns firing into the crowd. Jimmy pulled Itta away from the door when station security charged up behind them with batons and more stun guns.

Security waded into the crowd, swinging batons, following the buzzing fire of the stunners. The screaming became deafening, some of the refugees tried to run, crushing each other against the walls of the concourse, against the closing hatches to the access tunnels.

Station security and ship security faced each other across a pile of stunned and beaten citizens.

'. . . calm . . . you will be evacuated,' came the hissing voice over the PA in Federal. There was a moment when the place seemed almost to hold its breath, then the station security slapped gas masks over their faces, and, with a hiss, clouds of yellow gas poured from the vents.

The screams just got louder.

CHAPTER 13

WILLIAM WOKE IN an actual bed, clean sheets, a mattress that felt like a mattress not like a sack stuffed with potatoes and industrial waste. It had been years since he had lain in a soft bed. His tired eyes snapped open in the presence of a too-familiar chemical aroma; the smell of antiseptic, of hospitals, of places where people are healed, of places where people die.

He had no handle on a memory of how he got there.

'Good mornings, William,' the voice was male, or had a male timbre at least, it sounded old and superficial, nauseatingly cheerful. It was also out of sight, behind his head. Strange, it smelled like he was in a hospital yet every hospital he had seen before had the heads of the beds against the wall, nobody should be capable of being where that voice had come from; he craned his neck to see. There were bars behind his head. He stared to his left, to his right, a row of beds then bars. Past his feet was a space then another row of beds, beyond that more bars; empty barely lit space was behind them.

'Where am I, what the hell is going on?' William could hear the panic in his voice, feel the fear rising to heat his face.

'Don't panic,' the old voice said, 'I had you brought here when you collapsed.' The voice had lost some of its comforting quality as if 'paternal' was a costume that a voice could wear, as if voices could wear masks and the mask was slipping. A grating, metallic quality overcame the voice as it spoke, an inhuman quality, like a non-human trying desperately to sound human and comforting. When the mask fell off the voice became reptilian, cold. 'This is a hospital; not the prison hospital although there is nobody here but prisoners.'

'What?' William knew he sounded scared, confused. He fought down the fear, he had survived so much, what was the worst that could happen?

William could not remember having collapsed, could not imagine how he could have, there was nothing wrong with him he knew of that would cause a collapse. He fought to remember what happened before something had sent him into unconsciousness. The guards had come for him, he did not remember why, maybe they wanted to move him to another cell, maybe they just wanted to hurt him again.

He could not remember a beating, yet his ribs hurt. When he tried to move a hand to feel for a broken rib he discovered he was restrained. It hurt to move, he was afraid to fight the restraints and hurt himself more.

'I guess you could say,' continued the voice, sounding now like the wind through a long tunnel, cold, breathy and hollow, 'that it is a prison hospital but not the one you would have expected to wake in.'

'What am I doing here?'

'We will get to that later,' the voice said, 'but you need more rest if you are to get over the injuries those primitive-minded,

95

excessively violent guards inflicted. I will never quite understand your species' relationship with blunt violence.'

The tone suggested there were less-primitive, more creative ways to cause him pain.

There was a click, and a faint hiss, cold pain poured into William's arm through a cannula he hadn't noticed was there. 'No,' was all he managed to say. Heat poured up his arm towards his head, he felt himself getting drowsy, fought the blackness that chased the heat, flooding his head, then succumbed.

His return to consciousness was laborious. The fog in his brain would not clear. He wriggled a bit, found he was still restrained, the painful pressure on his ribs threw him awake. Someone was speaking, it must have been the voice that had woken him.

'We need a surgeon, a surgeon who knows things about humans, about human anatomy that might not be in the medical databases,' the emotionless voice behind William said. 'It says in your file that you are a surgeon, correct?'

William remained silent, he had no reason to trust anyone in the prison system, all they had done was hurt him. He hated that cold, distant voice, that false paternal tone, the breath like that of a lizard or a snake, though that might be just his imagination. If he was able to turn around what would he see? A scaled face, a flickering forked tongue, something so alien he would not even be able to make sense of the features? Last time he spoke to that voice, somebody, it must be the voice, pumped him full of sedatives, knocked him out against his will.

He tried to move, tried to remove the cannula from his arm, neither of his arms would obey the instructions from his brain. He fought with the last reserves of strength to sit up, to turn around and look behind him. Fought and lost. He prayed desperately that he had not been paralysed; while modern surgery could cure nerve damage, even spinal damage, he doubted that would be available to a prisoner.

His panic rose, flooding his body with adrenaline, every muscle was twitching although he lacked even the strength to shake. He did not know if he could stop himself from screaming, didn't know if he even wanted to stop himself.

There was an almost familiar hiss, like the voice of a snake, from above his shoulder. He turned to look, saw a strange box there, controls he did not understand and an IV line running down to the needle in his flesh. Heat poured into his arm from where he could feel the pressure of the cannula.

The drugs washed his thoughts, his emotions, from his head. His blank mind stared out through open eyes.

CHAPTER 14

LIEUTENANT DANIELS WANTED to be in the front, where the corporal was, seeing the danger first, taking the risks, saving everybody who came behind. That was, of course, impossible. Officers, especially the only officer available, should be back in the command centre but Shane flatly refused to stay out of the action. It was not like there was anywhere safe to command from on the station anyway.

The corporal went first, dragging himself into the dusty duct. They were searching for a mystery noise, a banging down the ducts that came and went, which could be a Conglomeration group who had somehow found a way behind them.

The station shook as something explosive hit it. The lights flickered and dimmed. Shane wobbled with the movement but with long experience riding in landers was able to stay upright. The lights came back on again, too bright, then settled.

Their communication was still shoddy, it glitched dramatically every time an energy weapon hit the station, so another man followed soon after, to relay messages. Soon after so did another until Shane was almost alone. Just as the last enlisted man crouched down to enter the crawl space a message came echoing up the vent. 'Lieutenant,' the tinny distant voice echoed down the duct, 'you have to see this.'

'Private,' said Lieutenant Daniels turning to the last man, 'take the rear, don't let anyone shoot me in the arse.' The private suppressed a giggle.

'Don't you shoot me in the arse either.' Daniels laughed then snarled, 'Seriously though, you shoot me in the arse and I will shoot you.'

It was a tight claustrophobic crawl, a head lamp lit the duct wherever Shane looked, the light shifting too fast from side to side with every head movement. Everything outside of the beam of light was dark, except for occasional disorienting splashes of light reflected from the shiny walls of the duct.

Shane reached one of the privates, he moved on when he was tapped on the boot, the next moved on when they reached her. It was a tight, warm space, filled with the smell of soldiers who had had their leave broken early, who had no way to keep clean, who might have been drinking when the alert sounded, who might be still hung-over. Sweat and stale alcohol, booze-sweat, a smell like no other. Another smell threatened to overwhelm even that odour, although Shane could not quite place it.

There was a squeal over the comms then for a moment the sound of plasma cutters and banging on the doors could clearly be heard over the comms. The Conglomeration were close to breaking through but there should be time enough yet.

By the time the opening from the duct was visible the smell was so nauseating only iron willpower could stop Shane from vomiting. The narrow vent opened near the top of a wall, where the corporal had obviously kicked out a grille, the floor of the room was about Shane's height downwards. The small troop of soldiers were standing in a knot, all facing the same direction, weapons at the ready.

Shane stared the way they were looking, at the pool of light created by the beams of their head-torches. There was a mess there, a stinking mess, with what looked like it could be people in it. The situation appeared to be under control so there was nothing to do but slide out carefully with the help of a private who stepped over without comment.

The corporal turned before Shane even spoke, lowered his gun and approached.

'Sir,' he began, 'we found these beings, these citizens. They appear to have been in this room for some time, they have a lot of stuff and, as you can tell from the smell, they have made a lot of mess.' His nose wrinkled. 'We haven't found an exit from this room except a maintenance hatch that has been sabotaged to stop it opening.'

'Who are they?'

Another explosion shook the station, loud enough to be audible even there in that hole. One of the beings screamed, a sound that to Shane sounded wordless. The corporal snapped his mouth shut until the echoes died away.

'We are not sure,' the corporal said finally, 'nobody can speak their language and their Federal is shit. From the mess and their sorry state I would guess they are stowaways. We would expect to see stowaways on ships though, not on stations.' Lieutenant Daniels gave him a look that left no doubt that, frankly, everybody knew that. 'They could be here between ships, but we can't be sure. One thing we do know, they can't get out.'

'Explain.'

'The maintenance hatch door locks have been disabled, sir,' he said calmly. 'The hatch can't be opened, not from the inside anyway, most of the people in here are not fit enough to climb out through the vents we came in, even if they had managed to break through into the ducts, which we know they haven't. Besides,' he sounded angry, 'the mess in here, the fact they are dying of starvation and dehydration, I would guess they simply can't get out. There's some evidence they had been beating on the hatch with something, which explains the noise we have been chasing at least.'

'Have you talked to them?' Daniels asked.

'We are trying, Lieutenant, but none of us have ever even heard their language.'

'Okay,' said Daniels, pulling out a salvaged officer's tablet, 'let me try.'

It was a long, meandering, patience-testing conversation, aided slowly by a translation app on the salvaged officer's tablet. It didn't matter how much both sides wanted to be understood, there was simply not enough language in common. Even the translation app struggled, and it was supposed to know every language in the Federation. Supposedly some words on each side of the conversation had no equivalent in the other.

Repeatedly both sides resorted to gestures in frustration when even Federation sign failed. From time to time Daniels broke away from the attempts at conversation and looked over to the closed hatch, glad someone was at least trying to get it open. They needed a way out of the room, they needed to escape from the smell as much as they needed to return to the defence now they had found the noise was not dangerous. A headache, from the smell, from the attempts to translate, was becoming an inevitability.

After what felt like hours but was probably only long minutes, fairly certain the strangers were no danger to the station, Shane walked over to where the corporal was supervising the attempt to break open the maintenance hatch. 'Any luck?'

'Whoever locked this hatch did not intend anyone to get out of here, we might have to climb out through the vents then open it from the outside,' the corporal said.

After a moment's silent thought, Lieutenant Daniels clicked on the communicator. 'Harper, how are you with locked and jammed hatches?'

There was a moment of silence, maybe Harper was thinking. 'Depends what's wrong with it, Lieutenant,' came Harper's timid voice finally, 'that is, sir, is it a hardware or a software fault?'

'It's not faulty, Harper, it's been tampered with, none of us on this side, the wrong side of it, can even figure out what is wrong. There are civilians trapped in here with us, otherwise we would just crawl out through the damned ducts the way we got in. Find some other hacker who knows the stuff you don't know, collect a couple of grunts for protection, on my orders, find hatch number—' The number was just visible in the bad light and needed to be translated to human numerals. The pause was embarrassingly long. '87201, and get the damned thing open. I would like to get back to defending this station now.'

Lieutenant Daniels turned back to the corporal, 'Corporal . . . Palmerston,' that was what it said on his name patch. 'I think I understand what's going on here. I think the trouble these citizens are in is not entirely of their own doing. I believe they paid someone they are unable or unwilling to identify all they had in the world to get them safely out of the war zone. They were brought here, smuggled on a freighter, locked in this maintenance area, they say they are waiting to be collected and taken to another ship. Whoever was supposed to collect them never did.'

'Shit,' hissed Palmerston.

'We have to look after them.'

'We can put them with the other civilians, sir.'

'Shit, the station was full of civilians, where did you put them, why didn't I think of them?'

Palmerston was silent for a moment, 'The sergeant, my sergeant, had us send the civvies to the shelter just before he died of his wounds. It's the hall in the middle of the station. I spent a lot of time on Jupiter Station One just before I signed up, I might even retire there,' he continued, 'it's a colony station, bigger than this one but certain things in all stations are the same. There is a relatively blast-proof box, well, a cylinder really, in the middle of these stations, big enough for the whole population and a few extra bodies if they are not too needy for personal space. There is food in lockup cabinets under the floor, enough air for about a week. Even if the station is destroyed it will take the Conglomeration a while to destroy the shelter. We can take our refugees there if the people hiding there haven't sealed it yet. They can't get to the food supplies until they seal it and they won't feel safe with it open so they might have.'

'We can feel and hear the bombardments,' Shane said, 'they will have felt them even if they could not hear them, I think we can assume they already have the shelter locked down, not that we have any time to escort these citizens to the shelter anyway. They will just have to stay with us and the other civilians we have in the concourse.' She searched the soldiers standing around but could not find what was needed on their insignia. 'Does anyone have medic training?'

One of the privates spoke up, 'I have medic class four,' he said timidly.

'That will have to do. Check these civilians over, see if any of them need medical support, ensure they are all safe to move.

I know you have no experience with this species but they must be in the Federal medical database which you, being a medic four, should have on your tablet. I expect Harper will be through that door any time now.'

©

A fast-jinking fighter, too fast, struck Romeo's heavy gunship a glancing blow only seconds after she exited the flight-deck. She could feel the heat even through the synthetic quartz viewport, even though it had mirrored instantly to deflect the radiation. She dodged faster than most would try in that brick of a ship, flicking the attitude controls faster than breathing. The ship that shot her must have been surprised to see a heavy manoeuvre like that. Romeo took advantage of that confusion, fired only a fraction of the ship's full power, saw the faster Conglomeration fighter disappear in a flash.

'Holy shit,' came over the radio, 'who the hell is flying that heavy?'

'Must be Romeo,' came another voice, 'nobody else can fly like that.'

Romeo almost laughed. 'Hey kids,' she said, 'I seem to have broken my delta to the point they won't let even me try to fly it.' There was a burst of laughter over the comms. 'They seem to think I might find it harder to break this one.' She laughed.

The transport cutters were still attached to the station. 'Anyone communicating with the station?' she asked.

'Yes, ma'am,' came a voice. It was her second, call sign 'Boxer', real name Bobby.

'And what did they say, Boxer?'

Another fighter came for her, she had to concentrate on that for a moment, returning her concentration to the radio once the enemy exploded. 'Sorry,' she said, 'what was that?'

'They are still attempting to repel boarders, Romeo,' said Boxer, 'they are ludicrously outnumbered but that friend of yours, Lieutenant Daniels, is still alive and holding ground.'

There was silence on the radio as Romeo joined the fighters; they had been momentarily swept away from the cloud of death around the station by the action. When she fell into formation with them, at the front as you would expect a heavy fighter to be, in the front where she liked to lead from, they turned back towards the enemy cutters. A swarm of enemy fighters flew towards them out of the shadow of the enemy battleships.

Someone screamed, 'Fuck!' It didn't matter who, they were all thinking it.

'If anyone is low on fuel or ammo this is not a good time to be in formation,' Romeo hissed over the radio, 'let me know if you need to return to base and rearm, refuel, or even if you are getting chicken.' Nobody turned back, nobody informed her they were low on ammo.

'Seriously though, I don't need anyone out here who is not willing to die with me, I don't need anyone too tired or hurt to fight and I don't need anyone low on resources. Now would be the time.' Surely everybody but her, fresh from the hangar, was low on fuel but they would not tell her that; they must have been terrified, she was, but they would never admit it. They would not pull out of the fight while there were humans in danger on the station.

They were all going to die.

CHAPTER 15

THE SUN WAS the bloodshot eye of a drunkard, what light filtered through the black smoke was wan and sickly. Walker surveyed the Country through dust-rimmed, tear-fogged eyes. He knew this place, or thought he knew it, knew that hill, that bend of dry creek-bed, that rock. If only he could remember how he knew it. What was that place, so close to his heart he knew it; so far away in his memories he could not place it.

He fell to the ground, sat cross-legged, stared until his eyes watered, listened to the song of the wind, felt the dust under his palms. The black dust was not right, he brushed it away, the sand was proper red beneath, that comforting red; Home. He buried his fingers in that red, felt the Country with his soul. He stared again at the grey-black landscape, imagined the desert oaks grey-green, the sand red, the spinifex copper and gold.

Home, that was the word for where he was. He was Home.

Instinct had led him, some force outside himself had driven him to this place in his grandfather's Country. He wanted to snuggle into the arms of the Country, hold it close, let it help him, let it heal him, but first he needed to eat, needed to find water. Tears burst from his eyes and watered the red sand, the black dust.

'Hello, I am coming Home,' he spoke to the air, to the dust, the rocks, 'this is my grandfather's place, I am Home, please, I am Home, I am family.' The Country did not answer, he hoped it had heard him under all that fallen black smoke.

It seemed to take a very long time to stand. Even in that short hiatus on the ground the black dust had settled on him, it wafted from him in clouds. Panicked, he brushed it from his clothes, ignoring the pain in his hands, the pain on his skin where he bashed and hammered at himself.

Somewhere near here, he remembered, was his grandfather's waterhole; he could remember being taken there, introduced to the place. The living water would be more powerful than this black dust; the living water would keep him alive, maybe he could stay here and get better. All he had to do was find that place and all would be well; his grandfather, his old people and the waterhole would look after him.

Taking bearings from the rocks, he would have run if he could, he staggered in the direction his childhood memory, his instinct, led him. Familiar terrain, his Country, sand, low scrub and spinifex, he walked it easily. Not far, he knew it was not far.

The feel of a smile on his face surprised him.

There the rock, the old grandfather tree, the other rock with ancient faint remnants of etching on it. A dip in the track, then the scrub got a tiny bit thicker. He stopped, listened, sniffed, searched his memory and his soul, somewhere near here was the waterhole he sought, where his great-grandfather was born. He listened, walked with eyes half-closed.

There! A small stain was before him, a patch where the sand was darker wet, the black dust was thinner there. He could see, could smell, could feel the living water rising to the surface.

Dropping to his pained knees, he scraped at the sand, pained fingers dragging moist sand away from the water. With every handful the sand felt a tiny bit damper, with every handful he felt the living water come closer. He dug a hole, knowing that was where to find the water of his soul. When his grandfather had died his soul had returned to this waterhole, he could feel it, could feel the warmth of an embrace in the sun on his shoulders, it had cut through the black smoke to drape itself over him.

Finally, he put his hands into the sand and felt water, it had pooled in the bottom of the hole. He dug a bit deeper and freed the spring. Water trickled and flowed into the hole, clean water, life itself was filling the hole he had dug. He drank the cool water, washed his face with it, careful to keep the black dust from falling in it. Relieved, he collapsed, lying in the warmth of the sun next to the living water of his ancestors.

CHAPTER 16

JIMMY SAT WITH Itta in a lonely corner of the concourse and watched fights break out over food, blankets and clothes, over a square metre of clear floor space in which to sit. Families fought families, for there was never enough room for a family to have space for all of them to lie down, or even sit together.

Members of families took turns sitting; often when someone had to lie down all their companions had to stand. They took turns defending their blanket-delineated spaces. Stronger people, stronger families, took room to spread out, kept it by force, while others sat, piled on top of one another, hugging their few shabby, likely worthless, belongings to them.

Eventually, Jimmy thought, the strong families would tire and a limited democracy of exhaustion would dominate. Nobody would be strong enough, one day, to hold more space than they needed.

Jimmy might have lost his mind if not for his friend, her skinny bird-boniness was nestled in under his arm, almost curled in on herself, a comforting presence, a powerful love he did not understand. He needed to be strong to look after her and her presence gave him strength. Her smile, the perplexed way she looked at almost everything, made him smile.

The ship carrying them on that last sprint towards safety, nothing more than an inter-system ferry, designed for short hyperspace hops to the next star but no further, had not the capacity for so many passengers. There would have been nowhere to sleep even when it had not been overloaded, once the refugees poured in there was not even enough room left to stand. Those on chairs had thought they were lucky, until the crush of bodies became so great that fights over those chairs broke out.

There was a crush, someone died, someone else was left broken, torn, crippled, unconscious maybe dying. The dead citizen was removed, the killers, nobody could know who the killers were, stayed on the ship.

Crammed into that ferry, everyone carrying everything they owned, the ship loaded to about three times its maximum capacity with bodies, they nearly didn't make it. The air had grown thick with breath, with sweat and fear, with the smell of people of multiple species who had gone too long unclean. The scrubbers, the air purifiers pushed to the very limit, the ship went on emergency air, then that too ran out.

A stranger breathed their last leaning against Jimmy; already weak, they could not tolerate the crush, the lack of air, they were held up for a moment by the force of bodies, their foaming face, their blank eyes just inches from Jimmy as they started to slide to the ground. They fell on Itta, knocked her down, bodies collapsing around them like dominoes.

There was a cry, then more and more until everybody was screaming. There was nowhere to shift the dead to, no space to place a foot, no hand-holds for the living to grapple so they could stand. Jimmy pulled Itta to him over a stranger who screamed and climbed over the people around him until he was seated, pulled the girl onto his lap, did not look at whatever he was seated on, did not want to know.

There was a palpable, indescribable sense of relief when the ship hit dock, when the faint sound of the engines, a sound they were no longer conscious of hearing, ceased. That relief was not enough though, they were still stuck in a great pile of bodies. Nobody had enough room to get their feet under them.

At the edges of the passenger compartment some managed to stand, Jimmy found room for his feet between the bodies on the ground and helped Itta to her feet. She rested her flimsy shoes on the relatively stable ground on top of his boots, grabbed around his torso like someone hugging a tree. He helped those near him to stand with the hand that was not holding Itta. There was a ripple of movement, glacially slow, as those standing helped others to stand, who helped yet others to stand.

More immobile bodies were found – living or dead, there was no way to tell; insensible or silenced forever, there was little difference. As one the gathered refugees stood immobile. For the moment at least united by their apprehension, knowing that there was not even enough room to fight.

When the alarm sounded to inform them the door was to open there was a sense of breathless relief, metamorphosing into cries when the doors did not actually move. There was a hiss as the pressure equalised between the ship and the station, Jimmy felt pressure in his ears release, felt Itta squeeze his hand in her pain. The doors still did not open. Something was wrong, they were on station power, there should have been enough energy to open the doors. Jimmy felt the panic flood through him.

The air smelled a fraction fresher, although it was still uncomfortably thin, the faintest tinge of ozone tickled Jimmy's nose.

Finally, the hatch eased open and those closest to the opening fell out, collapsing to the ground. People lost their minds to fear – they had to get out, get out, get out. Then came the blood-chilling cries of panic as the already crushed and crowded mob of bodies, three species, four if you included the two humans, united only in fear, tried to force themselves through a too narrow door all at once. Again, Jimmy heard the now too familiar buzz of stunners. When the screaming came he was ready for it.

The cabin seemed to shake with anxiety and anticipation. A voice came over the speakers, speaking Federal.

'Calm,' the voice said '. . . you will be *xchahg*.' Jimmy did not understand that word, what he did understand was that the announcement made everyone else anything but calm. He tugged on Itta's hand, drew her with him to the back corner of the cabin, as far from the door and the screaming, surging crowd as he could manage.

Few others seemed to have the common sense or the self-control to move away from the crush so everybody kept adding their bodies to the danger. Someone from outside removed the stunned, unconscious citizens from in and around the door, helped the bleeding and unconscious stand then more people tumbled through, screaming.

Slowly the numbers milling around the doorway decreased as people trickled out.

Jimmy did not want to be the last to leave, two humans would be too noticeable, someone might ask why he and Itta were on that ship, how they got there, where they were from. He did not want to answer for himself and he could not answer for Itta at all. She had latched onto him as if he was the only way she could stay alive, that might even be true; he held her hand like it was important, maybe it was.

He pulled her towards the doors, milled around with the sick and wounded who were left, holding Itta's hand, his blanket wrapped around his shoulders and over his head like a hood. Head down like he was incapable of looking up, backpack under his blanket so nobody could see he was better packed, more prepared, than the others, who carried their stuff in whatever they could find.

He kicked through dropped belongings, a torn plastic bag someone had carried their stuff in, a single shoe, some dropped precious food, what looked and felt like clothing.

Nobody paid him undue attention as he walked out of the hatch, past a pair of guards of a species he was unfamiliar with, armed with stun guns. There was a corridor marked off with ropes like the entrance to a ticket booth at a cinema back on Earth – Jimmy remembered going to a movie when he was little, weaving his way through a labyrinth of thick soft ropes to a counter faced with red carpet. Now people were lined up between the ropes, shuffling slowly towards a line of tables, stopping there to be interrogated by some sort of official.

The line before him grew shorter, the people, their bundles of everything they owned, disappearing one by one into a larger crowd that filled the far end of the concourse with a forest of bodies. Other ships must have come before Jimmy and Itta's ship had arrived, faster ships or from somewhere closer. Jimmy had a strong desire to flee, yet there was nowhere to run, and running would only increase his chance of unwanted attention.

Slowly, relentlessly, the table, the interrogators approached, until there were only a couple of people ahead of Jimmy and Itta. He wanted to crowd in on them to see what they were being asked, but that too would be stupid, so he just stood there.

It was their turn, there was nobody ahead of them, nobody to shield them from those prying eyes. He wanted to scream, yet would not.

'Passport?' The question slipped out from somewhere in the face before him in flat, unaccented Federal. All he could do was shake his head, he had no passport, no permissions to travel, no papers, no forms of identity at all. What papers he once possessed he had destroyed, dropped into a trash receptacle, hopefully the only proof of who he was had already, many days ago, landed in a molecular debonder. He had no idea who Itta even was.

Nobody asked their names. He was not aware of moving or making any sort of gesture, he said nothing. There was a sound like a grunt in front of him. Something that must be a finger pointed away to the left, he turned, there was another table there and someone, the same species as his interrogator, was beckoning to them.

He could feel himself shaking with fear, making Itta quiver too.

He pulled on Itta's hand and they walked to the table, towards their doom, towards his arrest, to unknown risk. Whoever was seated at the desk spoke to them rapid-fire in a language Jimmy did not understand. Jimmy had no clue why they were not speaking Federal.

Itta squeezed his hand, hard, maybe she did not understand either, it was neither English or Federal, sounded nothing like any other language he had heard. Standing still and silent, half insensible, he watched as hands, three-fingered and more delicate than those of a human, typed something into a tablet computer of some kind. There was a flash of light, must be a camera, he thought, too dazed to even care; of course they would photograph him before arrest. He stared at the being behind the desk in total bewilderment, what was he supposed to do?

There was a strange mechanical, whirring noise; a faint, familiar, whiff of hot plastic; more yammering in that befuddling language. He simply stood there, waiting for security to come take them away.

Then he realised, the official before him was waving a hand, something was clasped in those three long fingers. Without even thinking he reached out and took whatever it was that was being offered. The hands waved again, a universal gesture meaning 'that way'. He walked out past security and into the crowd.

Only then did he look at what he had taken. Two ID cards, one with his face on it, one with Itta's.

CHAPTER 17

THE OWNER OF the mysterious voice turned out to be a member of what humans insultingly called the Brainbug Alliance. William had heard of them, not a nation or a species but instead a loose collaboration of multiple species who cared only for science. He had no idea what they called themselves. Their faces were always covered in public, a mask and goggles, shade and mirrors, no features, every inch of skin covered by what looked like matt, opaque plastic in impossible black. The sigils of their allegiance, of their dedication to their profession, were printed on their masks in metallic copper.

His tormentor, his controller, was vaguely humanoid, would be heavyset if he was human and about six feet tall, his long robe or dress gave scant clue of his shape other than it being broad. He could be human, if not for that voice. No human could produce such impersonal sounds as that. He asked William to call him Jack. That was not surprising, it was the only human name many species knew.

Jack said he was a medical researcher. The building, if it was a building, they were in was a medical centre, a hospital, a research facility, perhaps all three, perhaps none of the three in any way humans would understand. Perhaps it didn't exist at all and William was still in the prison, trapped in a hallucination. Perhaps he was strapped to a bed, insensible, in a psych ward somewhere.

Mostly it appeared to be a research facility that used prisoners as research material.

Maybe, and William's gut lurched, they were in space; it was not a building at all but a ship or a station.

William felt he had no choice but to help Jack in his work, otherwise they would have left him strapped to that bed, fed from a tube, until the moment he died, which would almost certainly be many years away. He had no doubt they would keep him alive until he did what they wanted, until the solitude, the immobility, melted his resolve. The reason he knew that was because Jack had told him.

The halls William saw were stark, curved and featureless white, no decoration, no signage for directions, no windows, no door handles just white walls, white floors that showed no sign of his passing, white ceilings with blinding lights that seemed to have no recognisable source. He had no idea how anyone else navigated through the area, he was constantly lost.

Maybe the signs and markings everyone else used were in a part of the spectrum invisible to humans. That would go some of the way to explaining the faint bluish tinge to the light, the mild eye and head pain, like a permanent migraine, that came with it, like standing outside too long on a too-bright day.

Maybe there were no visual markers at all, maybe everyone else navigated by smell, by taste, by inbuilt GPS, by some sense humans were completely unaware of.

The doors opened when William walked up to them if he was allowed to pass; there was no sign of where the doors were until they opened. Maybe the doors, or whoever controlled them, knew who he was by identifying his face with an unseen camera, or by checking his smell, reading his DNA, examining his aura for all he knew.

He would wander without aim until a door appeared.

It was the same in the cell where he spent the nights, or what he assumed were the nights, there were no windows. If there were clocks they were kept from him or invisible; displaying the time in some part of the spectrum he not could see. Maybe they didn't care if he knew the time, or cared that he not know.

The door opened when they decided it was time for him to work and only then, closed when he walked back in after being dismissed. If it was time for him to go back to his cell, the doors herded him there. Once he entered his cell it closed and he knew it would not open again until they decided to get him up.

The lights would switch off when they intended him to sleep, switch on when they wanted him awake. He was a machine, an automaton, the lights were his on/off switch, the doors his controls.

He was getting confused about time, tired when he should not be, alert when he wanted to sleep, fog-brained when those in charge of the switch needed him alert. Maybe he was no longer on a wake–sleep cycle even remotely like twenty-four hours. He had seen the results of long-term adaptation failure before; it was going to drive him mad.

CHAPTER 18

'MY HUSBAND DIDN'T want me to sign up,' said a gruff masculine voice Lieutenant Daniels did not recognise off to the left. 'He threatened to divorce me, didn't reply to my letters all the way through basic.' There were murmurs, Shane could not understand any words but the tone was obvious. Most of them had left somebody behind.

Another voice floated out, calm and deep, like he was trying to out-butch the other guy. 'My wife loves me being a soldier, I think she hates me being in the house.'

'Probably sharing your house and bed with someone else while you are out here,' a hard woman's voice said. There was an explosion of laughter, momentarily overwhelming the discontented mumbling. A half-hearted scuffle broke out, surging like a wave through the bundle of infantry resting and yarning in the darkness.

'Nobody even cares if I live or die, I don't even have a wife to complain about.'

'Shut up, Shut-up.'

The troops needed rest, but Daniels let them talk, they needed to let off steam even more. The higher brass might disagree but there was no good reason to stop them tussling if they felt the need. Through the darkness they could hear the enemy sappers, or whatever the Conglomeration called them, trying to penetrate the blast doors – the buzz of cutting lasers, of plasma cutters vaporising metal, the hammering of improvised tools on the door. The troops were used to it; if there were no orders and no death coming your way you slept or dozed, or argued, half-heartedly, with your comrades.

The doors had been checked, their own sappers had welded them shut and then welded whatever metallic junk they could over the welds. There were table frames, pieces of sheet-metal, scrap from who-knows-where. If it was metallic enough to weld, they had added it to the mess accreted to the doors like coral.

Station security were encamped with them and would be at least a little useful for repelling boarders but they were not trained for this sort of fight, or for the nervous empty time soldiers were used to. Shane could see one of them, in a grey-green uniform, looking nervous, though with inter-species body language, who could tell?

At least station security had opened their armoury once the soldiers and Shane persuaded them. There might have been threats involved. Shane was the ranking infantry officer, it didn't matter if they reported they were threatened by the lieutenant; it was a siege. Any officer had the right to shoot them if they disobeyed orders.

Shane's husband had not approved of the army either. He hated the idea of the war, had not understood why anyone would enlist. They had yelled and fought, desperately trying to explain their far distant positions. In the end both had walked away in surly silence. Shane had enlisted the next day.

Perhaps if less angry, if thinking clearer, in less of a hurry, Shane would have tried for a commission as an officer.

He had refused to speak at all when Shane returned from the recruiting office to say goodbye.

He had never understood; Shane had done it for their children, for the country, for the planet, for ancestral land that had been stolen once and never would again. Allowing invaders from space to take the planet without a fight was unconscionable.

Shane regretted having asked if anyone had a spare helmet, tore it off, resisted the urge to throw it across the room and placed it carefully on the floor instead. She didn't want to know where it came from, whose helmet it had been, they were probably dead. Her hair was still in a perfect bun at the base of her skull, neat and out of the way.

It had been a quiet day when the Conglomeration attacked. Her son was at kindergarten, her hubby at work. The baby was asleep. Shane finished the housework, started work on her script, struggled her way through writer's block with nothing but her legendary bloody-minded stubbornness when what she needed was elegant subtlety.

A noise, almost silent as a cricket, clicked from her handbag on the couch. She ignored it, only a message, can't be that important. Then another, 'crick', and another. Then her landline rang, her mobile began drumming out so many alerts they merged together into one scratchy noise. In a final assault on her peace, her doorbell rang.

The door first, it was her neighbour. She was visibly terrified, her eyes spraying tears, her hands shaking with shock.

The landline rang out before Shane got there, she was left holding a receiver listening to the burr of the dial tone. She dropped it back onto its cradle and turned around.

'Shane,' the neighbour began, 'oh my god, Shane.' She degenerated into silent shakes, her eyes open but blank.

Her husband must have hit her again, Shane thought, one day she or her own husband would have to have words with him. Knowing him, the conversation would descend quickly into violence.

Shane reached out to offer whatever comfort contact could bring when the landline rang again.

'Shane,' the voice on the phone was almost screaming, it took her too long to realise it was her mother.

'Mum, what's wrong?'

'Oh my god,' her mother said, fear driving her words out too fast, into the phone, in a breathless tangled pile. 'They are coming, they are really coming, they don't want peace, they want the world, I think they want the world, they want to kill us all and take the world, what are we going to do, what are we going to do, what are we going to do, they are here, I heard them overhead, or was that ours, I heard them overhead. Shane, please, help me. They are here, I think they are right outside, they are really here.'

'Mum,' Shane interjected, 'what are you talking about?'

'The aliens,' her mother said, 'the aliens are here, everywhere, the sky is full of them, and they are going to take over, they are going to kill us all, their ships are everywhere, they are coming, they are here, oh my god, I need to find your father, I need to tell him I am sorry, I need to get out of here, I have to get out of here, oh god.'

'Mum, stay there, it will be okay, I promise.' Shane hung up and turned to her neighbour who stood still in silence, quivering, breathing rapidly like a scared bird.

'That was my mum,' Shane said, 'she reckons aliens are coming to get her, how funny is that?'

The other woman was shaking even more, now her head was quivering out of time with the rest of her, no it wasn't she was shaking it. 'No, don't tell me the aliens really are here, it's not funny.' Shane laughed.

Shane picked up her mobile. There were hundreds of new messages. She looked back to her neighbour, who was now nodding. Confused, she looked back to her phone, most of the messages were from the Emergency Contact system, message upon message about some emergency.

The most recent update was a situation summary, it started with a simple headline 'Caution, unknown numbers of unidentified objects have appeared in the sky above the world's largest population centres. So far the motives are unknown.'

'Oh fuck,' was all she could say before her mind rebooted, before her fear kicked in. She wanted to run out her door, she would have to take the baby. Her son, her husband, where the hell were her family?

In basic training, Shane had channelled her anger – the fury at the treatment of her people, the arguments with her husband – into the war. She was angrier, faster, a better shot than anyone else yet, somehow, generations had prepared her, she kept the anger under firm control.

She was a good writer, creative and stubborn. She had turned those traits towards learning to fight. Her solutions to military problems were unexpected, her bloody-mindedness did not let her not be the best. Whatever happened, anyone who wanted to take her Country, anyone who wanted to harm her children, they would have to go through her. She made sure to learn the arts of war; going through her was not going to be easy.

Eight years she had fought the war, stayed alive when others died. That was what her people did, they survived. Every fight she survived she got better at killing, better at staying alive. Every battle she survived made her more determined to get back to her family; too long she had been away from them. She regretted leaving her husband like that, leaving her kids without a mother, she would get back to him and to them if she had to win the war herself.

One thing surprised her more than anything else, hating violence is not the same as not being good at it.

@

As the fight for the station went on, Romeo had taken to rotating out pilots and their planes whenever they ran low on fuel. While the ground crew loaded fuel and ammo into ships, repaired what was broken, replaced worn parts before they failed, checked whatever could be checked, the pilots had a chance to sleep and eat. Sleep or eat, really; nobody had time for both.

Where the fuck were their reinforcements? When it was Romeo's turn to refuel, she had just enough time for a few moments sleep in an armchair in the ready-room. In sleep she dreamed, remembering the eve of the war.

When Perth was attacked the Conglomeration had bombed the city centre first, perhaps trying to weaken any potential defence or kill as many people as possible. As crowds ran they were hit with energy weapons, with incendiaries, with gas. Romany had been at home in the suburbs, sleeping off a big night drinking, a long night with friends who worried she was not okay. She woke to a message from the lover she had just lost, it simply said 'please forgive me'. The morning news told her of the attack, she decided enough was enough.

She left the city immediately. Her family – like many people from out bush she had a big family – were all on Country, they believed it would protect them, maybe they were right. She loaded extra fuel into the back of her car and drove as far as she could.

The drive out of Perth, out towards Country, towards familiar desert, to family, quickly began to look like a very bad idea. Roads were cut, blocked by crashed cars, by vehicles burned, cut in half, by traffic where there should be none, by military road-blocks, by war and death. She had to turn back, look for another way, more times than she could count. Eventually she had stopped completely where a traffic jam had formed seemingly in the middle of nowhere. Pulling over to the side of the road, she had closed her eyes.

By the time she woke the blue-white sky was bright where it was not filtered by the overhanging trees. She had parked between two gargantuan trees, completely by accident. She didn't even know how she had missed careening into them in the dark. To the passenger side was a forest, dappled light and dense green shadow; on the driver's side the bole of a huge tree then open space, nothing but knee-length grass, to the road.

Clouds criss-crossed the sky, long and thin, a matrix of white. She realised some were were contrails from planes; others, wider and solid, from some unknown craft.

A jet scorched across the sky, adding its lines to the abstract art overhead. It had come from the city behind her and was headed the same way as she had been before falling asleep. The traffic jam had gone, leaving behind a scattering of wrecks, some of them still occupied, anyone in them must be dead; some of them still burning, acrid smoke reaching into the sky like the arms of leprous beggars. There were scorch marks in the trees, on the grass, fallen leaves and branches, a large branch leaning against Romany's passenger door. Brush and grass still smouldered despite the rain overnight that had soaked the vegetation.

Somebody had fired upon the traffic jam. She was beyond lucky to be alive.

She started the car, too afraid to get out even to pee. She was hungry, thirsty and tired, feeling around on the floor of the passenger side she felt the crinkly supermarket bag she had stashed there. Inside was chocolate and cans of cola, the only food she had managed to buy at the only shop taking cash when she had fled the city. She could have bought more if she'd had a gun, or ammo, or something else like that to trade. But she would have to be stupid to give a gun up now.

If she kept it she could just take whatever she wanted.

Easing out onto the road she wove her tiny hatchback through the stopped traffic, ignoring the corpses still seated in their cars, some charred, some bleeding, some looking untouched – their heads hanging, their eyes empty of life. Her passenger-side wheels bumped over something soft, a person, must be, she winced and retched, closed her eyes, closed her mouth, swallowed the coming scream with the bile in her throat.

She must have been deathly tired to sleep through the attack that had killed so many, left so much destruction in its wake. It was only dumb luck and the huge trees that had saved her.

She wove her way around the corpses of cars, through smoke that edged its way into her cabin, forced its way into her lungs. Flame reached a fuel tank nearby, filling the air with heat and light and sound, spreading fire like a virus. Romany accelerated through the growing apocalypse, outrunning the spreading fire.

In her rear-view mirror the sky was afire. Eucalypt trees ignited, the flame spreading from tree-top to tree-top, the wind, thankfully, drawing the fire away. She stopped her car to breathe, to still her heart, to shut her mouth on another scream trying to escape her lungs. She tried to call her parents, her aunty, her brother but there was no signal, perhaps the phone towers had been hit.

Planes flew past, each trying to out-scream the others, more than she could count. On a whim, a foolish whim, a terrifying whim that might have not even been volition, she resolved to follow them. The pilots flying those planes were going somewhere; maybe it would be safe there, maybe there were people there, maybe she could join the fight from there. It might not be the smart thing to do but it was something.

When she reached a side road – no, not a road, a track weaving its incoherent way into the forest – she turned that way, still following the planes, or near enough.

The car bumped and shuddered, rattled down the road, winding between trees and scrub, dropping down pot-holes and bouncing back up again. The untrustworthy track seemed determined to disappear into the scrub entirely. It might just end at nothing, go from nowhere to somewhere even more remote. It might end in a ditch, or a clearing, a decrepit house of wood, home to nothing but spiders.

When the road bent the wrong way, away from the direction she had watched the planes fly, she fought down panic. When a track appeared that she felt was going the right way, even narrower than the one she was on, nothing more than wheel-ruts, separated by weeds and small bent trees, she took it. Branches scraped the paint off her doors, threatened her windows, endangered her tyres. Finally the car could take no more, a branch hammered through her windscreen, one of her tyres blew, she skidded off the track into the trees, thudding sideways into a spindly tree with a sickening crunch.

Her engine was still running but the car would not move, she revved the engine, thrashed it; nothing happened but noise. She tried to get out, the door would not open, she crawled, weeping, over to the passenger side and opened that door. Planes continued to periodically roar overhead, still travelling in the same direction. She grabbed what she could, her grocery bag of junk food, an empty water bottle, the ratty hoody that was the only warm item of clothing she had.

She followed the winding track as it wove through the forest growing ever more indistinct. Only the periodic screaming of planes overhead gave her any direction. When the track turned the wrong way and did not look like it was going to change again she struck out through the trees.

By the time the light of day faded she was completely lost. Only a few planes continued scorching overhead, their arrivals and departures so unpredictable and their crossing of the sky so rapid she was barely able to take a bearing. She had no light, nothing to light a fire, she cursed her stupidity. She tripped and fell over an unseen obstacle, a tree root, a fallen branch, a snake, a skeletal hand, there was no way she could have known which. Lying in the leaf litter she brushed wildly at her clothes; the fear of spiders and bugs, unseen, even unfelt, drilled into her brain.

She tried to walk, thumped into a tree, dropped her bag; leaned against the tree, hugged it, less scared of the bugs and spiders on the tree than the ones on the ground.

She was leaning against the tree, the bark abrading her face, when the faint green filtered sunlight woke her. The silence was terrible, there were no planes overhead, no noise at all bar the buzz of mosquitoes and the hiss of the wind. No planes.

What the hell had she been thinking?

She was in the middle of a banksia forest, the spiky grey-green leaves, the greyer trunks, with bark like cork, the only things she could see except for the lone gum she had embraced in her desperation. The sky was slate-grey overhead, despite the summer it seemed that more rain might be coming.

She had absolutely no idea where she was. All she knew was, she was not safe.

There was no use just standing there. She had been driving east when she turned left off the highway to follow the planes, so north made at least a little sense. The sunrise was to her right when she began, scraping through the thorny leaves, stepping on cracking branches.

It was hard going, she had never pushed through such bush before. She wondered how her people used to do it before the white people came, though this was nothing like the low scrub, mulga and desert oaks of her great-grandmother's Country, open space and red sand was more her thing. Her hands and arms were covered with scratches from pushing hard, thorny leaves away, her knees and feet hurt, there was not even good ground between the trees. She fell, stood and fell again, growing terrified she tried to run, and fell. Standing, she somehow managed to run again.

She barely noticed when the forest petered out, kept running wildly into grasslands until she came to her senses while the grasses whipped at her ankles. The sunlight, the sky returning to blue, cut her eyes. Before her was a grassland, studded with trees.

She kept walking north. There were more scattered trees in that direction but she could still see nothing else, other than more grassland. She stopped, she could not go any further in the growing heat. Finally she collapsed under a tree.

With an ear-bleeding roar, shaking the very sky, a flotilla of planes arced overhead, heading in the direction she had been walking. Diving to her feet, she ran, chasing the contrails and the noise-phantoms that chased the planes.

She had very little strength left. Every decision she had made since the war had begun had turned out to be wrong. She could have died when the ships had attacked the city. Running home to the bush had led her straight into an attack. Then, stupidly, she had wandered off into the bush on foot in someone else's Country.

She closed her eyes for a moment.

There was another new noise, savage, unrecognisable, a thumping, a roaring and the scream of a strange nightmare beast. A helicopter was hovering overhead. Unable to tolerate this new shock Romany's knees collapsed, she felt the long dry grass brushing her face, felt her tears watering the grass.

She woke in a green-sheeted hospital bed, drip in her arm, staring up at a green canvas roof. It glowed where the thick cloth was lit by scorching sun, the heat raining down from above faster than the desperate air-conditioners could remove it.

The doctors, the nurses, the orderlies looked military.

There was a metal meal tray on the table beside her. A bowl of soup, not steaming, it had probably gone cold, a dry bread roll, a glass of what must be juice. She devoured it, despite it being nearly tasteless.

Her phone was on the table, switched on, a message notification flashing. She loaded the message and tears fell, the lover she had drunk to forget, who she still loved, had died in the attack in the arms of somebody else.

A uniformed nurse strode over. Romany barely noticed.

'Miz Zetz,' the nurse said, 'I got your name from the driver's licence in your pocket. It's good to see you awake, you were not in very good shape when you arrived here. We are trying to save everyone we can.'

Romany wanted to keep eating but her curiosity was stronger than her partially sated hunger. Stronger even than the tears. 'Where am I?'

'This is a mobile hospital,' the nurse said, 'we set it up near an airstrip at a mine, which is now an air force base. We were actually here to treat injured pilots but we have started picking up strays.'

@

From there it was not far to Starforce. In Starforce she could try to forget the one she loved who had left her then died in another's arms. In Starforce she discovered what she was really good at. She was born to fly.

CHAPTER 19

IT WAS THE wailing that woke Jimmy, a high-pitched keening, like a mother missing a stolen child or a child refusing to leave a parent's fresh grave, like the memory of being held by someone you know you will never see again. He sat up, stared down the concourse from the corner he had found for him and Itta, a corner created by a wall and the familiar boxy bulk of a vending machine.

This one carried advertising in a language he did not know, with photos of a product he couldn't identify. He did not even recognise the Federation edibility code so it was extremely unlikely to be human edible.

Many of the other corners – where previously bodies had been jammed, masses of limbs and clothes, bundles of belongings, piles of trash – were now unexpectedly free of people. Only the bundles of belongings remained, vulnerable to theft. The citizens were all heading in the same direction, to a distant corner; he could see nothing beyond the multi-species wall of backs.

Itta lay beside him, eyes closed, peaceful, her sweet, dirty face inexplicably familiar. He missed other humans so badly any human contact was better than none. He had to leave to find them some food, maybe refugee services were giving out rations, maybe a charity was. She would be safe enough while he was gone. There was nothing at their camp to steal, plenty more people with more worth stealing, people weaker and less defended. Everybody knew Itta was protected and would be avenged.

Standing, he checked his pockets, he had both their ID cards. No card, no rations, he and Itta were lucky he had them.

They were the only possessions worth stealing from the refugees. There were people around who would change the photo on a card for as little as a ration pack. Maybe even for the promise of a ration pack once you had collected somebody else's rations. There were others who would offer to change the photo for the cost of a ration pack and then never return the card, sell it instead to someone with more to trade for it.

There were people on that station who would kill for a card. Steal someone's rations and you eat for a day; steal their refugee ID card and you have food to sell.

Their stay in the refugee camp had been uncountable days already and did not appear likely to end any time soon. His soul vibrated with the desire to go home.

He wove a meandering path through an open forest of citizens. The three different species stuck there were becoming as familiar to him as his own people, although he could still not understand a word any of them were saying. They were all facing the same direction, towards a corner, from where the terrible, nauseating wailing was coming. Even the refugee services staff, such as there were, were staring that way, they did not respond to Jimmy, he could get no food from them.

Through the crowds he wandered, they were motionless, some wailing as they just stood there, robbed of all volition but the desire to vent. Closer, through the wall of almost palpable pain, through the pools of slime, the tears, the ectoplasm of emotion. Around the standing, over the prostrate, shrugging off the clutching hands that were reaching out for any comfort they could grasp.

Clumsy tributes were scattered in a corner, religious symbols, the ash of burned belongings; few would be stupid, crazy or distraught enough to start a fire on a station concourse – yet Jimmy could smell the smoke. Around the ash was torn-out hair, magenta smears that could be the blood of a non-human. There were citizens prostrate on the ceraplastic floor of the concourse – skin, and clothes cut for a blood letting – they rolled on the floor, smeared it with their emotion, with their blood. Ash and blood painted them in patches of pink.

Jimmy could not wrench himself away from the spectacle of grief and pain; he could feel it, taste it, although he did not understand the words being wailed. He stood in silence, inexplicably feeling the pain like a weight on his whole body. Unexpected tears escaped from his eyes.

'Attention all refugees and citizens,' a voice speaking flawless unaccented Federal, so perfect it was almost certainly a machine, crackled through speakers hidden in the ceiling, echoing in the desolate corners. 'Anyone having friends, family, clan-mates et cetera on the refugee ship *Xsathaz* please stand by for an announcement.'

People were wailing, yelling, in different languages over the announcement so it was unlikely to have been the first time it had played. 'We have lost contact with the refugee ship *Xsathaz*. All available military and search resources have been dispatched and are searching but we do not expect to find the ship, there is no certainty that even remains can be recovered.' Well, at least the voice was honest.

Jimmy moved closer to the pile of tributes in the corner. There were pieces of paper covered with what could have been writing, rags and paper crafted into likenesses of what were probably flowers from a planet he had never seen, photos, so many photos of the dead, stuffed toys, religious symbols, a riot of shapes.

The sadness wafted over him like the smoke of a guttering campfire, there was a smell to the grief, like a wind bringing the aroma of death, like his memory of the time after a bushfire had passed, ash, cooked animals and rot. He could feel the grief on his skin, like the mist of a cold morning, like a sadistic breath. He could hear it like the lashing wind of a coastal storm. It overwhelmed him and he fell to his knees, he had not known anyone on that ship, yet he had lost so much, they had lost so many, their grief became his.

The announcement crackled and echoed from the speakers again.

Relief also flooded his mind. He could have been on that ship, might have disappeared, been destroyed, anything. Guilt followed, disbelief that he deserved to be the one to survive. He did not join in the wailing.

The next morning the concourse was in an uproar. No attack this time, unless you were counting the cordon of station security around the tightly packed mass of refugees. Some guards were unkempt, untidy, even dirty, they held their stun guns sloppily, they wore only the tunics of security uniforms; some not even that, they had badges, sashes, nothing else. The rest of their clothes looked slept in.

Jimmy suspected many of them had not been security when they woke up that morning in a cell or in a gutter. Some looked like they had not quite managed to sleep off whatever it was that had inhibited them the night before. They leered at the refugees, as if their desire for violence was barely contained.

Jimmy held tight to Itta's hand, there was no good trying to talk to her. The language she spoke when she spoke at all, the language she cried out in when dreaming, was not a language he knew even a word of. He had never heard it before; it was not like any human sound he had heard. Their only mode of communication, their only common language, was touch. He took her places by steering her by the hand. He held her when she was scared.

He suspected he was the only refugee on that station who had any notion what was coming next, he had seen it before, wished he could forget it. They were about to be moved on, violently. Past the thickest point of the security, in the doorway towards the food hall, was a heaving angry mass of citizens. They were silent, but they would not be so for long, Jimmy could already hear their shouting in his mind.

The refugees were soon to be forced back onto the ships they had been brought on by the crowds, by security, by xenophobia, by burgeoning hate. He glanced over to the hatch leading to the ship he had arrived on. It was closed, the purple 'locked' light glowing aggressively. Guards from the ship, holding stun guns and batons, stood in front of the hatch staring in desperate panic at the restless, murmuring crowd. There were not enough of them.

Things were about to get dangerous. Guards moved forward, herding the refugees. The angry mass of citizens roared. The refugees moved closer together then closer to the ships that had brought them there.

There was a pattern to how these things usually went. The station would ask the ship to take the refugees, the ship would refuse, then the station would ask more firmly and the ship would refuse more aggressively. Finally, the station would demand, and a battle of aggression versus stubbornness would begin, both sides believing they had the right to handle things their way. The ship could not leave until the station released the electro-magnetic grapples and it would not do that until the ship was loaded with the refugees. All the ship could do was lock their doors, which is what they had done.

It was possible that both sides would have hackers, although hacking the station clamps was as illegal as trying to gain access to a locked ship.

There could only be one outcome: the ship would open their doors. How long it took would be determined by the bloody-mindedness of the captain and the aggressiveness of the station.

The tension continued to ratchet higher until Jimmy felt none of the refugees would survive. The smell of fear from the three species was palpable, nauseating; the sound of fear, wailing and sobs, the screams of youngsters, made Jimmy want to cry out. It was hot in the concourse, one of the species trapped in there must get hot when scared, and they were all terrified.

Someone, then more people, then everyone surged towards the doorway, there was a sound Jimmy recognised as the buzz of stun guns, punctuated by wails of fear. The crowd, one huge multi-legged creature, then surged towards the ships, away from the door. They surged through Jimmy and Itta. The wave of panicked people separated them and Itta disappeared.

Scuffles broke out as people were knocked down and tumbled, scattered away from their loved ones, as people dropped their few belongings, as children and parents were separated. Somewhere in that scrum was Itta, he could hear her scream, an alien noise in a human timbre, no one else screamed like that. He stepped through a gap, around a wailing, flailing being, another was swinging a fist or some other fist-like appendage at him, he threw them past his hip, sent them spiralling into the crowd.

Jimmy could barely remember when they had evacuated his home city, yet he could remember it far better than he could recall his family. The authorities had waited a little too long, the first fly-overs from Conglomeration space fighters had begun, the first bombings, the first strafings with energy weapons. When a powerful enough energy weapon slices into an urban area, people splatter, buildings are cut and fall, cars melt into the tarmac, their drivers vaporising out of the exploding windows. Jimmy saw all that happen, he was only a child of six. He saw a glut of death, so much his mind could not understand it.

What was really terrifying to him was the people, fighting for the tiniest scraps of cover, prepared to kill to be the first to make it to safety. They jammed in the door of the underground train station, jammed so tight they could not get out, could not get in – they screamed, they flailed at each other's faces, more people pressed against them, they had no choice but to crush in, forced by the press of bodies behind. Blood was escaping the mass of people in runnels, wriggling, worming across the cracked concrete pavement. Then people started fighting, fighting to get closer to a door they could not possibly get through, fighting just to feel they were doing something to save themselves.

Jimmy had lost his parents in the press of the maddened crowd. He did not know what to do, another child crawled from the melee at the train station door, leaving a snail-trail of blood, then collapsed with a wet sound.

Terror consumed Jimmy and he ran into a building. He didn't know what he was really running from, where he was going, he just ran. When his path ended at stairs he ran down into the darkness, too scared of what was outside to worry what was ahead of him. The lights failed, maybe the entire town was blacked out, he crawled across a filthy floor in the darkness.

He stayed there so long, he dozed in and out of fearful sleep. When he was not asleep he was crying, sobbing, too scared, too tired from his fear to scream. His time down there in that cellar was eternal, before a faint flashing light approached.

By then he was too scared to cry out to the light, what if they were bad people bringing that light to find him? He hid his head under his arm, as the light came closer he suppressed the natural desire to scream, to bloody his fingers trying to burrow into the concrete floor. In fear and fatigue he fell insensible.

All these years later Jimmy remembered waking to see his parents sitting at the side of the hospital bed, though he could still not picture their faces. He found out later that most of the city had been destroyed, the people in the street and in the doorway of the train station had all died. The rest of his family had made it to cover together. The building he had hidden in was mostly destroyed, it was nothing but luck that had led searchers into his basement.

The business district of the city where he had been born was no more. He was in a temporary hospital in a military camp. It was some time, the tide of battle on Earth turning, before the city was considered safe enough for his family to return.

Remembering that in the emotional firestorm in the concourse, Jimmy was vividly aware of the danger. He struck out through the crowd, taking a swing at someone who had pushed him away; he didn't even care if his punch landed somewhere significant.

Pushing through the moving mass of bodies he saw Itta just as the crowd swept her away again.

'Itta!' he screamed over the roaring crowd, 'Itta!'

He thought he heard his name, forward and to the right, towards the direction of flow of the crowd. He did not know Itta had learned to say his name yet but who else could it have been? Forcing his way in what he hoped was the right direction he fell into the crush, felt a foot land on his shoulder, someone else trip over his head.

He tried to stand but was bumped back down by the weight of citizens, tried again and got to his knees. Someone fell down and to his side, they too managed to get to their knees, a look of pain in their face. Jimmy put his left hand on their head, grabbed another stranger's clothes with his other hand and began to drag himself upright. The fallen being cried in pain, flailing ineffectively at Jimmy's hand crushing them, the other stranger fell tumbling past Jimmy, pulled over by his weight.

The bruises on his body were getting bruises on them but Jimmy was not bothered by the pain, was not afraid for himself. He was terrified for Itta. He nearly fell again when his foot twisted on something soft, which emitted a scream. There was no time to look down even if he wanted to, someone bumped into him and he grabbed them, used the momentum of shoving past them to throw himself through a transient opening in the crowd. Tripping again, he tried to turn the fall into a dive through another gap, half succeeded, landing on something soft that wailed.

He knew that voice, without even looking he embraced the lump he knew must be Itta, pulled her into his arms, sat up and curled himself around her to protect her with his body as best as he could. The crowd flowed over them – it was like tumbling in the surf, being hit by an avalanche, standing your ground in a bar brawl, falling down the stairs; like being pummelled by police. It hurt and hurt yet he held onto Itta, protecting her small body with his own.

Itta was whimpering. Jimmy kept his voice behind gritted teeth so she would not know how scared he was. Almost unconscious, swooning in the heat, finding it hard to breathe, he felt someone land on him and roll off, felt someone else kick him on the way past, then, abruptly, the pummelling, the noise, the pain ceased.

Jimmy stood, lifting Itta into his arms in the same action, her weight was reassuring although she still weighed less than he thought she should for her height. It hurt to stand; he had taken a battering but he could remember beatings far worse. Around him was a mass of collapsed beings, some rising to their feet or at least trying to. Some looked incapable of standing, some looked like they shouldn't try to stand; some were moaning, venting their agony, others were ominously silent.

The door of one of the ships slid open with a prolonged, reluctant scream and a steam train hiss, then another ship and another lost their argument with the station. Maybe the captains had finally taken pity on the refugees, maybe the station had simply won the argument. Jimmy considered for a moment disappearing, opening a maintenance hatch and dragging Itta through into the uncertain darkness, fleeing into the bowels of the station, but he knew that it would never work. After expelling the refugees the station would be on high alert, if they found him and Itta they would split them up, he would almost certainly end up locked away somewhere.

Who knew what they would do with her.

Still carrying the scrawny bird-boned weight of Itta, reassured by the feel of her thin arms around his neck, he moved back to their tiny camp by the vending machine.

Doors hissed open, doors closed again, people wailed.

Jimmy packed the few belongings they had, his blanket, Itta's blanket they had wheedled out of some charity he had never heard of, some non-perishables they had reserved from their rations, mismatched cups, mismatched bowls, some nacreous, pus-green body-wash in a bottle with a shape no human would devise. His discharged tablet.

What he could he stashed carefully in his backpack. The blankets would not fit, he bundled them under his left arm. His fragments of cash, Federal credits and some random currencies he could not even identify were already in his shoe, their refugee ID cards were safe in the concealed inside pocket he had been surprised and delighted to find in his second-hand jacket.

Taking Itta again by the hand, she seemed calmer but he could not risk her wandering off, he walked towards the nearest ship. The hatch was closed again, the ship had gained a momentary advantage, but he knew the station management would get it open again, eventually. It would be best to be ready to get on before the ships tried to skip out.

CHAPTER 20

THE LIVING WATER had protected Walker, cool water bubbled up from the sand whenever he drank from it before carefully covering the hole with spinifex. He would stay there, in his grandfather's Country; he had no reason to leave when there was water. He was hungry but he could live a little longer without eating. The nagging pains, the bleeding patches on his skin were still there, he spat out teeth whenever he drank the cool water, yet he knew he could survive.

He slept in the comforting embrace of his old people.

A noise woke him from his sleep. He did not move, did not know yet if he should, if he could move, except to open his eyes. He heard it again, the faintest squeaky scritch of feet on sand. Too small a noise to be a person, it must be a small animal.

Reaching out, he found a fist-sized rock with his right hand, closed his fingers tightly over it, swung that hand in the direction of the sound. There was a squeak and then silence, he rolled over to see what he had killed. Small, furred, blooded by his rock, a rabbit, attracted by his precious water; given to him by his old people. He grabbed it, crawled away. A few body lengths from the waterhole, ten if even that many, was all he could manage.

Finding sticks and spinifex, and dragging a lighter from his pocket, he somehow got a fire lit. Held his aching body close to the penetrating warmth. He washed himself in the smoke, like his old people have forever, clean, grey and smelling of nothing but burned wood, a cleansing sacrament. Dropped the rabbit into the coals to singe off its hair. Lay beside the fire for the comfort, for the smoke, for the memories. Buried the rabbit in coals, covered over with sand. Slept in the smoke, like when his parents would take him bush to learn culture. Woke to the smell of cooked rabbit, found a stick to dig it out.

Eating rabbit, he felt a loose tooth rattle in his mouth and swallowed it with the meat. Hell, the rabbit was delicious. He wanted to smile. Collapsed into pained, uneasy sleep again.

He woke, did not remember his dreams, sun on his face, what a treasure. His open eyes found a hole in the black smoke, the sun peeking through. A stomach full of rabbit, the thin warmth of the sun to complement the dying warmth of his fire. All he needed now was a visit to his waterhole, the sacred living water to fill his belly with life.

It was both easier and harder to get back to the waterhole with a full belly. The nutrition gave him strength yet the weight of it made him sluggish. He wasn't worried, he had as long as he needed to get to his water. It was not far, it shouldn't be taking so long.

Where the water had been was slime, black, oily – like death, like the black smoke made liquid, like fear and clotted blood. It oozed into the hole, it smelled of pain, it glistened in the daylight until the smoke ate the sun again. Tears exploded from Walker's eyes as an unearthly scream tore from his lungs. The oily sludge in the bottom of the hole absorbed his tears as if they were inconsequential. He could not stop wailing, he tried but he could not, this was his grandfather's heaven, this was his very soul.

Finished.

CHAPTER 21

THERE WAS BLOOD dripping down the walls of the concourse, still wet, glistening and streaking, the blood of multiple species but most of it the dark red that came from humans. Lieutenant Daniels held back, crying inside over every soldier that had died, every soldier she'd ordered to their death. It would make all the troops feel worse to see their lieutenant, the soldier promoted from the ranks for being too badarse to die, crying, so she held her tears inside.

The last push, trying to re-close the blast doors and jam them, had been a mistake. She had tried to get the doors closed, save more lives, instead most of the people she had sent were dead or wounded. There was no chance of closing the doors now, there were too few soldiers left, she was not even certain there were enough alive to hold the barricades.

There was not enough blast door left to weld back together.

They were losing.

She was going to die here, they were all going to die here, in this station far from home, far from her family. It had been so long since they had been told even how the war was going, the propaganda had ceased, news from Earth had ceased, the news feeds in English and Federal were silent on the state of the war. For all Shane knew they were losing. Despite her time in the army, despite the desperate desire to protect her family and her Country that had pulled her from their arms, Earth might still fall.

Then her family would be dead too.

Maybe she should have stayed home, to be there when the Conglomeration inevitably broke the blockade and made another attempt on Earth. Then she could die standing between her children and the enemy, die knowing she gave her kids another few moments of life. She should die with her family, not here in this lonely station far from human space.

Family, Country, culture, she had been told again and again by her Elders that they were the most important thing. She thought she was fighting for them, thought she was doing the right thing. That was no longer quite so certain.

She was fighting for Country and for culture and she would never see her family or Country again.

Somebody out there was screaming, wounded, she would have to drag them to safety before they died, before their screaming took the fight out of her troops. No, she would have to send someone else, send them into the fire, into the melee, into danger. If they too failed to come back she would never forgive herself.

'I need a volunteer,' she said to the nearest corporal, 'to go get that wounded man out of the line of fire.' They had a family too, she could not leave them there to die.

'Yes, sir,' the corporal said.

'And I mean a volunteer, don't just choose someone, they might get hit too.'

'I will go myself,' the corporal said quietly and firmly, 'I have done this kinda thing before.'

Shane did not want to lose a good corporal yet nodded her assent.

She watched as the man walked to their barricade then crawled over on his belly. She had no idea how he managed to not injure himself on the various bent and broken things they had piled together. He crawled through viscera, over a motionless corpse, then he stopped, grabbed something or someone and crawled backwards through the wailing projectiles and hissing plasma fire.

He was slow, like cold honey oozing from a jar. Stopping abruptly, he crawled back over the screaming injured man, struggled with something she could not see, something caught on the wounded man's clothing, then crawled back and started dragging the man again. They reached the barricade and Shane rushed to meet them there, reached over the wall of broken furniture and bloodless corpses, grabbed the wounded man by his limp arm and heaved. She, the wounded man and the corporal landed on the safe side of the barricade in a heap as plasma fire splashed against it. A medic ran over in a crouch, she wished they had a doctor. The medic was a small woman, Shane wondered why she was not a pilot.

A bit like Harper really.

'Look after him,' Daniels told the medic sharply, 'then get back to the medic station.'

The sound of hell breaking loose became more deafening as Shane walked back to her command post, if you could call it that. All she had was a table, the only one not used to build or reinforce the barricade, and a couple of hard food-court chairs. The table was covered by boxy blinking and flashing consoles and half-dismantled electronics she could not even begin to understand.

Harper and another tech were head down in all that tangle-wired mess, talking loudly and incomprehensibly, almost shouting, to each other. Maybe they needed to shout for all the technobabble to be heard over the battle noise. Shane had no idea what they were up to but hoped it would be useful, prayed it would be useful; it had better be useful or she would lose her shit.

'Harper, how we doing?'

Harper looked up blearily, her watery, red-rimmed eyes seemed incapable of focusing. Her eyes opened wide when she realised who she was looking at. 'Sorry, sir,' she said, trying to stand.

Shane motioned for Harper to sit back down.

'You okay, Harper?'

'I'll be fine Sarge – sorry, Lieutenant – we have to get this done, it's important. Don't worry, it's just like, um, any other software project, I know all about not resting from those days,' Harper rambled. She sounded tired and scared, but confident.

'What exactly are you doing?'

'It was kinda your idea, Lieutenant. You said you want to kick them out of the airlock, well, we kinda took it literally, well, almost, kinda.'

'The emergency overrides are resisting a bit, Harper, not sure how long they will take to wrangle,' the other tech, a private, interjected.

'Sorry, what are you doing?'

'Done, it worked, oh shit,' said the private, before frantically tapping on a tablet. 'Not yet, fuck it.'

'Excuse me?' asked Daniels, irritated at the interruption.

'Hold onto something, Lieutenant,' said the tech private in a high-pitched panicked voice, just as a light flashed and a siren wailed in the concourse. Lights flashed over the heads of the Conglomeration troops trying to fortify the concourse.

Harper yelled, 'Shit not yet, you fucking idiot!' Her eyes wide with panic.

'Brace,' Shane screamed at the top of her voice, diving to the ground as, one after another, the docking clamps holding the enemy ships to the station blew with a drumroll of bangs even louder than the battle. The enemy ships violently disengaged from the station. The open hatches would normally slam closed when a ship unexpectedly disengaged but the Conglomeration forces had destroyed them when they'd cut their way in.

The blast doors were designed to slam closed in the event of the concourse decompressing, but they were so damaged and had so much random metallic detritus welded to them, no force in the universe would be able to close them.

A screaming sound, imported from her nightmares, louder than she could have imagined, filled the concourse. It rushed into her ears, threatened to tear her eardrums out. The force of the wind, as the air in the station rushed to fill a space it could never fill – all of space – threw first small items then larger over her head towards the open locks. There was an emergency tie-down in front of her face, she would have to let go of the meagre hold she had on the ground, with at least one hand, to attach to it.

The emergency tether all sensible soldiers kept on them some-where, even when not in uniform, was wound on a spool on her belt; she unspooled it with her left hand, feeling her right hand lose grip on the mesh flooring, feeling the ground slip under her right palm as she started sliding towards the open airlock. The decompression alarm must have been going off, though she could not hear it through the roaring of the wind; a blue-white light, heavy on the ultraviolet was flashing overhead. She was still sliding, the tie-down was almost out of reach.

Tether first, then breathe. She would only last minutes without air, but she would also last only minutes if she was blown out the airlock; and it would be a long trip back, dead. Blood streamed from her ears, from her nose, forming droplets as it was whisked away by the decompression. Almost too late, she clicked the carabiner on her tether onto the tie-down just as she felt the tips of her fingers slip away from her hold.

Whipped from the ground, she snatched at a body flying past, caught it, grabbed hold. Through the red flooding her vision she could barely see it was Harper, terrified and wide-eyed, untethered. There was nothing to hitch the girl to but herself. Spooling out the corporal's tether she attached it to a D-ring on her own belt, praying it would be strong enough, praying her own tether would be strong enough for two, that the tie-down would take the weight. She smacked Harper's dangling emergency respirator onto the girl's face and wished she had one herself or had kept her helmet on. The girl slipped from her arm, flew towards the open hatches, stopped suddenly, the line tightened with enough force to break bones. Shane's belt was being pulled two directions, the tethers and the dead-weight of Harper compressed her body, forcing her last held breath out.

Dangling on the end of a tether, the first link in a chain, Shane felt her lungs empty more than they ever had before as the air was pulled from her body. The world went redder then black as blood was pulled into her eyes.

'Oh shit,' Shane would have screamed if there was any air.

@

'What the fuck?' the exclamation came over the comms. Romeo had no idea who said it, looked around to see if there was anything interesting to see. She dodged a missile, cooked it with a short burst of her laser cannon, smiled when it vaporised, took a shot at a passing Conglomeration fighter, swung around, continued backwards for a while to see if anyone was behind her. Then she saw the Conglomeration cutters that had been attached to the station were drifting slowly away.

What the fuck indeed.

Both Conglomeration ships and the station were spewing debris from their locks. There was something familiar about the movement of some of that debris. She swore, all her favourite words, when she realised what it was. People falling, falling out into space.

'Code red,' Romeo almost shouted over the comms, 'forget the Conglomeration, we have station decompression, repeat, we have station decompression, immediately deploy emergency life-support to as many floaters as possible, we have less than minutes.'

'How do we tell friend from enemy?' A voice came over the comms.

'Flight Lieutenant Jones, I will explain to you what I think of that question in the gym later, I will not kill you because you can still learn. Fucking well rescue everybody.' Switching channels, she spoke fast, 'Attention, we have decompression in the station and the boarding cutters, deploy rescue ships immediately with pilots experienced in zero-g rescue in an active combat zone, prepare the medical bay to receive an unknown number of decompression victims from an unknown number of species.'

'Affirmative, Squadron Leader.'

She did not wait to see how fast they were jumping to send out the rescue ships, instead she turned towards the floating debris from the station. Some of the fighters had been closer and had not wasted time talking, they were weaving through the debris, dodging fire from the Conglomeration fighters, who were clearly less concerned about the floaters than the Federation were. There was no way for a Federation fighter to contact the Conglomeration so she hoped she would manage to tell them what she was up to through action. She also hoped what she was doing wouldn't look like she was attacking helpless floaters.

There were faint flashes as floating bodies, alive she hoped, were hit with the emergency life-support missiles. Experimental, there had not been many reasons to use them before and most fighters only carried six. Seeing a floater, she fired one of those plastic canisters, it hit, flashed as it engaged and almost instantly started expanding like foam until it was a bubble of opaque rubbery stuff coating what she hoped would be a survivor. She had been inside one of those bubbles before, there was a canister on her flight suit. If her cockpit was breached completely, if she was thrown into space, it would splatter over her and form a bubble full of oxygen.

Nanotech in the foam would produce whatever the floater needed to breathe. But not for long – two hours tops.

There were more opaque bubbles floating around now, and more floaters, she fired at them too.

'When you are out of life-support rockets, and only then, feel free to let the Conglomeration know, in the way we know best, what you think of them shooting at us while we are performing a rescue, while we are, in fact, also rescuing their people.' Romeo watched as one of her fighters fired a rocket at a floater then turned away, already firing at the Conglomeration fighters, before the rocket even hit. Romeo was firing and firing, hoping Shane Daniels was not one of the people out there in space. She was the last to run out of life-support rockets, she wished she had more to expend, there were still people out there dying, their blood boiling, the air exploding from their lungs.

In the cockpit of her ship, helmet visor over her face, she allowed herself to cry. Yet she would not allow herself to scream.

A human face floated past, blood streaming from his eyes, turning to red vapour then into nothing in the vacuum. He was so close she could have counted the wrinkles around his panicked eyes. She knew that face would never leave her nightmares, the face of a stranger, swelling, eyes popping out, the last air in his lungs boiling out through swollen lips.

He tumbled past, still twitching, as if his muscles were following the last order of a dead brain, the order to swim for safety, yet there was nothing to swim in. She had been the last with a rescue rocket, he had no chance.

She turned back to the battle, firing almost as soon as she turned at some prick who would rather have a shot at her than rescue their own. There was a flash as her rocket splattered the enemy fighter into fragments, she flew right through the expanding debris, felt the remains of the enemy ship hammering against her fuselage, frightening and satisfying in the same moment. For once she was glad she was flying a heavy, the thicker armour saved her life.

'Attention,' she growled through the comms, 'looks like the infantry have risked their arses to save the station, they might all be dead or out here floating, engage at will with the Conglomeration arsehole scum-buckets but do what you can to protect our rescue and salvage ships.

'We will not be abandoning this station. Let's hope the decompression shields deployed and there's someone alive in there.'

Romeo tried hard to forget that her best friend, the closest thing she had to a sister, was probably, at that moment, sucking vacuum.

@

Romeo returned to the *Yulara*, exhausted. The Conglomeration, demoralised from the decompression of their two boarding transports, and the loss of all lives onboard, had retreated – fleeing the battle despite still having the stronger force.

Almost as if they were waiting for the enemy to depart, Federation reinforcements arrived just as the Conglomeration entered hyper-space. At least the new arrivals could help with the rescue and clean-up and take over the salvage of the drifting Conglomeration cutters from the battered *Yulara* and her exhausted crew.

Romeo bounced from her cockpit, wanting to fly a recovery and rescue ship, to do what she could to recover the drifting soldiers and the civilians, but she must have looked like the walking dead. The chief petty officer in charge of ground crew called in the duty medical officer who immediately declared Romeo temporarily unfit for active duty. She returned grumbling to her quarters and promptly collapsed into sleep, too tired to even stay angry with the chief.

She woke naturally, well rested. Some bastard, likely on the medical officer's orders, had disabled her alarms remotely, had let her sleep. She had not been there to command her pilots for the mop-up, had not been available to rescue Shane. She grabbed a comms set and started talking too fast.

Turned out she had not been needed, her friend had been found by the recovery crew who hacked their way into the station, through the emergency spray-foam and inflatable plastic barrier that had filled the gaping hole. Shane had looked dead lying on the deck of the concourse, but she was an officer. Her file said so. When they detected faint signs of life, they called for a tank. Romeo was directed to the medical bay of a hospital station the *Yulara* had not even been docked to when she fell asleep. She sprinted there too fast, knocked a sailor flying in her haste, nearly slipped on the piece of deck that sailor had been scrubbing.

Shane was unconscious, floating serenely in a tank, the card read 'decompression'. As expected, there was no prognosis. She had lost some colour, everybody does in a tank but on Shane, almost as dark as Romeo, it made her look strange. A young white girl, in infantry uniform, was seated on a chair near the tank. She looked too young to be a soldier, until Romeo looked in her eyes; they were older than her clean, unlined face and filled with recent pain.

She was also kinda cute.

Staring blearily, tears in her eyes, it took the girl a long time to realise she was in the presence of an officer. Diving to her feet so fast she nearly fell over, creaking to attention, the girl nearly took her own eye out with a too-hasty salute. 'Sorry, sir, um, ma'am, I didn't see you walk in,' she said with even more haste.

'Please, at ease, please,' Romeo said, hating the military formalities, regretting wearing uniform to the med-bay. 'I'm just visiting like you, and we are from different services anyway.'

The girl still stood to very stiff attention, Romeo could tell she was not really fit to stand up. Who could she be? She thought she knew all Shane's friends.

'Please, sit down, before you fall down, no really, don't fall over.' Romeo gestured to the tank. 'She is my best friend, I just had to check she is okay, I have been asleep for too long.' She paused in thought, held out her hand, 'They call me Romeo.'

'Oh,' the girl said, her eyes wide, 'Romeo.'

'Hope that is not a bad "oh",' Romeo said, having heard the bad 'oh' many times. She sat down on the next chair. 'Hope you haven't heard too much bad stuff about me.'

The girl almost squeaked, the noise raising unbidden to her lips but not making it much further. It came out strangled. 'Oh no, ma'am, nothing bad. I was the radio operator, well not really, I was the technician, no, not technician, um.'

'The hacker?' Romeo asked with her cheekiest grin.

The girl blushed faintly. If she had not been so white, so almost blue, it would have been impossible to notice. 'Yes, ma'am, the hacker who got radio signal out to you, it kept falling out so the sergeant, sorry, lieutenant, kept me close. I heard what you said a lot of the time. You saved our lives.'

'Right, that would make you Harper, hi. I didn't save your lives, firstly I had a squadron, they helped, some of them died. Also, from the chatter in my ear-piece as I was running here,' Romeo said with a little grudging respect in her voice, 'I hear you were doing a pretty good job of rescuing yourself. You are the one who saved the station.'

'I didn't blow those ships off the station alone, I just helped,' Harper said a little too quickly.

'It was a soldier under your command, wasn't it? That's what I heard. You gave the orders, didn't you? You came up with the idea, I am sure. I have no doubt you did more than just help a bit and you would have done it yourself if you weren't too busy, if it wasn't such a big hack.'

'Yes,' Harper breathed, eyes downcast with pain, fear and shame, 'but it went off too early, we didn't have time to warn everyone, the private who was helping me died, thrown into space, Lieutenant Daniels nearly died, so many died, if you hadn't repelled the fighters who were bombarding the station I would have died helpless, suffocated, when the air in my tank ran out. They are going to court-martial me, I know it, I am going to go to jail.'

She was actually crying. Romeo itched to embrace the poor kid.

'They aren't going to court-martial you, it was a good idea, the only way to fix the deadlock. You guys and the station were doomed. You were the only person who could get rid of the boarders. It was your idea, your hack and it was brilliant, unorthodox, completely batshit bonkers – if I hadn't seen it I would not have imagined anyone actually doing something that stupid but scarily brilliant. If anyone was in trouble it would be the private helping you, he set it off too early, before anyone could brace.'

That was what I heard, thought Romeo, and if one of her pilots said something it was probably more accurate than the inevitable report will be. It must have been terrible, in a decompressing station without a suit, knowing her people were dying, knowing she might be joining them, watching people, machinery, everything not bolted down, throw itself into space. Thinking it was her fault.

Harper said nothing, just sat there with tears running down her cheeks.

'The lieutenant,' sobbed Harper, 'she saved me, she was dying and she grabbed me, tethered me to herself, put my mask on my face when I was too stupid and panicked to think of that myself. They say she will be okay in the tank but she might die. I would have died without her. I am sure she could have saved herself, I would have given her my mask if I had not been so scared.'

Romeo threw an arm over the girl, pulled her in close, nestled the teary eyes against her own neck.

'Ma'am, you are an officer,' Harper gasped, flinching away.

Romeo was confused for a moment. 'It's just a hug, besides, we are different services, different chain of command, nothing to stop us being friends.'

Harper must have been exhausted, she fell asleep with her head nestled into Romeo's neck. It was nice to hold someone, just hold someone. That was worth fighting for.

Romeo and Harper stayed at Shane's side for days, and then weeks, spending every moment of off-duty time there. Whoever got there first would wait, the other would message, check if they were there, bring water, or coffee for them both. They had their meals there, all of them if they were not on duty, waiting for their friend to be okay. Then Romeo realised Shane had become an excuse for them to spend every spare moment together. 'Let's go have dinner in the station food hall,' Romeo said suddenly, not aware until she said it that she was going to. It was a great idea though.

'What?'

'Shane is not getting better in a hurry, nor is she getting worse,' Romeo said. 'I pulled rank, played on my hero status,' she laughed, 'maybe I flirted just a bit, to find out. The medics, the tank techs, they all say she is going to make it but it will be another week at least.'

'Oh,' Harper said, the uncertainty showing in her voice. Then she sat up straighter, seemed more decisive. 'Okay, let's go have dinner, it can't hurt.'

They strolled through the familiar corridors of the hospital station talking. Harper had expected to be reassigned, instead they had kept her there, kept all of them there, waiting in that distant sector for an officer. None had come, there was a chronic shortage of human troops, an even greater shortage of human officers. That must also have been why they had tanked Shane in a hospital station rather than evacuating her to a hospital on Earth; why they had treated all the wounded on that station rather than evacuating them.

Romeo was glad. She had heard bad things about the hospital ships; there were even worse rumours about the state of medical help on Earth. Nobody she knew had met anyone who had been flown back to Earth in a hospital ship and then returned to the war.

Maybe it was a good thing, people returned to Earth were staying home safe, retired, the war over for them. However, surely some of them had wanted to return to battle.

It was only in places like the hospital station that she saw many members of other Federation species. For all its multi-species multiculturalism, the Federation still tended to keep military units single species, or at least put only particularly friendly species together. Humans, the newest members of the Federation, still had no close alliances, no close friends.

When Romeo left Earth, humans still had no vote in the council. She had not heard of that changing.

People of all species in the Federation were in the corridors in the examination rooms, the waiting rooms. Some so different to humans that it was impossible to even begin to understand their anatomy. None of them paid any attention to the two humans passing through the station like ghosts.

Romeo had managed to get her squadron temporarily assigned to this station as its fighter defence. She had people in the hospital, pilots who lost their ships, who caught fire bad enough for it to cut through the armour. Some of them would never fly again. Once they were patched up enough to survive the trip they would be going home.

She was short-handed with the losses, the wounded, even a couple of pilots due for discharge. There were no more human fighter squadrons for her people to join so it was easy for the Federation to justify leaving them at the hospital station until more pilots could be sent. Pilots and ships were on their way; they kept telling her that.

Reaching the station concourse, they went straight to the food hall and settled in at the only two-seater table that had seats for humanoids. Waving Harper back to her seat when she tried to stand, waving away the girl's protests with even more vigour, Romeo went to order.

'Well, I have food,' she said when she returned, 'though as always whether or not it is worth eating is a game of Russian roulette.'

'I've never eaten in the station here before, nor at the mess-hall, there's nothing we can eat at the mess. I have been living on ration packs,' Harper said, poking uncertainly at the strange blobby mass in the middle of the plate in front of her. It quivered in response.

Romeo knew what she was thinking but knew ration packs were worse.

Harper scooped up a spoonful of the gelatinous lumpy mass in the middle of the plate, but she could not quite raise it to her lips. It wobbled disconcertingly.

'Don't worry.' Romeo laughed, tapping the ear-piece she wore. 'I checked. This place generally succeeds at edible for humans but not at tasty. They haven't killed anyone yet that I have heard of, though one of the girls said that when she tasted one stew she wished she was dead.'

Harper laughed then, an honest laugh, it sounded clean of every other emotion but joy.

Romeo cherished the memory of that laugh through the next couple of weeks, through the peace they had before Shane got out of the tank, through their first tentative lovemaking, through the long discussions about family and dreams, through the return of Harper's platoon to the front with Shane officially commissioned as the lieutenant. Harper was promoted permanently to technical corporal, given a team.

The memory of that laugh kept Romeo flying, filled her with desperation as she fought to keep the skies clear, to give the soldiers on the ground a chance. Harper was her breath. She had never felt that way, that strongly, about anyone. That laugh would be what she would hold on to, what she would embrace, as she breathed her last. She would die before she let that laugh fade forever.

CHAPTER 22

WHEN JIMMY AND Itta arrived with the refugees at the next station, armed security were already waiting. The refugees were contained, imprisoned in one half of the gargantuan concourse behind temporary fences. They were fed barely edible multi-species rations, wrapped beige bars with the crest of the Federation embossed into them.

Planned for the nutrition and tastes of as many races as possible they were barely nutritious for anyone, barely edible according to everyone. The lucky ones got species-specific dietary supplements. It was easy for Jimmy to secrete some ration bars in his pack for later. He would have to be desperately hungry to eat them.

He might be able to barter them later.

Itta didn't seem to mind the bars, although Jimmy could not ask her what she thought. She was so tiny, so malnourished, had so little appetite, she had rations to spare. He stashed her spares too.

Jimmy had been identifying his fellow travellers by their clothes and accessories, by their groupings and associations, families and couples, big groups and small, it was only the broad strokes that were memorable. When they were reloaded into another ship he no longer recognised anyone around them.

A new ship, new passengers, it didn't matter to the authorities where they were sent, it didn't matter to Jimmy either, it was not like he had a choice.

'Human child, Earthling,' the voice was heavily accented, the tone might have been questioning, it was almost impossible to read. Jimmy looked around the crowd of strangers desperately. He had barely recognised English, he had not heard it for so long. He could not allow this English speaker to escape.

'Human child,' came the voice again, 'is Englandish your tongue, your language, I cannot tell from the colour of your skin or from the shape of your face, cannot tell where from on Earth you have come. I thought most humans spoke Englandish away from the human home system.'

Jimmy looked around again, then finally thought to look down. A cloaked figure was seated on the ground, leaning against the wall, the opening of a cowl pointed in his direction, the half visible face inside thin and not quite human-like. There was desperation in Jimmy's voice, 'Are you talking to me, talking English?'

The face within the hood was the same as one of the species Jimmy was stuck travelling with, people he still didn't know anything about. The clothes were different and distinctive. Jimmy recognised the robes. The speaker, if the words were coming from the robes, was an academy monk.

Jimmy had run into them from time to time. They were never rich, never poor, never dangerous and rarely in danger, for they had nothing to steal. They cared only about their research and could be good for a few credits if they were doing a survey and needed subjects. If they thought someone interesting they were sometimes good for a meal.

The academy had a strict policy of harm minimisation.

They would not, in a refugee situation, be particularly helpful.

'English, so that is what you call it, I sometimes get things wrong in your language. It is highly,' the monk paused, 'irregular is the word I think, the rulings they keep changing.'

'It gets us like that too.' Jimmy laughed.

'The human who taught me your language said it was the only language on Earth where you have to learn to spell it. They might have been joking, I could not tell, but spellings in English are so, chaos. I cannot understand why, if English is so irregular, it became the humans' dominant language.'

Jimmy didn't know what the monk was talking about. Nobody had ever taught him to read or write.

'Who was he, who taught you English?' Jimmy was consumed by a sudden desperation to hear something about home.

'She, yes, she, was a candidate for the academy. A, I think, professor on Earth, teaching us some Earth history, I can't even remember her name. She was studying race, species, relations, sociology you would call it, trying to find out why not every species gets along, why some are speciesist, even racist within the same species, I have heard you humans can be quite racist inside the species, you think skin colour means something. She might be a monk, as you call us in your language, by now, if her candidate, um, what is the word, thesis, that's right, if her candidate thesis is powerful enough.'

Jimmy didn't even know what a thesis was.

'I hope she made it, hope she passed the examinations you would call them. She was extraordinary, taught me Englandish, English, we were friends, I think we were friends, I considered her a friend, I hope she felt the same way. Why can't I remember her name? Never mind, it will come to me, we called her "Peace", in the way of the academy, for that is all she wanted, she hoped if she could work out why people hate she could find an antidote, find a way to stop us fighting the Conglomeration, end the war. That is the way of the academy, we name people after what drives them, that name changes if they change what they are studying.'

Itta let go of Jimmy's hand, sat down next to the monk, leaned into the corner formed by him and the wall. Were they a him, or a her, Jimmy didn't know. Perhaps their species didn't have sexes, they could be hermaphrodites. Jimmy did not want to guess.

'Please, young,' the monk paused again, 'man is it?' Jimmy nodded. 'Please, young man, sit with me a while.'

Was it deference to the monk that had cleared the space around them? Was it fear? It would be a relief to be uncrowded; Jimmy sat in the no-man's land, crossing his legs, looking in the black watery eyes of the monk.

'Sir, or ma'am, I can't tell,' Jimmy said, 'what is the correct address, what sex or gender are you?'

'That is important to you humans, isn't it? It's even embedded in your languages so you have difficulty talking to someone when you don't know their gender. Peace told me that humans are focused on sex a lot.' The monk laughed a disturbingly human laugh. 'And on sexes and gender. She believed it possible that this is the route of hatred. Humans are extraordinarily good at hate, which is why you are so feared as soldiers. You are unusually sexually distinctive. You have kept gender-divided jobs longer than anyone else, even longer than some species with extreme sexual dimorphism. Maybe distrust of the other right at the start, the other sex that is, might lead to other hatreds. I don't know. I do know that the hermaphrodite species are less warlike. Generally. My people are artists, poets, scientists.'

Jimmy nodded.

'Yes, we are hermaphrodites, and we don't hate the other. Maybe that proves Peace's theories, who knows. I was a poet before I met Peace, my academy thesis was a poem, now I have no time for poetry. Peace was inspiring, I thought maybe if I can find something that makes us all the same, maybe something similar in our language, I might be able to help end the war. Maybe I could find a language to describe peace in a way that was so compelling I could make peacefulness infectious. Peace was so inspiring, what a fascinating woman. I was a poet, now I guess you would call me a linguist.'

'My name is Jimmy.'

'Hello Jimmy,' said the monk, 'you can call me Professor Speech, or just Speech if you like, we have no equivalent to such unnecessary words as "sir" or "madam". I would like us to be friends. And who is your friend here, who is — is the word "snuggled"? — to me for comfort?'

'That is Itta.' Jimmy was surprised he had almost forgotten her. 'I found her all alone, she has nobody else so I am looking out for her. It was a couple of stations ago, she was wandering alone.'

'Hello Itta,' said Professor Speech, 'where did you come from?'

Itta did not respond, did not even look up, her face half-wedged between the wall and Speech, her hair curtaining her face.

Speech pulled back their hood. They were beautiful, soft fur of a glistening copper, large eyes in a flat face and a small round nose.

'I don't think she speaks English,' Jimmy said, 'when she speaks at all it doesn't even sound human. She doesn't speak Federal either.'

They were not allowed to stay on that station long. Troops on the way to the war poured in, battle-weary and scarred, dangerous and ugly in their bulky uniforms. They needed every resource, did not appreciate the refugees being in their way. They were moved on.

@

Next was a mainline station, near the densely populated core of Federation space, or on a major shipping route, huge and crowded; Jimmy had lost track of where they were or even if they were going in the right direction. He and Itta were probably the only humans. The concourse was so large that the flood of refugees had disappeared into a shanty town at one end, enabling the business of transport to continue unmolested.

Aware of the mysterious-looking grime on his clothes he scurried to the refugee camp, keeping to the walls, keeping his head down.

Normally mainline stations were too secure to pass through without being harassed by authority, or so Jimmy had heard. He was thankful for the cover of the refugees. He still refused to acknowledge he was now one of them.

Professor Speech was huddled close to Itta. They appeared to be talking, which was impossible. Approaching slowly, careful to not tread on anything, or anyone, he dropped his backpack on his thin mattress and thinner blanket. Speech looked up at him with eyes that might be sad.

'I have food,' Jimmy announced excitedly, applying a torn scrap of wet-wipe to the black grease on his hands. He pulled his haul out of the backpack, a couple of ready-meals for an unknown species; the codes on the packaging implied the meals matched human metabolism close enough to mean they could eat them, though they were unlikely to be palatable. He expected to regret eating them. There was also a vac-bag of something that looked like cooked meat and a can of something that was coded for Speech's species, if he correctly remembered the codes Speech had taught him.

Last out of his pack were some squishy unidentified pieces of fruit and vegetables they would have to be careful of if they decided to eat and, mercy of mercies, an overripe but intact banana. An actual banana. What the hell was a banana doing there? True, most species could eat them because they were little more than carbohydrate, but they were fragile; he could not imagine how it had made it to the core in edible condition.

'How resourceful, young human, you have found food for us all.'

Jimmy nodded. 'The garbage disposal system dumps into a molecular de-bonder and recycler.' Speech nodded in reply, but said nothing, it was the same as every other station. 'But there is a bottleneck here, a partially blocked tube, it's through a few locked doors, a couple of dangerous climbs, but I made it. The garbage just piles up there for a while. If you are careful, really careful, you can open a hatch just over the bottleneck and rummage.'

'Sounds dangerous,' Speech sounded worried, if Jimmy was reading the tone right.

'It is dangerous, very dangerous, you have to lean in, head-first, if you slip, well the tube is slippery and goes straight to a de-bonder. There might be a scanner to check for lifeforms, it would switch the thing off. In theory.' He did not mention that if it did detect him and switch off he would be stuck there in a slippery smelly filth-filled tube until maintenance and security pulled him out. He had no doubt they would then haul him off to jail.

He paused again but nobody else spoke, Itta was staring at the ready-meals with feral hunger. 'At least we can eat.'

'I hate this stuff,' Speech said, opening the can of food with something like a ringpull, 'I am nearly, barely hungry enough to eat it.' Pulling out a utensil a bit like a spoon they started eating.

Jimmy tore a ready-meal open with his teeth, he hoped it was enough for him and Itta, he was keen on saving the other one. It was horrible, it smelled like blood and pus, like a sick-bed. His nose wrinkled and his mouth revolted at the taste of it, but it went down. Itta didn't even seem to notice the taste.

'Itta and I have been having a talk,' Speech said with their mouth full.

Jimmy swallowed. 'I thought you didn't know what language she spoke?'

'I didn't,' Speech mused, 'but I do now, you could say I did always know it but did not know I did. I am not certain any of what I just said made sense. In any language. I know her language but her accent is atrocious, I don't know if it's because she is human or because she learned it in some backwater. It's almost unrecognisable, I failed to recognise it at first.'

'What did she say, where is she from?' Jimmy knew he sounded frantic. He could hear the words falling over themselves in their haste. 'Why is she out here in space alone, why doesn't she speak any human languages . . .' He petered to a stop then, out of steam, yet not out of questions.

'She doesn't know where she is from, doesn't know who you are, you are the first person she remembers seeing who has a shape so much like her.' Professor Speech looked bewildered and bemused. 'She doesn't remember any humans, which does not make sense.'

'I don't understand.'

Speech paused, maybe looking for the right words. 'She says her,' pause, 'parents would be the closest human word, her parents left her behind when the war came to her city, left her to scavenge with the pests and the abandoned pets. They were not human, her parents, they were, their species name for themselves is as unpronounceable in your language as it is in mine, or theirs to be honest, but they were not human, which is biologically impossible. She must have been adopted or fostered or some other thing like that. She had never thought to question why she looked like nobody else on her planet, why she looked not even slightly like those she called her parents.'

'I don't understand, I feel like I should, but I don't.' Jimmy barely breathed.

Professor Speech stared, open-mouthed and voiceless for a moment. 'I don't know if I can explain,' they said, 'I will try. Itta is human, obviously. She must have been taken from her human family so long ago that she had no time to learn human language. She was living with another species and learned their language as a native. If I know linguistics well enough, if I know humans well enough, she must have been not much more than an infant when she was taken away. She doesn't even know how to be human, or what a human is, all she knows is that you look a little like her, more like her than her parents anyway.'

'I was taken from my family too,' Jimmy said, 'they took me from my parents and sent me away. They said it was to school but it wasn't, it was to work, and work, I have never done anything since they took me but work. I have been away from my parents for so long I can't really remember them. I only know English well because I was in a house with other human servants, I spoke English there, and Federal, I had to speak Federal to everyone but the other humans.' He was angry for a moment, shook his head to clear it.

'Why didn't they teach her Federal, I don't understand,' Jimmy said finally.

'I think, what is the word, dream? No, that is not the word,' Speech mumbled to silence, then opened their mouth again. 'Imagine, that is the word, I imagine she was a bit of a pet, almost a child, adopted as a child, to be their child, treated more like a pet. Something like a pet or a child. They called her their child but never considered she was their equal, so she was more like a pet. It's a hard concept. Pet is closest. Humans keep dogs as companions if I remember rightly, we have the equivalent in our culture, they are loved almost like children but treated more like possessions.

'I don't think they intended her to have a full life, and existence outside of their pleasure, maybe what mattered to them was their status at having such a child under their control, as a possession. I think that's the right word. She was their equivalent to a human having an unusual breed of dog, or an exotic rare animal as a pet. I am sure there were no other humans on their planet, she would have been quite the status symbol.'

'When they took me away,' Jimmy said, 'they said they were adopting me and that I would be their child, that was not true either, they treated me as a slave, property. From the first day I was there in their house they made me work.

'I never understood why they didn't let me go home, didn't let me return to my parents, to Earth, why they kept me there. I am older now and I am beginning to get it, they just wanted me to work.'

Washed in the low murmur of citizens in the refugee camp, Jimmy wandered down the darkest corridors of his mind, maybe Speech was doing the same, maybe instead they were contemplating Jimmy, there was no way to tell from that unreadable face. Itta too was blank, staring into the middle distance as she did all too often.

'I can't even imagine what it was like for Itta,' Jimmy said finally, 'it was hard enough for me, but I at least remember my mother's face, I remember my father a little, I remember home, Earth. The colours, the greens, the blues, the smell and colour of soil, I miss them all. All the humans in the big house where I worked were all servants, all slaves, nobody was free. Itta was the first free human I had seen for so long, but she wasn't even free, she was worse off than me.'

Speech stared at Jimmy with an expression that he could not understand, the three of them fell silent. Suddenly the monk turned and spoke to Itta in what Jimmy assumed was her language. Itta replied so fast Jimmy thought he would find it hard to follow even if he had known any of that tongue. The exchange went on, the rhythm of the language hypnotic, Jimmy wandered lost and tired in that serpentine, labyrinthine sound, almost fell asleep.

Suddenly Jimmy felt skinny arms wrap around him, felt the weight of Itta on his shoulders. She spoke to him, the only word he understood was his name; she spoke again, still he understood nothing. He glanced at Speech, confused.

'She says thank you for looking after her,' Speech translated, 'she was lost and scared and nobody cared.'

Speech, as far as Jimmy could read their expressions, was sickened. 'She doesn't understand why they left her behind, she needed them and they left her behind. She is scared you will leave her too.

'She was swept up in the refugee migration, had no idea what was going on, where she was, what to do. Then you came and things were better.'

Itta spoke to Jimmy again, stared perplexed at the confusion written on his face. Turning to Speech she seemed, to Jimmy, to repeat what she had said, a short burst of sound, completely unfathomable.

'She says,' said Speech, 'she is glad she met you, you are the same.'

Jimmy nodded. He had no idea whether she meant they were both human, which was obvious, or both lost, both far from home, both alone. 'I promise, I will never leave you, Itta,' Jimmy said, surprising himself.

CHAPTER 23

WILLIAM'S LIGHT CAME on, it cut into his over-sensitive eyes even through closed lids, filling his vision with blood red and lightning blue. There was, as always, no clue to the time of day.

He lay there, with the light burning through his lids, yet did not move, lay there until the pain of the light was unbearable, until he could lie there no longer. They were not going to switch the lights off, they were summoning him. He rolled over onto his side, the light still there but not as painful.

He had no pillow, no blanket, the room was constantly almost exactly human blood temperature, so he had nothing to cover his face. He flung his forearm over his eyes instead.

He would have peace until someone grew irritated by his intent to stay in bed and found some way of moving him. Whatever they did to move him, it would hurt. He thought, although that hurt too, of Earth, of the time before his arrest, of his fractured family, broken even before they took him away. His home was probably gone; there was a war on. He could not hold on even to that, to a sense of home.

He could barely remember the sound of laughter, the voices of his children, the warm, long arms of his wife, those years in prison had almost taken them from him. Yet even that prison, as much as he hated it, was better than here, at least he'd had people to talk to, camaraderie with the other inmates, he would love to see them again, even the people who hated him. Even in solitary he had known that it would end one day and he would be back among people. Here the loneliness was eternal.

He had no idea when he had last seen a human face that was not unconscious or contorted in pain, strapped to a gurney in the lab. Or dead, so many of the people he saw were dead.

He had no idea if his hell was ever to end.

All he wanted was his family back, for them to be safe. He would die to defend them, to keep them safe. When they had come for his children there was nothing he could do. He had believed in justice then, had not believed in the need to die for them. He had been at work in the hospital, patching up the wounded, repairing the burned, doing his best for broken minds. The flood of wounded from the front line of the war seemed unending. When someone was wounded the under-trained, overwhelmed medics could do little more than patch them up and fly them home, they arrived in great ambulance ships, filled with blood and noise, the smell of fear and infection saturating the recirculated air.

The doctors and nurses performing triage called those ships 'meat-trucks'.

A few lucky ones, officers mostly, were submerged in tanks, in a honey-gold healing liquid as life-support hardware stopped them dying. Others were on beds, on stretchers, on the floor if the ship was really crowded. He had only been on an ambulance ship, a hospital hulk once, after that he had used his status as a senior surgeon to keep away, he delegated it to others.

He was taking a rare coffee break when a nurse arrived at a sprint, told him to come, come fast, he had a phone call. He walked briskly to the nurses' station, nodding calmly to everyone he passed, wanting to run to the phone but not wanting to cause a panic. A nurse handed him the phone, the terrified look on her face filled him with fear, he placed the handset on his ear, talked.

'They have come for your kids, Doctor,' the voice at the other end said in a rush.

'What, who has come?' He wanted to scream, yet he did not, the discipline, the habit of his profession did not let him.

'Hurry, they have come for your kids,' the phone went silent but for the sound of a scuffle on the other end.

Turning to the nurses he spoke as calmly as he could manage, 'Tell the director I have a family emergency, I'll be back as soon as I can.' He walked quickly, through those institutional cream halls, enforcing his false calm. Breaking into a run once he was out of the door into the fluorescent-lit underground car park he dove through the door of his car. Not his kids, damn it not his kids.

He was already speeding when he exited the car park, desperately afraid, almost certain he was already too late.

CHAPTER 24

WALKER WOKE TO the ground shaking. An earthquake, another bomb, the black smoke tearing the very ground apart. A scream rose unbidden, unstoppable, to his lips.

'Shhh, it's okay, you are safe now,' said a comforting female voice.

Safe, he could never be safe, not while his Country was dying, while he could feel the bones of his ancestors creaking.

His eyes burst open, staring towards the sky, but all he could see was a strange matt beige field, smudged, stained dirty. He was on his back in a vehicle of some kind. He turned his head to see more and his vision swirled black, his mind chasing his sight into the abyss.

He woke again. The car, it must be a car, was bouncing down a ragged, corrugated road. Firm but soft caring hands held him to stop the thrashing vehicle from throwing him from the thin mattress that barely softened the hard floor under his back. He looked up, between him and the roof of the car, he thought he had been in a car like it before, he could see a woman's eyes staring at him with concern over the top of a clean white cotton surgical mask.

'Where am I?' His voice sounded weak.

'We found you in the desert, you were dying.'

That didn't answer the question, thought Walker. 'Where am I?' he asked again.

'A troopy,' said the strange woman after a pause. Walker tried to nod but his neck hurt too much. Made sense, he thought he recognised it, troopies were the ultimate dream vehicles where he came from. This one had the seats folded up, he was on the floor. 'Our troopy,' she continued, 'we are taking you to Adelaide, maybe we can get you medical help there. I'm Kelly.'

'Walker. What—' he coughed, 'what happened? How did you find me?' The car hit a rough patch of road and he was almost thrown off the mattress. The woman grabbed his shoulders, rolled him back to the middle of it.

'We found you by accident. We were inspecting the bomb site, looking for evidence. We weren't looking for anyone, didn't think there were any victims, actually we assumed there would be plenty of victims, but not survivors.'

The woman squeezed past Walker and leaned into the space between the heads visible in the front. There were two people in the bucket seats there, silhouetted in the fierce daylight, their hats leaving no clue to the shapes of their heads, they could have been men or women. Kelly turned her head, whispered into the ear of the passenger who turned towards her to whisper back. It was a young man, with the beard of a much older man.

Walker tried to relax, despite the pain, despite the bouncy roughness of the ride. The car rattled, the panels were loose, the doors were loose, boxes and bags shook and hammered against the floor. The road, like so many through the desert, was so rough it was barely a road, barely even a track. His back was wet and he hoped the moisture was from the mattress not from him, hoped it was not blood or worse.

He knew it probably was his blood, his rotting flesh, he lay upon.

Suddenly they hit a harder road, maybe it was even sealed, the highway probably. The cacophony of the car turned into a light vibration, a comforting hum, he noticed then how much he had been bouncing. Walker felt something, blood or phlegm, catch in his throat, he coughed then he choked, hacked up something foul tasting into his mouth. He could not breathe. He felt something force open his mouth, tasted blood and a stranger's skin, felt something rough, a callused finger maybe, on his tongue.

He spat out the finger, turned his head away from it and spoke. 'There were no survivors, I'm finished.'

CHAPTER 25

'LADIES AND ENBIES,' Romeo said with authority she was not certain she felt to people she was not entirely certain she deserved to lead, 'we have been told this is the big one, it might be the battle that breaks our enemy, that ends the war. I don't even know for certain where we are but we have been assured the planet we are en route to is so important that taking it would cripple the Conglomeration's war efforts.' There was a chorus of murmuring from the ready-room, they had all heard it before but nobody was brave enough to shout 'bullshit'. The pilots, some of them replacements for those she had lost in the last engagement, sat with barely suppressed energy, they were almost vibrating with it, dressed in flight suits, helmets on their laps. They did not know when the siren would sound.

'Our bus is part of a battle group headed for the core of Conglomeration space, we are to provide escort for the troop transports, at least initially, orders will change.'

Romeo knew Harper would be with Shane on one of the transports, it made it that much more of a pivotal mission, though she would be in trouble if she told anyone that. She did not care about the war any more, she did not care about Earth either, she had not been there for so long, what she did care about was Harper.

She liked that girl a lot. She did not want to think of it as love but had to admit she felt something different this time. At the thought of Harper dying her gut clenched painfully, she was more afraid for Harper than she was for herself.

@

The floor hummed and vibrated under Shane's boots as she inspected her troops. It was a hard grey floor, nobody had bothered to cover it. They thought the grunts wouldn't appreciate decoration, but Shane would, she was heartily sick of Federation Infantry grey.

She wanted the war to end. She missed her husband and kids and her Country beyond words and regretted having left them even more. She had books to finish reading, a script to finish writing, a life, a career, a half-written novel on the tablet in her pack; backed up on her personal storage on the Federation cloud.

At least her family were safe on Earth. She had carried a photo of them with her for years, from camp to camp, from battle to battle, it had become worn, had accumulated dirt, had been nearly lost. Then in the battle in the mud, somewhere between running from the ordnance and making it to the evac, the photo had become so water-logged it disintegrated.

All she had of her family were memories. There were photos and other memories stored in the cloud somewhere but she was unable to access them for some reason. She needed to talk to someone about that; if she did not get access to her photos soon she would hurt whoever was responsible.

The ship's walls were the same colour as the floor, curving to an identical roof. If the ship lost its artificial gravity it would be almost impossible to know which way was up if not for the chairs, each area designed and designated for a species, bolted to the floor. Voices came over the speakers into the room, voices in a language Shane did not understand, they were not speaking English or Federal, they must not care whether the humans in the troop hold could hear the announcements.

Cargo didn't get to question where it was being delivered.

She glanced over to the other troops preparing for landing. Her platoon were the only humans in this ship, she had her orders, they had their orders, there was no need to communicate and nobody was even attempting to. That was okay. She did not want their fear, did not want the confusion of comparing their orders with hers.

The lander hit something, or something hit it, the floor jumped under her feet, she landed on the lap of her sergeant, a giant of a man, who grinned, a refreshingly honest grin, at her half-surprised, half-sheepish expression. She stood up, danced across the floor with the shaking and swaying of a ship that must be making evasive manoeuvres so erratic the artificial gravity was not keeping up. Her radio was switched to 'do not disturb', only emergencies that put her and her troops in direct danger would break through.

The last thing she needed was to hear ship after ship, lander after lander, go silent – the silence that implodes over the radio as ships full of sentient beings cease to be, the screams of the dying as their ships were holed, wasting their last breaths on futile vocalisations into the vacuum, the panicked voices of the crew as they lose control and their broken ships drop into the gravity well of the planet, to burn up in atmosphere or hammer into foreign soil, the pilot needing to make the decision, would his passengers prefer to know they are about to die or not?

The last thing she needed.

Returning safely to her seat, the first time she had been in the lieutenant's position on a landing, she grabbed the straps, was almost thrown from her chair, clicked the buckle, heard the whirr of electric motors, felt straps tighten until they were painfully tight, tight enough to steal her breath, felt the very shape of the chair adjust to her body. She was thrown into the straps again, as the ship manoeuvred under gravity, hung upside down from her chair as the pilot, what a prick, flipped the ship to dodge something, then turned back again, throwing her against the back of the seat. It was like being kicked by a horse. Someone, one of her platoon, vomited, stomach contents splattering on everyone.

'Nice one, Jones,' she heard her sergeant shout, 'next time try and aim better, you missed some of us.' Someone laughed. If she survived the landing all she had to do was fight a war. No, she thought to herself, she had to win.

Her family needed her and she needed them.

CHAPTER 26

JIMMY AND HIS friends were on the move again, Speech had applied for asylum on the planet below but, with the volume of applications the planet had received, they were simply refused without much explanation. Soon after the planet had announced a closure of their borders, Speech and Jimmy decided two of them would be better able to protect Itta so they stuck together as the entire refugee population of the station was forced back onto the ships they had arrived on.

Hulks was a better description; barely space-worthy, filthy wrecks would certainly be accurate. Nobody had wanted to get back on those ships, people fought and screamed, eventually those who could not be intimidated were forced, those who could not be forced were shot with stunners and dragged onto the transports.

'You are a resilient young human,' Speech said, 'you will survive this.'

'I don't know', Jimmy said, 'my luck might be running out.'

Speech nodded politely, their robes rustling faintly.

'I've been out here, alone, on the run for too long, I am getting tired, getting weak, now with Itta to look after I don't know what's going to happen. I shouldn't even be out here but I wanted to know where I came from, how I got there, who my real parents were. So my adopted parents kicked me out, I was homeless on the street on their planet, they didn't even tell me where my home planet was. Then I was arrested, I slept somewhere I shouldn't have, the police there didn't care who I was, where I came from.'

Jimmy glanced over at Itta, he had no idea who she was and where she came from, all he knew was that he cared, he cared about her like nobody had ever cared about him.

'They contacted my, well they called themselves my adopted parents, and they said they didn't want me back, it was only then, when they refused to take me back, that I found out where I had come from.

'Because of them I know where home is. That is where I have to go. Itta and I have to get to Earth,' Jimmy said. 'I can't trust the refugee ships will go the right way, I can't be sure when would be the best chance to run for it so as soon as possible is as good as anything.'

Speech was silent, Jimmy could not begin to guess what they were thinking. 'Yes, you should go home, maybe your family is there still, maybe they look for you, you could find Itta's people too, that would be harder as she remembers nothing, but you should try. You are humans, you belong on Earth with the other humans.'

'So,' said Jimmy firmly, 'we are leaving.'

'Not alone,' Speech sounded even more determined, 'I am going with you. I cannot do much good for the Federation right now, the war, it's changing us, it must be. What has happened to you two is wrong and yet the Federation I love was part of it. I can do one thing that is good, one little thing to make the Federation a better place, I can get you home, my language, my speaking, you need me.'

'I cannot ask you.'

'You didn't,' Speech interrupted, 'nevertheless.'

@

Down one end of the concourse, past the shanty towns of the homeless, the stench, the piles of refuse, some of them lived in, was a market of sorts. A ragged line of tables had been entrenched, kept clear of beds, of the sleeping, of trash by those who had things to sell, and sometimes by some muscle they had bought. In Jimmy's experience there were always people who would accept money to hurt other people, muscle was cheap. Some people would apparently hurt other people for nothing.

The only trash allowed there was the trash on the tables, everything broken, damaged, dirty, second-hand.

There were clothes, all of them ragged and much repaired, for more species than were in the concourse, many of the colour combinations intolerable to human eyes. There were bags and bundles, some little more than trash in which one's trash can be stored. Someone was even selling a disposable plastic grocery bag, as luggage. Among them were blankets, sorted by cleanliness, by state of repair, some with more messy patches than there was original blanket left.

Jimmy had seen people stabbed over a blanket, seen bags stolen, seen someone once try and barter their child, a squalling starving brat, for a clean synthetic blanket.

Maybe here, on these tables, was where stolen treasures turned up.

He knew he would die before he would give up his bag, before he would hand over his and Itta's last blankets. Nearly all the things for sale here were stolen. He knew that some of them had been killed for, knew that some of the patched cuts in blankets must be knife-holes where their previous owners had died in their sleep, some of the stains on the blankets were blood.

Jimmy had money to spend, he was careful not to display how much, not to reveal where it was hidden. He had scattered it over his body, even if he was killed nobody would get all his money in the time they would have to search him before they were noticed. Hopefully Itta would get what was left.

He walked over to the tables, showing he had interest in buying something yet careful to not show too much interest; trying with his expression, his manner, to demonstrate he had money to spend, but not too much.

Exuding as much false confidence as he could, he strolled down the line. He needed a knife, something to prepare food, something he could cut with, eat with, yet sharp enough to defend him and Itta, and Speech if it came to that, they had been helpful, deserved Jimmy's friendship. The knife had to be small enough to hide, if someone could see it they would certainly try and steal it, they would kill for it.

The stallholders viewed him with what appeared to be suspicion, they were all the same species, the dominant one on this station. He assumed it was that species whose planet they were orbiting over. If one of them was suspicious, untrusting, they all were – their expressions were so similar, maybe he was reading them all wrong.

One of them, at the end furthest from the entrance to the concourse, had a messier, fuller table than the others. Many of the items were mysterious, or at least they were to Jimmy, maybe to someone else they were valuable treasures, or maybe just species-specific toiletries. Turning so, he hoped, only the stallholder could see him he gestured the Federation sign language for 'knife' in front of his chest.

The stallholder stared for a moment. Jimmy thought he might be ignored; he didn't want to have to ask another. The more stallholders he asked the more people would know he was looking for a knife. Finally a hand sign appeared in the place between them, Federal sign for 'okay', or 'maybe', depending on context.

The stallholder gestured to the shadows behind his stall and Jimmy followed him, hoping he was not about to be robbed. Praying he was not about to be killed.

Jimmy was shocked when the seller showed him what he had for sale, it was so much like a human chef's knife it seemed impossible that it wasn't. He held up the sign for 'how much?'. The number flashed back, if it was local currency it was everything he had, if it was Fed credits it was more than he had.

He reached into one pocket, took out all he was willing to spend on a knife, it was less than half of what the stallholder was asking for. The stallholder gestured, it was 'no' with an inflection that seemed to cast doubt on Jimmy's intelligence. Jimmy took out a ration pack, a bar of muck with all the nutrients needed for a few different species. The code said it was edible by humans but it was so vile he failed to stomach one even when he knew it was eat or die.

The stallholder stared at it, did a gesture that asked 'and?', if it was sarcastic Jimmy couldn't tell. He reached into his pocket and another bar appeared, this one not coded for humans, perhaps coded for the species he was talking to, certainly coded for the majority of the species in the vast crowd of refugees, if anyone asked he would never admit where he got it from. Like a snake, the stallholder snatched at Jimmy's hand, the food, the money disappeared, the knife was dropped. The stallholder was already gone.

Carefully Jimmy took up a scrap of fabric, so dirty and ragged that even the desperate had not used it to patch clothing. It felt like an oily tea-towel but if it was he would have to be careful not to eat wherever it came from. It was filthy, the dirtiest piece of fabric he had ever seen. He wrapped it around the surprisingly sharp blade, stuck the parcel in his pants at the back.

Jimmy wove his way back to the main stall area. The stallholder who had sold him the knife was gone, someone else, a boxy muscular being, was watching their stall.

Jimmy began to suspect the ration bars were worth more than he had expected.

There was an oncoming roar like thunder, the sound of voices screaming in a language he did not understand. More voices joined in, it was deafening, he started running before his conscious mind even understood what was happening. A crowd was pouring in through the concourse entrance, yelling, throwing things, rotten food, bottles, anything they could find. The stallholders bolted, scattering into the panicking multitude. The attackers charged towards the camp.

Jimmy reached the camp only seconds before the attackers did, dashed desperately towards his narrow sanctuary between a pillar and the back of a chair. He, Itta and Speech had been safe there for a couple of days, but it would be no protection now. He dodged and dove, knocked over a panicked refugee who wheeled off into the crowd, fell when he could not bring himself to trample a child, rolled back to his feet.

He reached their tiny corner and held Itta in his arms, Speech was to his back, he saw an alien child fall, trampled, its desperate parent diving into the crush. He saw people in desperate fear striking out at anyone between them and the door furthest from the attackers. A hard, heavy object flew from the mass of attackers and collided with a hooded skull, their body hit the ground with a sickening crack. Multi-species, multi-coloured blood splatter filled the air in a rainbow haze.

Screams tore through the concourse, they would have echoed, Jimmy thought, if not for the crush of bodies absorbing the sound. Itta was on the ground, curled in on herself, Speech was behind her, their lanky figure twitching, ready to cover the small human if need be. Jimmy stood his ground between his friends and the crowd.

The tone of the screams was changing, hurting Jimmy's ears, a kind of keening like a dying cat, a whistling like a summons from human lips, a squalling flute. People were trampled under their friends and family, crushed against the wall, a wave of screams and blood and fallen bodies. Even if Jimmy, Speech and Itta wanted to run they could not, the wave of bodies had become a wall.

Jimmy could see the attackers clearly now. They were throwing bottles, bits of metal, whatever they could lay hands on; if there had been rocks in the concourse they would have thrown them too. He braced himself against the massive ivory ceremetal pole that helped form their sanctuary. Desperate, he extracted his knife from his clothes with one shaking hand, as horrified he might have to use it so soon as he was glad he had it. He unwrapped it and held it hidden, against the back of his leg, he did not want to let anyone see it before he was forced to use it.

Someone, their enormous liquid eyes open wide in fear, their soft mammalian skin flushed red, tried to squeeze into his corner, on top of Itta. Jimmy thrust his forearm between him and the interloper, he pulled the knife forward and held it in the stranger's face – he hoped a threat would be enough to prevent the need for violence.

The stranger dropped bonelessly to the ground at Jimmy's feet, wailed in what was probably panic. Jimmy reached down, not sure what he was trying to do. He didn't want to hurt anyone, just didn't want anyone crushing him or his friends.

Hiding the knife against his leg, he stood over the fallen stranger, staring out into the crowd. His guilt led to a desire to protect. Nobody was trying to penetrate his space, instead they were all flowing past him, pushing for the door, a great deadly crush of beings, a screaming mass of flailing limbs, flying mucus, splattering blood.

Jimmy knew that near the door, people were already dying. Tears of sorrow, of fear, of frustration, poured down his face.

He heard the flatulent, synthetic buzz of stun guns, searched desperately for the source of the sound; he could not avoid it if he didn't know where it was. Uniformed figures with stun guns were coming through the door behind the mob, firing as they came. Now those who had been attacking the refugees were in a panic. Jimmy saw one fall, face-first, before he heard the sound of the stunner that had hit them.

The rioters broke, throwing their weapons aside, some sprinted towards the bin corner, towards the flea market, others dashed towards the refugees wanting to disappear among them. Jimmy saw some drop to their knees, raise their hands, lower their heads in submission, aware there was nowhere to run.

None attacked the station police, who regardless kept firing. They shot rioters and refugees alike, maybe they had decided it was simply easier to control a room full of sleeping, stunned citizens. A stunner blast just missed Jimmy and hit Speech, who collapsed onto a screaming Itta.

Jimmy ducked down where the piles of the dead, dying and stunned hid him from the line of fire. The police were firing at hip height, hitting anyone standing. He looked at the knife in his hand, wrapped it quickly and stashed it in his bag, kicked his bag under the edge of his blanket.

Itta must have been aware what the danger was, she grabbed blanket and bag and scrunched them towards her, hugged them safe. Good girl. He had to trust she knew to stay there, stay still, stay silent.

The soup of noise continued, stunners firing, people screaming, people dying, he could not protect Itta if he didn't know what was going on, he rose into a crouch, half-stood to look over the piles of citizens. A light exploded in his eyes as if he had been looking at a camera flash, his limbs went rubbery, his muscles stopped working, he fell boneless to the ground.

CHAPTER 27

KELLY WAS GETTING nowhere, every test was a failure, she could only imagine she had not thought of the right test yet. She had tried every sensible line of enquiry and was just about desperate to start on some stupid ones.

'They call it a particle bomb,' Kris said, interrupting her thought, 'that is the best translation I can find, there is no word in English for what we have uncovered.'

Kelly strolled over to Kris, placed her hand on his shoulder, looked over his head at the screen glowing in front of his chair. He had been working hard at the translation, it looked from all the scribbled notes as if he had been taking detours through other tongues, translating by dictionaries, word by laborious, multi-syllabic word.

'Particle bomb?'

'Yeah, something like that, they have found, or created, or – buggered if I know – conjured from another dimension or something, extracted from spider shit for all I know, particles that are infectious. They dump some of them or the detonation of a bomb creates them – I don't know – they irradiate what is around them and that starts a chain reaction or something. The radiation, the radioactive particles, whatever they are, they make more of themselves from the atoms around them, which then expand outwards and infect other things.'

Kris absent-mindedly scratched his beard as he stared at the screen.

'Sounds dangerous, you might be talking about viral radiation.' Kelly knew she sounded almost as scared as the idea sounded ridiculous.

'Or prions, you know, well, the things that possibly cause mad cow disease, they are molecules, proteins, that act like viruses but they are smaller than a virus, not even as close to alive as a virus, they modify other proteins, buggered if I know how . . .' He sounded worried as well.

'But at a subatomic level, the new particles, these particles, like they are protons or neutrons that infect other protons or neutrons, but that is impossible.'

'Impossible to us, maybe not to whoever created this weapon.'

'You're right,' Kris said, 'maybe not to them.' The word bastards might have been on the tip of his tongue but it stayed there.

'I've tried all sorts of tests and whatever those things are they bugger up whatever equipment I use, viral radiation is the closest thing I can think of that could do so much damage to my toys,' Kelly said slowly and deliberately. 'So how do we stop it? How do we stop these viral neutrons or whatever they are from spreading?'

'I don't know,' Kris sounded panicked, 'but I assume whoever built the thing knows how to stop it. Though, maybe not. Admittedly when humans invented the nuke we didn't know how to clean up the radiation to make nuke sites safe again.'

'I know,' Kelly said, 'we can be so clever and so stupid at the same time.

'It could kill the planet,' she said, 'vacuum would stop it, having no particles, no atoms to infect would stop it, but no vacuum is perfect, it would only take one infected hydrogen atom, the vacuum of space has enough hydrogen floating around, maybe it could even infect photons, probably not. Even just infecting one hydrogen atom might be enough, eventually it would take out every planet in spacetime. Besides, ships land on Earth all the time.'

'I am not even sure I am reading their papers right, not even sure it's the right information. The hackers we got it from might have fed us the wrong info.' Kris sounded like he wanted that to be true.

'Kris,' Kelly's panic was overwhelming all her other emotions, 'we went near the test site, we breathed the air, we touched the ground, drank the water, we rescued that man, he had been in it for days, if it is that infectious, it is already in us.'

She looked into Kris's face, saw reflected there the fear that was pulling the gorge into her throat.

CHAPTER 28

THE NOISE WAS ear-damaging loud, Lieutenant Daniels switched on the noise suppression in her helmet, the thunder was cancelled down to a dull roar. Their refuge was a damaged, tumble-down aircraft hangar, half the noise she was blocking was the hammering of small-arms fire on the walls, it hit and hit and hit, the bullets breaking through with cracking noises, whining overhead until they hit the far wall. Most of the projectiles did not have enough energy left to cut through the walls again, they slammed into the far wall, ricocheting, falling, splattering, it was deafening.

The bullets that bounced off the back wall lacked the velocity to kill or wound but that did not stop them from hurting like hell when they were stopped in the end by flesh.

From time to time, aircraft flew overhead, adding their screaming note to the already deafening song. Random shells and poorly aimed bombs landed near the hangar with booms the troops felt rather than heard. None of them had yet hit the hangar, but it was just a matter of time. Then they would be dead.

What a screw-up. They had landed too far from the starport on the wrong side, their target, a control tower, was on the other side of the runways and landing slabs, a long sprint through open space. Certain death if they tried it. The lander crew, when they became aware of their mistake, simply told the human troops to tough it out, unloaded them then flew off for the next troop drop. The hangar was the only cover they could find.

Then they discovered there were more Conglomeration troops in that tiny spaceport than they had been told to expect.

Shane wanted to call in an airstrike or even a bombardment from space but they were supposed to be taking the facility undamaged. Or at least with as little damage as possible. She crawled through the maelstrom towards the death rattling through the wall. Most of the fire, if not all the fire, was coming from the direction towards which she was crawling, the direction of the control tower and the spaceport offices, the safest buildings. There was a slight lull in the enemy fire, the hammering slowed, though it did not stop. She crawled all the way to the wall, looked for the lowest bullet hole she could find. In the dust her unit were throwing up with every moment, sunlight cast a thin god-ray through the hole, she watched the dust motes dance, waited to see if the noise would calm further.

It didn't. Her troops fired through gaps in the covering walls, through windows before running from the return fire. The Conglomeration troops didn't so much fire back as fire constantly. She raised herself up on her elbows and placed her eye at the bullet hole. The air was filled with smoke, the light weak and pained, the setting sun casting a reddish glow on the haze. Across the runway was another hangar, and before it, protected by steel barriers and sandbags, were the Conglomeration forces who had Shane's platoon pinned down.

If she was in their position she would keep the enemy down until artillery or air support arrived. Then her platoon would die and it would be her fault. None of her people would make it home and it would be her fault. Earth would fall, her children would die and it would be her fault. She knew that to be untrue, if the war was lost it would take more than just her to screw it up, but she could not stop feeling it.

She peered through the tiny hole again, squinting to see more in the waning light, in the waxing smoke. Something was moving behind the Conglomeration barricades, and a bit to the side. She stared some more, trying to interpret the play of shadows, the swirl of red-glowing smoke that was all she could see of this new thing, some part of her must have known what it was, must have known it was important.

'Oh shit.' She hated being right, the smoke swirled away; her view cleared for a moment. A bunch of humanoids, smaller than average humans, were hauling something to the barricade. She half-recognised the shape, understood it well enough to respect the danger, to feel her stomach lurch with fear. It was a field weapon, a heavy plasma cannon or an artillery piece of some sort, a tube, a tube on simple wheels.

'People,' she roared as she stood and ran towards her unit, 'get ready to move out immediately. Sergeant with me.'

'Sir,' Sarge snapped without hesitation.

'They are bringing some sort of field cannon, a siege weapon into firing range, it might be a plasma cannon, or a projectile weapon, it might throw kittens, I don't care,' she snarled, 'they are too close, there is virtually no cover between us and them so it doesn't matter what the gun does, we are sitting ducks.

'Those Conglomeration dickheads over there have so far shown they can barely hit a barn, we know that because we are stuck in one, but now that is all they have to do. That is why I want you to get our people out of here as fast as you can, we head north, the open space of the runways, the landing pads, it narrows there. We cross the open space in the cover of twilight, the cover of night if we are that slow, and double back. If we get a chance, we will hit the Conglomeration forces from behind, otherwise we will go wide around them, head for our objective. If we can get there we will fortify, buckle down and hold that bloody tower.

'We need to keep them distracted while we move out.'

'Yes, sir,' Sarge said.

'Make it happen, Sergeant.'

'Yes, sir.'

'Volunteers, you understand.'

'Yes, sir.'

'I mean it.'

Lieutenant Daniels moved to the back of the hangar, climbed into the back of the commandeered troop transport she was using as a command post. She wished someone in her unit knew how to drive the thing; unfortunately, its controls were completely alien. There were people in the Federation who would risk their lives to get their hands on Conglomeration tech in working order so they could learn to use it or go mad trying; none of them were there with her. Sarge had a team, well, two techs and a specialist driver, on it and so far they hadn't even managed to find the starter.

'Harper,' she said, 'how's communications?'

'Sir, we have some flaky comms with the ships above and none with anyone on the ground. Basically we pick up our fighters when they are approximately overhead but no more than that. From the sound of what we are getting it's even worse up there than it is down here, they are getting hammered.' Harper sounded more worried than Shane had ever heard her.

Shane put her hand on Harper's shoulder, 'Don't worry, Corporal, there is nobody in space of any species who can outfly our Romeo, she will clear the sky above us, then she will get us out of here, then when it's all over you can meet her on the carrier.'

It would have been silent at that moment if not for the hammering of small-arms fire.

'Because of the amount of fighting going on in near orbit, it is nearly impossible, certainly too dangerous, to get a comms ship, a fighter or a relay satellite geosynchronous above us. There seems to be a low-level interference on ground level comms as well. Until our people in space can get a relay into orbit above us we have no off-planet communications at all,' Harper said.

'Unless we take the tower,' Shane mused.

'Unless we take the tower,' repeated Harper.

Shane and her soldiers moved through sheds and hangars, past abandoned tools and half-dismantled equipment, over dust and concrete, as quietly as they could, not ghosts, too heavy booted for that, they were whispers, were rats in a garden shed, relying on the hammering of small-arms fire, the 'whomp' of the cannon to hide their small sounds.

They jemmied open doors quietly, kicked them open when that didn't work, hoping the sound of the guns would cover it, trying to time the noise for when they thought the cannon would fire.

When there was no building to move through they dashed between buildings, desperate to get under cover before someone was seen.

Twice they were forced to turn back, look for another path. Only discipline stopped the front of the group doubling back into the middle, from turning into chaos.

Behind them the hammering of small-arms fire hitting the hangar, like hail on a roof, rose to a deafening roar. Shane did not even want to imagine how it must feel back there, in the bare cover of the hangar. One of the volunteers, staying behind to make the enemy think the platoon was still encamped there, fired back, a rattling of an Earth-made machine gun. Shane heard a plasma cannon, a 'fwarp' like a chord on a nineties synth, then the hiss of air being obliterated by heat like that of the surface of the sun.

The Conglomeration cannon fire hit the building, Shane could imagine the carnage; parts of it would have been thrown like shrapnel, other parts would have melted, sprayed lava-hot metal that burned all in its path. The sound imploded into silence, everybody stopped firing, everybody held their breath. The soldiers Shane had left behind, volunteers, diehards, holding the line, were surely dead now.

Air rushed back into the space left by the evacuation of the air superheated by the plasma explosion. It sucked past them like a breath. There was a faint crack.

Then someone started firing again in the hangar behind them, then another. Shane sent a message over the comms to the rest of her platoon, they were too bunched up, they had to get their arses moving. If the operators of that plasma cannon started spreading their fire to the buildings near the hangar she would be among the first in the line of fire. She had to wait until the troopers ahead of her moved.

The space before her cleared, she moved forward through a door into a dusty hangar filled with damaged atmospheric fighters and landers, heard the people guarding her back begin to move after her. Then another 'whomp', the plasma cannon had fired again, the ground shook beneath her feet, dust danced into the air and was caught in the evacuating wind, the breath of the dying hangar, flung away towards the distant unseen door.

Again her people started firing in the hangar behind them. She was shocked that any were still alive within that ruin, under that barrage. She knew they would be no longer even trying to aim, just lying prone emptying their guns, reloading and emptying again.

She imagined some of them must be enduring wounds, splattered with molten metal from the blasted walls, bleeding from shrapnel wounds. Yet still they fired. If any of them survived it would be a miracle; it was a miracle any of them were still alive now. In the depths of her soul she was crying for them already.

'Everybody, we have to keep moving,' Shane said into the comms, 'we have to move faster, when the enemy realise we are on the move they'll start looking for us. If we are really unlucky, if they are smart, they will start smacking this entire side of the airfield with plasma before they even bother to look.'

'Yes, sir,' she barely heard Sarge reply through the hissing of the comms, the hissing of the air rushing back into the plasma-burned sky.

'Our friends back there are ready to die to give you a chance,' Sarge said with authority, if they were not trying to be quiet he would be bellowing, 'let's not shit on their sacrifice.' Again the plasma cannon sang, again the wind pushed Shane in the back, harder this time; the attack was closer. The enemy were starting to widen their bombardment.

'Everybody move,' said Shane into the comms.

@

The ship was filling up, a riot of noise and so much smell; four species in fear, pheromones and bodily evacuations creating a miasma that might not clear for the entire trip. It was nauseating, painful, acrid, acid, bitter all at once like a thousand unwashed people living in a sewer. Unconscious citizens were piled just inside the door where the guards had dropped them, nobody had the strength or the desire to try and move them.

A pool of liquid, might be blood, might be vomit, some other unpleasant secretion, a mix of fluids, spread from the pile. Perhaps someone inside that pile was injured and bleeding, crushed under all that weight, perhaps they had injured themselves fighting security before the stun guns hit them. Perhaps instead fear or the after-effect of stunners made them soil themselves. Nobody desired to investigate, instead they turned their backs on the wounded and stunned, seeing to themselves, to their family and friends.

Itta looked like she wanted to scream, her eyes wide, nose wrinkling under the assault of the smell, she shivered like a trapped bird under Jimmy's comforting hand. Speech was left without words, their nostrils closed against the smell, they panted through their just-opened mouth. Jimmy wished he could do that too. He took a relatively clean square of cloth out of his bag, not much more than a rag, folded it in half corner to corner and tied it around Itta's head, covering her nose and mouth.

Jimmy had only just recently learned to read Speech's expressions, it was surprise on that increasingly familiar face as the hermaphrodite turned to look at him. Jimmy shrugged, Speech returned with their species' version of a smile, an open mouth like a surprised human.

Speech sat down next to Itta, Jimmy could hear them murmuring. He tried to not let it upset him that Itta, the only other human he knew, spent more time with Speech.

More and more people poured into the ship's hold, it was already full, there was nowhere for people to overflow into. Another crush, then the panic when people discovered they were trapped, realised they couldn't breathe. People tried to get out the doors, which closed, suddenly, violently. Someone had a limb in the doorway, it was torn off by the sudden closure. Inhuman screaming tore through the hold, increasing to a deafening volume as more voices joined in.

The screaming would not stop.

Citizens were everywhere, crowding around, some of them seated on the deck, others standing, crowded together. Scattered around the deck people were pushing others out of the way to claim small camps, laying blankets on the ground, fencing their tiny domains with piles of their belongings. Fights broke out over those tiny scraps of land, those ragged rectangles of deck, each micro-war brutal, bloody and short.

The screaming would not stop.

Jimmy stood on the edge of their blanket, knife half-hidden at the ready. Someone screamed nearby, loud enough to be heard over the background wailing, as a swaying knot of citizens broke, some landing on a blanket camp, on top of the people set up there. People set up close but nobody tried to muscle in on their corner. They had barely enough room to spread out a blanket, there were three of them, it was probably just not worth the effort.

The screaming would not stop.

Jimmy tried to ignore the blood, the screams of the wounded, the angered screeches of those who had no piece of ground to make a home on. A fight surged towards Jimmy, he held his knife behind his back in his left hand, held out his right to fend away anyone who stumbled his way. They did, two of the long-limbed aliens, Speech's species, furred and scrawny like spider monkeys but with beautiful, trustworthy faces. They lost their footing and staggered as they wrestled. Jimmy stepped towards them to repel them as they approached, they were taller yet he was far heavier, he threw them from their feet, they tumbled back into their own groups, nothing more than a tangle of limbs.

Jimmy tumbled, rolled back to his feet, returned to his blanket, to his camp, his safe little piece of floor. Itta was staring at him with eyes gone huge, Speech was armed with a bottle, held by the neck like a club, eager to help whichever way they could. The rank air burned Jimmy's lungs, he held his knife, stared at the people around him, wondering who would transgress on his space first, who would he have to hurt. People stayed back, to his relief.

There was wailing from the pile near the door, a group of the hooded and masked people were kneeling around a prostrate member of their own people. They began crying, a lament. Someone was dead.

The screaming would not stop.

@

A day later a whistling had broken through the silence, through the faint moans of the sick, the despairing, the dying. It was not very loud but it was insistent, unending. No matter what other sounds overlay the noise it continued.

'I think it's an atmosphere leak,' Speech said, 'I have heard it before on a station, the air leaving through a micro-leak.'

'Oh shit,' replied Jimmy, 'that's not good.'

Jimmy could feel the air getting thinner, hoped that was only his imagination. Voices murmured in languages Jimmy had no comprehension of; rumours must have been flying, people must have realised what the noise meant. Voices flowed in waves, floods, a flash flood of fearful voices overwhelmed even the whistling.

Someone ran over to the intercom, beat on the button to activate it, yelled into the microphone. There was no response that Jimmy could identify, no reply, no sound from the intercom at all. The hand beat on the button again and again, smashed the cover over the emergency alarm button, hammered on the button until it cracked. Nothing happened to prove that the button was working.

The whistling had continued, for days, days and nights, a relentless squeal of doom, a haunting sound. Beings searched desperately for the source of the noise, finding it eventually high up the wall of the hold, near the ceiling. Jimmy ran over when he heard the exclamations, saw the limbs pointing.

He hoped he could help in some way, hoped there was a way to seal the hole, to keep them all alive. People momentarily forgetting their species differences formed a ladder of their flesh, Jimmy among them – human size not being heavy enough for the bottom of the pile but too big for the top, he ended up halfway up the wall.

Jimmy felt the weight above him like the mood in the ship: depression, despair, impending doom. In the end one of the cloaked citizens, one of those with a covered face, climbed the pile, the limbs must have been twigs under all those clothes, they weighed so little Jimmy could barely feel their weight on his back when they climbed him. Despite that, the weight above him was almost unbearable, he heard voices above, hoped they were working out what to do with the hole.

The ship lurched – no, that was not possible, they would not feel it there in the hold, protected by artificial gravity; maybe the artificial gravity was giving out. He felt it again before he realised what it was, the beings below him were collapsing under the weight above them, his support was buckling. When it finally collapsed, the ladder of people falling into a mass of flesh, he did not have time to throw himself clear, he ended up again somewhere in the middle of a pile, it felt even heavier than the more structured pyramid before.

Speech and Itta dragged him out, helped him stagger to their tiny camp on the deck.

'They failed,' said Speech in a voice that Jimmy thought unnaturally calm. 'It's still leaking.'

Jimmy merely nodded, he could hear the squealing, the whistling, the wails of the terminally terrified all around the hold. Someone banged on the door connecting the hold to the crew areas of the ship, futilely; if the crew were not responding to the alarm button, the intercom, the decompression alarm that must be sounding, they were not going to respond to the soft wet sound of limbs on a pressure door. Jimmy looked over, the door was smeared with blood from flesh beaten to bloody ruin.

The crew had stopped inspecting the hold, they no longer cared or they knew it was decompressing and had cut it off from the rest of the ship. The crew would survive even if their passengers did not. Jimmy sat despondent on his blanket trying to conserve oxygen, around him everybody was doing the same. Someone was still screaming, over the other side closer to the whistling noise, there was a thud then another as someone – family, a stranger, an enemy, there was no way to know – knocked them down, beat them unconscious, saving everyone's oxygen.

It would only be a matter of time, Jimmy thought, until it was decided that there would be more air to breathe for the survivors if there were less people breathing. He was not going to be the one to make that decision but he would defend his people. Anyone deciding Speech or Itta needed to not breathe would be the ones losing their lives.

Jimmy just lay there, slept as much as he could, for days, crawled when necessary to vomit into the waste receptacle or the toilet. When he was really little he and his family had holidayed in a town a thousand metres above sea level, he could not remember the name, where the air was thinner. He had not understood until later what altitude sickness was, that the thinner air higher in the atmosphere left him feeling short of breath, low oxygen eventually made him vomit.

Slow decompression felt just like altitude sickness and just like altitude sickness exercise made it worse. Even trying to stand was intolerable in the end, he stayed on his back as much as possible. Eventually he was not able to even crawl off his blanket to vomit, lying on his side he emptied his almost completely empty stomach, felt the blanket under his shoulder dampen.

He woke in an emergency infirmary in an area he did not recognise. He was clean, wearing a hospital gown that was species-specific only in that it required at least two arms to slide through the sleeves. He was alone, no sign of Itta and Speech, they must have died, why would they leave him alone? He had no bag, no clothes or blanket, none of the belongings he needed to survive.

When he was fit enough to walk they ejected him from the infirmary into the corridor of a station he did not recognise, still wearing the disposable hospital gown. Barely covered by it, he staggered towards the other refugees. Faces, cowls, eyes turned towards him as they must for everybody as they returned from the infirmary, every eye must have been searching for those they had lost; all looked away when they saw it was only him. Then there was a wail, a voice shouting his name. His eyes followed the voice. Speech was waving, Itta's tiny form was running his way over belongings, over people if they were not fast enough to get out of her way. She didn't care what she was stepping on in her haste.

Carrying Itta, he returned to his friend, without him they had no safe camp, just another blanket among the others, in the middle of the crowd. His bag, mercifully, was there.

@

Jimmy just sat there; not even thinking. When they had arrived on station they were not told where they were. The refugees had almost not reached that station at all, after a nightmare trip, nauseating odours, excruciating claustrophobia and an unstable drive.

There had been dead on the ship and nowhere to put them, many had not even awakened from the stunning, from being dragged onto the ship. They were piled up by the door to rot, their smell, putrid and vile, had filled the air until Jimmy woke wanting to vomit and never quite recovered.

The smell was sucked up by the air circulation system, run through filters and scrubbers, but that would not have been enough. When the captain sent a crew down to clean up the worst of the mess in the hold they refused; refugees were instead press-ganged into it.

Limbs fell off when they were used to drag corpses leaking rot; the bearers of the bodies adding to the smell with their physiological reactions to the situation: nausea, evacuation of digestive contents, fear pheromones. One dead being was no more than liquid putrescence wrapped in what was left of their skin. It was like carrying an overfull plastic bag full of rot, the skin inevitably tore, rot and gore spilled all over the deck.

The bodies were piled in the airlock, the weight of those on top crushing more decay and filth out of those beneath. Jimmy would have backed off if he was not already against the wall, people backed onto his blanket. He lacked the energy to repel them. He collapsed on the blanket, Itta embraced him.

Those who had carried the dead refused to clean up the gore and rot on the deck, one was stabbed repeatedly with a pain prod until unconscious. Still they would not move so the crew pushed them aside and 'volunteered' another group to clean up. The pungent smell of cleaning products cut through the smell of death and fear; the result was terrifying and eye-watering.

Cleaning finished, an alarm and flashing light warned the passengers who turned their backs. The cleaners dumped all the filth and the dirty tools in the air-lock with the bodies, the door ground closed. Another alarm and the airlock contents were evacuated into space. What was left of the bodies after the liquids boiled away in the vacuum would soon be frozen.

CHAPTER 29

WHEN THE LIGHTS came on again, William no longer had the courage and strength to resist. He should not have tried to resist last time; it had cost too much. He felt his face gingerly, winced at the piercing pain on his cheekbone. It must be fractured at least.

The guards had been about human-shaped but heavier, their pleasant faces belied their brutality. The fact they seemed to enjoy beating him was proof they were more human than most species. They had not looked at his face while they kicked him.

His breath jerked into his lungs at the pain, the cruelty of it all. That hurt too, he realised, at least one rib was cracked. If he resisted them again, already injured like that, he was dead.

The mess hall door appeared then whooshed open at his approach. He had never, in all the time he had been in that place, seen anybody else in that room. Either nobody else ate there or they removed everybody else before he was allowed to eat.

There was nobody there this time either, the white chairs were empty, on the table in the centre, white like everything else, was a plate of what he thought they must consider 'food'. It would be nutritious, that he was certain of, it would be warm, they seemed to understand that humans preferred hot food but couldn't bring themselves to make it actually hot.

It would not, however, taste much like anything he considered worth eating. If he was lucky, it would be bland and tasteless. 'Tasty' was not always a good thing; there had been food so awful he was tempted to have his taste-buds surgically removed.

He felt fortunate the food was pleasantly bland, the blinding white room silent and empty. It was, as it had been every meal, just enough to be satiating and he had no doubt it would have all the nutrients he would need. He marvelled at the scientific cruelty of this place. Starving him to death, giving him malnutrition, would be too uncontrolled, too easy, and would teach them nothing other than how long humans could live undernourished.

They did not want to starve him, they wanted to break him yet leave him capable of working for them.

He would not be surprised to discover they were starving someone else in another part of the station to find out how long it would take them to die.

The over-bright lights overhead flashed once, a warning; it was time for him to go to work. Back into the hallway, through the door at the end, there was a room there a lot like a hospital nurses' station but for the fact that he could recognise none of the monitoring equipment. He looked at the people there as he passed, every face a different species, none of them looked back at him.

Why would they?

Past that was a ward, empty, the beds made up for humans with sheets and pillows. Eventually he reached the ward for prisoners. The door opened at his approach, he was expected. Attached to the ward was the lab, with equipment to record every fragment of data from the death of a patient; the real reason why the prisoner ward was there.

There was a prisoner there, or a patient. It was impossible to tell whether he had been brought there for experiments and the experiments were killing him or they had brought him there to study whatever was killing him. If he was sick the disease that was destroying his body was virulent, indescribably damaging. He was bleeding from his eyes and nose, what could be seen of his skin was blotched with purple-black shapeless stains; if they were bruises they were the darkest bruises William had ever seen.

The man on the bed writhed in a weak, half-hearted way, opened his mouth as if to speak. Nothing came out but black-red drool. It ran over his lips, down his cheeks and stained the pillow beneath his head. It seemed there was nothing inside his open lips other than a shapeless, wet, red-black cavern.

'There is nothing you can do for him,' Doctor Jack said behind William. William turned to stare at his tormenter, whose mask was on. 'He was caught up in a nasty bomb blast and his cells are dissolving at a – what would you call it? – a subatomic level.'

Jack was still, like a robot or a statue, in a way no human could manage. William wondered what was behind that mask, under those plasticky clothes.

'What could do this?' William asked; he had never seen anything like it.

'Fearsome technology,' Jack said. 'I don't understand it myself, I am a medical researcher not a weapons researcher or physicist. I can, however, see its effects quite well. We have been sent this patient so I can try to understand how this poison, this weapon, works, see what effect it has on living tissue. Maybe we can save others who are suffering from the same condition.'

William stepped closer, staring at the wounded man, wondering what could destroy someone in such a way. The few areas of flesh visible between the bruises had a strange sheen, they did not look like human flesh any more, more like the skin of a frog, moist and slimy. Only the eyes looked human, or one eye looked human, the other was clouded over the pupil and bloody around the white. William could see those eyes begging him; he knew the man dying on the table would beg for help if he could clear his mouth of blood and talk.

The dying man spat and coughed, blood bubbled from his mouth, sprayed into the air, rained down on his face. Some hit William, splattering his hospital scrubs. The blood was too dark, like it had already clotted although it was still liquid.

The man on the table tried to speak, made nothing more than a gurgling noise, coughed again and started choking, his eyes filled with terror.

'Now,' said the doctor from across the room where he was preparing a trolley, 'let's get started. Euthanise the specimen.'

CHAPTER 30

SPEECH HAD CONVINCED the captain of a ship to take them in. Jimmy had not understood how, had simply handed over all the ration packs and money he had as partial payment, agreed to work to pay for the rest of his passage. He did not mind washing toilets, cleaning the crew kitchens, his labour and his belongings bought passage for him and Itta; Speech was working with the crew as a translator.

He didn't even really know where the ship was going, just knew it was heading closer to Earth, closer to home. Closer to his parents who he hoped would remember him. The smell of the bodily secretions of multiple species followed him everywhere as he worked, but that was okay, they were leading him closer to home. Speech had arranged it and Jimmy had to trust it was true.

©

Jimmy rolled out of his too-soft bed when the alarm sounded, a piercing, nauseating sound, not quite right for human ears. Itta, on the top bunk, was still sleeping, or at least appeared to be. He didn't know how she did it, in a comfy bed she could sleep through anything. He had not yet worked out how to wake her up consistently.

Dressing as fast as he could in the uniform they had cobbled together for him, he walked out of the cabin. The only good thing about his uniform was it showed his muscles; he had put weight on with the decent food in the crew mess, with the labour that was buying them passage.

Speech was already in the staff mess, daintily eating something Jimmy did not recognise. The other cleaners on Jimmy's team were seated together around a table, every one of them a different species, every one of them completely uninterested in getting to know Jimmy. He was pretty sure Speech was only getting up early so Jimmy would have someone to eat with.

He stomped over to one of the food machines. He had cleaned the food preparation area for the passenger dining rooms more than once, the machines there were almost identical. Waiters brought the orders into that room, entered them into the machines which then produced the food, people plated it to look nice then the waiters delivered it to the table.

'Good morning, Jimmy,' Speech said as Jimmy sat down at the table holding two plates, a burger and a side-salad on each one. That was the real surprise, seeing the machine produce crispy green stuff that looked and tasted exactly like lettuce. The best thing about working on that ship was the food.

'Morning, Speech.'

'I trust you slept well.'

Jimmy shrugged. 'Yeah, well, I had little choice, by the time I finished working I almost fell asleep walking, I didn't even have the strength left to eat.'

'You are working too hard,' Speech said as if it was not obvious, 'you should rest before you get sick and fall over.'

Jimmy shrugged, it was a waste of time trying to explain that there was no way the crew manager was going to let him rest. Speech knew they were working him two shifts a day, his and Itta's, knew that was eighteen of the twenty-seven hours of a day in ship time. Between work, eating, looking after Itta, trying to learn her language, he didn't have any other time, nor did he have any other choice.

Speech knew all that but didn't realise Jimmy was sleeping only about three hours a night. Jimmy had no idea what their response would be.

Jimmy ate, if he did not get enough food in as fast as possible he would regret it later, there was not really even time to talk, he had to be at work soon. He didn't know what the burger was made of, didn't really want to know, but it tasted exactly like a burger. He had not gotten ill in the month he had been on that ship, so it must be digestible.

Finishing his burger, he moved on to the other one, then picked the best bits out of both salads.

He didn't want to work, wanted to return to his cabin, return to Itta, take a few more precious moments to work on a common language. Itta was learning Federal, more useful unfortunately than English; she had electronic books downloaded on Jimmy's old stolen tablet and – well, he hoped she was studying hard. He was trying to learn her language, Speech was helping but Jimmy was making very little progress, it was just too alien and they had not found any ebooks or apps to help.

He was also too busy, had no time for study. He was not going to give up, was not going to stop fighting. He went to work.

CHAPTER 31

What passing bells for those who die as cattle?
Only the monstrous anger of the guns.
Only the stuttering rifles' rapid rattle
Can patter out their hasty orisons.

– WILFRED OWEN, ANTHEM FOR DOOMED YOUTH

SUCH NOISE, THE rattling panic of semi-automatics, the hammering of explosions, the screams that sounded like a throat tearing, the wails of the dying on both sides of the line. It would not stop, it would not stop and Shane was in the middle of it, part of it, one with the noise. Someone in the front screamed, someone else shouted 'Medic!', she hoped the medic would hurry, someone carried a wounded soldier, so covered in blood, face so contorted in pain, they were not recognisable. Their scream preceded them and then their scream followed them.

Shane didn't want to be an officer, to make the decisions that sent all these people to die. She crouched down in cover, itching to throw herself in there, to die with them, to die for them. It might be best if she just died, if she sacrificed herself to give her troops a chance, better she die rather than them.

'Lieutenant,' her sergeant's voice came over her comms, 'we have taken losses, but not as many as them, we are still outnumbered but pushing them back,' there was a crackle and a scream from somewhere, then the guns started again in earnest and she could barely hear him.

'If they break don't push them, Sarge, don't chase them, let them run. All we have to do is get them moving, take their cannon and their position.'

Sarge laughed over the comms, 'Yeah, all we have to do.'

'Our first and only priority is the control and communications tower, that is our target.'

'Yes, sir.'

'However, we just can't have them hammering the tower with that cannon once we are in there.'

'They will bring another cannon, sir, or if we are really lucky a tank.'

'I know, Sarge.' And she did, they would come and then they would come again unless they were busy elsewhere. All her people out there, the ones she sent in to die, were doomed. She would die too, at least that would be a relief, because if it all went wrong, if she had sent all those people to die she would be better off dead, she could not live with it. Luckily the enemy were probably going to take care of that.

She thought for a moment, cried for a second – hoped nobody would see her tears – if she died she would never see her kids again;

she would leave them without a mother. Not that; that would be worse than dying.

Things had gone approximately to plan. They had snuck across the landing field under the cover of twilight, when the light from the sky was brighter than the shadows, when most eyes found it difficult to adjust, until they were almost behind the enemy. They had stopped, silent, and she had sent a coded pulse over the communicator. Those they had left alone in the hangar stopped firing. The Conglomeration troops waited a moment for the firing to begin again then some of them pushed forward to the hangar.

That was when Shane had ordered the attack from behind.

She would never be used to the blood, the guts, the pain. Nobody had prepared her, nobody could, for the gore of scientific slaughter. Not even the war poems she loved, that had inspired her to be a writer. She imagined what the world, the universe, would be like if cultures spent as much energy on almost anything else as they did on finding new ways to kill each other.

Her thoughts drowned in blood.

She had long ago stopped counting how many of her platoon had died, how many she had sent off to their death. She did not want to think how many more would die before the Conglomeration troops broke and fled. No time to bury the dead, they were left wherever could be found that was out of the way.

She turned and stumbled, exhausted and in despair, to the temporary medic station she had ordered set up in an office. It was not what you would think of when you thought of hospitals, the noise of the battle was barely reduced by the thin walls, it seemed even louder among the stretchers and the soldiers lying on the hard ground. So many wounded, all trying to make no noise, to show how strong they were, to not scare each other; many failed, the screams would not stop.

Someone Shane didn't recognise, though she thought she should, looked to her face, she could see relief and hope crawl over theirs. Someone else held out their hand, she reached out and took it, squeezed it, held it for a moment. A medic shook her head, tears glistening on her cheeks, pulled a blanket over a slack, bloodstained face. The other soldiers, those still conscious and coherent, looked away.

'You need to rest, Lieutenant,' said someone kindly, 'we can't have an officer who is so tired she can barely stand.'

'I'm not tired,' said Shane.

'If you are not tired then you are suffering from something far worse, something that maybe sleep will not cure,' they said, 'nevertheless you need to rest, it is safe here, more or less, as safe as it is anywhere right now and you need to rest.'

'I'm okay,' Shane snapped.

'You are not okay, you are tired, you look worse than tired, the sergeant can take care of things until you are fit for command. Either that or I can get a second opinion, someone to help me declare you temporarily unfit.'

Shane turned and glared at the medic, then looked around. There was a soldier, a young woman; Shane was that young once but she was not a soldier then; she had a kid who must be almost that age. The young woman was only half-conscious, most of the expression on her face was clouded by sedatives, but what was left was fear. Shane sat on a chair next to the girl, took her hand, as cold and moist as an oyster. 'I will rest here,' she said.

@

'Lieutenant,' Sarge's voice woke her from ill-considered sleep, 'the enemy ranks have broken, we have taken their cannon and their fortifications.'

Shane sat up straighter in her chair. 'Well done, Sarge,' she said into her comms, hoping she did not sound too groggy. 'If you are thinking of pursuing, don't. Don't let anyone chase them down. Our objective is still the tower, send some people to secure it.'

Switching channels, she spoke again, 'Harper,' she waited for the 'Yes, sir' before speaking again. 'We have taken that plasma cannon, get someone on it, highest priority, we have no weapons techs, not officially but I am sure you have friends who would love a crack at it.'

She stood up, creaking, switched channels again. 'Sarge, Harper is getting some techs and hackers to try and work out the controls for that damned cannon. Do we happen to have anyone trained, even slightly, in artillery?'

There was thoughtful silence on the comms, then Sarge spoke, 'There's a corporal, he's been bucking for a transfer to artillery for a while now. For some reason they have not let him transfer.' Sarge laughed, a surprisingly clear laugh lacking in cynicism. 'It might be that he likes blowing shit up a little too much.'

'Tell him it's his lucky day then get him to pull together a team, people he thinks might be able to help him aim and fire that thing. He should run all his selections past you, of course, send him to Harper, together they might be able to work out how to fire it.' She didn't think either would be able to work it out alone.

Switching the comms controls to general chatter, she walked into the offices at the base of the tower. Some of her troops were taking a well-deserved spell, eating, resting, having wounds tended to by the medics. She passed through them, talking to those who looked her way, showing no fear, they did not need to see she how afraid she was.

This battle was over, they had routed the enemy, but no doubt the Conglomeration forces would be back. This was their home planet, they had everything they needed and would have a powerful desire to take it back. Shane and her troops only had what they had brought with them, and they were settling in for a siege.

Unless, of course, the enemy decided they needed the airfield less than they needed to stop the Federation having it. In that case, they would bomb it flat with Shane's people in it.

Sarge was over by the plasma cannon, supervising or just making sure they could see he was there if they needed him. Except for the shape it was completely alien to Shane. The controls, even the practicalities of the technology, the material the wiring was made of, the shape of screws, the composition of the casing, all that and probably more was unfamiliar.

Harper and a couple of techs already had the casing of the cannon torn open where the controls had been. Harper, the smallest of the lot, was half in, half out of the casing, festooned with what was probably the wiring. Soldiers stood at the ready in a ragged half-circle, guns pointed at what must be the direction the enemy had retreated.

Sarge turned at her approach, reading her presence before she made a noise. 'Sir,' he said, 'we have not tried to fortify here, they have not turned back yet, Harper and her friends are hacking into the cannon for now, just while waiting for more orders. Over there,' he pointed at a skinny man with a grenade launcher, 'that's corporal Chen, his friends call him "Boom", he tells me he has actually passed the artillery specialist exam a couple of times and can't work out why he never got his transfer.'

Shane nodded. 'Corporal Chen,' she said firmly, the sound leaving silence in its wake as everyone jumped belatedly to attention, 'let the record show you are being field-transferred to artillery until such time as command have had an opportunity to review that appointment. When Harper has your toy sorted out, get your team together and get that thing moved over to the tower.'

'Yes, sir,' Chen replied with a little too much enthusiasm. He looked at her with a faint smile on his face.

'Sarge,' she said, quieter, 'get your people together to prepare to hold that tower, we need to fortify it so we can hold it, we can't rely on reinforcements for a while.'

'Yes, sir,' he said with a dangerous grin.

'And when it looks like Harper has the cannon in hand send her into the tower. We need her to patch the comms through that Conglomeration tech.'

@

'This is Lieutenant Shane Daniels,' crackled the radio, 'calling from planet-side, please tell me there is someone up there who speaks English, or Federal.'

Romeo was so surprised she almost failed to dodge, almost. 'Holy shit, tidda,' she whooped into the comms, 'don't tell me you took that goddam tower already?'

'Already? Shit, it felt like days. Yeah, well, maybe we got lucky, maybe my troops are just that good. More likely it's the bad temper of humans, and the Conglomeration arseholes down here just pissed us off a bit too much. Maybe those Conglomeration fellas are all a bunch of whiny wussbags and all ran away as soon as they saw us.'

Romeo hammered on her console, banging out the pre-planned code telling the mothership that at least one spaceport, one of the smaller ones, and its control tower were taken.

'Maybe they got a look at your angry face and fucked off.' Romeo laughed. 'I dread to ask,' she switched to Shane's private channel and spoke with false calm, 'but did that Harper girl make it to the tower?'

'Squadron Leader Romeo,' a voice tore through the comms, 'take your squadron and overfly that starport, check it is safe and ready for landing.'

'Yes, sir.'

Quickly she switched back to the tower's channel.

'Tidda, I got interrupted,' she said, worried, 'did Harper make it?'

'Romeo, how the hell would I patch my comms through the tech of a Conglomeration tower without that girl? I'm not smart enough.'

Romeo smiled. 'Well then, I have new orders, apparently I am coming to visit the sky above you. This here delta sucks in atmo but a girl has to do what a girl has to do.'

@

Shane stood at the ground level door of the tower and stared out at what she could see of their defences. They were good, but not quite good enough, yet. Broken Conglomeration fliers, cars and trucks they could not quite work out how to drive, sheet-metal torn from surrounding buildings, and other unrecognisable junk, had been moved with human muscle and hand winches, welded together using portable plasma torches, bolted together using salvaged spare parts, even, it seemed, cable-tied together, gaffer-taped, super-glued, fencing-wired. Well, her people were resourceful.

What they had made was a raggedy, uneven battlement around the base of the tower, leaving enough room for her troops to encamp and from there defend the rest of the spaceport. The sappers they had were still hard at work fortifying their barely adequate defences, the more bored among the privates were helping. Every minute the Conglomeration left them alone made Shane's unit fractionally safer, better defended.

Artillery Corporal 'Boom' Chen and his team had bedrolls unrolled near their cannon, which was facing the direction the prior owners had fled in. Shane watched as Sarge appeared and disappeared, moving around the camp so fast he looked like he had a teleport device. Abruptly he was at her side.

'Lieutenant,' he said to her with a soft but penetrating voice.

'Sergeant,' she said, biting back a startled breath, refusing to show she was startled, she could imagine his grin at her lack of reaction, 'how are the defences, how are our people?'

'Morale is high, nobody expected to take this whole starport so fast, well it's not much more than an airport, it was mostly a fighter launch site, but getting control of this place so easily made everyone's whole war. We've lost some good people but the medics saved quite a few lives. Even a couple of the volunteers we had left in the hangar made it back, lucky bastards or as tough as boots.'

'Both,' Shane said. 'So we are relatively safe, they apparently have nowhere nearby to launch fighters and bombers to hammer us with.'

'I don't know how far they will have to send air support to get us. We have sappers frantically fortifying this tower, welding plates over the windows, that sort of thing, anyone off duty is resting in the tower offices, Boom is drilling his team in operating that cannon, we have test fired it once so we know we can but we don't know how much charge it has or how to charge it. Yet. Harper is in the comms office. No power in the universe would get her out of there now she has made radio contact with Romeo.'

Shane laughed.

Sarge had a smirk on his face, spoke quieter, 'She's in love with your best friend, that could get complicated.'

Shane shrugged. 'Better than boring.' She wondered for a moment how he'd worked it all out, then remembered he was a sergeant. He was smiling.

'We have found some anti-aircraft guns, at least that is what they appear to be, smaller plasma cannons, rapid fire, that can't even be aimed at ground level. I have some people on it, mostly Harper's friends, the ones who worked out how to fire that goddam cannon, trying to modify the controls so we can use them, once we disable any automatic firing mechanisms they might have.'

'Oh shit, that would not be fun if they auto-fired at any friends we hope are incoming.'

Sarge shrugged again. 'We could always just smash their cameras or detectors, cover them with duct tape or something.'

Shane nodded, duct tape, another human invention to make it to the stars, fixes everything. 'Good.'

Comms switched on suddenly. 'Lieutenant Daniels, this is Squadron Leader Romeo requesting a fly-by.'

'Permission granted, I had better tell my kids not to shoot at you,' she switched channels again, 'if any of you mob have those anti-aircraft guns working, kindly refrain from shooting at our fighters about to fly overhead.'

CHAPTER 32

'I'LL NOT FINISH up here,' Walker breathed; every word sounded like the last thing he would ever have the strength to say.

Kelly glanced over, startled by his voice. He was standing, he should not be standing, frankly he should already be long dead. Bloody tears had congealed in blackened streaks on his gaunt cheeks. There were black stains on his chin where he had thrown up whatever he had eaten as blackened bloody gunk, he was starving to death. Even if the poison stopped melting his flesh the starvation would kill him, if the dehydration didn't. How he had any working organs left was a mystery.

There was no look of pain on his face, only despair and determination.

'What?' Kelly asked, uncomprehending.

'I want to go home,' Walker said, then coughed blood into a hastily applied cloth, 'I don't want to finish here, I will not finish here, I want to go home.' He sounded adamant, the strength in his voice was waxing, the strength of his conviction, the most energy he had shown for many days. He should be dead.

'You are dying, Walker, we can't save you, you are going to die.'

'If I am going to finish, I want to go home, I want to finish up on Country with my old people.'

'You won't make it,' Kelly said, 'there is no way you can make it, even if you had transport you will die.' She was deeply moved. She abruptly understood why her family had wanted to return to poisoned land to die.

'Why?'

'You are too sick, you will never make it.'

'No,' Walker said, his voice sounded like something between a breath and a hiss, 'why did you bring me here to this place? I don't belong here, I belong there, where you found me, in my Country where my old people are.'

'You didn't save me, I keep telling you that.' He didn't sound dejected or depressed or resigned, he sounded content to die.

Kelly felt the guilt keenly, she had tried to do good but he was right, she hadn't saved him.

'I'm going,' he said, then took a step towards the door.

Falling in a spray of black mist and blood he started to crawl, leaving a trail of blood, of black pus, the ruined atoms of his contaminated cells. He would not even make it through the door. Kelly stared, her face felt too tight, she heard the faintest of sounds, looked down, there was a drop of water on the touch-pad of her laptop. Tears were pouring down her cheeks.

She launched to her feet. She was lifting Walker from the ground before she was aware of what she was doing, he was so light, he seemed to be made of feathers. She helped him to his feet, turned him around to look at his blood-streaked face. The pain she expected to see there was absent.

'I will take you home,' she said, deciding she would even as she said it. Somehow, she knew she would not be coming back. Wiping away her tears she looked at the damp streaks they left on the back of her hand. Coughing faintly, she tasted blood.

Her tears, smeared alongside a bruise on her hand the colour of cancer, were red.

@

It was hot, Kelly's hands were so coated with sweat it was hard to hold the wheel of the troopy, her clothes were stuck to her back and arms, to the seat. She looked over, Walker was asleep, more likely unconscious, in the passenger seat. He did not look like he was going to make it.

There was a noise from her bag. Ignoring the law, there would be nobody to bust her out here anyway, she took out her phone and answered it.

'Yeah, it's me,' she said.

'Where are you, we have work to do,' said Kris over the phone. 'Where's Walker?'

The car hit a bump, the previously well-maintained highway was rough.

'Kris,' she said, 'we took that man from his Home against his will, yes, I know he was unconscious, I was there. We wanted to save him and we didn't, we can't, he's dying and there is nothing we can do.' She swerved slightly to avoid a stinking dead kangaroo as she listened to the phone. Belatedly, she realised the kangaroo corpse was streaked with oily black. 'I'm taking him home.'

She wished Kris would listen. She would not be going back, even if Kris found a cure, even if he had already found it. It was over.

'What about the work, we are so close to something, we can make them pay.'

'The work can go hang, I don't care. I have left my notes, you have the blood and tissue samples. I can't do much more, my heart is no longer with the cause.'

Kris spoke fast, he sounded worried. 'It's still hot there, you are going to get infected. You will get sick and there will be nobody to bring you back here.'

Again she listened, politely, showing her irritation on her face but not letting it get into her voice when she spoke again.

'It's too late, I am already infected, I have started coughing blood. I am dying and I intend to do something right while I still can. Before I can do nothing ever again. If I could make it back I would, but I won't, and, well, to hell with it and to hell with whatever sort of arsehole would make such a weapon.' She hung up the phone and threw it over her shoulder into the back of the troopy. It clattered, the back of the casing came off, the battery bounced separately across the floor.

'To hell with you,' she screamed into the air.

She glanced over, Walker was looking at her, the whites of his eyes were blacker than his irises.

'I'm taking you home Walker, I don't know if it is going to be any good for me, don't know whether I am going to make it back to Adelaide after that, but I am taking you home.'

'Why?' Walker shook his head laboriously, struggling to speak, 'why would the Conglomeration drop that thing on Alice Springs? There were no Starforce bases there, nothing except civilians. There was not even much work there these days, not many people there. I don't understand.'

Kelly shook her head slowly, red and black tears trickled down her face onto her chest. She struggled for words.

'They didn't,' she said finally.

Walker looked at her blearily.

'They didn't. We think somebody in the Federation wanted to test a weapon, they wanted to test what it would do to people, but they had to do it far from the prying eyes of their own law. They couldn't drop it on the Conglomeration because then they would know such a thing existed.' She shook her head, the runnels of blood throwing droplets to the sides. 'You were expendable, expended, the Federation thought nobody would care. Earth is not even a full member of the Federation, only a provisional member whatever that means.'

'Shit,' Walker said, 'not again.'

'Yeah, Maralinga,' Kelly said, 'that's my old people's Country.'

'Stop, please stop the car,' Walker whimpered. Kelly hit the brakes.

Walker fell out the door and staggered a few feet away. With a horrible gut-wrenching hack he vomited on the red earth. The red and black gore painted the earth darker, it smelled like rot, like death.

Kelly dove out her door, ran around to Walker, placed her arm around his shoulder as he was wracked with retching and sobs.

'I don't know what to say,' she said, 'I can't tell you everything will be okay, that you will live, I can't even tell you that your Country, your Home, is going to be okay because unless the Federation decontaminate it soon it won't be. This poison is killing you, killing me, killing the land itself.'

Walker's legs lost all their strength, he collapsed in his own blood.

'My mum told me,' Kelly said, crouching so she could keep her comforting arm on Walker, 'that when the old people were dying after the Maralinga bomb they did not fear for themselves, they feared for their Country, that the Country would die, that the weapon they had tested there would never let the land recover. I wondered what it must have felt like, knowing they were returning to Country when they died but the Country was dying too, knowing they could never return to Country alive. I think I almost understand, Country will never be the same now.

'I have never been to Country,' she continued, 'it's been hot since they nuked it and will be forever.' She felt hot tears on her cheeks.

She helped Walker to his feet and to the car, helped him climb in, then wondered how she would get in the driver's side. If not for the fact they were both dying, it would be a perfect day. The spinifex glowed, a golden almost pink, the sun, cooking the ground, also gave the world a golden tinge.

'You have to let them know what happened here,' Walker said as he climbed back into the passenger seat, smearing black blood on the frame of the door. 'That's more important than going home, because I can't really go home. Please tell them what happened here.' He went silent, Kelly looked over and saw he was asleep, or unconscious again.

The car moved on, carving tracks in the black dust. Nothing was going to stop it.

@

Walker had been dying for a long time, no point being dishonest about that, had been dying when she had picked him up in the desert, dying even before they met. Now he was dying at speed, rushing towards his death like to the hands of a loved one; he would not last much longer. He was, however, happier than she had seen him in the short time she had known him, he was even smiling.

The meagre fire of spinifex and mulga she had lit was crackling and sparking a couple of metres from the troopy, throwing its glow onto the sand, casting fingers of red onto the desert oaks lit from the other direction by the first light of day. Embers danced in the darkness, flying up to join the stars, the embers in the sky.

Walker lay between the flames and the car, he had rolled in his sleep and was facing her when Kelly exited the vehicle, a safer place to sleep than the contaminated, infectiously irradiated ground. Not safe, merely safer. There was a slight contented smile on his wracked face. We must be close to his Country, Kelly thought, that was the only explanation.

'Morning,' Walker said, his eyes not even open yet.

Kelly jumped in surprise, took a moment too long to respond. 'Good morning, Walker, you seem better today.'

The wind was talking in the voices of ghosts, whistling through the spinifex, making the needles of desert oaks dance.

'Not better,' he almost whispered, 'still dying, but I can feel my Country, feel my old people talking to me.

'My Country is waiting for me,' he said, 'I can feel it, I am nearly home, it's still there, it's sick but it is still there. My old people need me, we need to look after that Country, need to make it safe again. I can hear them, my old people, they came to me last night, told me they are still here in Country, even though our Country is sick, they are still here.'

He fell silent again, for what felt to Kelly like an age. In the almost silence only the wind sang, brushing through the spinifex in a rush to reach Kelly's ears, it sounded like the grass was talking.

'Where else would they be?'

Kelly stirred up the fire with a stick, lay a log on it, thinking. The particle bomb could destroy Walker's Country, might destroy the continent, the planet, there seemed to be no limit to how far the destruction from such a terrible weapon would reach. Her world would die in that black sludge and there seemed to be nothing they could do about it, the black grease would infect the sun, turn it black and dead. She would not even be there to watch the planet expire. She would be dead long before the planet died.

At least she would not have to watch.

'Not much longer,' Walker said. Kelly had no idea whether he was referring to how long he had to live or how long it would take to take him home. 'Soon I will be back in Country,' he continued, maybe he had heard her thought, 'and soon I will be finished.

'I can feel it,' he breathed, 'I can feel my home, can feel my old people, it isn't dead yet, my Country, you can't kill my Country, strong Country, stronger than that bomb. I worried that the old people might have left. They might have left and I will be all alone in that place without my old people. If the old people had left I wouldn't blame them. It's okay, even if I am alone in Country I will be where I belong.'

Kelly stood by the fire, opened two cans of beans, a can of hotdogs, nestled them in the coals at the edge. There was nothing to say and Walker had returned to his habitual silence. She realised it was truly silent, no sound but the faint crackle of the almost expired fire, no rustle and whisper of wind in the spinifex, no flutter and twitter of birds, no buzz of insects, no scritching of lizards in the sand. Except for Walker's assurance she would have thought the land they were in dead.

They ate in silence, the steaming beans poured into plastic bowls, the hotdogs poking out with a jauntiness that bordered on the obscene. They had no utensils but plastic sporks.

'I hate beans,' Walker mumbled as he fell back on the dust, dropping his bowl, piercing the ground with his spork.

CHAPTER 33

SHANE DANIELS WATCHED from the control tower as a transport landed and disgorged its supply of troops. They were not humans, they were not even of a species she had encountered before, only their uniforms in Federation grey, pink and yellow indicated they were on the same side. Behind her she could hear the commands sputtering and hissing over the radio; there were many more Federation supply and troopships waiting to land.

Guns and troops had been landed, ground vehicles and artillery, tanks and trucks. Hers was the only Federation-controlled spaceport on the planet, the only place troops could land with control tower guidance and without losing whole ships to anti-aircraft fire. She had command of the whole spaceport until she was relieved, if that ever happened.

A code flickered over the radio, a rapid array of squeals and clicks, one she recognised although she was not trained in air-traffic control. She flicked on her comms. 'Harper,' she said, 'you might want to stop what you are doing, unless it's going to explode, and get down to the landing pad.'

A squadron of deltas was cleared to land, she watched them fly in, holding perfect formation. The commander was last, their landing ostentatiously perfect. The pilot climbed out, threw her helmet to a member of the ground crew who had landed only an hour earlier in a shuttle. Shane smiled when the tiny form of Harper ran from the tower, dashed across the tarmac past smiling soldiers and threw herself into her lover's arms.

@

Romeo lay with Harper in her arms; finally, Harper in her arms, she was building dreams for the first time in her life, building a life for the first time. Because Harper was in her arms. Generations on the riverbed in Alice Springs, years in the town camps, years watching her people die from the drink, from despair, from violence perpetrated on them by the whites, by each other, all that was slipping away, because Harper was in her arms. Not even the sex was important, not at that moment, because Harper was in her arms. For so long it had all been about sex, when a woman was in her arms; after the sex, it was over, she no longer needed anybody.

Not this time, this time the end of sex was the beginning of the desire to hold on and never let go. Nothing else mattered; not the war, except that it could pull them apart; not her family, except that she wanted them to love Harper like she did; not Earth, except that the planet had given birth to the woman she loved. Love – she had fought it but it had eaten her alive, now if it killed her she would die happy. Harper loved her.

Stupid white girl, thought Romeo, she had no idea what she was in for.

@

Shane was wearing her best formal uniform and the biggest smile she could remember having had, for many years, on her face; it made her face muscles hurt, it pulled a fresh scar on her chin tight. She was going home, not forever, just for now, she was being rotated out for some extended R and R. The Conglomeration had not quite been beaten into submission but the tide had turned, though not all outlying planets knew it yet.

The war was all but over, yet the fighting continued, scattered and eternal. Those who had been for more than one tour of duty, though, were going home, rotated out. The emergency was no longer so urgent.

She was staying in, she was on leave but was not ready to leave the infantry. Shane did not trust that the war would not flare up the moment a big mob of Federation military retired. Maybe the war had twisted her, she could no longer see a life out of the military. Her leave would give her a chance to see her children, whose growing up she had missed, but at least they were safe on Earth. Maybe she could finish her book, work on a script.

Maybe she could get a training command on Earth, stay there for a while. Maybe if she was training on Earth she would have enough time for her family and for both her careers.

Her impending leave was not why she was smiling.

Romeo was in her finest dress whites, impossible blinding white, medals festooned over her chest. Her face shifted too swiftly through emotions for Shane to read them all – happy, terrified, confused, confounded, delighted, lost, all were there with others that were not so clear, not so easy to name. Every look of consternation on Romeo's face just made Shane smile wider.

'Never thought I'd see the day, tidda,' said Shane. Romeo looked about to panic.

'Shut up.'

'You are a lucky girl, she's lovely,' Shane said, giving her friend a hug. 'Now, let's go get you married, before you change your mind.'

The non-denominational chapel on the ship was so full there were people standing at the sides, at the back. There were people outside who had failed to even get through the door. The seating was split, it made Shane smile, not bride's family–groom's family, rather it was split infantry one side, fighter pilots and navy the other. It was beautiful in a way, a block of infantry grey, an aisle, a block of Starforce white. Only Starforce would be so impractical as to wear white, on infantry it would be brown in moments.

Shane and Romeo entered through one side door; Harper, looking tiny and young in her dress uniform, and an officer from signals, her witness, came in through the other.

The room was silent as only a room full of military sitting at attention could be. There were incredulous looks on some of the faces, especially on the fighter pilot side. Smiles erupted in pockets and spread like a virus. Laughter seemed just under the surface.

The fighter pilots seemed united in a bemused disbelief that Romeo would ever marry.

Yeah, Shane felt it too.

CHAPTER 34

THE ORDERLIES WERE not human although they were vaguely human-shaped. It was rare to see non-humans on Earth so William could not identify their species. They were about the same height as average humans but slightly heavier built, maybe they had evolved on a planet with slightly higher gravity, maybe these were particularly powerful specimens of their species. It did not matter.

William pulled a sheet over another ruined, blackened, melted human face; a human conceit that he was perfectly aware none of the non-humans would bother with. They were dead so who cared if their face was covered? William cared. The black greasy mucus, dissolved flesh, soaked through the white sheet almost immediately.

The orderlies waited impatiently for him to walk away. He wanted to say a prayer but could not think of anything to say, he did not know this patient, this specimen, this thing dead on a stretcher, did not know their culture, their religion, only knew they were dying of a disease, a disease he had not come any closer to understanding. He did not know what could be causing the disease; all he could do was identify it. He did not understand death either but knew he would know it when it came for him.

He knew that thing on the gurney would not be going home to their family, would not be buried, would be stored for whatever information might be extracted from their tissues in the future. If there was a way to store them without the contamination escaping.

He could not continue to think of these human-shaped masses of dissolving flesh as people, that way lay madness.

There was no action he could take to make things better. The orderlies wheeled the sheet-covered trolley down the corridor between the beds, past the other dying 'patients'. Later that body would appear in the autopsy room for more study and an empty clean bed would appear in the place the dead had just vacated.

Even later another dying person, always human, would appear in their place so they could be scientifically examined, not healed. The 'patients' were not being studied as they healed, they were being studied while they died.

Nobody else seemed even slightly interested in healing people.

He was consumed with a desperate desire to clean the contamination, the blood and black filth from his skin, to burn his scrubs and be clean. The shower room next to the lab was the only place they had given him to get clean. He stripped down, dropped his clothes in the recycler, turned the water on maximum heat and pressure and stood under it for as long as he suspected they would let him. There were clean scrubs ready, he put them on. Fearful, he looked down at his hands, there was a black spot, tiny like a melanoma, red-black like death itself, a tiny drop of oily black blood oozing from it. He wiped away the blood with a swab, calmly walked to the sink – of alien design, it was oval with a constantly flowing fountain of water in the centre. He placed his hand under that flow of water, filled with disinfectants, and prayed there was a cure they were keeping from him.

CHAPTER 35

THE SHIP DISGORGED Jimmy, Speech and Itta into a dirty grease-smeared, rubbish-strewn concourse. Here and there were knots of decrepit citizens, multi-species groups. Jimmy could not read anyone's mannerisms but he assumed they were up to no good.

Poverty was not the cause, was not an excuse for the state of the station. Jimmy was poor, he had been in poverty-stricken stations before. There was something else, a wilful dirtiness, an intentional unpleasantness. He looked around some more; there was more than one species living in that filth so it was not a cultural thing.

'I do not like this place,' Speech said in Federal.

Jimmy didn't either. Something about it set off warning bells, the instincts that kept him alive. There was a smell, unidentifiable, as nauseating as rancid Parmesan cheese, as penetrating as over-boiled cabbage.

The hatch hissed closed; they would go no further on that ship, it was scheduled to go no closer to Earth. Jimmy hoped getting off here was not a mistake, the only reason the ship was stopping was to refuel for a long run between stations. No other crew exited from the hatch, not even to grab a bite of non-ship food, not even to have a drink in the unpleasant-looking bars.

'I need to find us somewhere to stay, somewhere free or at least as cheap as possible.'

Jimmy had not needed to find a secret place to sleep for a long time, had never tried to find a place to hide for all three of them; not without the inadvertent assistance of a mass of displaced people. He imagined in that station most of the grey-legal places to sleep were being slept in already.

'We have some money,' said Speech hopefully, 'we both got paid a little for our work on the ship—'

'Can't,' interrupted Jimmy, 'we can't spend that money finding somewhere to stay. We need it for food, we need it to find passage further, if we spend it on somewhere to sleep it won't last. We can't stay here and looking around I doubt there is much work to get.'

Jimmy knew they would have to move before they looked too confused. Confusion, looking lost, was like blood in the water.

'Let's find the food hall, if there is one, first,' Jimmy said, 'we can regroup there.'

Speech nodded and they slipped out of the concourse, following signs in Federal, and what Jimmy assumed was the local language, through blast doors, towards the commerce area.

There was no separate food hall, the food stalls and vending machines were scattered among stalls and small shops selling traveller-specific items so cheaply made they could not be trusted to do what they were intended to do. There were stalls and shops filled with stolen junk.

Everything on station, despite the poor quality, was more expensive than Jimmy had seen it anywhere. He could not recognise any of the food available. Jimmy would have to search their menus in detail to find out if there was anything he or Itta could eat. Crappy low-quality spacer food at crazy prices was the special of the day.

'We need to get the hell off this station.'

Jimmy walked over to a bank of vending machines. There was one that sold purified water in plastic bottles, good to know even though all three of them had packed bottles of water when they left the ship. No other vending machine held food humans could eat, except one: a vending machine version of the food machines on the ship. He flicked through all the menus in Federal, it was painfully expensive but thankfully the machine took Federal credits as cash.

He returned to the table where he had left his friends, carrying chips for Itta and the cheapest edible thing he could find from the vending machine for Speech. 'I am going to go explore. I need to find out what I can get my hands on without money, find out what I can. You two stay here, look after each other, watch my bag.'

It was not long until the concourse was far behind him, the shops and businesses, the offices of shipping and travel companies, got shabbier and shabbier, then the rest of them were closed, not just closed, closed down, the doors locked, the displays covered over.

It was strange to see closed shops in a station when space in a station was so expensive.

The corridor of closed shops led to a dead-end, the hatch ending the corridor was welded shut, the warning lights telling him vacuum was past that door. Walking back past the closed shops he checked every one of them, none had atmosphere. Then there was a maintenance hatch, it was square, as tall as his waist, the tell-tales said there was atmosphere on the other side, it did not look like the lock was engaged. He forced the jammed hatch open and crawled in.

@

Jimmy was more uncomfortable than he could ever remember being, and his life had never been easy. The hidden room – box, crate, shipping container, whatever it was, he, Itta and Speech were hiding in, in the hold of a freighter – was cramped, dark and constantly damp. There was wet metal under his arse, the blanket he had folded under Itta was soggy, the walls were running with condensation.

Itta was so distressed she had long ago fallen completely silent. He tried to talk to her, in English, Federal and the few words of her language he knew and although he could hear her breathing, was certain she was alive, he got no response. Speech was in no better state, for a time they had been talkative, then uneasy silence had descended.

Jimmy could find no exit from the room they were in, it was sealed from the outside, a crate, a small shipping container, a coffin. He remembered crawling into the box, in a room at the back of the loading area of the concourse. He remembered them sealing the box, felt the box being lifted on a loader of some sort, then nothing. Both he and Speech had been foolish, had assumed they were being boxed just so they could be smuggled onto the ship without Federation police finding out. No way they would have ever guessed they would be spending the duration of the trip locked in it.

Luckily it was not cold, and there was some sort of ventilation so they could still breathe. The packaged junk food, all the food they had, had run out already. Jimmy had given his water bottle to Itta and started licking the slick walls for water.

Lying back on the damp floor of the box, Jimmy prayed to the gods of his slavers, though he could not believe in them, for deliverance from that hell.

Speech had found the people smugglers, or the people smugglers had found Speech, looking for a way to make easy money. Speech had found them, Jimmy had stolen the money to pay them. He pilfered wallets, he broke into vending machines in quiet corners. He broke into small, poor shops, even mugged a smaller, older member of a local species.

He hated himself for those vicious, opportunistic thefts, but he had to get off that station and he had to do it quick. Speech was so desperate to escape the station they didn't even ask where the money was coming from. Jimmy had no idea what the hermaphrodite was gaining staying with him and Itta. He asked but the answer was non-committal, slightly confused, lines of questioning went nowhere, in the end he simply gave up. Speech being there was just a fact.

There was no time, no night or day in that darkness, that absolute darkness, the only break they had was Jimmy's tiny flashlight and the light of the tablet until the batteries ran out. All this light did was make the darkness feel more complete, more oppressive, when turned off. They slept when they were tired, woke when they woke, when more than one of them was awake at a time they spoke. After a time the darkness stopped them talking then eventually Jimmy stopped thinking. He could hear voices in the darkness, hear them talking though none of them was talking to him, they were so distant, so muffled he could not determine even if he knew the language they were speaking.

Somehow, not knowing the language, barely able to hear them, he knew they were talking about him. It was quite likely that he was going mad. Finally, after an eternity, the crew cracked the seal and opened the box. They were still in flight, Speech translated, the crew were letting them out to wander in the cargo hold. They had vacuum-sensitive cargo beside the 'passengers' and there was no reason now they were in hyperspace, out of reach of inspectors, that they should not show kindness to their 'passengers'. They were expected to be grateful for these moments out of their box.

There was still not enough light to see by; not enough for humans anyway, and Speech was not faring any better. Jimmy knew that other species saw light differently; maybe to the people who were flying the ship it was brightly lit.

The short time outside, so dark, so cold, was not long enough to completely restore Jimmy's composure before the travellers were locked back in their box for the long light-speed commute to the main Earth orbit space station. No one bothered to tell them how long they would be back in that box for.

CHAPTER 36

For it's Tommy this an' Tommy that, an' 'Chuck him out, the brute!'
But it's 'Saviour of 'is country' when the guns begin to shoot;
An' it's Tommy this, an' Tommy that, an' anything you please;
An' Tommy ain't a bloomin' fool – you bet that Tommy sees!

– RUDYARD KIPLING, *TOMMY*

THE STATION WAS new, everything was too shiny, some of the surfaces
were still coated with plastic film; why someone had not bothered
to peel it off was a mystery. Actually, the real mystery was why
kids or bored soldiers had not been peeling all the plastic off,
thought Shane.

It's like popping bubble wrap. Nobody can help themselves.

She itched to grab a loose corner, she could see one, and pull
but it would not be becoming behaviour for an officer. She almost
couldn't stop herself.

Harper and Romeo were out there somewhere, on the station. They had taken a different route home, enjoying a pleasure cruise for their honeymoon. Shane checked her tablet, the ship carrying her friends had just arrived; if she hurried she could catch them at the arrival gate.

She beat them there, she could see them at customs, lined up with hordes of Federation citizens, their identity packets in hand, their bags ready for the inspectors to check. It must be a shock to them, she thought, arriving on a passenger ship, going through customs like civilians.

The military had their own gate, nobody ever checked ID or bags. If someone got off a military ship it could be assumed they were who they said they were. It was assumed they were carrying no contraband. It was also assumed they would be carrying a weapon, unlike on the civvy side where weapons were banned. The military would take care of any breaches, and the person who committed them.

Shane had Harper and Romeo's sidearms, they must feel naked without them.

There was a knot of refugees in the corner of the concourse, Shane had seen them more and more on stations lately; a dirty group, seated on mattresses and blankets, piles of belongings in the middle of each smaller group. Station security, faceless in visored helmets, were guarding them. She did not want any trouble this close to Earth.

From a distance the refugees looked human-shaped, but filthy, she would have thought it impossible to get that dirty in a sterile station. She could not tell what species they were under that grime.

They looked so human.

People were everywhere, Shane could not remember such a busy station concourse, so many people, so few of them were human. Not much military either, instead there were the ubiquitous interplanetary business-beings, carrying their culturally specific, strangely shaped communication devices and computers. They slept on benches waiting for shuttle flights to Earth below or a hyperspace flight to another station.

Among them were a few pleasure travellers, carrying bags or with their bags at their feet. Some of them looked rich or at least their clothes and belongings looked expensive. Others appeared humbler, carrying little, like backpackers or young people exploring before taking up business back wherever their home was.

There was something wrong but she could not quite determine exactly what it was, maybe there were a few too many non-humans there, not enough humans. Maybe she was just being speciesist, she had to guard against that feeling. The station security seemed too paranoid, too authoritarian.

Even wearing a uniform she could not quite eliminate her deep-seated fear of police and uniformed security.

They were leaving her alone, except for suspicious glances at her sidearm. She was in her uniform, they were rightly wary of an off-duty soldier. There was something wrong about their wariness, however; she felt too strongly that she was being watched.

Where were all the humans?

Shane was distracted then, bemused as her friends, Mrs and Mrs Harper-Zetz, shuffled slowly with the civilians in the queue, holding their minimal bags. None of the station security were human, which was strange, they had arrived in human space, the security at the checkpoint should be her species. It took a little too long for Romeo and Harper to get through security; Romeo looked irritated.

Harper made it through security first, rather than wait for her wife she ran to Shane, dropped her bags, dove in for a hug. 'Hello Harper.'

Shane hugged her back, ignoring for a moment the difference in their ranks. Shane looked over the smaller woman's shoulder, security were staring at them with increasing interest. She hoped it was just because Harper, out of uniform, was embracing a soldier in uniform.

Romeo, looking irritated, finally cleared customs, walked over, dropped her bags on top of Harper's and joined the hug. Shane felt like a giant, she was tall for a woman, near six foot, her friends were both about the same below-average height, like perfect bookends. She felt a wide unconcerned grin spread across her face.

Her best smile in years.

Later, Shane Daniels was waiting at immigration. Nobody had told her, yet, why she needed permission from them to return to Earth. Everything continued to make absolutely no sense. So she waited. The being before her was dressed in Federation administration pink and yellow, with the requisite Federation insignia. Shane thought, despite herself, that they looked like a carp. Everyone in Federation administration uniforms looked like carp.

As opposed to her, who, after days trying to get permission to return to Earth, looked like crap.

So she waited. She reached the front of the line, again, handed over the required paperwork, in dense Federal legalese she could barely understand. It seemed intentional, so did making sure there was no legal aid available. Luckily the army provides, both officially and via the buddy-of-a-buddy network.

The citizen before her took the papers, flicked through half-heartedly, stamped the top page with a stamp Shane could not see properly and handed it back. Shane stared at the stamp, it may as well have been hieroglyphics, or traditional Mandarin, she had no idea what it said.

She raised her eyebrows in consternation as much as in aggression, glanced at the faceless bureaucrat – they were not really faceless, they had a face like a human's but thinner and noseless, their eyes were purple with huge pupils. They nodded in the direction of another counter.

Shane knew when she got there she would be handed more papers to fill in.

Romeo and Harper joined her, the same look on their faces as Shane knew she must be wearing on hers.

'We have fought a war, we survived a war,' Romeo said.

'You didn't fight, not really, not way up there in space, slacking off,' Shane said before poking out her tongue.

'Shut up.' Romeo took a half-hearted swing at her friend, pulling the punch as if she was scared to let it connect. 'The point is that we have survived a war and this fucking bureaucracy is going to kill us.'

'They gave me back my papers and directed me to another line,' Shane sighed, 'again.'

'We were headed for another line but decided it was lunch time,' Romeo said. 'Actually my beloved wife was wondering if you would like to join us.'

'Yes, I will join you for some sort of meal. Though I don't actually remember having breakfast, so I don't think I should be considering myself to be having lunch yet.'

'I imagine that's what they call brunch,' Romeo said.

They left the crowded immigration office. 'I didn't even know they had opened up Earth to immigration,' Harper said as they approached the food hall, 'there are so many citizens here.'

'Surely most of them are just visiting Earth – business, pleasure, sightseeing, checking stuff out, who knows,' said Shane, hoping it was true. She did not want to think about it.

'Come to Earth,' laughed Romeo with an edge of hysteria, 'stay on the station, wait in lines, for days, it's an experience people from all across the Federation are—' She paused. 'Lining up for.'

They laughed as they sat down at a table, though there was little mirth in their laughter. They were lucky to get a table at all. After getting her food Shane guarded the table while the still ecstatic newlyweds went to get their food. They looked so cute, holding hands like that.

They returned and the friends settled in to eat, silent but for the clatter of cutlery. All three had experienced too many interrupted meals in the military; there would be plenty of time to talk once they had food in their bellies.

'Once we go meet each other's parents,' Harper said, throwing a dazzling yet innocent smile at Romeo, 'I am quitting the infantry.'

Shane had already half expected that. 'What are you going to do with yourself then? Housewife?' Her sarcastic tone produced stuck-out tongues from both of her friends.

'I've applied for a masters in Xeno-engineering at Luna City University, might be able to transfer from that to a doctorate, I have a pretty good chance. I want to be at the cutting edge of adapting Conglomeration technology to our uses.'

'Nobody can hack like my missus,' said Romeo proudly, 'she's almost scary.'

'What do you mean, *almost*,' Harper finished that off with another tongue-poke. All three women laughed again. Shane noticed the noise was attracting attention from station security, she turned half to them, made sure they could see her rank insignia, her medals.

Suddenly the security ran off, all of them, fanned out into the arrivals concourse with precision and efficiency that told her they wished they were military. Shane had a perfect view of what was happening. Security ran through a beaten-up hatch into a ship. Soon after they dragged out the crew in handcuffs. They did not look like the sort of crew Shane would want flying a ship she was on.

Smuggling, she thought. Then security led out a couple of humans – a young man and a girl, bedraggled, dirty and knot-haired – and a tall lanky humanoid in academy monk robes, along with a couple of citizens of a species she had never seen before. One of the humans flinched, tried to cover their eyes like someone who had not seen light for a while. It took her a moment to realise that the smugglers were smuggling people.

Romeo tapped her on the shoulder. 'What's up?'

Shane realised she had been staring. She shook her head. 'I was just looking at those humans – they must be refugees.'

'That's odd,' Harper said, turning to look. 'Why would humans need to be smuggled to Earth? Earth is their home.' She frowned as she too stared at the dismal group. Romeo shrugged and, in an obvious attempt to lighten the mood, said, 'Maybe they just got sick of doing paperwork.'

CHAPTER 37

PHONE SIGNAL WAS flaky at best out there in Walker's Country. Kelly stared and stared at her phone, willing the signal bars to switch on, but at that time of day her hope was futile. It was slightly ludicrous that after humanity had joined the Federation, after earning a place in the stars, gaining access to technology capable of building the particle bomb, phone signal in some places still sucked. Not just in the middle of nowhere either, there were still dead spots even in the middle of the bigger cities.

Close to sunset, when the shade of the desert oaks and mulga grew long, when the sun was in the direction of the nearest phone tower, the flaky signal dropped out to nothing.

She had no way to call Kris and tell him what was going on.

Walker was not yet dead, though he was so close it was getting harder to be certain. He lay, on a blanket on the soft bone-dry red sand, a windbreak fashioned of spinifex casting a shadow on him in the late afternoon twilight. His face was towards her yet she knew he was beyond seeing, there was nothing left in his eye sockets but the red-black slime that had broken through his skin in globs.

Kelly coughed, caught the black globule from her throat in her hand, threw it to the red dirt in disgust. It landed, rolled, picked up dirt. The sun set, there was a miasma even to the air, it turned the sunlight the colour of congealed blood. Not long now and the sun would stop fouling the phone signal. Not long.

She woke in full dark, the stars so bright, the Milky Way, in the moonless dark, all it is dreamed to be in the mescaline dreams of poets. She put the phone on speaker, dropped it on the dashboard of the car before sitting in the driver seat. Kris answered on the third ring.

Kelly could barely speak.

She listened to him for a moment, he said nothing of consequence so she stopped him.

'Listen to me, Kris, I told you already, I'm done.

'I returned Walker to his Country, he is dying, I doubt he will still be here at dawn, I don't even know how he has lasted as long as he has.

'I'm dying too, even if we find a way to stop the infection I have too much organ damage.

'I am going home, to my great-grandmother's Country. I have always wanted to see it but it was too hot, always too hot, it would be death to go there. I am already dead, I may as well just go home, my real home. They tested nukes there, on my ancestors' Country, they say they got all the people out but we know different, family of mine, family I never knew, family that never got a real chance, they died here. We know hundreds died. What's the fucking difference?

'I'm sorry, I can't help you any more, Kris, maybe you can find a cure for yourself, maybe the Federation has a cure, but I don't know if they will give it to you; either way I am dead. I am going home. Walker was right, there is nothing else to do. There's nothing more for you to do than just say "goodbye".'

Kelly's hands were leaving blackened bloodstains on the steering wheel of the troopy, but still she drove on. Walker had died on Country, holding on longer than she had imagined possible, still breathing when most of his body was a ruin. She had left him there, mere moments after his breath stopped. Her great-grandmother's Country was just ahead.

CHAPTER 38

JIMMY FELT THE terror tearing into his soul, Speech had been taken away from them, there was nobody to help him. He held Itta in his arms as tight as he could, unsure what he would do if they tried to take her away too. He would fight; he would lose, he would die.

The cell was too small for both of them. If he gave up Itta there would be more room for him; they told him that in Federal. The light was constant and bright, painful after the low light of the ship's cargo bay, after the darkness of the crate they had been hidden in like animals. He closed his eyes, covered them with his coat, which they had inexplicably left with him, the light was still painful even through the fabric.

The representative from the department of immigration had been disdainful. 'You will be transported off station, there is a detention centre in Saturn orbit,' they had said in accent-less Federal, 'you will be detained there until your case is heard.' He had no idea what would happen to Itta, they had no translator who could speak her language, no way, so far, of talking to her.

In a quite pathetic attempt to confound them he failed to mention that Speech could talk to her very well.

When they had been taken he had said Itta was his sister, it was a spontaneous statement, made completely without thought, possibly risky. In hindsight, he thought, it was quite clever: they might let them stay together; it might keep her safe. Neither of them had ID, beside the refugee cards they had been using, the immigration police might not even be able to find where they had come from. Unless their DNA was on record, unless they were being sought by the law. Jimmy was certain somebody was looking for him, he hoped communications between government departments over the great distances he had travelled was not that efficient.

He would die before he let them return him to slavery.

Jimmy had been in far worse situations, though not with a child to protect; at least nobody here seemed particularly intent on his bodily harm. Since he had been taken from his parents on Earth, he had been working or on the run without end. It was almost a relief to have been finally caught, almost; although he feared what they would do to him, he knew he could relax there for a while, the worst had already happened. He just wished he knew where his backpack was, he felt naked without his stuff.

The door opened, someone came in, dressed in what could have been a Federation police uniform if it was not so ragged and faded. Jimmy did not understand a word they were saying, why were they not speaking Federal? He shrugged to indicate that and they shrugged back, gestured for him to follow them. Taking Itta's hand, he did.

The guard led them down corridors to as big an open space as Jimmy could have imagined in a station, wide and long but with ceilings only a metre above his head. There were tables bolted to the floor, stools as well, round and backless, both the chairs and tables had one columnar leg each. Almost every species could make some use of a stool. As far as he could read so many different mannerisms, everybody looked dejected.

Many if not most of the beings in the room shared the ragged desperation Jimmy associated with refugees in their features and in their belongings. Running from horror they had found new things to fear. There were even family groups, little and big members of the same species detained together. The children must have been terrified.

Others were the sort of degenerate petty law-breakers and wanderers who had once made up Jimmy's peer group. They were the most dangerous, they would find ways to steal, to smuggle, to con even there. They also had more to lose, many of them would be criminals, wanted like Jimmy, some of them would be wanted for the simple reason that they were simply no longer where they were expected to be. Like Jimmy.

Speech stood up in the middle of the room and waved to them. Jimmy almost dragged a terrified Itta to their friend, who had followed them into danger for no benefit to theirself. They wound through the tables, past and around the occupied stools. They were all occupied, every stool, there were more detainees in that vast open space than there was available seating.

Most of the people Jimmy passed reacted, either flinching in response to the blow they expected or preparing visibly for a fight. He simply ignored them.

Jimmy reached Speech and half-sat on the edge of the table between the hermaphrodite's left side and the nearest chair. Itta climbed into Speech's lap, snuggled into her friend's shoulder.

'You doing okay, Speech?'

Speech looked at Jimmy. 'My apologies, Jimmy, young human,' they said politely, 'I was unable to secure you and Itta a seat. I could have fought harder for one when we came out to this place, everybody at once, it seems to be the daily routine to leave our rooms and come here, but I didn't know if you would be joining us.'

'It's okay, Speech,' Jimmy said, aware that his non-aggressive friend was lucky to get a seat at all without Jimmy's muscle and human reputation to help. Jimmy had stood his ground many times, many of those times a being he had never met had looked at his face, identified his human features and simply melted away into the crowd. It was as if 'beware of the humans' had been scrawled everywhere across the entirety of Federation space in a language or form humans had not learned to read.

Something had been bothering Jimmy. 'I don't get it, Speech,' he said finally, 'I am returning home to human space and to Earth. I expected problems returning because I had run away, I did not expect to be arrested for attempted illegal entry.'

'Yes, it does not make sense,' Speech agreed.

'How can it be illegal entry to return to my home?'

CHAPTER 39

ROMEO STARED AT the news feed on her tablet, rubbed her eyes in disbelief, kept reading.

'Fuck!' She threw the tablet on the bed and rolled to her feet. 'Arseholes,' she yelled to nobody in particular.

Leaving the room at a run, she mashed on the screen of her phone with her thumb raised to her ear. 'Hun,' she said, 'where are you?

'Stay there.' She hung up and dialled again. 'Shane,' she almost shouted over the comms, 'meet me at the food hall, we have a problem, it's happening again, like in the old days.'

@

There were hundreds of people squeezed into the corridor that led to the immigration office, crowding the space, leaving no path to the door. They were all human, that was even more worrying than the news. The air was thick with the miasma of anger and fear, the people surged forward and backward in waves, the heat of the crowded space flushed faces, dripped sweat onto the floor.

Shane had not even been aware there were so many humans on the station. The sound of them, worried voices in conversation, in whispers, exploding into shouting in pockets, the shouts moving up and down the corridor in waves, people raising their voices to be heard over people shouting next to them, dying back to whispers again.

Shane stood at the front of the trio, she was the biggest, she was a grunt, she was intimidating. She was in her charcoal-grey service uniform, as was Harper. Romeo was in a flight suit, her uniform whites would get too dirty. A wave of silence spread down the corridor to the office as everybody turned to look at them.

'I am Captain Shane Daniels of the Federation Infantry, with me is Wing Commander Romany Zetz, call sign Romeo.' Ahead of them pockets of order appeared as military or retired military stood to approximate attention. 'We intend to enter the office down this corridor to determine what the problem is. Please make way.'

Slowly the crowd before them parted, intimidated citizens crowded closer together to make room, in other places people with military bearing pushed civilians out of the way. Occasional voices said 'Sir'; someone said, 'Go get them, Cap'n'; someone with the physique and nervous twitches of a fighter pilot said, 'Holy shit, it really is Romeo' then the hall was silent. The door at the end was closed. Shane buzzed the intercom.

There was no answer. She buzzed again.

A voice came out of the speaker. 'Due to policy confusion and overwhelming numbers of complainants this office is temporarily closed.'

Shane sighed and pushed the 'speak' button. 'Hello,' she said with false friendliness, 'I am Federation Infantry Captain Shane Daniels,

I have restored order to your entry hallway,' she heard Romeo snort with suppressed laughter behind her, 'and would like to enter to discuss this unfolding situation with whoever is in charge.'

The intercom remained silent, she imagined them arguing on the other side. The wait seemed interminable.

With a click and a hiss, the door unlocked. Shane turned to the people behind her. 'Romeo and I are going inside to get to the bottom of this. Corporal Harper,' she said, then pointed to a random person with military bearing, 'and you, could you please wait here and maintain order in the corridor. Try not to shoot anyone.' People looked at Harper's waist, then looked at the officers, then backed away a bit as if noticing for the first time that the three of them were armed.

Shane and Romeo stepped through the door.

From what Shane could tell, the staff inside were terrified. They were cowering as far as they could get from the door while still at their stations. Not one of them was human; the only humans in the offices were those few who had been inside when the riot outside began.

The few humans were seated, looking both scared of the riot outside and smug, because they were inside. When they saw the two women walk in in military uniforms, fear spread across their faces. Shane heard Romeo snort her laughter out her nose.

Shane marched up to the first counter.

'Tell me, first,' she said with a voice that suggested not answering would be bad for the citizen's health, 'are the rumours true that nobody will be allowed entry to Earth who is from a race only provisionally in the Federation?'

The being behind the counter looked at Shane and their expression changed; they might have been afraid. 'Yes, that is my understanding of the situation at this time.'

Shane reined in her anger. 'Humans are only provisional members of the Federation, yes?' She raised her hand to indicate she did not really want an answer, 'Therefore humans will not be allowed to migrate to Earth, even though we came from there, even though I have a house and a family there?'

The clerk behind the counter looked terrified.

'If you wait over there I can have someone see you when they are available,' the clerk said finally in perfect, too perfect, Federal.

'I have a better idea,' Shane said frostily, placing her hand on her hip just above the butt of the gun at her side, 'how about you get someone out here right fucking now. I can wait.'

Shane and Romeo followed the thin being in a Federation administration uniform as they wove through the desks towards a back office. She had no idea what gender, what sex this being was, or even if this species had genders or sexual dimorphism.

She had to admit, and she hated herself for it, she found it easier managing someone when she could at least identify their gender. She couldn't really work out how to ask.

Finally they were in an office, with someone who could at least give them answers. Shane had no experience with this species, she could not tell if they were intimidated by her presence, her military rank, Romeo's rank, their guns.

Probably the guns.

'What seems to be the problem, Captain?' The being in the office paused, looked over at Romeo, 'Wing Commander?'

'We have just been informed,' hissed Shane, 'that citizens of provisional members of the Federation will not be allowed entry to Earth, despite the fact that we were born there, despite the fact that it is our home, that we have always lived there.'

The bureaucrat before them, whose face seemed featureless, or at least had features humans did not understand, spoke from that disturbing nothing. 'We can't just have anyone landing on Earth,' they said, 'it is to be a luxury retirement estate for returned soldiers, soldiers from the full-member planets of the Federation, we don't want any riff-raff, to use a human word, settling there.'

'It's our planet,' Romeo hissed.

'You joined the Federation,' said the bureaucrat, 'it's the Federation's planet.'

'You fucking arseholes,' Shane said, 'I went off to fight your war, *yours*. I left my family, I have a husband, a son, a daughter, they are still on Earth, I can't even get the comms to connect a call to Earth to contact them.'

'Provisional members are not allowed phone or email contact with the planet previously known as "Earth",' said the being before them. 'I can't help with that but I can help with one thing,' they brandished a tablet, 'I should be able to find out where your family are, I can get a message to them, maybe they can join you here, when you find a place to settle you can take them with you. I am sure the infantry will allow you to take them on base, wherever you are placed next.'

'This is madness,' Shane was almost screaming, 'why should I need to find somewhere to settle? That is my planet, my home, below. My family are down there.'

'I have now checked the records, you have no family on that planet.'

'Excuse me?'

'You have no family on that planet.'

Romeo held Shane's shoulders, stopped her lunging over the desk; she was stronger than Shane had expected. 'Are you fucking kidding me?' Shane said. 'Where are my family if they are not on

Earth?' She struggled and writhed in Romeo's hands. Then she stopped, she knew she could overpower Romeo in seconds but her friend had the right idea, punching this bureaucrat would not be helpful.

'I'm sorry, you will have to ask the Department of Human Services, this is immigration, we do not have that information.' The bureaucrat looked down, acted as if Shane and Romeo had already left.

CHAPTER 40

WILLIAM WAS IN bed again, a cannula in his arm, the tube running to a complicated-looking device. This time he was not restrained. He simply lacked the strength to get up, lacked even the strength to sit. When he tried to move, his moans were so loud and heartfelt he shocked himself further into wakefulness.

'Good morning, William,' said Jack – he sounded cheerful.

'What happened?'

'You collapsed. The viral, I suppose viral is the best human word, condition we are studying got its claws into you, you were dying. I am almost glad you were infected,' said Jack, sounding delighted. The light of the room reflecting off his goggles made him look even more sinister than normal. 'You have been a great help and, bearing that in mind, I have received permission to test the cure on you. It is already being injected into your arm, hopefully we will see exciting results.' What remained unsaid, thought William, was that even if he died the results would still be exciting for a scientist.

He lay back for a moment, praying, although he did not truly believe in a god, praying that the cure would work. So tied up in his fear, so occupied with his hope, the incongruity of the situation took a moment to work its way into his mind. 'Hang on,' he almost shouted, 'how long have you had this cure?'

'We had a version of the cure before you came here, though we have not until now tested it on your species. I am sure you can understand why I am so excited to test it on you.'

'What, what do you mean? I thought we were trying to heal people, trying to find a cure, or something? Trying to help people with this disease.' William knew his voice sounded frantic, but it would be a waste of energy to even try not to sound panicked.

'Don't be stupid, we don't need to find a cure for the condition, we always had it; we have been studying the effect of the particles, of the disease. We need to know the effect on living tissue and we have had fascinating results. Your job was to keep the subjects alive so we could study the effects of the disease on them for as long as possible. You get to test the cure because you have been helpful, and I can't continue this work properly without you.'

William had suspected for a while that the facility was not really about curing the disease but what Jack was saying made him hate himself.

'Rest,' Jack continued, 'let the medicine do its work. You will feel better soon. It would be best if you slept.'

There was a hiss, William had heard it before, heat flooded into his arm, leaving behind a leaden cold that paralysed him. He felt it flood across his body. It hit his head and he slipped into blackness.

He could feel the two forces, the killer disease and the cure for it, fighting a battle over his body. It was like having armies march through his system, his veins were their highways, his organs their battlefields; they fought and re-fought, their battle lines moved back and forth, neither seemed capable of winning. He had never been in battle but he had read history, he knew that the trampling of feet, the explosions, the fires had left many green lands ragged and dying.

He was the Somme, he was the fields of France, he was Nagasaki, he was the Dardanelles. He was Emu Field, he was Maralinga.

He did not know if he would survive, regardless of which side won.

Even if they were to allow him out of bed, even if the door would open so he could walk out, he did not think he was capable of standing; walking away was out of the question. He could only lie there while the battle raged, when the war ended what was left of him would emerge. Maybe the warring chemicals were remaking him like a caterpillar in a chrysalis, his flesh would dissolve into de-structured chemicals, and what was left of him would reform, becoming something living, but not necessarily him.

He might end up as an amoeba.

Jack walked in, stared at his chart, the lenses of his goggles dark. William was not sure he could speak, he tried anyway, nothing but moans came out. Jack walked over and poked at the touch screen of the monitor, flicked screens faster than William could follow. William wanted to ask what was going on, was desperate to know if he was going to live, but nothing but moans came out again.

Jack was about to leave so William screamed. Liquid, pus or blood, undifferentiated cells, maybe just water or spittle, sprayed from his mouth and rained down in a fine mist onto his face.

Jack looked at William, writhing on the bed. William could see himself reflected in those goggles – thin, pasty, near death.

'Sorry, William,' Jack hissed with politeness that sounded transparently fake, 'how unpleasant of me to not talk to you. The treatment seems to be working, it is stabilising the infected atoms, returning your atomic structure to close to normal. There has been some tissue loss, some cells will certainly continue to be too damaged to function, you might lose some organ function, but when we have you stabilised we can use nano-bots to rebuild what can be rebuilt.'

William thrashed on his bed, felt his skin peel from his back, felt the bed get sticky. He tried to talk again, tried to cry out. No noise came out this time.

'I will let you rest,' Jack said in a voice that sent shivers down William's tattered spine. 'Good night.' As Jack left the room the light flicked off, leaving William feeling like he was already dead, in a fetid, foul-smelling darkness. He suspected, to his horror, that most of the smell was coming from him.

CHAPTER 41

JIMMY NEEDED SPEECH'S help, the forms in Federal were written in dense legalese, the small print almost too tiny for him to read, the blocks of text intimidatingly massive, the sentences too long. Speech had taken pains to teach him how to read but his language skills were not quite up to the challenge.

'It's almost as if they are trying to make it harder than necessary to apply for entry,' Speech had said. Jimmy had been thinking the same thing.

'I still don't understand why I am having to fill in an application for refugee status,' Jimmy replied, his eyes aching and watering. 'That's my home planet down there, shouldn't I have immediate, automatic access?'

'I don't understand it either,' Speech mused with a shrug. 'I have never heard of anything like this anywhere in the Federation, not that I follow the news, I have always concentrated mostly on my work for the academy. Local news, from any planet, generally had no effect on my work so I didn't need to study it.'

'I want to go home,' Jimmy was disgusted with the whine in his voice, 'I want to find my family, I want to find Itta's family. There must be records somewhere of where I came from but the Human Services Department say there are not, that I have to get a DNA profile. They can find my family from that, or at least narrow it down a bit. I submitted my DNA, I took Itta to give hers too.'

'It might help,' mused Speech.

'The problem is that I am wanted on another planet for absconding. They might get my DNA profile and just arrest me.'

The light in the library was oppressive, something about the colour or the reflections made Jimmy's eyes feel tight. The pile of paperwork teetered, leaning towards him like a bully ready to attack. Speech was staring at Jimmy with concern on their face. The display on the wall, showing Federation time, moved far too slowly. He did not know if he could hold on.

'I have to go to my appointment with Human Services now, let's see what they have for me.'

'Best of luck, are they seeing Itta today too?'

'No, this appointment is private, and hers will be too, except for a translator. They will only talk to her or her legal guardian. I have no idea who that would be. I think they are going to try to separate us, foster her out again.' Jimmy was tired, and angry and worried. He knew there was a risk he might become the monster others believed humans to be.

'If I don't come back, look after her, okay?' He made sure to sound calmer than he felt.

Speech nodded, opened their mouth as if to speak yet nothing came out.

He walked through the once clean corridors, full now with detritus, living and otherwise, and unnameable stench. The detainees had mostly found places to call their own. They all had cells, but when they were not locked up they found somewhere to mostly sit and do nothing. Refugees sat in spots they claimed – a corner, a table in the mess hall, a scrap of ceremetal floor.

Jimmy was strong, fit, aggressive, he had managed to claim an actual table in the library for Itta, Speech and himself. Speech felt comfortable there, among the e-readers, the computers, the magazines, a few paper books. There his friend, when not trying to get asylum on Earth, taught Itta Federal, tried to teach Jimmy the unintelligible tongue Itta talked. The table was useful, a flat surface on which to spread out their forms, fill them in. All Jimmy cared about was returning to Earth.

The whole detention centre was starting to smell, Jimmy suspected it was suffering from intense overcrowding. Damp patches had developed in some corners, growing mould. He wrinkled his nose but could do nothing else to block out the stench.

It was a long walk from the library to the Human Services office.

'We have not yet found your family,' the bureaucrat behind the desk said when Jimmy finally arrived, 'the linkup to the rest of the Federation is currently unreliable.' Jimmy suspected they were lying, they just didn't want to tell him where his family was; there was no reason for the linkup to be failing again. This was the Federation, an official Federation facility, not some backwater on Earth.

Looking around the room to distract himself from his desire to scream he realised the room was as blank as a new piece of paper, nothing on the ivory ceremetal walls, nothing on the mid-grey desk of the bureaucrat before him but unfathomable controls for a computer.

'We do have some good and somewhat surprising news for you, young human.' It took Jimmy a moment to realise the voice was talking to him. He looked back at the being behind the desk.

'In the office yesterday it made us all smile, such good surprising news, it makes the job seem worthwhile; the sort of thing we, in administration, live for.'

Jimmy wondered what news beside 'We have found your parents' or 'You have been authorised to return to Earth' would be good news. He had checked the laws, the system controlling their lives, with Speech's help. He could apply for entry to Earth on his own, he might even get it; once there he could look for his family, look for Itta's people. However, if he could prove he had family there it would be a lot easier, human services or immigration would attempt to reunite them.

'It seems you have a sister, and we have found her. You match genetically for both parents. Isn't that fascinating? We think it is amazing.'

'I didn't even remember a sister,' Jimmy said. 'How did you find her, I thought the connection to the rest of the Federation was not working properly?'

'She is here, on this station, that's amazing.' There was no emotion in the voice of the bureaucrat that Jimmy could read, no change in tone to match the excited words. How could he have a sister he didn't even know existed? Were there that many gaps in his memory?

Could he even trust his memories of Earth, of his parents?

'Who is it then?' Jimmy knew he sounded as confused as he felt.

'She came in at the same time as you, when we ran her DNA at first it identified her as having no family, no known guardian, she was not reported missing or anything. Her name on our computer is "Itta".'

Jimmy shook with emotion he could not even begin to fathom. He had been looking after his sister all this time! How could that be? She must have been taken from their home, their parents as well. He ran out the door, frantic, happy, terrified, overwhelmed, he had to get to his friends, to his friend and his sister. He had a sister.

@

Jimmy entered the library at a sprint, nearly bowling a stranger over in his haste. He slowed down before he reached their table.

Speech was there, looking, from what Jimmy could understand of those alien mannerisms, worried. 'How did your appointment go, Jimmy?' Speech said with a tone that appeared to be an attempt at human jolliness.

Jimmy sat down at the table, rocking his chair forward and back with anxiety and excitement. 'They say they have found my sister, Speech.'

Speech just stared at him. 'I didn't know you had a sister.'

'I didn't know I had a sister either,' Jimmy continued, 'but I do.' He stopped, out of breath and feeling slightly ill.

Speech looked at him with an expression that might be inquisitive.

'It's Itta,' Jimmy said after long silence, 'she's my sister and I never knew.'

'Are you sure no part of you knew?' asked Speech. 'Something, some instinct made you look after her even though you had never met her before, something compelled you, maybe it was you, your knowledge that you were related. Some part of you must have known.'

Jimmy worried he was going to go mad. Her would not be the first person in the detention station to lose their mind. Every other day somebody would be taken away, sedated, more often than not somebody would take their lives. It was no place to be, that detention, there indefinitely, time stopped but still moving, lives over for people not actually dead.

Itta walked in, smiling the strange half-smile that had lately become her habit, her eyes were as sharp as pins. Jimmy dove to his feet, half smothered her in an embrace. She spoke, he could not quite catch what she said, were his emotions making him forget everything he had learned of her language?

Speech noticed his confusion. 'She is asking if you are okay.'

'Yes, I'm okay.' He squeezed her tighter, emotions he could barely understand let alone articulate overwhelmed him. Hot tears ran down the clammy skin of his face, he knew they were dripping on Itta's dreadlocked head. She was tensing up in his arms and he knew he was holding her a little too tight, but he could not stop, he wanted to never let her go. She was the only connection with his lost family he had ever found.

'Speech,' Jimmy said, 'please help her understand, please translate. I am lost. Itta, oh my god Itta, I found out today, you are my little sister, you are really my little sister.' Jimmy was silent as Speech spoke rapidly. He hoped his friend was getting the translation right, that his sister was understanding, that Speech could explain the bits Jimmy had not said.

Itta was silent for a moment. She pulled out of his arms, stared him straight in the eyes. He could not read the expression on her beautiful face. He studied her to distract himself from his anxieties. He could see it now: the surprising similarities in their features. How had he failed to notice it before? If only he had imagined he might have a sister, he would have eventually realised that sister was Itta.

Itta was silent. He let go, stopped trying to squeeze her to him, either she would believe she was his sister or she would not. He wished she would say something.

She reached up and touched his face. Stared some more.

They stood there, three statues. Jimmy staring into Itta's face; Itta's eyes examining Jimmy like someone trying to read a book in a language they have only just started to learn; Speech, watching them both. Speech moved first, turning their head to look at Jimmy, then at Itta.

Itta finally spoke, too fast, manic, almost frantic and then threw herself at Jimmy, threw her arms around his neck. 'She said you have always been her brother,' Speech translated, 'she is glad you see it now.'

CHAPTER 42

'HOW DID WE get fooled again?' said Shane. 'Everybody on the planet, on Earth, has fucked us over for hundreds of years, why did we expect the Federation to be any different?' She and Romeo stormed down the corridors with Harper in tow. Beings caught before them melted away from their fury. When they reached the Department of Human Services, they stopped so abruptly Shane wobbled.

'The paint's still wet,' said Harper. Shane was uncertain whether she meant it as a metaphor or literally, she was not going to touch the paint to find out. It did smell like wet paint in the hall.

Buzzing the door, Shane shook with anxiety and anger. The door opened and they swept in before anybody could stop them. The bureaucrats inside had no idea what was coming. Romeo followed Shane, nodding to her wife. Harper peeled off and walked briskly down the corridor.

'I am from the planet below,' Shane growled at the bureaucrats, 'I was born there, I lived there all my life until we joined the war, my children and my husband are there, I left them there to fight your war.'

The bureaucrats before her seemed to have no idea what was going on. Shane wondered how long they had been working with Human Services. Did the department even exist yesterday?

Shane was suddenly furious with herself; she had never bothered to ask anyone what the war was about. She had assumed that the Federation were defending themselves against the Conglomeration but what if they were not? What if the war that humanity had been dragged into was just another stupid war; what if the Federation had attacked the Conglomeration?

The bureaucrat nodded, the sort of faint nod you use to calm a crazy person by pretending you are listening. Must have learned that one from a human.

'I have been told that not only can I not return to my home planet but that my family are no longer there. Kindly tell me what the hell is going on.'

'Name and address, please.'

Shane answered.

'That address no longer exists,' the bureaucrat said. 'I have initiated a search algorithm looking for any reference to that address.'

'What?' Shane felt worry beginning to override her anger, felt the anger return, felt her last vestiges of control start to wither.

'The address in question shares co-ordinates with the Perthtown Estate, a new estate for returned soldiers. I'm afraid anything there, any buildings – if you can call what was there buildings – everything has been removed, the land was cleared for the estate.'

'What?'

Silently Harper returned, with her were two soldiers from Shane's unit. They were armed.

The bureaucrat stared, as still as glass, Shane could only assume they were terrified. She would be if she were them. 'I am just looking now for your family, the family you claim to be on the planet below.'

The world was spinning, Shane did not know what blow would happen next, did not know if she would survive it. Harper and Romeo moved to her sides, the two infantry soldiers stood at her back.

'Your children were found to be without a mother, their father was working long hours, it's a clear case of neglect, they were taken to an orphanage. From there they were fostered out. I'm afraid they have left the planet below. I am not authorised at this time to inform you where they are. If you fill in these forms we can begin an enquiry.'

Shane's pistol was in her hand before she knew what she was doing. She pointed it at the bureaucrat's face. Romeo reached out, snake fast, using the reflexes that made her a great pilot. She took the gun. Shane swung at Romeo, missed, dropped but did not hit the ground, held up by the infantry at her back. They lowered her to her knees, picked her up, carried her out.

@

'There are blocks all through the system,' Harper said, 'some of them seem unintended, dead-ends left by poor programming, others seem intentional, designed to make it harder to gain access to the sort of information you are after.'

'Are they on to us already?' asked Shane. 'They must have been trying to block me from the very beginning.'

'I don't think it's personal, Captain,' Harper replied, 'I think they have made it difficult to access all human data, all data on Earth, and communications over all human networks. I just don't know why.'

Shane stared at Harper and the two people helping her. On her left was a private from the infantry, even younger than Harper, the insignia of a signals private on her arm, she was taking a great risk being there, she could face a court martial. Past her was a civilian, as pale as milk with their ramrod-straight black hair in a loose greasy ponytail.

From what Harper had explained, the private was piggy-backing on Harper's access attempt, helping when needed; the civilian was watching the wires for evidence someone had noticed their intrusion. Two of Shane's soldiers were loitering in the corridor, seated on the couches, playing cards and appearing to drink beer, ready to buzz her phone if someone official headed their way. Romeo, well, she had no idea where Romeo was but she was hopefully doing something useful.

They all faced courts martial if anyone discovered they were attempting to hack into the Federation databases. Nevertheless, they were there; their loyalty to Shane, to humanity, to each other, superseding their loyalty to the Federation or to their military services.

Even Harper was doomed if they got caught; she had tendered her resignation from the infantry but her discharge papers had not yet arrived. Everything was electronic, she had expected her exit papers immediately. It was possible they planned to reject her resignation.

'The first bit was easy,' Harper said, almost to herself, 'all we had to do was get out of the station's firewall and read the uncensored news. I didn't even know censorship was so common, that so much was kept from us, but it is. There are systems in place to block or censor news based on species and planet of origin. They even seem to block the military a little bit more; they use a code on our tablets; on our accounts. Maybe officers get more news than grunts, did you notice anything, Cap'n?'

Shane shrugged. 'I don't really read the news, I wish I had. You enlisted – what? – three years ago, Harper?'

'More like two, Captain.'

'Was any of this going on when you left Earth?'

Harper was silent for a moment. 'Not that I noticed, sir, but I wasn't really paying attention, I have no family I know of and I was in a bad way.'

'I wish I knew how long this has been happening.'

'Shit.'

Harper hammered away at her computer a bit more, concentrating intensely. Shane did the only thing she could to help, she waited in silence.

'Sorry, things got a bit hairy for a moment there,' Harper said eventually, her casual tone belying the obvious tension in the room. 'I had to run the news feed through a translator, it says that Earth is now earmarked for the senior races of the Federation, mostly as war veteran estates. Any humans already on the planet are being mostly ignored but being a provisional member species we cannot own land in the Federation so all land ownership from before we joined the Federation is invalid.'

'What the hell,' Shane wanted to shout it louder but that would be dangerous.

'They are building estates for their war veterans with total disregard for what was there before.' Harper sounded tense, too tense, Shane hoped she would not make a mistake. 'That's all we know for now. We haven't found out anything new about your kids,' she paused, 'or found your husband.'

Shane stayed silent, didn't want to distract the hackers with her panic. She had plenty of practice at staying calm, she had been fighting a war for nearly a decade. She had been fighting a war for a Federation that didn't consider her to be a citizen. Her blood ran cold. Humans had done this to other humans in the past, so why did she expect better from the Federation? She sat down on the only chair left, an armchair, she thought too soft, she did not want to fall asleep.

She woke a short time later feeling surprisingly refreshed. She checked her watch, she was not certain what time she fell asleep but surely it was nearly two hours ago, maybe longer. Harper's hands were still dancing a tarantella on her tablet, someone had broken out a laptop, as powerful as what they would have called a supercomputer when humanity had joined the Federation. There were empty paper coffee cups about, still faintly aromatic. Shane was suddenly desperate for coffee. She found a full cup, a long black, just what she wanted, next to her chair.

'Yes, that coffee is for you,' Harper said without even bothering to turn around, 'long and black just like you.' She laughed a twitchy little gallows laugh, a soldier's laugh. Shane joined in.

Inhaling the seductive aroma first Shane took a small sip. The time it had been sitting there had cooled it to Shane's preferred coffee temperature, just above that of her skin. She hated hot coffee and hated cold coffee too. Well, not hate, she could never hate coffee, even bad coffee. That taste, then the caffeine hacked its way through her system, executed a blitzkrieg on the cobwebs in her brain.

The civilian hacker was still sitting at the table, working on the laptop with one hand and a tablet with the other. Harper now had two tablets, Shane had no idea where the extra one had come from, the private was curled up asleep in a corner, perhaps it was hers.

The door opened without warning. Shane's reflexes were wired, she had her handgun in her hand, aimed at waist height in the direction of the door before her ears even registered the sound. 'Honey, I'm home,' came Romeo's artificially jovial voice. She looked down at Shane's gun, smiled. 'Hey tidda, don't point that at me, I brought burgers. If you shoot me I might drop them.'

'I am so fucking sick of burgers,' Shane replied, almost surprised to see her gun in her hand. She slipped it into its holster. 'Surely on a station orbiting right above Earth there is something else to eat.'

'Possibly not,' Romeo said, 'but you do get a better class of burger.'

Shane unwrapped the meal, suddenly starving. Romeo was right, she thought, biting into her meal, it was a better class of burger, better than what she had eaten most of the way through space. What she really wanted but had never seen on a station was pizza; in eight years the only pizza-like thing she had eaten was the frozen crap they sometimes served in military bases.

Even automatic food machines, those nanotech miracles that could make pretty much anything, made woefully crappy pizza.

She decided to make her complaint public. 'I would kill a stranger for a decent pizza.' Mumbles of agreement flowed around the room.

Everyone was silent, even the tapping on screens and keyboards had slowed down. Shane noticed Harper was typing one-handed while eating with the other hand. Hardcore. They were nearly all military, none of them wanted to jeopardise their meal, nobody spoke.

Shane was first to wake in the morning. The hackers had been quite late at it, Romeo had not wanted to go to bed alone.

The station had an unpleasant feel to it as Shane marched a little too fast through the corridors. It was only breakfast time but security were very much in evidence, searching bags, requesting

ID. Shane gave them a look, stared them in the face, they left her alone as she walked into the food hall. There were people everywhere, humans for the most part, lost and confused, teary-eyed and bewildered people with their bags at their feet.

She shopped for food fast. It was not a good time to dawdle. She had to stop herself from running as she returned to their room.

Harper turned around as Shane dropped the fast-food bags on the table, an unreadable expression on her face. 'What's the matter, what have you found?'

'I had feelers in several computer systems all across the Federation networks,' Harper explained, 'they are set to inform me if people stumble across my hacks or one of our names comes up, or your kids' names or your husband's name. There was a sudden spike, starting with this.' She leaned over, highlighted a section of text on her notebook computer and turned the screen for Shane to see.

'New-Manus Station Detention Centre: James Daniels, AKA Jimmy Daniels, moved from general population to solitary confinement, punishment for assault. Izabella Daniels, AKA Itta, under temporary guardianship of Academy Monk Speech.'

'What?' Shane almost screamed.

'I did some more digging, New-Manus is a detention centre for civilians caught attempting to enter Earth illegally, it's in Saturn orbit but where among all the junk around the planet is a mystery.' Harper was speaking with a tone someone would choose if they needed to talk someone else down from a high ledge.

'What were they doing there?'

'I don't know, the only thing I am sure of is that they must have arrived in this system from outside of it with no papers. How they got off system in the first place is beyond me. Every refugee has a unique code, and now I have their codes I am able to mine the net for more information but it's taking a lot of time. Also,

I am not sure their refugee ID numbers have been consolidated with their files from home. I am digging but it's not going well, it's also risky, it might set off alarms. It's getting harder to cover my tracks.'

'At least we now know where they are,' Shane said with determination, 'we can plan to get them.'

'Romeo is already on it,' Harper said. 'She was out the door the moment I told her what I told you.'

CHAPTER 43

THE WAR IN William's body that had threatened to take his life, that had left him so ravaged, seemed to have ended; the peace left in its wake felt slightly unsettling. He did not know where he was, his eyes were gummy, hard to open, he was not in a bed. He found it near impossible to move, like trying to swim in honey. After what seemed like an age, he wrenched his eyes open, felt liquid press against them; far thicker than water, like syrup, like glycerine. He could see but only just, it was like trying to look out of a mug of beer: yellow, slightly cloudy.

His eyes adjusted to the gloom, strangely the liquid in which he was suspended did not hurt his eyes, he could keep them open as easily as he could in air. Easier in fact, the strange liquid lubricated his eyeballs better than tears, he could go on without blinking for longer than he thought possible. Stranger than that, he did not need to breathe, or he was breathing liquid, which was impossible.

He became aware of his lungs, of a heaviness in them, he seemed to have adjusted to this new condition before waking, he had no particularly strong instinct to cough out the syrup. Fighting down a wave of panic, he seemed to be in no immediate danger, it was only his instinct against being trapped that was freaking him out. He tried again to see what was going on. Outside the liquid were shapes and patterns that implied a room filled with electronics, with machines. Small lights flickered on and off out there.

It was like being a bug encased in sap, turning slowly into amber, waiting for a million years to become jewellery.

Must be a full-immersion tank in the hospital, he had seen them, had seen military officers being decanted from them. This seemed different. He was vertical, not prone; the liquid was thicker, a different colour. The machinery attached to the tank was bulkier, more advanced; it was to the machines he had seen before what those machines were to a hospital bed.

Some paranoid people claimed that the senior races of the Federation had life-support tanks backed up by nanotechnology and were keeping them from the others, from humans. The machines the human military had access to were merely life-support and chemicals to assist with healing; the more advanced machines, if they existed, would save thousands of lives. He had always thought such theories too paranoid, surely if such a technology existed all members of the Federation would have access to them.

He had been wrong. He hated them for that, hated himself for trusting in the Federation.

Something moved in the room outside his tank. A voice echoed, too loud, into his ears.

'Hello William,' said the voice and he wondered how it penetrated into his ears through the tank he was in. 'I hope you are feeling better. You were unconscious, we thought it a good opportunity to discover how humans would tolerate a full-support nanomachine tank. I came as soon as the machines recorded an increase in brain activity. How are you feeling? I admit to being deeply curious how the program for the nanos is working.'

William didn't think he could talk, his lungs were full of goop, he was breathing goop, how could he talk? He decided to try, it felt strange, his mouth shaped words, his lungs pushed the goop out through his vocal chords. 'Ggarghg,' was all that came out.

He tried again, 'Where?'

'You are in another wing of the hospital, the wing closest to my ship, to be precise.' William realised it was Jack speaking. 'By the time we had the viral radiation under control we realised it was too late. You had quite extensive organ damage, you would not survive. We brought in the tank from my personal research ship, we wanted to see if we could modify the chemical mix to support human life and reprogram the nano-bots to repair human tissue.'

William shook, could feel the blood-warm gelatinous mass he was held in rippling slowly in apparent sympathy. 'Why?'

'Why what?' Jack asked. 'Why did I save you? It was the best way to research using a nano-tank for a human, you were available, you are unlikely to be able to tell anyone about it. Also, you have been useful, I would hate to lose your services.'

'Why?' William tried to scream. 'We have soldiers, sick people, why have you not tried the nano-tank before?'

He could see Jack was walking towards the exit from the room, not answering, he yelled a formless, wordless noise. His tormentor stopped.

'This tank,' Jack said, 'the nanomachines, they are not meant for such as you. You ungrateful human, you should be thanking me for saving your pointless life.' Then the room outside was empty.

Many days later, he had no idea how many, he was decanted.

@

William sat on his cover-less bed, lifted his heavy head from his hands, stared at the bowl they made. Were they even still his hands? He was no longer even remotely certain. They were the shape of his hands, they moved like his hands when he touched something; when he rubbed them together they felt like his hands both as the subject and as the source of the feeling. They were not his hands, it was not his skin. Something was wrong with his skin, a faint pearlescence, a gloss like he was made of plastic, or a statue cast in resin.

He hoped it was just his hands, a fool's hope, there was no reason why only his hands would be affected. There was no mirror in his room, no phone or tablet to photograph himself with, no way to find out how far the albedo spread on his body. He slid up the sleeve of the garment they had dressed him in, shapeless like a cross between hospital scrubs and pyjamas, designed only to cover against nakedness. His arm was the same as his hand up as far as he could slide his clothes. Raising the hem of his shapeless shirt, his stomach, now hairless, was the same colour, had the same sheen as the rest of what he could see.

He raised a desperate hand to his head, felt a smooth glossy dome where hair once was.

It was as if every cell of his skin, his whole body maybe, had been replaced. What fearsome technology was this, that could take him away at an atomic level and replace him so well that even he could barely tell?

'We had no template for human cells,' Jack's voice broke through his reverie. He had not heard the alien approach, had not heard the door open. Sneaky bastard. William looked up, startled. 'What have you done to me, what have you done to my skin?'

'We had to improvise, design a template on the fly using software for other species. It seems to have had an interesting side effect when it comes to the texture of your skin. Well, actually it seems to have left a pearlescence on your skin where previously there was none.'

'You fucking arsehole,' William screamed, 'you were just waiting to experiment on me.'

'Why am I an orifice you humans use to excrete from that's currently fornicating?' There was a heavy pause then Jack spoke again, 'I assume it is an insult from your tone and the inexplicable disgust with which you humans regard your bodily functions. It doesn't matter, I saved your life, you might not look completely human any more, you might not be strictly human any more if I am to be honest, but who cares? You are alive.'

'I care,' William hissed, 'I care and so will the people back home. My wife and kids will care when they see me like this, people on the street will know I am not human any more.'

'It doesn't matter.'

'It does!' shouted William.

'It doesn't matter,' Jack said, 'because you will never see any other humans outside of this facility again. You will never leave here.'

Jack walked out then, leaving William screaming to a room empty of everything but his own noise.

CHAPTER 44

'WHAT DO YOU think of our chances?' mused Shane as the tiny ship headed towards the looming station. The station name and number that would normally be written building high on the station bulkheads, even though to an incoming ship it was unnecessary, was missing. The station showed up on their radar, a massive object; one of the biggest stations in human space, it was the biggest station Shane could ever remember seeing. It was tagged on the display as a Federation asset, the transponder beacon was definitely transmitting, yet beyond that nothing, no name, no hull number.

It was Romeo who answered as she manoeuvred the tiny ship. 'Well, assuming this is the right place, and assuming we can somehow dock with it, and assuming your kids are still there, well,' she paused, 'it's a bloody big station with, I don't doubt, a correspondingly large bureaucracy. Then again, you are the hardest bitch I have ever met, and as determined as hell, or should I just say really pissed off, I don't think it makes a difference, I don't fancy their chances.'

'We've been pinged,' said Harper sitting in the comms chair, 'they want our ID with a thinly veiled automatic threat that this station is off-limits.'

'Do what you have to do to get us in there, get us docked and I will take care of the rest,' Shane said then raised her hand as Romeo made to speak, 'I am going to talk to them before I do anything drastic or permanent.'

'We are going to talk to them, I am not letting you go in there alone,' hissed Romeo, 'and as much as I like your grunty friends they are not as charming as me, they can wait in the ship until we need them to extricate us, with lots of the bangs and booms and screaming you grunts love. I look forward to the noise. Hopefully most of the screaming will be other people.'

'I need you to keep the ship warm for a fast get-away.'

'Bobby, better known as "Boxer", here,' Romeo tapped the shoulder of her co-pilot who Shane only knew in passing, 'will keep the ship ready to go. They can fly this tub almost as well as me anyway.'

Boxer's head was shaved, they were dressed in a flight suit, leaning back jauntily in a chair, feigning boredom while sipping from a mysterious can of something. Their knuckles were scarred and gnarled, perhaps a clue to how they got their call sign. 'Thanks, Romeo,' they said, 'I think that was probably a compliment.'

'If you are sure,' Shane said, 'it will be pretty boring to try to do this legally.'

'It will also be dangerous to do this illegally,' Romeo said, 'and that is why you need me, I can help chat them up, then I can help you gun your way out. Don't argue.'

'You're going armed?' asked Harper.

'I might be batshit crazy,' laughed Shane, 'but I am not stupid enough to go in there unarmed.'

'Shit,' interjected Harper, 'their docking computer is trying to repel us, it keeps telling the ship computer to turn back.'

'Keep her on manual,' Romeo said, 'the station is trying to take control of the ship.'

Harper's hands were a blur as she tapped frantically on touch screens and control pads, some of them jerry-rigged into the ship's systems roughly with wires and black electrical tape. The ship lurched, levelled then lurched again as Romeo wrenched at the controls. 'You can do it, baby,' Romeo said, 'come on, Harper, my love, you can do it.' The ship lurched again, throwing Shane off her feet, the control stick shook itself out of Romeo's hand and settled into an unsettling shudder.

With breathtaking suddenness, the ship stopped thrashing and Romeo wrenched it back under control.

'We have access, the station thinks we are a maintenance crew coming in to check the atmosphere scrubbers.' She shrugged. 'It was the only thing I could think of, the only thing I could do fast enough. If there are any sentient beings monitoring the system they might question why a ship that was fighting their computers suddenly became a maintenance ship. It must look really suss.'

'You got us there, that's the important thing,' said Shane, 'I will take care of the rest. I am going into the passenger compartment to let our little gang of troops know what is going on.'

There was only one door, a pressure door, between the tiny crew compartment and the slightly larger passenger area. Shane passed through it and was immediately surrounded by her waiting friends – infantry barely days from the front, some of them retired, others on leave. 'Ladies, gentlemen and others,' she said, 'we are about to dock with the station, they think we are a maintenance crew but that ruse will only last long enough to dock. Romeo and I will go in and have a little talk with the staff and demand my children back. If they return them without a fuss we walk away; if they don't, we threaten them – yes, we will be armed. If that fails Romeo and I will negotiate with extreme prejudice, guns a-blazing – if we have to draw there will be no going back, I will call you and let you know, you are then to come in after us, assist us if you can, help us get out if that's necessary.'

'What about security and whatever?' Shut-up asked, 'we need a tech.'

'Harper volunteered to go in with you if it comes to that,' Shane said.

'She just doesn't want to be separated from her missus,' said Shut-up with a smirk.

'Shut up, Shut-up,' someone said.

There was a shudder that almost knocked them off their feet, then a clunk as the docking clamps on the station grabbed on.

@

Shane was certain the receptionist was surprised at the sight of an officer from the infantry and a wing commander from Starforce in uniform but she could not read that species' emotions. Romeo's hair was freshly buzz-cut, Shane's in a tight bun. The receptionist's gaze moved to the ceremonial yet very real sidearms in their holsters then got stuck staring at Shane's gun as if it would strike out and kill them on its own.

'I am Captain Shane Daniels, this is Wing Commander Romany Zetz, call sign Romeo. I apologise for the subterfuge of landing here under the pretence of being a maintenance crew but it was imperative that we were allowed to land.'

The receptionist looked up suddenly and stared Shane in the face. Shane smiled internally as she saw a new emotion in the being's eyes; hopefully the confusion she was hoping to see.

'I understand that you have my children.'

The confused silence deepened. Shane thought that mouth, so dark red it looked lipsticked, was about to say something foolish, instead it stayed shut. The receptionist gestured to chairs in the waiting area; Shane imagined the being, a bureaucrat usually far from danger, was terrified. They picked up a phone as Shane and Romeo walked to the waiting room and stood in a pointedly military 'at ease' stance.

Shane imagined the wait was to irritate them, to make them give up and leave, make them lose their tempers and do or say something stupid. Whoever thought that was a good idea, making them wait as a kind of torture, clearly had no experience of the military – the infantry are world champions at waiting. Shane and Romeo waited, standing as if their time did not matter, waited like only a soldier can wait, like automatons switched off, awaiting further orders.

Both wore unobtrusive ear-pieces. Shane was listening to comms from their ship, mostly her small band of troops keeping her abreast of their preparations between the bullshit all soldiers talk when idle. They were still familiarising themselves with the guns that the gun smuggler had provided, at a frankly obscene cost, guns that were technically legal in the Federation. Modified hunter's dart-guns with technically legal loads, which were only legal because of a loophole.

They were technically non-lethal, although if you hit most species with more than one dart they were as dead as someone hit with a projectile. They also had a couple of stun guns, used for station policing, and some service pistols. A complicated Federation law allowed all humans to carry handguns if they were active military personnel or whenever they travelled anywhere unsafe.

The broad definition of 'unsafe' was another loophole.

Shane had an antique Earth pistol in the ceremonial holster on her belt; legal for a certain value of legal. Shane was willing to risk it. Romeo's was more modern, made of resin and plastic, the technology was just as ancient.

Romeo, Shane assumed, was listening to her wife; it was so cute.

Eventually someone stepped out of the door behind the reception desk. Shane could not identify their species, she was constantly surprised by how many different species constituted the Federation. She would have expected humans to control an immigration centre in Saturn orbit. The new arrival leaned over and spoke quietly with the receptionist, stood again and walked over to Shane and Romeo.

'What can I help you with?' they asked in Federal.

'I am Captain Shane Daniels, this is my friend Wing Commander Romany Zetz, we have been fighting in the war for the last eight Earth years, I in the infantry, her in the Starforce. I have received word that my children are here in this facility, I am not leaving until my children are returned to me.'

There was silence. Shane had no idea what was going through the bureaucrat's mind, she could not begin to read their expression. They stared. In a human it would be reasonable to imagine they were deep in thought, trying to work out how to handle this, how to make these humans go away. The silence went on too long – Shane was capable of just standing there but had no idea how this other being was managing it.

'Allow me to check your files, um, Captain,' they said finally. 'What are the names of your children?'

'James Daniels, but most people call him Jimmy, and Izabella Daniels.'

'I will be back shortly, please wait,' the bureaucrat said before walking away.

Shane and Romeo again waited patiently though it was not long before the bureaucrat returned and beckoned them through the door. They were led to what looked like an interview room, though it was too neat, too clean, as if they had opened an empty room and frantically adapted it for the coming interview while Shane and Romeo waited.

There was a table, organically round with a single leg that made it look like a white, flat-topped toadstool. There were chairs around the table, one chair and a stool close together and another chair directly opposite the midpoint between them. None of them matched.

Shane did not sit, standing at ease beside the stool, staring at where the bureaucrat's head would undoubtedly be when they sat down. The look on their face when they sat and saw Shane's eyes already locked on theirs without her moving was indecipherable but she could imagine what it was doing to them. It was not her first time pulling that trick.

'Ah,' said the bureaucrat, 'your children, yes, they are here. Your oldest, James, is in solitary for attacking and nearly killing another detainee; your youngest, Izabella, who calls herself "Itta", is being looked after by the academy monk who had accompanied them into human space. This is necessary as the monk is the only being on the station who can understand Itta's language.'

'Excuse me?' Romeo interrupted, 'I am sure there is someone who can speak English, how can you have a detainment facility in human space if nobody here speaks the dominant human language?'

The bureaucrat looked down at the tablet in their hand again, they seemed to look for a very long time. 'Izabella does not speak English or Federal, she speaks,' the bureaucrat vomited out a long string of noises that Shane could not even begin to construct into a word.

Shane's future was a long corridor with too many doors, she was being herded down the hall, waiting for a door to open. Most of the doors led to disaster. She did not expect to be given a choice, would have to take the only door that was offered. In her mind, she was armed, ready for war.

It was foolish, she thought, to train humans to fight, to give them guns, mess with their heads until they could do nothing but fight, then take their future away. If her children were not returned to her she would have nothing left to live for but getting them back. It would not matter who or what got in her way.

The bureaucrat, a different unreadable expression on their face, looked down at the screen again. The room was silent but for the faint sound of soft flesh tapping on the glass of the touch screen and the measured breathing of the two humans. Shane waited with false, forced patience, trying not to scream, trying not to dive over the desk and grab the being by what they had been using for a neck. It might take time but she was sure she could find a piece of anatomy to squeeze. She could keep trying until she got it right, eventually she would find somewhere that would hurt a lot.

She calmed herself again, worried her thoughts would show on her face.

It went on too long, despite her military bearing, despite her training she could feel herself twitching. Romeo looked at her, the touch of her friend's eyes like a calming hand on her shoulder. She realised her hand was twitching slowly towards the handgun at her side. If she drew her gun all hell would break loose; it was not yet time.

Eventually the alien before them looked up and spoke, 'I have been forced by the contents of these files to refer your case to a higher member of my department, please accompany me to the waiting room and you will be seen as soon as possible.'

'How about we wait here and you bring someone now?' Romeo asked, it did not sound like a question. The bureaucrat must have been around humans enough to recognise the menace in her voice, they stopped mid-way to the door, turned around and stared. The room was dangerously tense, Shane could hear her own heart, beating too fast, almost drowned out by the bass 'whoosh' of blood in her ears. She felt close to losing control, soon she would fall into a pit painted adrenaline red; she would act before thinking.

They had her kids.

Romeo seemed aware of her loss of control. She did not reach out physically but somehow Shane could feel the pressure of her friend's love and concern for her. She calmed herself, desperate to retain her composure. The bureaucrat walked out of the room, a little too fast to maintain the pretence that they were in control of the situation.

Years of military experience helped Shane just stand there.

She stared at nothing, not even at the blank walls, her eyes focusing instead on the empty space before the walls. Her eyes may as well have been closed, but if she closed them she knew she would lose control. Nothing was more important than maintaining her composure until she had her kids.

The wait extended abusively long, she was becoming tired, her left knee kept twitching, she could feel it but hoped nobody could see it, her feet were sore but nobody else would know. Romeo was silent, only her friend's breathing and her undeniable presence told Shane she was not alone.

The door opened and a figure walked in; as thin as a human skeleton and slightly too tall to be human, they were almost naked, grey-skinned, wearing only a pair of shorts that looked like cut-off and hemmed suit pants. They wore those pants with the faint discomfort of someone habitually naked and only wearing clothes as a concession to the presence of humans. Shane could not remember having ever seen this species before.

'Good afternoon, Captain, Wing Commander,' they said. Their face was almost featureless, it was hard to see from where the voice was coming.

Their Federal was without accent, flat, as if they had trained in making their voice sound like it could be from anywhere in the Federation. Humans used to do that, a long time ago the English speakers in broadcast radio trained in an accent-less dialect so that nobody in the British Empire would find their accent alien. Maybe that explained the accent, or maybe this was a member of the mysterious race who had founded the Federation, developed the language from their own. They were legend, no humans even knew what that species were called.

Shane pointedly ignored them.

'Good afternoon, Captain,' they tried again, holding out their hand for Shane to shake. Shane ignored it, she could not read their expressions but hoped they were confused by her refusal of such a human gesture.

'Your children are here,' the stranger said, 'but I am afraid you cannot take them with you. They have been removed from the planet because they did not have parents looking after them. Your son absconded from where he was an indentured servant, he needs to return there to continue his punishment for the crime he committed.'

'And what crime was that?' demanded Romeo.

'He ran away from home, from the foster family who were caring for him. In the process of his escape, he stole from houses, from shops, he slept outside, had no dwelling – in the society that had cared for him all those things are crimes. He was tried and sentenced to twenty years as an indentured servant.'

'My daughter?' Shane suppressed her almost overwhelming anger, practice had taught her to not show any of it on her face or in her voice.

'Your daughter was travelling unaccompanied. We have contacted the family who had adopted her and they have stated they no longer wish to have her back, as is their right on their planet. Your son applied for guardianship of his sister and received it, he is now her guardian and therefore she will be returned to his home with him.'

'I am their mother,' said Shane firmly, 'I would like to take them with me.'

'Your children were motherless, abandoned, you were off-planet and their father was working sixteen hours a day. We had reports they were being neglected and had to act to protect them.'

'I was off-planet defending the Federation against the Conglomeration, I was fighting the war to keep the Federation safe. I have not spoken to my husband, he is missing too, but I am sure if he was working such long hours he had a damn good reason. He was a medic, I am sure he was patching up the wounded. You took my children but I am going to forgive that, ignore that crime. I am their mother. I am right here, right now, I am taking them with me.'

'And where will you take them?' smirked the bureaucrat. 'You cannot return to Earth, it's a retirement centre for full citizens of the Federation and I can see from your file that you, like all humans, are not a full citizen. You have few choices, none of them would be suitable for your children. You certainly cannot take them with you into the army, they cannot be left behind while you fight.'

'Enough,' shouted Shane, pulling her handgun from her holster. She pointed it at the bureaucrat. 'Bring me my children, I am taking them with me.'

'No,' said the bureaucrat in what sounded like an emotionless tone.

'They're my children,' Shane shouted.

'Not any more,' came the dispassionate answer.

Before she could pull the trigger, a stunner buzzed, the citizen before her collapsed.

Romeo lowered her stunner, raised a communicator to her mouth, 'That's a go,' she said calmly.

CHAPTER 45

JIMMY HELD ITTA tight as they were dragged down the corridor. With his other hand he grabbed at every hand-hold he could find. Whoever had built this station had dragging prisoners down the hallways in mind, every edge was rounded off, leaving nothing to hold. Itta was screaming her chilling inhuman wail.

Speech had tried to stop the guards, tried to keep hold of Jimmy and Itta, had fallen stunned in an untidy tangle of long limbs and robes. Jimmy heard other detainees scramble, some away from the guards, others towards his friend to help, to turn Speech on their side, to keep his friend breathing.

He grabbed an open doorway. The guard's fingers, slicked by sweat, slipped off Jimmy's forearm. The guard fell against the other and they both fell. Jimmy found his feet, held Itta's hand, ran, staggering with the fear of it, almost tumbling when his footing slipped. He was not sure why he was running, they were on a station in space, where would he go?

He lost his grip on his sister, tumbled and came up running, heard her feet pounding down the corridor behind him. Half turning to look back, he saw the guards raise their stunners, point them at him, saw Itta stop and face them, get between him and them, saw her foul their line of fire, saw them try and fail to correct their aim, heard the stunners buzz, saw his sister fall.

He stumbled to a halt. Itta was on the ground, convulsing. She was too small to safely take two stunner hits at once; if he knew that, they knew that. He ran to her side, fell to his knees, felt his bones grind. He turned her to her side, cleared her tongue from her throat. She was not breathing, her heart was not beating. There was something he remembered from his childhood, something he had seen once, something his father had shown him. Forgetting the guards, if they stunned him they stunned him but if he ignored Itta she would die, he pounded on her chest, he breathed into her mouth, he pounded on her chest. On and on, beating her heart for her, breathing for her.

He pulled his mouth away as she vomited, held her shoulders, waited until she stopped thrashing, picked her up, held her in his arms. She was insensible, immobile. Standing with her in his arms he stared at the guards who had their stunners aimed at him. He stared them in the eyes, defiance on his face. They stared back; one, then the other lowered their guns.

They gestured in the way they had been walking. This time Jimmy lacked the drive to resist.

@

Jimmy walked slow, he used the weight of his sister as an excuse; stopped walking in protest when they used a pain-prod against him. He had heard of them, a prisoner who had been through the prison system before ending up in detention had told him – he did not think they had the right to use them in immigration detention. They threatened him, threatened to hurt Itta, he walked on, told them that if they used the pain-prod again they would have to take their chances with him because he would rather risk his death than be prodded again.

It hurt.

He told them that if they prodded him with that thing again they would be forced to kill him. They would have no idea whether or not he was lying. He knew they probably wouldn't want to have to fill in the 'oops we killed a prisoner' forms.

From what he had lately learned about the Federation he was fairly sure it would be a really long form.

They were in a part of the station he had never seen, there were no scuffs on the spotless walls, few scuffs even on the white plastic flooring. They walked in silence, the threat of prods, of stun guns, of the plasma rifle that one guard had retrieved, were enough to keep Jimmy moving. He did not fear for himself as much as he feared for Itta; without him she would have nobody to protect her.

A door opened to darkness at the end of the corridor with a sigh. When they passed through that door lights flashed on and stayed on, bright blue-white, they lit a huge open space. It looked like a station concourse but empty, nowhere for people to wait, no vending machines, no chairs. Only the hatches, which matched the Federation standard for ship to station access, gave clue to the room's use.

There were six hatches, all closed, all but one showing the pale-blue 'disengaged' light, the last one proclaiming there was a ship there but the hatch was locked. The hatch unlocked with a clunk when they reached the middle of the room.

'This is your ship,' a guard hissed, 'it's not safe to have you here.'

'I'm fine,' said Jimmy, 'I want to be here or going home to Earth, not on another fucking ship.'

The guard shook their head, another human gesture that had made it to the stars, 'It's safer for *us*.' They almost dragged Jimmy and Itta towards the distant door.

CHAPTER 46

THE LOW SCRUB, it didn't even reach her knees, the red sand, that was home. She could feel it, hear the voices of her ancestors. Maybe it was Walker's lessons, he had taught her without even knowing it, maybe it was her proximity to death, but she felt more in contact with her people, with her Country, than she had ever felt in her life.

Kelly stood next to a sign, what could be read among the flaking paint and flecks of rust said 'Kuka Palya, Ngura Wiya' in her great-grandmother's tongue. 'You can hunt here but don't camp here' was the nearest translation she could think of. Maralinga.

It was here, in the 1950s that the British Empire tested nuclear weapons, lit the sky like a thousand suns, made black smoke and poison sand, turned the red sand into fractured green glass. Australia was already an independent country before the testing began, Kelly did not understand why another nation was allowed to bomb here, why they did not bomb their own home lands.

White people had thought it empty, this Country, it was just desert, no good for them, no good for sheep, cattle or wheat. White people had thought it empty, useless, thought it would not matter to anyone if they destroyed it forever. It was someone's Home, this Country, sacred land. All land is sacred to someone.

Her Country was still not clean, if she was not already dying it would be fatal to stay there, a slow death of cancer, of radiation poisoning. It had happened to her people before, they did not know what radiation was, did not know it was a sickness in Country that kills, a sickness that will stay there forever. To create such a thing, a nuclear weapon, so destructive, something that contaminates all it does not destroy must take madness.

Why the hell would anyone think creating a nuclear bomb was a good idea?

Stupidity never changed, it seemed, even within the Federation.

It did not matter if her Country would kill her slowly, she would not live long enough to care. It did not matter if she got radiation poisoning, if it made her blind like it had done to so many Anangu in the past, if it gave her cancer. She was already dying from the vile Federation weapon and would not live long, maybe only days.

Climbing, with a groan of pain, into the troopy, she fired up the engine and drove into the contamination. Contamination travelled with her.

CHAPTER 47

SHANE DANIELS HURDLED the stunned guard without even slowing, behind her pounded her too-small army. She just hoped it would be enough troops to penetrate the station and get her kids back. Good thing not many are needed for a hit-and-run.

The first victim, the bureaucrat who had rejected her application, had fallen so fast they might have not even known what was happening. She had broken out of the interview room door and her troops stormed through reception, leaving unconscious bureaucrats behind them, to get to her.

Alarms sounded, painfully noisy in the enclosed space of the station, of a pitch that humans found nauseating. Someone had thrown Shane a helmet and she screwed it onto her head, switched on noise suppression, the siren was reduced to a whisper. She turned, saw the relief on Romeo's face through the plastic of her infantry helmet visor, the soldier who had thrown her friend a helmet must have already activated noise suppression for her.

Everyone but Shane and Romeo was masked under their mirrored visors, the cameras would not capture their faces, she hoped the security system would not be able to identify them from their shape, their size, their movement. They had decided to destroy all cameras they saw just in case.

Beyond that they would have to rely on Harper.

There was a door leading to the detention centre at the end of the hall, a secure door with a pair or guards in front of it. Darts flew past Shane's shoulders, one hit each guard and they dropped. Shane bent over and searched them, there were no keys; she took their stunners, handed one to Romeo, checked the load on the other. The door was secure, no lock she could see but there was a keypad.

'Give me a moment,' Shane heard Harper say from the back.

'Boring,' said Shut-up, 'always waiting for tech support, there's not even anyone shooting at us.'

The door buzzed then beeped, it opened inwards. Shane gestured with a nod of her head, 'If you're so bored, Shut-up, you can take point.' Someone behind her laughed.

Shut-up edged forward just as stunners started buzzing, the tell-tale sparkle of light blasted towards the door. Shane was first to dive for the ground and started firing as she fell, her weapon singing like a cicada. All of her people were fast, or the guards couldn't shoot straight, nobody went down and soon only one stunner was firing down the corridor. Shut-up fired and that too went silent.

'Was that better, Shut-up?' someone asked.

They moved slowly up the corridor, the officers and Harper in the middle of the group. There were two unconscious guards on the ground. The soldiers in the second rank took their guns and cable-tied their hands together, injected each of them with the contents of a disposable syringe, while the men at the front watched for more attackers. They moved on, through another door and into the detention centre.

The smell hit Shane like a punch in the face, the smell of human secretions and fear but something else even more powerful. There was a guard station on the left, the door open, a wall of monitors showing scattered civilians in rags. Shane studied the screens but could not see her children, did not recognise anyone. Harper connected her tablet to the computer with some sort of adaptor and hammered on the screen until the alarms stopped.

'Nearly there,' Harper said as stunner fire erupted down the hallway, 'keep them off me and I will get us in.'

Shane and Romeo could hear the noise of stunners right outside the door, light flashed and sparkled. There was an answering splash of sound from the far end of the hall, stunners, then something else, a meatier sound like throwing a steak on a hot barbecue. Shane would never forget that sound. 'Plasma rifle,' screamed Shane, 'everybody down!' There was a chorus of answering thuds as everyone took cover.

'What the hell are they doing with a plasma rifle in a station?' asked Romeo.

'Please take out the idiot with the plasma rifle,' Shane said calmly out the door, 'before they punch a hole through the bulkheads and we all die.'

There was the sound of firing, the insect sound of stunners; from the other end the cheap keyboard sound of the plasma rifle answered. One of Shane's soldiers rose to a knee, took aim with a dart-gun, fired at the same moment as the plasma rifle sounded again, then fell with a singed shoulder. 'Plasma gun is down,' said someone else as the sharp-shooter cried out. Someone crawled over, knelt beside the wounded man, checked the damage.

'Only a light flesh burn,' they said over the secure comms. 'I've seen worse on chefs' forearms, you lucky son of a bitch.'

'It fucking hurts.'

'Burns do, but you won't even need a hospital.'

There was silence in the corridor, Shane waited for shooting to break out but it didn't. Crouching down, she stuck her head out the security station door. 'All good out here?' she asked bemusedly.

'I got shot, Captain.'

'I know, it hurts but you'll live. Okay, as soon as Harper has broken into security, which should not be long, we will move on. First, though, someone confiscate that plasma rifle, we can't have some dickhead guard shooting holes in the station.'

'What the hell is it even doing here?' asked Shut-up, his whining tone distinctive.

'You heard me say "dickhead",' Shane replied, 'let's leave it at that.'

@

Shane Daniels kicked the door so hard it almost fell off its hinges. Through the small window she could see the guard's face, saw the shock as the door hit them hard, sent them flying back. Shut-up went through the door first, shot the fallen guard with his stunner to make sure they would not get up. Romeo rummaged through their pockets, took out a stunner, a ring of keys and small plastic things.

Someone expended a syringe.

'Electronic keys,' said Harper, glancing at them, 'you tap them to a reader and they open the door, like the ones we have had on some buildings on Earth for decades.' Romeo nodded, threw the key ring to Shane who was still looking for someone to shoot. She was not disappointed, someone charged out of a side corridor and she snap-fired, barely looking before she pulled the trigger. Her stunner gave a warning 'beep'.

'My stunner's low, who has a spare?' she asked abruptly.

'The guard you just shot probably has one,' said Romeo.

Shane holstered her stunner, walked over, grabbed the stunner in the guard's holster and took it.

The group moved on, Shut-up in the lead. They disarmed the guard on the floor up the hallway, took their keys, bound their hands. Shane injected this one herself. They went through another door, then a short corridor before another door. Through that one an open space, as filled with people of more than one species as it was full of smell. Shane did not know how they could stand it.

'Shut-up, secure the area, everybody stay sharp, there are a lot of ways into this room, a lot of cover for the total bastards who run this place.' Shane was barely able to contain her anger and anxiety.

'I am looking for two refugees,' she shouted loudly in Federal, the anger dripping from her voice, 'humans, brother and sister, I know they are here, where are they?' Nobody spoke at first, some turned away, then a voice came from the centre of the room.

'Do you mean Jimmy and Itta?' asked a soft voice as it moved towards her. Its owner was revealed, tall and thin in academy robes. 'They are my friends,' said the monk, 'my name is Speech, we travelled here together, I was trying to help them get home. You look a little like Itta; are you their family?'

'Yes, I am Federation Infantry Captain Shane Daniels, I am their mother. I thought they were safe on Earth with their father until I tried to return home. Please, if you know where they are, please tell me.'

'The guards took them,' said Speech calmly, 'that way,' they pointed. 'Someone said it might be a loading concourse for bigger ships.'

Shane gestured and her troops started silently, cautiously down the corridor Speech had pointed to.

'Thank you, my friend,' Shane said, 'thank you also for looking after my kids. I will try and come back for you. If I don't make it, if you need anything, get in contact through the infantry, ask for Shane Daniels, they will find me.'

Shane turned and chased her troops up the corridor, stolen stunner in hand and ready.

CHAPTER 48

Therefore still their eyeballs shrink tormented
Back into their brains, because on their sense
Sunlight seems a blood-smear; night comes blood-black;
Dawn breaks open like a wound that bleeds afresh
– Thus their heads wear this hilarious, hideous,
Awful falseness of set-smiling corpses.
– Thus their hands are plucking at each other;
Picking at the rope-knouts of their scourging;
Snatching after us who smote them, brother,
Pawing us who dealt them war and madness.

– WILFRED OWEN, MENTAL CASES

IT WAS IMPOSSIBLE to find a rope. William did his best to twist one from bandages, feared it would not be strong enough, that it would snap, unravel. Nowhere to hide it, he wrapped it around his torso under his scrubs. Someone left the dispensary unguarded for a moment, he slipped a multi-species tranquilliser syringe into the waistband of his pants.

He waited, not knowing if he was being watched, if there were cameras in his room, waited for dark, pretended to sleep, hoped there were no night-vision cameras.

The lights switched off. He slipped the syringe from his pocket, unwound his rope. It felt strange not to have it twisted around his torso; he checked by feel if it was still twisted, still strong.

Sitting back against the wall, his thoughts, his emotions, consumed him. He could barely remember his children at all. When he fought for them – hand, fist, elbows – it had not been enough; they took his children anyway and put him in prison too.

He could not live like this, in this place, not knowing where his wife was, not knowing where his children were. He wanted his family back, yet that was impossible. He would be trapped in this place, until old age and misuse took his life slowly; a threadbare life, a pointless life, dissecting dead people, euthanising others, murdering them. If he resisted, if he fought Jack, the guards would hurt him, scientifically, skilfully, until he obeyed or died.

He closed his itchy tear-filled eyes, tried to remember his daughter's face, his son's. How many years had it been? He could not even remember how long it had been since he'd last seen them, could not remember their faces. There was nothing, only darkness. Then something came, the face of a dying man, then another dying man, and another, then a dying woman. The only people he could remember were all dying of the disease that had almost killed him; a disease he had only survived by becoming no longer human.

He was no longer human. The disease would take all his people, eat his family. They would all die.

He could not fight it.

Tears squeezed their way out through his eyelids, dampening his cheeks as he started to wail. He had a family, children, a wife – she loved him, he loved her; he could still feel the weight of her in his heart, the weight of the love, the weight of her soul on his. He did not even remember what she looked like, saw only blackness when he tried to remember her. Flailing at his memories he found fragments that he could not quite grip, a wisp of smell, a fragment of voice, the feel of her lips on his.

He would never see his family again.

Taking the syringe in hand, he felt for his vein, stuck the needle in, was barely aware of the pain, pushed down the plunger and felt leadenness flow from the needle into his body. Quickly, before the overdose took hold, before he could not move his limbs, he twisted the rope around his neck, twisted the stainless steel body of the syringe into the fabric and twisted that too, pulled the rope tight until he could not breathe. He forced himself to let go, sat on his hands. As his mind faded he was glad he could not remember his family; if he knew them still, if he had hope, he would fight to live, would untangle his neck, call for help.

He did not.

He waited to die, he could not breathe, he smiled, he waited to die. His soul, what was left of it, would escape his body and return to his Country. There he would join his old people. His wife and kids would be there one day too.

CHAPTER 49

THE DOOR WAS locked, Shane Daniels tried key after key on the touch plate but the door would not open. 'We forget,' she hissed finally, 'that unlike physical locks these can be switched off remotely.'

'I'm on it,' said Harper confidently as she walked forwards. 'They can be switched back on remotely too.' She squinted at the code on the lock, touched the screen of her tablet and started typing. 'I guess they could even be opened remotely.'

'We've made it all the way through the station and this is the first time we've found a disabled door.' Shane stared at the door as if she could burn through on will, and the heat of her anger, alone. 'I have no doubt that they are waiting on the other side of it, get ready for a fight.'

She closed her eyes, a moment of darkness, of peace. The rustling of soldiers checking their weapons, the soft sound of fingers on a tablet, breathing were the only sounds. How did it come to this, waiting outside a door to fight the Federation, whose army she was a part of, to get her children back?

A beep, followed by an electronic buzz caught her attention, she opened her eyes.

'Got it,' said Harper as the door opened.

Shut-up was through the door firing before Shane even said anything, just as quickly he fell as stunner fire splashed against the door frame, lit the air, came sizzling through the open door. Shane dived through the door, landed behind Shut-up's unconscious form and fired over him at the knot of guards. A young man, a young human, dressed in rags, was holding a bundle in his arms nearby. He dropped to his knees, protected the bundle with his back.

'Every guard, everybody not human, in that concourse needs to go down right now!' Shane hollered before firing again into the guards, who returned fire, their stunner fire hitting the wall behind her. The guards scattered, leaving the human kneeling in the middle of the room, trying to take what cover there was. Everybody with Shane hit the deck, firing at the guards who were running, standing, rather than diving to the ground.

A ship access hatch was starting to open, she could hear the hiss of its pneumatics even over the buzz of stun guns, the whoosh of darts. 'Someone seal that hatch,' she hollered, 'whoever is coming through there is unlikely to be friendly.' Someone said 'Yes, ma'am' and there was the sound, the flash and burn of plasma. The hatch squealed as the emergency close engaged and started melting as shot after shot from the plasma rifle hit it.

Shocked silence descended upon the room.

'I can't believe you actually did that,' said Shane.

'Why not, Cap'n, it worked didn't it?'

'I have already nearly been sucked out of a holed station once this year.'

'Sorry, Captain.'

'It's not fun, ask Harper.'

'Sorry, Captain.'

Then the guards started shooting again.

The noise was terrible, the light migraine-inducing, Shane's troops crawled and fired, crawled and fired. The guards checked their shots carefully, fired at vital parts, torso or head; the soldiers, better trained, knowing stunners and tranq-darts worked even if they hit a finger, scored more hits. The sound quietened, Shane climbed to a crouch, raised her hand in the 'cease fire' hand sign, waited until her troops stopped firing. Silence descended.

One of her troopers, she could not see who through the mirrored visor of their helmet, stood first, drawing fire; nothing, Shane stood next, more nothing. She gestured for half the troops to stand, the other half to cover them.

Shane walked over to the fallen humans, or at least they looked like humans from a distance. She was irritated by the smell of the station air, the burning stink of ozone, the sound of the ventilation. She pined for the sound of the breeze through banksias. She was sick of living on the inside of a fridge, the light was too blue, not enough like the light at home. She wanted nothing more than to return to Country.

Except getting her children back. She would not be returning to Country without them. She could not decide whether she hated the Federation more for its betrayal or herself more for leaving her family, for trusting the government, any government, would not betray her. History should have taught her better. She considered her future. Even if her identity and presence in that station had not been recorded, the fact that her children were about to go missing would be. All she wanted was to take her children home, to find her husband and take him home too, to sit on the beach in Country and watch the sunset turn the water to fire, to sleep under the stars. That was the only reason she had gone to war. When the Conglomeration threatened Earth, they threatened the land of her ancestors.

A guard groaned and moved, she fired her stunner without even aiming, no longer caring if over-use of the stunner could kill that species, cook their brains. Another rolled over, she fired again, shouted 'Secure these arseholes, make sure you inject every one of them' and walked on without even checking if any of her troops had responded.

She walked calmly to the humans on the ground. The little girl looked about ten, maybe twelve, though she was malnourished, tiny, if not for the dreadlocks she looked like a photo Shane had seen of her mother at that age. There was dirt on her face, her clothes were ragged, she was twitching, shaking, unconscious in what could be a stunner hangover. Shane rolled the girl onto her side, made sure she was safe, moved on to the boy, no, man; he looked to be six feet tall, skin colour that decades ago would have been called café au lait, wavy brown hair, red-orange at the tips like all her family's hair.

If she squinted she could see her son's face. He was unconscious, probably caught a stray stunner hit.

She could hear movement, hear the 'fwip' of cable-ties as they were tightened around wrists and ankles, hear people dragging bodies, she hoped they were alive at the same time as not caring if they were all dead. A noise suddenly, too close, she turned, raised her stunner, saw it was Romeo. 'Sorry, tidda,' she said.

Romeo smiled. 'Yeah, well I'd be tense if I was you. Those your kids?'

Shane smiled a crooked smile, forced, uncertain. 'They must be, they look like my kids, well, the girl looks like my mum did, the boy, the man, looks like my son, like James, Jimmy, if he had been through a hundred kinds of hell.' Her son had the scars and the burned expression of a veteran, not the sweet face of her child. For the first time in years, for the first time since the first friend she was forced to bury in an unmarked grave, she felt her eyes stinging, felt tears burn down her face, hit her chin, cool then fall away.

Whoever did that to James deserved to pay dearly for it, but Shane doubted very much they ever would. Karma is a bitch, payback is a bitch, mostly because neither of them ever did what you wanted them to.

It was her fault. She had gone to war, gone off to protect them, protect their homeland, four years she'd signed up for. Those four turned to eight, she had lost count. Her leave to return to see them was never granted. Now her children, who she had fought to protect, were traumatised and lost, her husband was missing.

She reached out and touched her son's shoulder, his eyes abruptly opened, he turned, tried to raise his fists. He was too weak. Shane pulled her helmet off, wanting his terrified eyes to have a chance to see her face. There was nothing on his face but confusion.

'Medic,' Shane screamed, 'now!'

Jimmy tried to raise his hands to fend her off. 'It's okay, Jimmy, I'm your mum, I have come to get you, to take you home.' She hated herself for that lie, she could not take him home.

'Mum?'

He sounded confused, Shane did not know if it was because he was stunner-drunk or if he did not remember her. She reached for him, and he flinched away. 'I'm sorry, I shouldn't have left you. I'm so sorry.'

Someone ran up, crouched next to her, she hoped they were a medic. They held a tablet over Jimmy, stared at the reading. 'Stunner hangover,' they said, 'he should be okay.'

Jimmy was staring at Shane.

'Mum?' he asked again. 'You came for me.'

Shane nodded.

Jimmy fell unconscious again.

She had her kids, she was armed, she would get them out of here. She would do whatever it took, somehow she would make it to Country with them. Anybody who tried to stop her would die. Once they made it home, they would simply disappear. Anyone from the Federation who came looking for her would also disappear.

Her son was too heavy for her to carry and he was unlikely to be able to stand and run or fight any time soon. 'I need a stretcher and some volunteer stretcher-bearers,' she said in a firm voice.

'Volunteers, get over here,' shouted Harper, 'finally a use for big men, we can't spare four people so we need the biggest two.' Harper was unfurling a stretcher, she hit the button and it went rigid. Two men, the biggest two, grabbed the stretcher and walked over, helped Shane roll Jimmy onto it.

'Big and strong like his mother,' one of the men said, the other giggled.

Shane holstered her stunner, slipped the empty one into her belt. Crouching she reached out, grabbed the girl, her daughter, pulled her into her arms and stood. The girl was feather light, a bird in hand, a feather pillow with bones.

'I can barely carry my child and hold a gun,' she said, 'if there is anyone planning to stop us, I will be about as effective as you lot generally are. That means you mob have to be twice as dangerous as normal because I will not be able to drag your arses out of the shit.' Her troop laughed. 'Let's get back to our ship and the hell out of here.'

Shane did not care how her troops were managing the retreat, she was too busy carrying her daughter. She had missed their childhoods, she had known that was a risk when she'd joined up, though she had not intended to be away so long, thought she would be allowed to return to Earth. She thought the Federation, or at least some members of the Federation, had deliberately not allowed human soldiers to go home.

Her children had missed their own childhoods, her son was a man, his face hardened and pained, wherever he had been it had not been pleasant. Someone needed to pay, yet she knew that bill would go unpaid.

She was in the middle of the column as they reached their ship, protected from the front and back.

As they left the station, Harper set off a logic bomb she had set hours before. If everything went to plan the station's computers would be wiped, their memory destroyed by the targeted virus. The only record of the attack would be in the wetware of the guards, the universal anaesthetic her group had carried in the disposable syringes had a normally negative side-effect of scrambling the memory of pretty much every Federal species. There should be nobody in there with a clear memory of who attacked them.

It did not matter, Shane no longer believed in the Federation.

CHAPTER 50

SHANE WAS DOZING in the chair in front of the communications console, lulled half into sleep by the chorus of electric humming noises – air-circulators, engines, computers, all added their notes to the chord. Romeo was driving, the ship was so much like a bus that Shane thought of it as driving not flying. Harper was doing what Harper did best, mysterious things with machines and screens.

'Hun,' Harper said with an uncertain tone, 'I think I have finally found a way to hack into the phones on Earth.'

Shane woke so fast she almost jumped, was bolt upright before her eyes were completely open. Romeo gestured for Boxer to take over the controls, got up from the pilot's seat, put her arm around her wife, gave a squeeze. 'How long, baby?'

'If it works, minutes.'

@

A phone rang in Kelly's troopy, it broke the concentration she needed to keep the car on the white pounded sandstone track. The car bounced off the track, skidded to a stop in the spinifex and sand. It was not her phone, the ring was wrong, an old-fashioned phone sound from back when people had landlines. She turned off the roaring, rattling old diesel.

She climbed between the seats towards the sound, rummaged around the gore-soaked mattress, among discarded packaging and supplies. There was blackened pus and drying blood on everything, she fought the urge to vomit before she realised there was as almost as much pus and blood on her skin and clothes as there was in the car.

The phone stopped ringing but she kept digging, maybe it would ring again. Her hand, digging in the wet refuse, touched something hard, cold like glass. She gripped it, pulled it out. It rang again, without thinking, she answered it, felt blood and pus hit her face.

'Hello?'

'Where's Walker?' the voice on the other end was gruff, hard but female. 'Who the fuck are you?'

'Um, hi,' replied Kelly, 'I'm Doctor Kelly Christian.'

'Is Walker in hospital?'

'I'm not that sort of a doctor, I am a physicist. Who are you?'

'I am Romany Zetz,' came the voice on the phone, 'I am a Wing Commander in the Federation Starforce, off-planet right now fighting a fucking war. There seems to be a communications blockade to stop people calling Earth from off-planet, this is the first time I've been able to get through in years.' Silence, a bit too long, there was a crackle, a hiss on the phone, no, the sound was too digital, like a compression artefact. The voice returned. 'I'm Walker's sister, where the hell is he?'

'I'm sorry, so sorry,' Kelly said, 'Walker is dead, an experimental weapon was dropped on Alice Springs and he was caught in the blast.'

The silence returned to the other end of the phone, unless that was breathing, light sobbing and tears at the other end. It seemed to go on forever. Kelly wanted to hang up, wanted to end the wait, the silence, the breath and the crying.

She waited, this stranger on the other end deserved that at least. What she really deserved was to talk to her brother, to Walker, but there was no chance of that.

By now he was probably a black, greasy smear in rapidly dissolving sand.

'Sorry,' said the tight voice on the other end, 'I'm not coping with this so well, I'm off-planet defending the Federation.' Silence. 'Meanwhile Conglomeration fuckers killed my brother.'

Kelly knew she would have to speak carefully, knew words were dangerous, knew also she had to tell the truth, the time for lies was gone. 'The Conglomeration didn't bomb Alice,' she said with a measured tone, 'the Federation set off the bomb. They were testing it. I was investigating the blast, trying to prove what had happened when I found your brother.'

'Those fucking bastards,' screamed the woman on the other end of the phone before the line squawked then went dead.

'I still can't get your husband, Captain,' Harper explained on the verge of tears. 'I can call his mobile but nobody is answering. I called your house and it says the number is not connected.'

Romeo was driving, her mouth thin, her eyes burning. Shane had nothing to say to either woman that would make anything bearable. 'Call every hospital in Perth,' Shane said, 'and find out if there's a William Daniels working there. I know they said he is not on-planet but they could have lied. I'm going to check on my kids.'

In the hallway she ran into Speech, the refugee academy monk who had been looking after her kids. 'Thank you for helping my kids,' Shane said, 'I am sure they would not have made it all this way without you.'

The hermaphrodite stared her in the face, the wafting of their robes in the breeze from the slightly over-enthusiastic vents the only movement. 'It's terrible the way the Federation has treated you humans,' Speech said, 'you fight with them, for them, for us, you follow our laws, the laws of the Federation I once loved, and yet we treat you like you are not our equals. Your children should never have had to live the way they had.

'I did not save your children, I did not look after them, though I helped look after Itta. There are many times I would have died, would have been robbed, there were many terrible things that could have happened but they did not. I did not save your kids, your son, Jimmy, saved me, kept me alive.

'It's the same in the Federation, we helped you humans when the Conglomeration attacked you and then you joined the war, our war that was only your war because they invaded you. I am sure other people can see it, humans have a better record at fighting than any other species, you are used as shock troops, as special forces, you are sent in when nobody else can do it. Yet often you are kinder than most others. You are primitive and violent but that's not the same as savage, Jimmy did not have to look after me, yet he did.

'We in the Federation think of your people as primitive, Captain. If you are then maybe the rest of the Federation should try being a little more primitive.'

Shane stared at that alien face, saw something like a human expression from someone who had been watching humans, living with humans, maybe someone who loved humans. 'Would you like to join me when I check on the kids?'

'I would be honoured, Captain.'

They walked further down the narrow corridor to the last hatch, the Federation symbol for infirmary on the door. Inside were two beds, Shane's kids lay on them, except one of them was no longer a child. They slept, not even thrashing any more. The medic could not work out what was wrong with them, the infirmary computer, with analytical programs for nearly every species in the Federation, sapient or not, could not work out what was wrong with them. At least they were sleeping peacefully. It had only been a couple of days, maybe it was just the stunner hangovers, coupled with starvation and emotional trauma. Until they could be taken to a hospital all the infirmary could do was keep them alive.

The tubes in their arms, mouths, noses, were doing precisely that.

'Do not cry, Captain,' Speech said, 'you have done all you can.'

Shane had not even been aware she was crying, she had been doing that a lot since she'd found her kids. It felt like the tap that had been turned off for so long had been used now and, no matter how desperately she tried to shut it off, it kept leaking. She had done what she could to save her kids. Maybe all she could do would never be enough.

Somewhere between little and no choice, Romeo and Boxer carefully edged the ship towards the station. 'Station, this is the *Vagabond*, ready for connection.' There was a moment of nothing then they felt the ship shudder like a car going over a speed hump as the station's docking arm grappled the ship and pulled it in. Lights blinked on as they connected to station power, station air, station waste management.

'I don't want to do this,' Shane growled. She pulled her antique nine-millimetre pistol from the holster in the small of her back and checked, again, it was loaded.

'I know, Shane,' replied Romeo, 'but your kids are still unwell and we don't know what is wrong with them. You need to get them to a hospital, this station is pretty far from the mainline, far enough from Earth too, it should be relatively safe.'

'I have their fake IDs and yours set up, Captain,' said Harper, 'here are the cards, they should get you on the station, get your kids into hospital, they should be safe enough there. It seems unlikely that such a dump of a nowhere station will have good security software, good enough to break through my hacks, that is.' Shane took the cards, they looked real enough, she had no idea how Harper had made them so quickly with the equipment on the ship, did not want to ask.

'I also have a concealed carry permit, fake of course, for that handgun.'

Checking the charge on her stunner and running a diagnostic, Shane slipped it away. She would have to go in alone, the tiny army she had used to get her kids free had returned to the infantry, their supposed R and R over. Assuming they had been drunk the entire time, nobody in the chain of command would ask where they had been. She was still technically on leave.

Not even Speech would be going in with her, even though they would add respectability and could help with translations. It was too risky, the monk was a fugitive and Harper had no idea where to begin in forging their ID card. Shane forced herself to stay calm as Harper, taking the comms station, pretending to simply be a comms officer, informed the station infirmary that there were sick humans on their ship, immediate medical assistance requested.

She settled down to wait.

The ship's contact bell chimed, someone was at the hatch, 'It's a medical team,' said Harper, 'letting them in.'

Shane met them in the corridor, led them to the med-bay, they fussed around the kids. 'Looks like malnutrition, exhaustion and a heavy dose of stunner hangover. There must be depression or some other combination of mental disorders complicating matters,' said one of them.

'Looks like resignation syndrome,' said another.

Another turned to Shane, she did not know their species so could not tell if it was disdain, concern, or even nothing at all on their face. 'How did this young man and this child come to being hit with stunners so many times they both fell into a coma?'

Shane thought quickly, talked slower. 'There was a raid and boarding attempt by pirates.' She had heard a lot lately about pirates harassing ships so she thought it was a good lie. 'I think they were trying to take slaves, we repelled them but the kids were shot.'

The medical officer made the gesture that in Federal sign was the rough equivalent of a nod. Shane could not be sure whether they were acknowledging what she said or agreeing with her.

'Who are you?' one of them asked.

'I am their mother,' Shane replied, handing over their ID cards. She hoped they were good enough. The physical cards were imperfect but the information behind them on the Federation network was near enough to perfect.

One of the medics looked up from their med-scanner. 'If you are their mother can you explain how the young girl came to be so malnourished?'

'She's been at a boarding school, I am in the process of suing them for neglect.' It was not like they would check, thought Shane.

'With your permission we will move these humans to the station infirmary, there we will be better able to restore their health.'

'Go ahead,' Shane said, hoping they would not hear or recognise the suppressed fear in her voice.

Shane watched in near panic as Izabella and Jimmy were loaded one by one onto gurneys and wheeled away. She followed, in civilian clothes, her stunner concealed in a handbag, a knife in her boot. It was strange to carry a handbag again, like a normal person. It was hanging almost where her holster would be on her dress uniform, she might be fast enough with the stunner if she needed it.

The station had a sinister atmosphere, everybody seemed to be staring, as much as Shane could understand expressions and body language, they all seemed affronted by the presence of a human in their midst. Watching for potential attack, Shane slowed, wished she could risk being in uniform, wished she was in a mainline station, although that would be riskier for her kids. She wished she had her platoon at her back. She briefly lost sight of the medical team in the crowd, crossed the concourse through the crowd as fast as possible to keep up.

Shane knew she should not run, it would catch attention. Nevertheless she was walking fast enough that people she passed in the corridors stopped as she passed, turned to stare. She could not slow down, her fears had changed to urgency, it was hard enough to not run, not sprint, not knock people over in her desperation.

She reached the hatch with the medic symbol on it, pushed a big blue button next to the door. The door whooshed open.

Two beings stood inside, in front of stools, each had a screen, a computer, a tablet, it didn't matter. The room was otherwise empty.

'My children were just brought here,' Shane said.

'Names?' the receptionist's Federal was unaccented. They sounded like the perfect sort of machine voice that the Federation used a lot.

'My name is Jane Smith, my children are Jimmy Smith and Izabella Smith.' Shane hated using the kids' real first names but they might wake while she was not there, someone might ask them for their names. She hoped they were smart enough to not use their real family name.

She realised suddenly and to her disgust that they probably didn't even know their family name.

One of the receptionists tapped on the screen in front of them, the other stared at Shane who again could not read the expression, did not know if stares from that species were polite or insulting. She tried to not be affected by it, but it was beginning to irritate her. She stared back. Luckily the other one spoke before Shane lost her temper.

'Your relatives are in intensive care, we will inform you when they are placed in beds where you can visit. Until then you will need to leave.'

Shane nearly screamed with frustration but instead gave them her number. It was a fake phone number linked to her fake ID that was routed through several networks before it rang her phone. If Harper was good enough, and so far she had been, the number would never connect back to any part of Shane Daniels' identity.

'If there is any change, if you move them, if they wake up, anything, call me,' Shane said.

@

Shane left her cabin, walked through the short, now too familiar corridors into the bridge, if it deserved the title. Romeo was sitting in the pilot's chair, tipped back so far she was almost lounging, her eyes closed, she looked asleep. Harper was at her station. It had been a simple comms station when they had acquired the ship, now festooned with wires, studded and warty with rectangles of plastic in every imaginable shade of beige and grey, it was far from being a simple comms station any more.

She hoped Harper understood it all at least.

'Morning, Shane,' she said, sounding tense, there were thoughts behind her voice that she didn't want to say.

'Is it?' They both laughed. Shane continued, 'What have you been up to while I've been asleep?'

Harper looked nervous, there really was something she didn't want to say, something she was afraid to say, something she couldn't say. 'I am still confirming what I found out, I don't want to say.'

'Out with it,' Shane snapped then wished she hadn't, forced herself to calm down. 'I can tell it's about me and I would rather know, rather you didn't try and protect me.'

She unclenched fists she did not know she had clenched.

Romeo sat up, stood and walked over to Harper, put her arm around her wife's shoulder. She looked Shane straight in the face, her mouth thin. 'I love you but if you hurt my wife in any way, I will kill you.'

Shane held out both hands in a gesture of peace.

'I had information alerts out all over the place,' Harper said, 'feelers, network search term alerts. I have been watching hacker gossip, I have been asking around in chatrooms, across the darknet. The Federation did not understand humans very well. I reckon it was only days after we got access to the Federation networks that someone worked out how to build a second hidden network piggy-backing on it, secret and illegal.'

Shane nodded but said nothing.

Harper continued, 'I had alerts out everywhere with the search term "William Daniels", and about two hours ago there was a hit.'

'Her notification interrupted our rest,' said Romeo, her smile still carried the scars of finding out Walker was dead. Shane did not envy the late-night conversations, the talks they must have been having after sex, the talks they would have for years after sex, when the post-coital storm of emotions made it impossible to block what they knew, what they happened. The talks they would be having instead of sex when it all got too much. Shane wondered if Romeo would ever have a real smile, a smile without qualifications, a smile without pain, again.

She was almost glad that, until she found her husband, she had nobody to inflict herself on.

'I am still confirming, still chasing clues, but it seems that your husband was arrested trying to stop them from taking your kids. He was locked up in a prison on Earth, charged with assaulting an officer of the law and with resisting arrest. He was there for a while then he disappeared again. It was easier to pick up the trail after that, once someone is in the prison network they can't completely disappear. It seems he was transferred to a hospital station, I can't tell from the codes if it was a prison, a hospital or a research facility.'

The room fell silent, except for the hum of station air, the faint cricket chirps letting them know all was well; all was well. Shane waited, survival had taught her patience; shell-shocked soldiers who were considered well enough to return to the war had taught her patience. She suspected Harper was trying to find the words to say something Shane would not want to hear, she thought she knew what it must be, could almost smell the fear. It must be bad to make her friend fear her.

'I think he's dead,' Harper said finally with a flinch like she expected to get hit. Romeo appeared ready to get between her wife and her best friend, to protect one from the other.

Shane's eyes felt too tight A single hot tear flowed down her cheek. She realised she already kind of knew William was dead. Why else had he been so hard to find?

'I am not sure what happened,' Harper continued, 'but it looks like he might have killed himself.'

@

Everybody was watching as Shane Daniels strode down the corridors. Voices whispered in the local language, that she could not understand, and in Federal, which she wished she couldn't. 'Why won't the humans go home?' was one thing she heard, 'who needs them anyway?' 'They smell, they're stupid', 'We shouldn't have welcomed them to the Federation'. She heard them calling her a 'petroleum-age savage', a 'violent animal', 'warlike barbarian' – hardly fair, the war had started long before Earth joined the Federation. Everyone in the station looked away when she looked at them.

The tension in the recirculated air was so thick she felt she could move faster walking on it rather than through it.

She strode down the corridors, upright military, eyes front – not a conscious decision, not to make a point. She was on automatic. She did not want to look at their accusing faces or hear their voices.

She turned a corner, up an elevator that had emptied as soon as people saw she wanted to get in, down a corridor where nobody would look her way. She stopped before the medical centre, breathed slowly, deliberately, hit the 'door open' button.

Reception was unchanged, Shane walked to the receptionist to the left.

'I am here to visit Jimmy and Izabella Smith.'

They said nothing but tapped on their screen for a while, looked up at Shane, saw the expression on her face and tapped again.

'There is nobody here by those names,' they said.

Shane felt the blood rush to her head, heard it pounding in her ears, the air flooded from her lungs. 'What do you mean? I am their mother, they were brought here by a medical team.'

'The identities under which those individuals were entered into this facility were false. Routine DNA testing revealed that the male was James Daniels and the girl was Izabella Daniels, also known as 'Itta', both of whom were missing from New–Manus immigration detention centre. Their identities have been corrected on our system.'

Shane breathed slowly. She had lost friends; watched people die, killed them herself. Never had she felt her lungs clench like this. Her family had seen children stolen, the white-man had stolen her Country. Never had she felt so close to losing her temper. Her hand was in her handbag, fondling the stunner inside.

'Nevertheless, I am their mother and I would like to see them.'

There was more tapping on the screen, they looked up from their work to stare Shane in the face.

'Captain Shane Daniels,' the receptionist said, 'our surveillance system has been put on high alert and has positively identified you. Security are on their way to escort you to the military police for questioning regarding how those children came to be in your possession. Please remain calm.'

She fired without thinking, without even knowing she had pulled her stunner from her handbag, the receptionist fell without a noise. Shane turned her weapon on the other receptionist, 'I don't have long because of your friend so I don't think I will take kindly to obstruction. Where are my kids?'

The receptionist stared at Shane, whose eyes were large, black and liquid, like deep tannic pools, dangerous places that hid spirits, beasts, that hid death. 'Where are my kids?' Shane growled each word like the slow beat of a drum. 'I have never seen your species before so I have no idea what a stunner would do to you. I don't think you know either.' Every battle, every person she had killed for the Federation, every soldier she had failed to save was imprinted in her voice.

'They are not here, Captain Daniels. James was returned to the place from which he had run, he still has years of bonded labour to complete there. He has returned to his home. His sister, of whom he is currently the legal guardian, has been returned with him. Their ship is already gone.'

Shane stared, could keep nothing from her face. The expression on the receptionist changed, still Shane could not read it, it was as indecipherable as the look on a cat's face.

'There is no point getting angry,' the receptionist said, 'I had no responsibility for what happened, I merely do my job here.'

Shane felt the buzz of the stunner firing before she was conscious of pulling the trigger. The receptionist fell, collapsing like a marionette with its strings cut. Shane had not known for sure you could actually see red, that you could act without knowing what you were doing, until she came to – kicking the unconscious receptionist in what would be their ribs if they were human.

Screaming 'arseholes' at the top of her voice she stormed through the door into the hospital wing.

There were two beds configured for humans, they were empty, the coverings removed, there was no evidence her kids were there, no evidence they had even woken before being removed. She grabbed her phone, smacked the big-red-button app Harper had installed – it had 'Don't panic' written on it. She wished she could take the advice.

'Harper,' she almost shouted, 'they have taken my kids again, find them.' She hung up, she could hear the door to the rest of the station opening.

Harper did not stop typing to talk, Romeo knew it must be serious. 'They took Shane's kids again.'

'Oh fuck.'

'Security has been deployed to the med-bay.'

'Oh fuck, how many?'

'Lots, could be all of them, no, it's not all of them, some are heading for our hatch in the concourse.'

Romeo grabbed a comms handset and nodded to Harper, waited for her to connect. 'This is the *Vagabond* requesting permission to disengage,' she said while slipping into the pilot's chair.

There was a crackle over comms then the words 'Permission denied, this station is under lockdown.'

'We can't just abandon Shane here,' Harper squeaked.

'We have to,' snapped Romeo, 'if we and our ship are detained by security we will be unable to rescue her. Also, if we are free we can chase whatever ship took her kids. We cannot allow ourselves to be boarded and detained under any circumstances.'

'Speech is still on station.'

'Requesting emergency disengagement,' Romeo shook into the handset.

'Boxer's still on station.'

'Bobby can take care of themself.'

'Denied,' replied the station. Romeo looked over and saw that Harper was desperately at work, hammering at the screens on her heavily modified console. She knew better than to talk about the situation, knew her love was on it, knew she would do whatever she had to do.

'Doors locked,' Harper said, 'we are in lockdown ready for launch if I can get us off this station, as a bonus it would be impossible for security to get into the ship, unless – crap,' she silently tapped on screens again, 'unless they have a hacker who can get us open.'

It was a tense wait for Romeo, unable to do anything but wait while Harper worked. She pulled out her phone, called Shane, no answer, she was probably fighting for her life.

Then, with the suddenness of a breath, the disengaging symbol flashed onto Romeo's console just as a clunk echoed through the ship. Romeo reached out, instinctively taking the controls and easing them away from the bulk of the station. The space around the station was full of ships that Romeo had not noticed when they had landed, refugee hulks, luxury yachts, small cruisers, like the *Vagabond* but newer with the Federation police logo, small freighters. A delta flashed past then turned on its axis and boosted back towards *Vagabond*.

'Private vessel *Vagabond*, you are ordered to surrender. Return to the station immediately or stop manoeuvring so you can be boarded by Federation Law Enforcement. Private vessel *Vagabond* . . .' the sound ended.

'You didn't need that distraction,' Harper said as Romeo settled into her seat and started dodging.

@

Shane had shot her way out of the infirmary, they had expected her to surrender when ordered to do so, three of them were sleeping before they even knew she planned to resist. They had been out of cover, out of position, unprepared. She stepped over sleeping bodies, taking every weapon she could see.

Pity none of them had plasma rifles, cutting lasers or projectile weapons, stunners were safer in ships and stations but nearly impossible to threaten with. With an expression halfway between a grin and a grimace Shane snatched the pain-prod one of them carried; she could threaten with that if she didn't mind hating herself.

Smacking the pain-prod against the wall again and again she grinned when it finally broke.

Most of the available security had been sent to apprehend her so there were few people trying to stop her as she returned to the docking bay where she had left her ship. Security were guarding the door yet strangely they were not trying to gain access and impound her ship, arrest her friends. Then she saw it: the 'engaged' light was dark, her friends had abandoned her. There must have been a compelling reason.

Security trying to access the ship was a damned compelling reason.

She ducked back down another corridor. If she was lucky no eyes had seen her on the security camera, the security computers would take time to analyse the data and find her. If she moved fast enough she could stay clear.

She moved fast, causing distractions, keeping security on high-alert, shooting them down seemingly at random so they would be too scared to relax. Then she went quiet, suddenly, disappeared, they searched all the ships they could as she hid in a duct. They held all departures as she casually lay on her back in a duct and ate an emergency ration bar from her pocket. They searched all ships on the station as she watched them through a tiny hole in a wall. They panicked as she slept in a crawlspace.

It was only when they had stopped freaking out, when security had been awake for too long and needed sleep, that she re-entered the public areas of the station, wearing damp robes and a hood stolen from the washing machines. She had paid a fixer more than she could afford for a meeting with a smuggler, paid that smuggler all the rest of her money to get on a ship. They had not said where they were taking her, she had not asked, all she needed to do was get away clean.

CHAPTER ZERO

KELLY HAD FOUND an old tripod for a camera, in the spare-wheel well of the troopy, the black matt paint chipped off in places showing the shiny metal underneath. It might have even been hers, lost, long forgotten. She improvised a phone mount for it out of sticks, fencing wire and gaffer tape, the holy trinity of improvised engineering. She was leaning against the greasy tyre of the car.

She reached out, hit the icon on her phone, started streaming.

'My name is Kelly Christian,' she said, staring right into the tiny camera lens on her phone. Her eyes were blurred with tears. 'I am dying. Long before the Federation can find me, long before they can stop this transmission, I will be dead.

'Some weeks ago, agents from within the Federation – scientists, military with assistance from the highest echelons of the Federation Council – detonated a new type of bomb on the city of Alice Springs on Earth. The damage done was extensive and immediate. It also had a slower-acting component, a form of viral radiation that devastates everything it touches, anything made of atoms at a subatomic level – stone, water, flesh – all are vulnerable. Infected atoms emit particles that infect other atoms. Everything is vulnerable. Some days ago, I have forgotten how many, it got its claws into me.

'More people have died from this weapon than we have been able to count, we may never know how many as the action of the weapon will dissolve everything, leaving no cells, not even any molecules intact to identify as human. Eventually, if left unchecked, the weapon will destroy all life on this continent while infecting the rock of the land itself, it will eat the rocks, move to the water, move to the core of the planet. If nobody stops it the entire planet will dissolve, it can then move on and destroy the entire galaxy, maybe the universe.

'I sit here now, knowing I will die, knowing also that my death is going to be streamed. I have had help, I have made plans. There is no way to stop this stream through the Federation networks, there is also no way to get to me, to stop me physically before I die, I am too far from the nearest anything for anyone to be sent. I sit here now, in my great-grandmother's Country, I sit here and now you will watch me die.'

Leaving the phone on, Kelly leaned back and closed her bleeding eyes.

@

Nothing picked at Walker's bones, gleaming whitely in what looked like a man-sized patch of black grease. There was nothing there to scatter his bones, even the eagles had ceased flying over where he had died, too cautious, too scared to place feet on the ruined country. Soon his bones would dissolve, already they were greying in patches, ageing a thousand years in days. There would be no trace of Walker, save his breath on the wind.

@

The sand was white, not the red she loved, not the colour of the sand at home, on Country. Romeo could not go there, could not return home, yet. They would look for her there, they would expect her to go there. She could not go home anyway, the particle weapon had made it too hot. They had seen it as they were burning in through the atmosphere, it was on every service on the Federation network, they had watched the woman who had tried to save Walker die.

The sand was white, an almost unnatural white that reflected like glass, casting splinters of light into eyes abraded to tears by the blowing sand. Harper stood breathing heavily, water running off a flight suit that was a touch too big for her onto the sand.

Romeo pulled a waterproof bag out of her flight suit, pulled her phone out of the bag, tapped a command, waited for the confirm button, tapped that too. 'Ship is secured and powered down,' Romeo said.

Harper looked up at her. 'If I set it up right,' she said.

'You set everything up right,' Romeo said, pulling a bundle out of her flight suit, unrolling it to reveal a huge duffel. 'You always do. Let's get out of these suits and find a road.'

@

The sign inside the main airlock had once said 'Luna City University' but students had made a joke of painting over the I and the T in city for so many years that maintenance had stopped bothering to fix the vandalism. It became the school's nickname and then stuck. There was extra agitation in the plasteel and ceremetal corridors, even more noise than normal. A fierce rebellious energy was burning through the student body.

From hand to hand the discs transferred, from email account to email account the emails flashed, from server to server, copy to copy, the data propagated. IT students created shadow servers within the network, data clouds spread thin across entire buildings full of desktop computers. Tablets were slaved together remotely, without their owners knowing, creating tangled matrices.

Others, resourceful but lacking the tech skills, hid discs in holes in walls, in waterproof bags in water tanks, in toilet cisterns, in hollowed-out books in the library. Soon there were so many copies of the data, proving the Federation bombing of Alice Springs, in Luna C__y University that the only way to get them all would be to raze the place to the ground.

That would not stop the Federation from attempting to stop the data there. The Kris files, as the students knew them, could not be allowed to reach the outside world.

Data security noticed the increase in bandwidth almost as soon as it happened. Two hundred and thirty-seven students were attempting to email the files to contacts outside human space at the same co-ordinated second. Data security attempted to close the gap, dedicating all their staff to the breach.

It was during this distraction that a hacker known only as 'Yagan' broke through the firewalls and streamed the entirety of the Kris files onto the Federation net. The data spread across the networks like a fire.

@

Just another dodgy room in yet another filthy backroads station, barely utilitarian, a bed and a microwave, a desk, a chair and a power coupling. Shane Daniels found it adequate after so many years in the military. They took cash even though it was illegal to do so, that was perfect.

Shane pushed back the flimsy desk chair, looked at her tablet. There was text, a letter, and a 'send' button but that was all. Old habits die hard, she decided to proofread it one more time.

'To nobody, to everybody,' the letter began.

'Before the intervention of the Federation, when humans had control over their own world, their own affairs, "terrorism" was a word that threw more fear into minds than so-called terror attacks. We were so scared of terrorists we let the government do almost anything to protect us from them. So scared we even gave up many of our rights, willingly, to escape the fear of terrorism.'

Checking the load on her handgun she slipped it into the holster on her belt, behind her back. She let go, moved her hand away, her coat dropped over the holster, hiding it perfectly. Her stunner was charged, she carried that openly on the right side, it never hurt to look a little dangerous in the sort of circles where she was going to be forced to travel.

'We joined the Federation and humanity rejoiced, we would have the stars as our playground, the Federation would save us from ourselves, stop the terrorists and the wars, fix our broken environment. The Federation had saved us from the Conglomeration, we, the people of Earth, were glad, even delighted, to fight with the other peoples of the Federation to defend the citizens, and ourselves, against our common enemy.

'Certainly, there were humans who fought against the entry to the Federation. New terrorists. Racism took on a new urgency when it was no longer just humans with different skin colour they were fighting against.'

There was a noise outside, she checked the security camera feed. Nothing.

'I was one of those who believed that the Federation was bigger than race or species. In my time in the military I would not have hesitated to violently stop anyone of my own species who had engaged in speciesist language or behaviour. I believed in the Federation.

'The Federation never believed in me. They have killed my husband and kidnapped then tortured my children.

'I now understand the terrorists, I understand their fear. We have been betrayed, the senior races of the Federation do not see us as their equals, although we believed they did. They let us believe they did. Our "friends", our "allies", have snatched our land, taken our children. I fought for them and then they took everything from me. I am going to take back what I can, I'm coming for my children; anyone who tries to stop me will have cause to regret that decision. If anyone reading this has had anything to do with hurting my children, when I have them I am coming for you.'

She stared at what she had written. Her finger moved towards the 'send' button that would, if the hackers who had risked their careers to help her did what she asked, transmit her letter across the entire Federation. Once the letter was out it would be mere minutes before they traced her; that was a side effect she could not quite eliminate. She froze, stared at the tablet. Reached out, flicked on the keyboard app, started typing.

'We have been betrayed.

I no longer believe.'

She hit send, waited for 'message sent' to pop up on the screen, nodded to herself, picked up the tablet, smashed it against the edge of the desk, turned and walked out the door.

If in some smothering dreams you too could pace
Behind the wagon that we flung him in,
And watch the white eyes writhing in his face,
His hanging face, like a devil's sick of sin;

THE OLD LIE

If you could hear, at every jolt, the blood
Come gargling from the froth-corrupted lungs,
Obscene as cancer, bitter as the cud
Of vile, incurable sores on innocent tongues, —
My friend, you would not tell with such high zest
To children, ardent for some desperate glory,
The old Lie: *Dulce et decorum est*
Pro patria mori.

– WILFRED OWEN, *DULCE ET DECORUM EST*

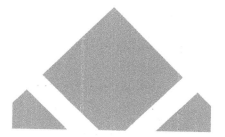

Author's Note

THIS IS A work of fiction yet it is influenced deeply by historical events.

Thanks are owed, as always, to the works that influenced this novel. Anna Haebich in *Broken Circles* for the story of the children taken from families while their fathers were at war. This happened to Noongar people, my people, it is unimaginable that it could ever happen to anyone but Aboriginal people. Archie Roach in the song 'Munjana' for the isolation felt by people taken from family and country.

The Stolen Generations affected Aboriginal and Torres Strait Islander communities badly. It will be many generations before the after-effects of these government actions end. My family were never stolen; my grandfather hid my father from the government and in the process removed us from culture. We are still working to return.

One of the strongest influences on this work was the history of my own family. My grandfather and all of his brothers enlisted during World War II. I have no evidence that they suffered from racism after returning from the war but it seems certain. I never met my grandfather or any of his brothers – my grandfather died when I was a baby – but I can state this, neither my grandfather or any of his brothers received war land or, I believe, pensions. When recently I visited my grandfather's grave I discovered it to be unmarked, lacking the soldier's memorial it deserved. This is not uncommon for the graves of First Nations soldiers who fought in World War II.

I have made reference to Maralinga and to other sites where the British tested nuclear bombs. The inspiration for that section came from the touring exhibition 'Black Mist Burnt Country' and the catalogue the curators produced, as well as from numerous writings on what happened there. Official records state that all traditional owners were removed to safety before the weapons testing, it is well known that that is not true.

Respect is owed to the traditional owners of Maralinga and to all Anangu communities. The people who have lived around Maralinga for tens of thousands of years might not be able to return safely for tens of thousands of years.

The final influence was the poetic works of one of my favourite poets, Wilfred Owen, who fought in World War I and died a week before the Armistice. His works, written in the trenches, made a lie of the belief that war is glorious. History tells us his mother received the telegram informing her of his death as the bells rang out celebrating the end of the war.

Acknowledgements

I WOULD LIKE to thank my Noongar ancestors without whose resilience I would not be here today. This novel was written on the road and in Naarm in the traditional country of the Wurundjeri people of the Kulin nation. Thank you to the elders and communities whose Countries inspired this work.

I would like to thank Hachette Australia, who published *The Old Lie* and my previous novel, *Terra Nullius*. Robert, you are a wonderful man and your faith in me enables me to work with confidence. Thanks also to Thomas Saras, Fiona Hazard and Louise Sherwin-Stark at Hachette.

Project editor Karen Ward and publicist Alana Kelly, you have both been amazing and I am sure I have been driving you both insane.

Ali Lavau and Deonie Fiford, you both did an amazing job of editing and Grace West, you have designed another totally incredible and striking cover. Grace Lucas-Pennington and the team at black&write! Thank you for your editorial feedback.

Lily, again I could not have done it without you, volim te.

Finally, huge thanks and love to everybody who read *Terra Nullius*. Writers are nothing without readers.

CLAIRE G. COLEMAN is a writer from Western
Australia. She identifies with the South Coast Noongar
people. Her family are associated with the area around
Ravensthorpe and Hopetoun. Claire grew up in a Forestry
settlement in the middle of a tree plantation, where her dad
worked, not far out of Perth. She wrote her black&write!
Fellowship–winning book *Terra Nullius* while travelling
around Australia in a caravan. *The Old Lie* is her second
novel.

hachette
AUSTRALIA

If you would like to find out more about Hachette Australia,
our authors, upcoming events and new releases you can visit
our website or our social media channels:

hachette.com.au

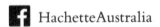 HachetteAustralia

 HachetteAus